LOVE
Deception
in HARTFORD
HOMICIDE
Constitution State

J. ALEXANDER

Love & Deception

J. Alexander

Love & Deception
By J. Alexander
Copyright 2014 by J. Alexander

Acknowledgements

First & Foremost, I must praise the Higher above for all of my blessings. I am extremely thankful for the abilities to write what dwells in the mental cavity of my being, and through immeasurable diligence and determination, I am now out- living societies claims and predictions that once a bad seed, always a bad seed. I have come such a long way out here in "CORRUPT CUNNUCK" a.k.a. "HOMICIDE HARTFORD," and feel (La-Z-Boy) comfy in my present standings as a man, father, son, friend, and life partner. That being said, WALKWITMEH as I tour guide you through the illicit life of KORY & KEONNA BLAKE---GOD BLESS MY BIRTH PLACE HARTFORD CONNECTICUT...2014.

J. ALEXANDER...

My first s/o goes to my precious mother, Mrs. Marie Gray. You are my truest blessing. I could not have made it through certain storms without your assistance in the weathering process. I could not have asked for a better Mo'father. In addition, even through all the letdowns, misfortunes, and embarrassments I have caused you over the years; it was my desires to turn to the streets, not your misrepresentation as a parent. I sincerely hope now, that your baby-boy is making you proud. I LOVE YOU MOM!

POPS, you are still my dude, no matter why, or what separates us! Until we reunite, ONE-UP!

Wassup sis, Ms. Deanna Howard, it's imperative that I extend this verbal hug for the 42 years of appreciation and sibling rivalry...all smiles! You are the best, LOVE YOU TO DEF, HOLLA @ MEH!

To my son, Javon "Young $paid" Gray, if you only knew how deep my love and admiration runs for you... So proud of how you've turned out young. You did it without trailing in my footsteps; instead, you use your intelligence, wit, upbringing, and personal experiences as a voice through your muzik. Always keep it 100 with yourself...you are destined for stardom. Continue to do it "STRICTLY FOR YOUR DOUBTERS." ONE-UP!

Awe...my rarest jewel, Secret Shanelle Gray, in my absence I have imagined how life, your growth was without a fatherly figure around to raise and protect you over the years. SOOO... SORRY FOR ABANDONING YOU POOH! However, you have grown into a beautiful energetic young-lady only a dad could appreciate. I LOVE YOU MORETHAN YOU COULD POSSIBLY KNOW. MWAH, STAY YOU MY LI'L GEMINI, AND EVEN THOUGH WE OFTEN BUMP HEADS @ TIMES, YOU ARE FOREVER GOING TO BE DADDY'S LILTTE GIRL! Gimme kissey...stanka butt-butt, lol.

Last but not least, my best friend, soul mate, fiancée, and lover; words cannot explain what I feel for you. 20-years you have rode shotgun by my side, but now it is time we strut side-by-side until the wheels fall off. Might I add, most women abandon their significant other due to a state of loneliness, but you stuck it out for eight-long-years, kept money on my books, made many   long drives to various parts of the world to uphold our bond, down to answering every single call I made from prison and I want you to know, I LOVE AND THANK YOU DEEPLY, Mikia L. Eady! I am definitely DRUNK-IN-LOVE!

FRIENDS: Avenue Ave; Ahmed Gibson; Carti & Jay(mix-tape stand); Charlie-Boy; Dime (Bedrock); my brutha Damon Dum Hill; Edwin Rivera; Fred; Frank Puzzo; Corey Jahmal; Djuan Davis; Head (bedrock); Jinkx (Bridgeport); Marlon Lawrence; Meech80/Miz (Rochester, Ny.); Nestodagreat (N.H.); Obama (Flint); Boogie; Catman; Popeye; Trell; Rosey; My Guy Spike; Taz; Tim Robertson (thanks homey); Ty Hightower & Lil-Bit; Brandnew; Andre Hudson (POTZ); Toby(forty-deuce); Mega; Chubb; Chan; Buck; Aj Williamsbey; Tee-Tee & Summer; Villain (Yammy); Antony(Rig Lyfe); Natasha McIntosh; Tiff & Trell; Rae Bae Roye; Ivette Vazquez; Mila Carrion; Kisha Lee & G-Money(Va.); Kendra Mrshoney Littleton; Melissa Black Widow Colon; Tina Mathis & Malcolm; Alasia; Judy Cruz; Maurice; Carlos Gray; Prina & Charlene Smith; Christina & Shootaboy Luc; Kashan Klien (Mi.); Jamale Nicholson (Oh.); Stackz (Pa.); Free Swerve (Jersy860); Trap Beats; Seanan Wooten; Dooney Man; DJ QT;

FAMILY: To all of my in-laws, The Copper/Anderson's thanks for your undivided love & support over the years. Renee & Eric Edmunds; Jamal & Janeeta; Deneen; Shanna; Charmaine; Alexis; Auntie Viola; Auntie Vanessa; Uncle Jr.; Pretty; Melquan, Malaysia; Charles & Michael Hite; Rick Anderson; Tyus & Aaliyah; Bunny; Bernett Anderson; Shaun; Terry & Keisha; Debra & Bridgette Fleming; Parnell; Dominique TheCashQueen; Antwan Smith; Meechie; Tyshaun Taylor; Pinky; Uncle

Patrick, Latoya & Aaliyah Ledbetter and my second-son Tyrell "Boo" Hightower, miss you young. Hurry-up home! SPECIAL S/O TO THOSE WHO PREVIOUSLY SUPPORTED MY LAST PROJECT, "HALFWAY CROOKZ": Dum; Obama(Mi.); Charlie; Toya; Kea-Kai; Chrissy; Marge; Chris; Germaine Scott; Monique; Yolonda;

Kawanna, CoCo Flow; Star; Wes; Marlon; Renee; Snail; Jinkx(B-port); Freddy Sanchez; Debbie; Wiggz; Black (Va.)

BOSSLIFE/MDC FAMILY: Young $paid; Ty-Nitty "TheProducer"; Trevor Lloyd; Tyrone"TyStylles"Davis; Quan"Riza"Ware; Marlon God's-Gift; Apollo; LateNightSnacks; Badnews Greedy-Gang; Mook;

AUTHORS/PUBLISHERS: G-Street Chronicles; Nikki Urban/Diamondstoneproductions; New Era Books; Cole Hart; Shiana Lesa Jones; Roy Glenn; My Favorite Author Al-Saadiq Banks; Rocky-Rose; Kenya Whiter-Black; Lisa Muhammad; Felisha Bradshaw(Grapevine Mag); Siren (for a great review); Papaya Sistah's On Lit (for a great review); Real Queenb Divas; NeNe Capri;

Now onto my new home, family, and label mates, K. Ellis Publications/Mz-Robinson Presents: MzLeebra Clark; Trappelean Mista; Tenele Coc Daauthor and Recognize Ringo (great cover art).

S/O to my publisher: Author Katavious Ellis, for taking the chance on the unknown. It is my pleasure to write under your tutelage, advisory, and company amongst the others. THANKS FOR HAVING ME!

This is to Mz-Robinson for reaching out to me in a time where I felt stumped in my writing career, due to unfortunate happenings. You have provided me with a platform where I now feel comfortable and confident about my writing again. Through many talks, my pen-game has been rejuvenated back to its proper element...above the rim (in my 2pac voice.) So without further ado: THANKS UH BILLI, Mz-Robinson.

~J. ALEXANDER~

Prologue

It was a blistering cold February night in the state's capitol. The murder rate had risen at a disturbing count, which was starting to pose not only a threat to the Mayor and Governor's seats, but the community as a whole.

Bodies of both genders were being slain in what appeared to be vengeful, cold-blooded, murderous killings. Although, a strict curfew was sanctioned by local authorities, the death toll rapidly increased despite the heavy police presence throughout the city.

With no solid leads, witnesses, or clues to what, or perhaps why, these bodies were popping up all over the city, the killer was seizing what little life, hope, freedom, and safety the H.P.D. had to offer its citizens.

After fourteen unsolved homicides throughout Hartford, the unknown killer had taken control of the night, and the city by leaving trails of mangled-bodies and pain stricken families with unbearable grief and sorrow.

Chapter 1
Careful What You Ask For

As rookie patrolmen, Michael Henson and Emmit Hall, canvassed the area of 60 Woodland Dr., an area known for drugs and prostitution, a duress call came over the radio from dispatch, advising them of reports of loud noises and screams coming from a vacant apartment.

Henson, who was known as Li'l Mike, to his fellow officers, was riding shotgun tonight, so he responded to the call. "Dispatch, this is 1-Adam-12 in the vicinity, approximately 10-feet away."

"Roger that 1-Adam-12. Back-up four minutes out. Proceed with extreme caution." Debbie, H.P.D's 3rd shift dispatcher, advised. Debbie knew the threat the two rookies were up against tonight; this particular project was full of the worst breed of criminals Hartford birthed and housed to date.

Officer Henson laughed the warning off as if it were a gut-wrenching joke from Kevin Hart. He stood 6'2" solid. His skin was a rough chocolate, and though he had a major problem with acne and large feet, he had no problem meeting women. Quite the comedian, Henson, was well known around the department for his practical jokes and never taking things too seriously, such as tonight's call. He was hard-bodied, and portrayed a tough guy façade since the academy. He also surpassed most of the records held by veteran officers, graduating at the top of his class and making him a star in the making on the force. The simple obstacles and shooting range was a walk in the park and tonight's call was one he yearned for over the past twelve months, an opportunity to put all his training and natural skills to work.

"Let's move," Hall ordered.

"Sounds good!" Henson shouted, with much energy. "Let's go!"

"One of these days, Lil Mike..." Hall began. He stopped mid-sentence when he noticed a dark figure leap over a white Honda Civics' hood with ease and gun in hand. "Hey...look," Hall shoved his partner in the side, his eyes glued to the dark figure, but it was too late, Henson had hopped out before the squad car came to a halt, taking chase after the figure, eager to apprehend the assumed assailant.

Hall brought the blue and white sedan to an abrupt stop blocking in two parked cars. Although officer Hall was tonight's designated driver, he took the initiative to radio in the call, then hurriedly snatched his Billy Club and joined the pursuit. Hall was not as enthusiastic as his partner was, there was a strange feeling coursing through his veins, a combination of nervousness and what others would describe as fear.

A few feet away, Henson struggled to keep up with the quickness of his fleeing target. It wasn't that he hadn't acquired the best training, nor was he out of shape---it is just that their assailant was in better shape. It became a nightly ritual for him to stalk, prey, assault, and then murder his prize only to flee at a cheetah-like pace leaving minimal clues or reasoning as to why the Prince of Darkness knocked at the victim's door. However, for his reward, he would take some type of trophy from his conquest.

Officer Henson had surprisingly shortened the distance between him and the fleeing target. He could now see that the dark figure wore a large fitted hoodie that covered his entire head. The only true visible characteristic about the 'evil beyond the veil' was the metallic-silver streaks lining his footwear that kept the chase thus far.

"Freeze! Stop…Or I'll shoot!" Henson ordered, his voice echoing in the still of the night, lungs begging for relief.

It was as if the sprinter had earplugs jammed into the tiny crevices of his ears, or he did not respect the law, because he only sped up his pace infuriating Officer Henson further.

Lagging behind was Officer Hall, too far behind to identify their assailant's gender. Male or female…Young or old…His only point of pursuit was the fast-shuffled sounds of coupled feet against the grayish-black tarmac in the back of the housing project's leisure areas.

"If this guy only knew what he was up against, he'd end this chase," thought Kory Blake. Kory was the killer they chased and he was luring the officers into a darker, unlit area to heighten his kill stats. It was not his original intent to shed the officer's blood. He had not expected them to arrive at the scene so quickly, but blood is blood and a police officer's blood is very rewarding in his realm.

Chapter 2
Officer Down---Officer Down

"I said freeze!" Officer Henson shouted into the numbing atmosphere a second time, his body temperature rising with every step as his Fruit-of-the-Looms dampened against his pale skin.

In response to Henson's request, the urban stalker glanced over his left shoulder revealing the slightest possible trait of his identity and possibly the last one Henson would ever witness in his lifetime. However, the reality of the nocturnal peepshow shook him far worse than any horror-flick he had witnessed as a kid. The circumference within the large hoody was empty, no face to remember, no face to identify, nothing but darkness, a non-existent image.

In a heroic attempt to subdue his target, Henson twirled his metal baton, lunging horizontally at the target's feet. However, unlike the hundred and some odd attempts back at the academy in which this technique worked superbly, tonight, the evasive target easily hurdled over the metal rod. It was the extensive training of the urban stalker that enabled him to land on both feet with the timed precision of a chronological Swiss Bulova stopwatch. It was the lengthy days and nights in the high school gym, that prepared him for such things. He was part of the state's elite gymnast surpassing many of his teammates to sit alongside eight others at the finals where he took home six gold medals by his lonesome. His training as a gymnast, coupled with the martial arts he diligently studied as a youth, gave him a great sense of speed and patience. Kory Blake was built from the beginning of conception to be a dominating force at whatever sport he chose to indulge in.

In mid-air, he managed to retrieve his sidearm; a silenced 9mm Ruger that housed 17-armor-piercing shells illegal in the U.S. because of their lack of respect for authority and damage they were known to cause to police vests.

There was only a split second between Henson and his target. With very little light casting in the rear of the projects, Henson reached for his heavy-duty flashlight. "Ahhhh...." He belted out, feeling the gaping hole in the middle of his palm. He had been hit by an armor-piercing shell, lucky to even still have a hand to masturbate with, that is if he made it home tonight.

"Shots fired...I repeat...Shots fired! My partner has been hit. Where's our backup?" Hall panted, into his shoulder mic. He was now close enough to have a clear view of his partner and see he had sustained some direct hits. His fear had been replaced with worry and concern for his partner's safety.

"Two minutes out," dispatch relayed.

"That's not good enough!" Hall fired back still in pursuit, his flashlight in one hand and his service revolver in the other.

"This is it pig, your final destination," Kory laughed. "But as they say, everything happens for a reason. Wrong time, right place!" the man in black recited, as he stood over Henson who was doubled over in obvious pain as blood leaked like a running faucet with no way to shut it off.

Even through the tight black ski mask, Henson could see the coldness in Kory's eyes. Pain, death, heartlessness, and mass murder were all he assessed from the killer's empty irises. No remorse whatsoever. Before Henson could finish his silent prayer, Kory whispered two bone-crushing shells into his skull.

The low muffled acoustic sound of silencers gave Kory excitement every time his life-takers spoke.

Officer Hall was just in time to see Henson's lifeless body become one with the cold pavement, which would also help slow down the decomposition of Michael's body.

"Officer...Down, damnit!" Hall's heart ached at the awful sight of his partner. "Officer... down! Where's my...!" He attempted to say, as the Kevlar vest he was obligated to wear while on duty, happily attracted shell after shell like a magnetic surface, leaving several holes in his torso for the coroner to examine once his body reached the medical lab.

Before Officer Emmit Hall's life faded away, Kory so kindly lifted his mask revealing his sacred identity. Something he would always do as a last-minute rite for his victims. The worst part was the shock Emmit received before passing out which was the sickening olge Kory wore, as the remnants of his existence slowly faded away. "Life's a bitch---then you die!" voiced Kory in a brilliant chuckle.

Jogging away from the bloody scene as if he was warming up for an Olympic meet, the chance of him being caught at this point became very slim. After a quick thought of the death penalty verdict he would be sure to get if caught, Kory sprinted off like the great Carl Lewis making this his 10th serial killing.

Chapter 3
The Bloody Aftermath

The entire Woodland Drive Projects, formerly known as Dauntless Lane, was overly populated with swarms of nervous tenants, spectators, and reporters, but mainly Hartford's finest. Although the majority of the department's finest crowded the area where two of their fellow colleagues had been slain in the line of duty, the main focal point was at 78 Woodland Dr. which is a vacant bi-level apartment.

Inside, was a naked, blonde-haired Caucasian woman sprawled out on a large cardboard box. She was in the position of an angel. Her arms were spread outward, equally level with the other, while her slender bronze standing apparatus' was spread eagle revealing a full golden-bush covering her forbidden parts.

Flash after flash after flash, the homicide team snapped photos of the body while forensics collected all the evidence they could find. It was hard not to stare at such a phenomenal body that God created, only for it to return to Heaven's crib in such a demeaning fashion. A path I am sure wasn't written in her eternal GPS.

"Okay boys and girls…Let's get this wrapped up!" First Sergeant Detective Wayne Mosley ordered, as he and his partner, Yolonda Young, 2nd grade detective, walked onto the chilling scene.

The crowd scurried at the order given which concluded the free peep show.

"Hey Londa, get a look at this," Wayne suggested, never looking up from the corpse.

"Oh my goodness….Is that," she gasped. "Is that?" Wayne cut her short by answering her question.

"Sure is CBS news reporter, Melinda King, why weren't we advised of her identity?" Wayne shouted, searching the massive crowd of onlookers for an answer. "Pretty face, big boobs…Who'd a missed it?" The dry humor rolled off his tongue like water on a rain-x'd surface, fast leading nowhere.

"Well at least we can say it's our boy 'Killa', seeing the letter 'K' he viciously carved in her abdomen." Yolonda quickly noticed.

"Yeah…Just like all the others. Well I've seen enough. Let's go check out our fallen soldiers." Wayne suggested, taking the first steps in their direction leaving the corpse in the coroner's care.

"After you. Hey Sam…" Yolonda called out, "let me know as soon as you find something useful." She bided, now hovering over Samantha, the Chief Medical Examiner.

"Will do, I'm quite sure Mrs. Howard is going to flip out over this one." Sam mentioned knowing how belligerent Deanna M. Howard, the State's Attorney, could get over such unsolved premeditated torture killings. It was true; Mrs. Howard possessed the nastiest attitude when results were not produced because it was always her job on the line. Moreover, Samantha had seen firsthand how wretched the State's Attorney could be.

"Whew…Who you telling, please don't hesitate to call me girl." Yolonda had also dealt with the devil on several occasions. After relaying the brief message, she strode off to the crime scene several feet away where two slain police officers lay dead.

Chapter 4
Ha…Ha…Ha…, You'll Never Catch Me!

This crime scene was just as heinous as Wayne expected. The scene was no different from your everyday drive-by shooting between two rival street gangs, only these two individuals were police officers. He was in fact relieved to see that the crime scene was being handled with such intensive care. Yellow numbered cones were being placed at the exact locations where each spent shell casing once lay.

"Damn…Seven malicious shots are what cut down these officers?" Wayne mumbled to no one in particular. He held a small steno-writing pad in his left hand. He had a black paper mate pen held tightly between his right thumb and index finger as he collected all the investigative notes he would need in order to solve this senseless murder.

As he further searched for any visible signs or clues about whom had the gall to shoot down two officers and a top news anchorwoman, his mind drifted back to many other crime scenes where a single, unmistakable set of footprints were left behind, almost implying, Ha ha….You'll never catch me.

Crouched down on one knee, Wayne observed the footprint closely as he did every other scene, when Yolonda quietly walked up. "You mean you're not going to take a personal photo this time?" she asked, clutching her navy-blue 3¼ trench coat tightly before crouching low beside him.

"I thought about it…, why should I?" He answered never looking her way. For some reason he was fixated on the footprint.

"Because it's habit, Wayney and one that might solve this murder, but not if you change up your methods," she elaborated. Yolonda and Wayne had become quite the duo; they were very close to say the least. Their work had brought them together in a sibling sort of way. Each knew what the other was thinking more times than not. It was fair to say, she knew he was making a bad decision when not photographing the body, which was right on the mark.

Wayne knew she was correct when she questioned whether he would take the photo, but after seventeen bodies and no real leads, he was beginning to lose faith.

"I guess you're right, Londa," he acknowledged; then used his I-Phone to photograph the print; storing it numerically with all the others.

"We're going to catch this scumbag Wayne. He'll slip up soon, and we'll be right there to nail his ass." Yolonda assured; at least she hoped so.

She had been a 2nd grade Detective for eighteen months now, surpassing several other prime candidates. It was her degrees in criminal law and psychology from Harvard that helped seal her position in the homicide division. She was the first body in, and always the last body out. She had no social life whatsoever. When she accepted the marriage proposal from the department, tying a bind that she vowed never to sever, anything but police work took a back seat; promising a career with no adultery. Married to her work was an understatement.

At thirty-two years old, 5'10", 141 pounds thick, her walnut-brown complexion was hard to resist, not to mention, her full lips, curvaceous hips, and voluptuous bottom. On most occasions, she would style her shoulder length hair in a ponytail with a wooden Chinese pin holding it neatly in place, crowning her the Venus Williams of police officers throughout her department.

"You know Londa, this case is starting to weigh me down. I'm thinking of retirement soon after this." He confessed with a heavy sigh. For both detectives, this one particular case had sucked at least 10 lbs. out of them. Morning headlines, headaches, jumpy episodes and lack of sleep, were fought off with jumbo-sized cups of coffee, which was ingested on the hour alongside non-prescribed, over-the-counter No-Doze. For the most part, Yolonda remained focused, but it was Wayne who was beginning to slip behind the likes of this 'KILLER', not to mention all of the bashing from their colleagues over the case.

Yolonda smiled, "Hush all the tired, laid back, beach resort talk, until this is all over. You know we have to bury this bastard first. Come on…Javas on me."

Chapter 5
Tears of Endearment

"**L**ive…Special news broadcasting. We are on the scene of yet another horrid murder involving three dedicated and much appreciated voices of our community who now lay deceased behind me. Just a few feet away is a lady whom we've come to love, enjoy and rely on when obtaining most of our daily and most controversial news and updates is Melissa King," Lasandra Love reported then sighed heavily. She had lost her editorial mentor, someone she held as a prestigious person and valued deeply.

"Also, amongst the slain, were two rookie patrolmen."

If up close enough, the stream of tears cascading down the almond shaded face of news reporter Lasandra Love would surely cause any 300-pound linebacker to follow suit.

"Melinda King was found right there in a vacant apartment, obviously overpowered by her attacker, then murdered." She pointed as she turned towards the apartment.

"Do they have any leads Mrs. Love?" Someone from the Hartford Courant yelled out.

"At the moment, all details are sealed due to the investigation." She answered.

"Hey…Is it the infamous 'Letter K Killa'?" Another respected journalist shouted over the other reporter's questions. The North End Agent had been officiating more of the cities crud in their column lately, and he was eager to get the lead story.

"Sorry, but I can't comment on that one either Ben." Although she wanted to blurt out, 'hell yeah,' the info was red taped to the public.

The scene dramatically switched from the even side of the projects to the odd, where Lasandra reported about the two lives that were cut short in the line of duty. Even at 2 A.M., the Mayor, Governor, and Police Chief, were summoned to the atrocious scene. However, all of the attention seemed to be focused on the two slain officers, which was expected.

In a small huddle, stood the three men-of-power conversing, undoubtedly, about the three homicides and what could possibly be done to stop them. With not too much to go on but footprints, there was nothing they could do.

As the Mayor stood firm, displaying his expensive $800 Brooks Brothers overcoat that was feathered by the early morning breeze, his hard bottom Brutini's gathered a light shadowing from the morning dew. Whatever substantial evidence at the scene that was obtainable needed to be gathered quickly, as the skies prompted a chance for early showers.

The three officials shook hands and promised to gather some relevant information that could possibly assist in leading to an end of the malicious string of serial murders. The Mayor, Governor and Police Chief each rode off into the early hours in a black Lincoln Town Car. All three men were soaked in their own thoughts.

Chapter 6
Sexy Candidate

Inside the Park Place Towers, Kory's enormous penthouse was covered in a thick fog and smoke from the stand-up shower and an expensive Cuban cigar burning in a crystal ashtray that rested on a swivel, three-tier glass end table.

Kory Blake sat on his imported mauve couch nude basking in the most recent edition of the CBS news. Had he known that killing two cops would have drawn the overseers of Hartford out of their foxholes, he would have long ago targeted the boys in blue. However, they were just an added bonus in the 'game of death.' The essential names on his particular list were calculated with vengeful choosing.

There was a time in Kory's life where he swore payback would be a bitch, and in droves of blood.

He carefully studied Lasandra's voluptuous body wrapped in the tight Shearling coat, that even through its thick covering, he could read her measurements; she was definitely a looker.

"You handled that well Mrs. Love and a whole lot better than a sacred lover would have imagined." Kory said while picking up his glass of Conjure and orange juice and downing the remains.

Kory wondered if anyone knew about their lucid affair---it didn't matter though because he did. He knew all about his victims, it was his job to get to know them in depth.

His job was to study every detail, large or small because it would support his quest for vengeance. Everyone played a significant role in his madness, even though it was unbeknownst to them.

Satisfied with his viewing, Kory used the DVR remote to rewind the broadcast to the beginning, and then masturbated, becoming one with Lasandra.

"Keep up the good work Mrs. Love, and you'll soon make the list," he said, caressing the stem of his penis as he headed towards the shower. He had special plans for tonight.

Chapter 7
Bragging Rights

After hand stroking himself into a blissful climax, Kory stepped out of his sandy-brown tiled standup shower, which is one of his favorite places in his condominium. The room temperature was oven warm. It was a calm 81 degrees Fahrenheit, which was just the way he liked it.

For no apparent reason Kory suddenly gazed at the coffee brown towel set perfectly overlapping the circled gold ring that hung securely by a 3/4 sheetrock screw, and decided to air dry. Everything about Kory was odd and peculiar.

In a naked stride, Kory found himself shadowed by a mirrored duplicate of his muscular body. He was a rock-chiseled sculpture made for the cover of Men's Fitness. Out the corner of his eye, he noticed the blood-soaked brassiere that belonged to the late Melinda King, his eighth kill. Soon after, Kory realized that he had forgotten to salvage the bra in its proper housing as keepsakes for later proofing.

Two feet away was a walk-in closet full of clear, Rubbermaid containers that housed seven other blood-soaked outfits he kept as game souvenirs; half of the accredited scoring in his game of death. After neatly storing the bloody keepsake in the container, he placed it on top of the steeple of evidence. With a satisfying smile, he envisioned every single kill with great admiration. Thereafter, with a feeling of contempt, Kory began to dress.

On the average, Kory's attire consisted of linen, silk, gators, suits, and other high-end trends; however, it was a casual affair tonight. Laid across the king size waterbed, was a pair of Polo purple label slacks, a 2x wool Polo pullover rugby, with a deep hood and leather drawstring, which he was going to rock over a black tee. Keeping the ensemble in a particular designer fashion, a pair of black ¾ leather Polo boots with a strap would complete tonight's look.

After splashing on some of his favorite cologne, he grabbed a huge stack of singles and an alligator-skin billfold full of hundreds. Last, but not least, after applying a light layer of Sporting Wave to his hair, then a black doo rag, Kory, thuggishly, put on a black scully and shot to his garage.

With the push of a button, a 2010 760 Li roared to life. The instrument panel glowing neon-white as the newness of the BMW's interior emitted a European endangered species scent. It was obvious a prime animal's skin and life was substituted to ensure the operator and owner rode in the most exquisite, comfort possible.

"Call Keonna," Kory demanded to the onboard cellular system, as he pulled out of the parking structure.

As Kory controlled the wood grain steering wheel, the phone rang at a low decibel inside the foreign whip, his thin leather gloves snuggled tightly against his large hands. Suddenly, a soft, hypnotic voice serenaded the cabin of the flagship as he sailed down Park Street.

"Hey big bruh...You call to brag?" Keonna answered.

"Never that...But now that you've mentioned it, that does put me at eight, not counting the two pigs in a blanket."

Keonna laughed. She was well aware of the current stats where she was only lagging behind by one kill.

Subsequently, the two cop kills would surely total a double point advantage at the end of their sick, twisted, vengeful 'game of death'. "You never cease to amaze me Kory. It really doesn't matter because I've already seen the news. By the way, that Mrs. Lasandra Love seemed very distraught, you know with Melinda's death an' all."

"Yeah...And?"

"You plan on playing captain-save-a-hoe?" She knew how Kory felt towards beautiful woman, especially those with long hair.

"Not sure, haven't really put any thought into it." He replied, driving by a group of street hustlers on Park and Zion Street.

"Humph!" She knew better. "All right bruh...We'll talk later. I've got business to tend to."

"I guess you do... Love you!" He chuckled, happily.

"I love you too!"

The call ended.

Chapter 8
Risqué Departure

After making the acquaintance of the Chief State Treasurer through Craigslist, he and Keonna Blake had been sexually active two, maybe three times a week. Ramon Grumenthu was a well-respected man of power. His judicial ties were endless within the constitution state. He had faithfully been married for twenty-three years, sharing the parental duties over their four kids which consisted of three boys, one beautiful girl, and last but not least-three aggressive Rottweilers as pets.

Now reaching his 53rd birthday, he decided he would rather spend the night rolling around the sack with his weekly mistress instead of the norm, which would have consisted of having dinner at a five-star restaurant with his family, then an endless night of tossing and turning. His wife Patricia was aging and no longer turned him on, nor craved sex, she was satisfied with just simple hugs and kisses. The thought of a long stretched out flannel nightgown nearly caused Ramon to vomit, as he sat inside the hot tub of his suite at the Goodwin Hotel.

"KeKe…Where are you?" Ramon called out using the pet name he had given her months ago, obviously ready for his birthday gift.

"Coming Ray-Ray…Gimme just a second," she promised, cooing like a young prep school girl.

Keonna was rolling some haze and had just popped a bottle of Moet Rose`. The audio system softly played one of Dream's new hits. Yeah, how ironic, she thought, that the R&B Killa would be serenading them at this particular moment in time. Clad in a soft-pink teddy with matching bikini and some stylish four-inch Giuseppe heels, Keonna demonstrated a sensual look. Always sexy, but careful when in Ramon's presence, Keonna wore gloves and tonight a sheer white pair graced her fingers.

Keonna was beyond beautiful. She had the most sensuous brown eyes, light-cinnamon skin, and a set of 36DD breast that sat high up on her chest with no extra support. Her thin waist measured a remarkable twenty-two inches, which molded perfectly into her thick thirty-two inch bubbled eye candy. She was a man's walking playground.

As she headed towards the bathroom, she lit the Purple Haze and took several deep pulls. She let the blunt rest between her full Mac-glossed lips. In a sultry strut, her moneymaker danced with every step she took and Ramon was completely mesmerized by the risqué display, which appeared to be in slow motion. Nevertheless, it was not surprising that she helped to kick-start his limp penis from its undeveloped stage to an erect state of being. Even with the Viagra, his rod only reached a mere 5½ inches. He regretted never having the surgery to lengthen his love stick, especially now that he's found his sweet cinnamon twist, Keonna.

"Hey you…Miss me?" She teased the elderly man entering into the room.

Keonna could clearly see that Ramon was overly excited and wanted to feast, but tonight was special, one he would always remember.

He licked his lips almost tasting her sweetness. Keonna took great pleasure torturing him over the course of their secret rendezvous.

"Come 'ere!" Her index finger ordered him like a parent ready to inflict a physical beating to a child.

At this point, Ramon tried to shake the dirty thoughts of what he wanted to do to her, but they would not leave. He had a bad thing for her.

"Get in, it's nice and warm KeKe," he urged, through a lustful smile.

"Here, take this while I step out these shoes." She mustered, passing the haze off like a football to a running back. She wanted him extra nice tonight.

He accepted the thick-bat with ease and begun sucking it like it was a Pall Mall Gold, inhaling every bit of the smoke. Amazingly, he never choked or gagged. It was as if he pre-tamed the potent herbal. He had it under his full control long before she offered it to him.

His eyes became wide as saucers when Keonna sat on the toilet, legs wide open and her camel-toe stared him dead in the face. After getting off the toilet, she guzzled some Rose` then passed the fruity passion off to Ramon. After he accepted, he downed it in its entirety. Trails of Moet trickling from his mouth to his gray and white chest hairs. Keonna smiled, and then licked the extra champagne from his person causing his pink-nipples to harden from her supple touches. Ramon was definitely a born again, freak and it was all because of Keonna. This is indeed the type of lifestyle I'm willing to get used to, he thought. She had obviously set-off a fire in his sexual seclusion that desperately needed unleashing and it was soon to be unveiled.

Keonna took the sleek bottle from Ramon, and then stepped out of her bikini. Dancing to a melodic tune inside her head, her movements mimicked those of an exotic belly dancer.

She placed the bottle onto the floor, and then squatted very low until the bridge of the bottle disappeared inside her plush cellar.

"Uuhhhh…" She moaned, staring Ramon in the face.

"Ramon…Ramon," she softly sang.

"Ramon…Ramon!"

"Yes KeKe?" His voice mimicked a scared hostage of love, caught and bound by the neck, hands and feet willing to do anything for his freedom.

"You like what you see?" Her eyelashes feathering as she spoke. "You like what you see, big-boy?"

Stuck, unable to respond due to the X-rated show, Ramon simply nodded. His muscle further expanded to its full potential, a length it had not been in years, and he loved it royally. Things like this, he had only heard about in the golf club's locker room while amongst his uptight coworkers. Appreciative that he would finally get the chance to visit this sexual plane, he intended on fulfilling all of his wildest dreams.

Keonna sped up her squats. Faster and faster, she squatted onto the length of the bottle all while watching Ramon puff on the potent relaxer.

"Ooooh…Ooooh!" she cried, nearly at her climax.

She could hear Rhianna's new single throughout her every thought, as she wound her hips to the beat.

Falling into the mood, Keonna's eyes closed for a brief moment. Upon opening them, she was faced with his pink stiffness. His eyes were petite and chinky and he was salivating at the mouth. Still massaging the Rose` bottle with her vaginal muscles, she took Ramon's pink, peppermint stick into her mouth. Keonna, herself knew, she was 'bout it, down for whatever when it came to sex, but this sexual act was going into the archives for later use.

"Mmm, mmm!" She moaned, through wet slurps enjoying the pleasure of stroking him with the slightest usage of her teeth.

Ramon's eyes were somewhere lost in the back of his head. He was gone, high and tipsy. He was in a place Patricia could never send him, and he enjoyed it fully.

Her strokes sped up, both on the bottle, also his phallus. She was at her mark waiting to hear the sound of the gun blasting off to release her tidal wave of cum into the sleek bottle.

"Uumm, ooh, oooh mmm..." She moaned, as her fluids oozed out heavily.

Finally, Keonna had broken her sexual barrier, but she was not the selfish type. She continued her stride on Ramon's dick, only she now inserted the bottle into his rectum, giving him a glass enema. Strangely, Ramon was not only inviting, but he was really enjoying the ass fucking at the moment. What really fucked her head up was when he backed up to the toilet, then sat down and rode the bottle like a cheap trick off 59th street in New York.

Now freaked out and bored with the party, Keonna dug into her breast and eased out a three-inch surgical blade and with a swift slice, she severed his dick from his aging body. A loud scream escaped from his vocal box just before she brought the sharp blade across his throat. Streams of red serum squirted all over the bathroom floor. He was dead before his wrinkled neck tilted backwards making the slit even larger.

Keonna was strikingly quick when she sliced the letter "K" deep into his chest. Satisfied with her work, she wiped everything down with some bleach she held in a small receptacle that she kept in her bag. It was a keen move on her part in case she ever happened to leave any DNA behind. After collecting all of her garments, belongings, and anything else that could draw some heat to her door, she threw on a blonde wig, a long black designer coat and a pair of dark shades, and then left the suite.

Passing a door attendant, she said, "The Chief State Treasurer doesn't wish to be bothered. He's got a lot of shit on his mind."

Chapter 9
Blake History

As the night's skyline aged with darkness, the late day sunshine withered away respectfully with every churning hour. Still, as local authorities strenuously tried to conclude and solve the terrible and suspenseful mystery behind the letter "K" killer, the malevolent minds of two siblings stirred a serious panic throughout the city. The killings were very similar to the Atlantic City child murders, only Hartford's victims consisted of some prominent and a few less fortunate citizens in the middle-class brackets.

Kory traveled the grim streets of Hartford, unnerved by what the newspapers, T.V. and radio broadcaster had to say, it only fueled his fire and thirst for vengeance.

With every street corner he passed, he viewed the many struggling youths as they sold the Government's poison, continuing the stagnated future of so many. It angered him to drive by every ten or so odd businesses, buildings, tenements and restaurants, only to see a liquor store that had not discriminated against the legal age limit when vending the poisonous liquid serums to today's youth.

Though it is true, Kory enjoyed the savoring taste of marijuana and premium liquor when his desirable crave demanded he indulge. It was a habitual addiction he knew how to control. As the oil-black BMW eased its way through the night's windy air, Kory sipped every so often from the pint of Remy V.S., letting the warmth of the cognac soothe his throat. Pulling on a perfectly rolled blunt stuffed with purple haze, he entered the parking lot of the newly owned and renovated Teezer'z. He co-owned the club with a close friend. He had an important business meeting to attend to and a little shopping to do.

Kory and Keonna were born into money, so they were able to indulge in a lavish world of no limits and infinite spending to a high caliber. Their birth parents were Nathaniel and Kaitlyn Blake and before their untimely demise, they smartly invested in the stock market. They also built their family corporation, Blake Industries, a nationwide tool & die company that held a strong place in many of our states today. Blake Industries became such a popular hit and investment, that the top members of Exxon thought it would be a profitable move to purchase 25% of its shares and back the Blakes by naming the family business a subsidiary of Exxon, which of course is one of today's leading Fortune 500 companies. Back in the 70's, their totaled capitalization topped at $4,000,000,000 U.S. dollars, though today, Exxon easily ranged at $250,000,000,000.

The Blakes also had shares in Westinghouse Electric and Anheuser-Busch. Together they owned over 500,000 shares. It was a very wise investment, at such a low commitment, back then. Kory and Keonna were only toddlers when the Blakes suddenly found themselves at the end of a mountain ridge in the San Fernando Valley one late night. Nathaniel never saw his life ending in such a tragic way, but through thoughtful planning, Nathaniel ensured that his offspring would live well by his will. It was so well put together that the James' adopted the two children in hopes to someday acquire what shares the children rightfully owned back into their family for the sake of the James' legacy. It was not enough that they were already a name amid the elite, being James Electric, sitting second fiddle only to General Electric, the world's number one entity.

As Kory and Keonna grew older, so did their desires to understand why and what happened to their natural parents. Despite all the under minding of William and Carroll James after gaining full custody of Kory and Keonna, they also met a fate in the lap of fire when their ten-million-dollar home burned to the ground back in the 80's, not a decade later. The end result was that this accident was also ruled to be a suspicious death. Naturally, custody of Nathaniel and Kaitlyn's offspring stayed within the James grasps as, John Jr., and his wife Elizabeth James assumed custodial duties. Things were cool until James and Elizabeth relocated to Hartford, CT.

John James quickly devised a new plan for obtaining some dead-presidents by opening up a large brewery just outside of the city limits and making Kory president. Kory somehow through numerous negligent background checks on their employees happened to stumble onto some unknown relatives who were also old friends of his late parents. They were able to give him some insight as to what could have really happened to his parents on that dreadful night in California. When Kory approached James with his findings, the entire scenario was downplayed to merely lost family members trying to stick their hands out for the Blake's riches.

Kory was no dummy. He let things die down, but Keonna and he were slowly planning to assure that their parent's death was not in vain and avenged ten times worse.

Chapter 10
Friends, Some Old...Some New

Pulling up to Teezer'z, Kory immediately noticed the parking lot was extra full tonight. He also noticed the silver sports package added to the 2010 S600 Mercedes Benz amongst the crowd, so he knew Robert Krammer had to be somewhere inside enjoying the explicit world of exotic dancing. Twice a month the two would enjoy each other's company, while conversing about ways to seize the twenty-five percent John James controlled in Blake Industries, and possibly all of James Electric, if things went accordingly.

Kory and Robert became good friends and were nearly inseparable after a board meeting involving all of Blake Industries' major shareholders. Things around the company had been showing classic signs of scandal lately. Along with Kory, some felt the need to address certain issues. Unbeknownst to them, John James and a few others had been conspiring in the looms of darkness where Robert Krammer had fallen victim to what John deemed phase-one of their fiendish plot. During one particular meeting, things got very heated resulting in Robert Krammer being stripped of his 15% voice within Blake Industries.

"This is a hoax," shouted Robert, hearing the accusations brought fourth concerning him signing into a falsified share agreement. "Pure crockery!" He continued heatedly.

"Sorry, but it's right here in black and white. In addition, I can strongly assure you that an expert has authenticated this signature and it belongs to you. Now you see, the only problem is, that you placed your John Hancock on a fraudulent document and the penalty for that clearly states that you immediately forfeit your shares back, where they'll go up for auction by the end of the business day upon finding," stated John James.

"Let me take a look at that!" Through a tight face, Kory carefully reviewed the document as his eyes bucked with curiosity. By the last page, he had seen enough to know John James was correct in his findings. However, the most important fact was that the lawyer who had drawn up Robert's share agreement had passed away several years ago. Not seeing the need to scrutinize pass paperwork, no one had considered the fact that there could be a false paper trail tied into Blake Industries.

After studying the document, Greg Hollins, Blake Industries in house lawyer, agreed that it was indeed a fake. Kory then ordered Greg to examine every other share agreement by the end of the working day.

With all that having taken place during the meeting, Robert calm and collectively cleared out all his personal belongings and was escorted by security off the premises.

Kory had a much bigger agenda. He scurried to catch up to Robert who now stood in a distraught manor awaiting the arrival of his vehicle from the valet.

"Hold on Robert," Kory tugged at his forearm.

When Robert saw it was a friendly face, he lowered his defensive shield. He knew the Blakes were good people.

"Hey, careful there. I thought you were…"

"John James," Kory quickly said.

Even through Robert's smile, Kory could see the hurt and pain in Robert's gloomy eyes. Kory had never witnessed a grown man on the verge of tears until now, but surprisingly, he held the torrent back. Kory thought that Robert was a trooper that is until he realized where his future lied.

"I guess you read my mind…What's up though?" Rob wondered, a stream of tears now cascading down his face.

Kory offered him his monogrammed handkerchief and then invited him for a drink. After a few hours, they devised a scheme that would possibly get the Krammers back what they deserved and all of Blake Industries.

L♥D~ L♥D~ L♥D

Kory stepped out of his car and opened the rear door. It was chilly and the cold air was nipping at anything radiating heat, so he grabbed his black leather pea coat to help keep him from being frost bitten. His swagger was as usual, above par. Yanking his black scully as far as it could go over his ears, he sauntered towards the Teezer'z entrance where he now welcomed the club's heat. Through the door, he received several head nods from other well-established cats in the game. Whether legal or illegal, Kory was that dude and demanded his respect.

They spared no expense reconstructing the new Teezer'z. Its current owners had an elaborate vision; one that would attract the city is most well-spoken for ballers and executives unlike the old Teezer'z. He co-owned it with a very good friend of his that was currently serving out a lengthy prison term in a federal prison. Kory was CEO, seeing while in the Bureau of Prisons, Spaid was restricted from owning or gaining profits from all entities. The two went back like hide & go seek, real sandbox types. Their friendship was exclusive and genuine, but most of all their friendship was built off loyalty. To this day, there had never been any trust issues for Spaid when it came down to acquiring what profits were owed to him. They were passed on to him through his better half, who periodically collected his share as promised while he was gone away.

Deeper into the establishment, Kory found Robert courtside the dancing stage making it rain. Kory smiled as he made it to his usual table in the corner of the club. "Shake Your Tail Feather" was blaring throughout the concert speakers as Mo`nay captured every man's heart and bankroll. The pole seemed to enjoy the way Mo`nay rode up and down its length. She was one of the club's best dancers.

"Excuse me; will you be having your usual tonight boss?" Molasses inquired, standing in front of Kory in nothing but some red Jimmy Choos. Her breasts were thick and round with minimal sag and her sacred garden was neatly shaved very low where you could easily notice the 2-carat diamond piercing through her clit.

"Yeah, but make it two bottles Mo`." He smacked her on her ass as she sauntered off, her switch causing each cheek to bounce.

By the time Mo`nay finished her set, Kory had downed half of his Rose`.

Shortly after, Robert found his way over to Kory's private booth. "Wassup Rob?"

"Dude, you already know, I'ma tear that chocolate bunny down, tonight…" His words slurred.

"Oh, I know. I saw you push that wad in her G-String. You all right though. How's the wifey?"

"Uh, who? You mean that money hungry bitch, Bethany?" Robert hesitated, and then made sure his 100% cotton shirt was intact. "You know how it goes Kory, when they assume the well is dry they find another drill." He said, remembering the day Bethany walked out.

"Sorry to hear that Rob, did she take the kids too?"

"Oh no, not Beth. Said she couldn't afford it. They had to stay with their sorry ass father!"

Kory felt sorry for his friend. He'd always known Bethany didn't have Robert's best interest at heart, long before she propositioned him with an act of fellatio, something Robert had yet to experience from her. Bethany was a real looker. At 5'6", she had beautiful long blonde hair, the most exquisite ocean-blue eyes and shapely legs to anchor her round bottom. Bethany could easily have any man she desired and at that time, Robert happened to be it. Nevertheless, after learning about his recent termination from Blake Industries, she no longer saw a future with the man.

Kory shook his head in utter disgust. "Aye, I assume your little stash has gotten low, so I set aside two-hundred grand for you. You and the kids can use the mansion out in Wethersfield also."

Kory rarely frequented the place and was thinking of putting it on the market. He had several pads to kick back at whenever he chose, so letting Robert and the kids utilize his expensive abode was nothing short of true friendship, no skin off his back.

"Thanks pal, you know I got `chu once we handle John James." There it was that slurring again. Robert's speech clearly displayed signs of his drunkenness. "Yeah, handle John James…" He repeated with pure venom in his eyes. The James' had turned his family's world inside out and he wanted blood.

Even with the boisterous music blaring, Kory looked around weary of unwanted listeners. He was just that careful in everything he did, always looking to tie loose ends.

"Don't worry about it, that's what real friends do. Now this thing with Robert and Elizabeth will happen, but on my time. Until then, you're covered financially. I've got several other projects I'm covering in the city," Kory advised, never revealing the details.

"Okay bruh, I got 'chu! How is Keonna doing? I haven't seen much of her round lately," he blurted out of nowhere, which heightened Kory's threat radar.

Kory eyed his drunken friend before responding.

"She's been around, mostly entertaining the city's social network," he smirked, knowing better. "You know how she loves to throw down."

Kory was very protective of his baby sister. It was more so about her safety when it came down to men in general. Therefore, he definitely was not easily inclined to discuss her in any degree.

"I sure do!"

"Aye, here's that number you needed."

Kory passed a folded piece of paper across the table and Robert quickly accepted it.

"You finally got it, I see. Not sure how, but you did. This is a very good look. I'll let you know what comes out of this as soon as I hear something back."

Kory shook his head in acknowledgement. He was peeping a new piece of eye candy walking their way. He figured her to be 5'7"-5'8", and she was thick all over, except in the mid-section. She had a butter-almond complexion with slanted eyes, which almost made her appear Chinese. Kory had never seen or heard of a china girl with a thick curvaceous body. She obviously had to be mixed.

Finally, her sensuous saunter halted at the booth. She also appeared to have a little class and respect for herself. She was dressed more conservatively than any of the other females in the club; wearing a halter-top, a pair of tangerine-orange boy shorts and matching heels. Her halter-top only exposed her two erect nipples both of which you could hang a coat off. After throwing her long hair to one side, she introduced herself.

"Hello gentlemen, my name is Ashanti, but my stage name is Desire." She smiled widely, her thirty-two' straight and white as oyster pearls.

"I can see why," Robert burst out. The sexual thoughts controlling his speech. "Damn."

Kory shrugged his broad shoulders embarrassed by his partner's actions, although he should not have been. He was quite use to his sexual ways when it came to women of color. He had a strong fetish for thick, beautiful women. It was Ashanti who felt like a ton of bricks was lodged in her stomach as it churned out of control when she recognized she was meeting her new boss.

"How are you Shanti?" Kory questioned, with a slight smirk, while casing her voluptuous sculpture, his thoughts clearly explicit.

"I like that. My grandpa used to call me that all the time," she shot him a warm smile in appreciation.

"Well I'll find you another nickname to go by seeing another man; especially your gramps used that one."

"No...No, please call me Shanti. It has a special ring to it," She insisted. "Can I get you another bottle, sir?"

Robert looked at Ashanti, then at Kory. He was puzzled.

"Yes, I know Rose` cost $200 a bottle, but Mr. Blake looks well worth the purchase."

"Sure, we'll have two," Kory nodded, leaning into a more comfortable position in his booth. It was just a ploy on Kory's part to see how much Ashanti craved his acquaintance. He would refund her money one day later down the line.

Without a second thought, Ashanti's large ass bounced as she glided over to the bar.

"Damn Kory, you go at it like that, huh?"

"I mean, look at me. You know if you had some tits and a phat ass, you'd throw it at me too!" He laughed, as Robert punched him in the shoulder.

"Well…I've got a date with Mo`nay, so, I'll get with chu Playa…Playa!" He voiced playfully.

"No doubt, drive safely. Better yet, let Mo`nay handle the wheel tonight." Kory suggested. He did not want Robert driving in his condition.

"Oh, I plan on it," Robert laughed and walked off.

L♥D~ L♥D~ L♥D

Kory and Ashanti kicked it until closing. She begged to be his cushion for the night and of course, he obliged. Ten-minutes before rolling out, Kory stopped to holler at a couple of heavy-hitters from around the way. Dudes he has grown to know from pick-up games at the YMCA since relocating to Hartford from California.

"Wassup Noot?" Kory said.

"You playboy," Noot replied after sipping from his drink.

"I see the big boys out to play tonight. Wassup Mega, Chubb, Shaun. D`ayum and y'all got Tru, to cash in some of that '88 money?" Kory stated paying homage. The four men were by far your elite when it came to the Game, getting out unscathed with plenty to show for their hard work in the streets.

They all smiled knowing Tru's money was long.

"I'm feeling what you and Spaid have done with the new spot," Mega added, as he checked out a fly Mami prancing by.

"You better chill out Meg, wifey probably out riding, strapped up, and ready to catch you slippin'," Kory teased. "But look I'm out. Y'all stay up and keep it green." Kory said.

As he exited club, Kory noticed two trucks side by side. One was a gold Denali, the other a milk-white Audi C7. Just looking at the Audi, he knew it was Deezy, Onk and Breeze. The Denali belonged to the kid Coco from Brook St., also known as Bedrock, a well-known cocaine block. Stuck in his stare, he was caught off guard when Ashanti crept up behind him.

"Damn girl, you almost caught a bad one," he explained showing her his silenced .9 mm.

"I guess so, but I'm from the P.J.'s too."

She pulled out an automatic 9-shot .380.

"You better watch that one Kory, she's a killa!" Someone yelled.

"I see dat."

Kory blew some warm air into his coupled hands, as they made the small hike down the steps. After pointing out his whip to Shanti, he unlocked the doors and suggested she warm her kitten.

"Aye peeps, if y'all ever decide y'all wanna flip some of that street money into some untouchable shit, holla, I got 'chu."

"No doubt playboy, I see dat Wall Street shit's treating you real good," Onk said. You could see the brisk night air billowing as he spoke. He was the one to watch, even if you thought you were tight.

"One-Up!" Kory finished, making his way towards his vehicle where the reward of the night lustfully sat warm and waiting patiently.

Once inside the BMW, Kory took his place behind the wheel and examined Shanti's beauty further. "Hey, is it cool to leave my whip here?" Ashanti asked, staring into his melodic eyes.

"Fo' sho, but give me the keys. I'll have it flat-bedded to your spot."

She watched as Kory got out, placed her keys under the driver's seat, and then made a call to whom she presumed was a towing company.

As soon as Kory made it back to his vee, Shanti seductively asked, "Sooo, handsome, where we headed?" She wore the sexiest expression that a man could stand.

"If you gotta ask," he paused, "nowhere."

Shanti shrugged. "Umph." She reached over grabbing his dick through his pants and then finally pulled his prize out. Kory rode away enjoying the delightful warmth of her mouth against his chocolate stick.

Chapter 11
Hard Press

John James, the only living heir to William and Carroll James, awoke to the slobbery warmth of saliva from his outgrown St. Bernard. They had a very unusual, but typical bond. Bratford was used to the morning ritual counting back ten-years, though lately John James had not been laying his over achieved body in his large bed. As of late, he had been consumed with board meetings and the decisive planning for the final undermining seizure of Blake Industries. Never satisfied or one to settle, it was his envy, greed and lust that drove him into such a strategic state. When it was all said and done, he would also make sure he defrauded Kory out of his shares within James Electric.

He had been spending countless hours inside the plush comfort of his private office, where he would fall fast asleep on a lay-z-boy, with his beady eyes too heavy to keep open.

Through outside sources, John James learned that Kory was breaking new ground. However, he didn't know exactly what the young billionaire-boy was up to at this point. He did take close notice to the ample amount of time that Kory and Robert Krammer had been sharing recently. He also learned that Kory had added some extra lawyers to his cabinet, who were paid to keep close watch on the former ones. It was a pre-caution he picked up from the late Biggie

Smalls, his favorite rapper. Definitely, a tactic he felt was well worth the huge retainers he set forth.

"Get down boy!" John James yelled in Bratford's ear. Bratford continued to lick his master, disobeying his orders. "Okay, okay boy...I miss you too!" He rubbed the large dog under his slobbish muzzle with a wide smile. After a moment of uncontained affection, he somehow got Bratford to go and retrieve the morning's edition of the Hartford Courant. Even in the deep woods of Glastonbury, John James had several inner city newspapers delivered on a daily basis, which was a required piece to his evil enigma. After accepting the newspaper, he flicked off the hot slob Bratford left on the front page and immediately found the stock market section.

Next, he brought his 60" Sony plasma to life, quickly tuning into the Bloomberg/Market Watch to view the morning stock exchange ticker. He was pleased to notice General Electric was still at $20.60, as well as IBM held at $137.37. What did seem odd was how Mobil fell by 3½ points and Standard Oil of California, which he just recently bought 50,000 shares at 12.50. It was really nothing to be concerned with though, that was how the market worked.

In the midst of glory, John felt exuberant, more so rejuvenated seeing how well J.E. was doing, stable with no decline in the current forecast. Throwing one leg after the other over the edge of the bed, he now stood up groping himself while studying the vast flow of water cascading into his fabricated lake from a small waterfall that stood 7ft. above a mass of green pine trees. It was too early to chase his crave for cigar smoke, so he gallantly paced the hallway floor of his 6000 sq. ft. home alongside a cheerful Bratford, until he reached the dining area where Elizabeth and

Isabella, their housekeeper, enjoyed fresh croissants and premium select coffee.

"Hey pretty ladies," he cheerfully greeted the two female specimens.

With a look of embarrassment, Isabella turned her head noticing John's morning erection.

Unaware of Isabella's gushy feelings, he stared confusingly at Elizabeth shrugging her sleek shoulders. The loaded weapon in his pants not once being a motive in her disposition.

It was not until Elizabeth innocently gestured towards the bulging print in his briefs that he realized he had not urinated this morning.

"Oooh," he uttered, turning slightly to the left using the Hartford Courant to shield the obvious. "It's okay now Isabella, I've put the beast away." He joked taking his place at the breakfast nook.

"Yes, it's okay Isabella, he's sitting now," Elizabeth advised. "Babes, what's got you up so early?" She added with emphasis.

"Bratford, of course. It's a good thing though, because now I have a jump on the numbers and we're doing extremely well."

"So what about…," She covertly looked out her peripheral at Isabella, "you know who?"

Despite the fact that no joke had been said, he had to laugh at how his wifey tried to conceal certain things from Isabella, even knowing she spoke not a lick of English except yes sir and no sir.

"You mean Kory and his pesky sister?"

Elizabeth held no restraint as she swayed her head back and forth at her husband's ignorance. He could be so shallow at times, which may very well be the cause and effect to his future downfall.

"Yes, I guess so John!" She spoke with her voice disturbed and out of normal context.

John's awareness became piqued after hearing the tone and display of annoyance from his wife. Not to mention he detected a change in her behavior whenever Isabella was in the room. Her usual calm, cool, loving demeanor would morph into something short of snobby and 'til this day he couldn't put his finger on what was triggering it.

"Well yes, I have meetings today and most of tomorrow also. He's gotten two new attorney and they seem to be checking all of the work and accountability of the ones he already had working for him," he sighed, and then continued sipping the Columbian coffee. "It's like he trusts no one, I tell you!"

"I guess he's smarter than you think John," she replied smugly.

"Guess so, but let's see how smart he is once this new plummet is implemented and he sees the decline in profits. Well, I've gotta run, meeting Jordan and Brice in a few."

"Golf, I presume?"

"How'd you guess?"

He stood up, and then poured the room temperature coffee down the drain.

"It's Saturday, John! You, Kory, and the rest of the boys meet up and test each other's manhood. I swear if they were selling bottles of testosterone, you'd have a wine cellar full."

"I've got enough juice, sweetheart," he said groping his wood with a huge smile as he and Bratford left for a shower.

"So disgusting," Elizabeth thought, and then in an instance, she got a good glimpse of Isabella eyeing John's playful antic. However, there was no cringing whatsoever. "Come on Bella, Let's swim." Elizabeth ordered.

Chapter 12
Drunk'N Luv

In the peaked hills of Wethersfield, CT., sat four-acres of pristine property where the enormous abode belonging to the Blakes rested. Perfectly manicured shrubs and rosary bushes surrounded the property. A black iron gate secured the modern day fortress.

In the second floor master bedroom, Mo`nay lay comfortably atop a snoring Robert. They had a fun-filled night of drunken sex and drinking that began on the dark roads of Hartford and ended with Robert and Mo`nay knocked out on a king sized bed. Robert's snoring actually caused Mo`nay to wake out of her slumber. After a quick glance of her surroundings, she recalled the sexual night they'd shared.

Fully awake now, she nudged her leg over his feeling his limp member. She playfully licked at his nipple with soft wet strokes causing him to squirm unknowingly. He was out of it, knowing she had to go further to awaken the beast, she threw the down comforter to the floor exposing their nakedness, then stuffed Lil' Robert into her warm mouth. By the fifth slow stroke down his shaft, they had both fully awaken.

"Umm..." He moaned eyes slightly ajar.

She had a vicious death lock on his hot link, as she accepted his round helmet deep into her throat. Pushing his calves up into his stomach gave her full access to his balls that she twirled in between her free hand like golf balls. Robert hadn't felt this good the entire time he was in wedlock with Bethany. He found it sad that this type of treatment could only be found in a dimly lit strip club, but it didn't bother him to splurge one bit. In his world, he felt he deserved such treatment.

"Oooh, oooh! Yes…yes, jus' like that!" He begged and begged, pushing her head from the back, hard and fast. She sucked his thickness like a champion, never missing a single stroke. The slurping sounds were enough to drive them both to climax during any morning session, however you had to put in massive work or be a magician to get him to nut once the show started, which Mo'nay had no quarrels with.

Mo'nay continued her assault on his cock all while massaging his balls. At the same time, he was enjoying the softness of her breast with his right hand while the other rested on the back of her head. Knowing he would never cum this way, Mo'nay climbed on top and slid down his pole accepting every inch slowly.

She interlocked her hands with his allowing him access to her thick nipples, which he sucked with hurriedness. Bucking like a wild bull, she rode his length with rapid speed, the air inside her womb creating a loud farting noise, their skin slapping in an orchestrated concerto during their passionate sex drive.

Robert locked onto her winding waist, pulling her up then down, controlling the velocity of the movement.

"Ahhhh, Ahhh, Ahhh, Oooooooh! Harder! Harder!" She cried. "Yeah, yeah, yeah." She chanted, enjoying her dick shamelessly.

"You like that huh? You wanna ride daddy's toy don't you?"

He drove his 4x4 deeper into the wooded forest never thinking there would be an end. The path was endless, a trail of infinite land. The sheets were soaked with sweat and the room was engulfed by the smell of sex as the two ravaged each other. Somehow Mo`nay got Robert to unlatch her nipple and she quickly spun around with him still lodged deep inside her womb, her mouth now pacifying his toes as her ass plopped up & down his oily shaft. The more she bucked, the more his head thrashed from left to right. She knew the toe sucking had a major part in it, so she added another toe to her warm mouth, as he helped her thick ass slam hard onto his dick.

"Yeahhh daddy, yeah!" She yelled releasing a volcanic orgasm down his pole. Then three hard thrusting strokes later, he shot a pocket of semen into her womb.

They both lay there in a heavy panting session, as she continued to lick his feet and wind her curvaceous hips. It was some of the best sex she had ever had.

Five or ten-minutes later, Robert's phone began to summon him. Too tired to move, he let it ring but it never stopped. Eventually, Mo`nay got up to get it. Robert could care less; he was paralyzed by her pussy.

"Hello?" She took the courtesy of answering.

"So I see you claiming papers now?" Kory said into the phone.

He knew what Robert went through, seeing he had also experienced Mo`nay's toe curling action, only he was too strong for her pussy game, which always only resulted in an extra $500 and cab fare.

"Not sure yet, but...I'll put 'em on. Bye." She smiled, handing Robert his phone.

"Yo!" He managed.

"Wassup Rob. Who was that, Bethany?" He joked.

"Now you've never heard me slur after sex with Beth, you know exactly who that is!"

"Anyways, 'bout to go swing the clubs with the boys, you coming through?"

"Don't think I'll be able to make it. I'll catch you later though."

"All right, be careful Rob, she's deadly!"

"I know..."

L♥D~ L♥D~ L♥D

The sun was definitely putting on for the city. The skyline was vibrant and picturesque, posting a wide rainbow effect just below the clusters of white-fluff.

It was a perfect day to parade an expensive car around, which is exactly what Kory chose to do as he displayed his 2010 aluminum-grey Lamborghini Gallardo through town. He had on a pair of tinted sunglasses, some casual plaid Polo shorts, with a crisp white V-neck tee. He even went as far as Polo oxfords.

His mood was mellow and calm, although his desire for blood flushed his mental. He quickly lit a blunt to add more ease to his posture. He had major plans and goals for the future and Keonna was urging him to speed things along, however, speed would not accomplish or gain all that was due to the Blake dynasty. The people who cheated, stole, deceived and murdered their parents would forfeit everything wholesome and endearing to them. It would be blood for blood.

As the quarter-million-dollar time capsule turned into Keney Parks Golf Course, Kory could see that several others had also come out of their dwelling to enjoy a hole-in-one. A young caddy quickly saw dollar signs when the sports car halted.

"Excuse me sir, my name is Sean and I'd like to caddy for you today Mr. Blake."

He'd taken notice to the rear plate as the vehicle approached.

Kory stood still and observed the young man for a moment, then said, "You're new Sean."

"Yes sir I am. Doing a little side work to pay for tuition." He replied modestly.

Kory smiled, he thought it was strange seeing a young black kid looking to do caddy work here at the club, but he admired the kid's ambition and drive. He just hoped he was worthy of the strenuous task, especially considering whom he would be pairing against.

"Sure, no problem Sean, my clubs are in the front seat."

Sean quickly grabbed the bag of clubs then loaded them into the golf cart.

"Are you meeting anyone today or teeing alone?" Sean inquired, seeing no entourage in tow.

Before Kory got a chance to answer, a Dodge Viper and a new Cadillac SLR pulled up beside them. It was Brice and Jordan. They hopped out and their usual caddies ran up to earn their weekly stipend.

"Hey, wassup Kory?" Brice mimicked Kory's Ebonic lingo.

"Out early today, huh, Kory. Shit, we usually have to call and wake you up bro." Jordan stated.

Kory brushed it off as usual; he was accustomed to their idiotic slurs. He was, and would always be one up on them; as so, he was banging both their wives whenever he felt the need to slut around.

"Wassup Brice, how's Janice?" He smirked.

"Fine, I'll tell her you said hello." Brice frowned feeling some type of way at Kory's remark.

"Jordan…Jordan what's crackin' playa? It's 'bout time to trade in, naw upgrade that Dodge, don't you think? I'm sure Susan is very terrified in that thing," he smiled widely. "Make sure you tell her hello also, and the pie was very thoughtful." It was apparent Kory's comment went clear over Jordan's head even with the sly remark he made.

"Yeah, you're right. She has been complaining about it. She wants a Volvo or some fucking wagon, but you know that'll never happen!"

Kory shook his head at how pitiful John James' two flunkies could be at times.

"Where's John?" Kory asked.

"He should be pulling up soon. He had to stop for gas, but he told us to get started," Brice answered.

"Well then, let's get it started," Kory suggested and the three golf carts rode off.

L♥D~ L♥D~ L♥D

Unexpectedly, John James noticed a canary yellow box on 22's as it swerved into the service station, and the finest female specimen emerged in her most elegant stride.

"Damn girl, you looking fine as always," John James said as he poured on his charm, complimenting Keonna. He always had a thing for the slender cinnamon twist, despite their age difference.

"Stop it James," she blushed batting her thick eyelashes. "I thought you were swinging the iron today?" She flirted a tad bit, noticing the bulge forming down below.

"Oh I am, I just had to stop to filler-up real quick, but I saw your Hummer pull in so I paused to say hello."

He was there waiting on an important client, rather investor. He hoped the investor would not pull in and crash the party because it could prove detrimental to his future.

Keonna was no dummy. She saw John's Aston Martin a mile away, so she pretended to need some fuel and a beverage. She could see the sweat beads forming over his brows, he was clearly nervous.

"Well...James, I'll be seeing you around, I've gotta get moving." She said, casting a tainted smile.

"You take care, Kee!" He sighed heavily, as the birdcage on wheels skirted out the lot. He wasted no time hopping back in his coupe where it was cool and comfortable.

Not more than thirty-seconds later, a dark-blue sedan pulled up behind the Aston Martin. The driver of the sedan got out, then into John's sports car.

"Is everything okay? You look flush, like you've seen a ghost John-James."

He did, it was Kee driving back the other way in traffic, and he just hoped she was not paying the lot any mind. However, it was hard to tell, seeing her windows were obscured with black film.

"I'm cool Harry. What 'chu got for me?"

Harold shrugged his shoulders because he knew how stressed John could be at times. He sat a brown attaché case over his lap and pushed in the 3-digit code to open it up.

"Here, a $100,000 like you asked. Now do we have a deal?" Harry questioned wearily. He had done what John

James asked of him and produced the final payment as required, which totaled $1,000,000 untraceable dollars.

"Of course Harry, would I stiff you?" He gave him a stern, but cunning look.

"No, I don't think so. So how long before I take over Blake Industries?" He wanted a date and he wanted one soon.

"Soon Harry... Soon."

Almost forty-five minutes later, John James rode across the minty green pasture, finally stopping at hole number three. His cockiness and charismatic nature went into second gear immediately.

"Hey boys, miss me? I see you've gotten a new caddy Kory." He joked after stepping out of his golf cart.

"Looks that way Jamie." Kory replied, sarcastically.

Brice and Jordan chuckled at Kory's pet name for his friend when he tended to go overboard.

"Cute, Kory." He responded.

"So where were you all this time Jamie, you know we tee off at 11:00. Business perhaps?" He threw it out there to fuck with him.

John James immediately assumed Keonna alerted him, but she had not had time; she was off stalking her next victim.

"Uh, no, my baby over heated and I stopped to add some antifreeze."

"C'mon, let's swing." Brice intervened.

L♥D~ L♥D~ L♥D

It was 3:30 p.m. and the group had finally conquered their 18th hole, and called it quits. As Sean escorted Kory and his clubs to the car, Kory informed him that he had a job not only on Saturday caddying, but also somewhere at his office, and then tipped him with five c-notes.

"Thank you Mr. Blake and I'll definitely be here on Saturday, bright and early, I'll also be looking forward to working for your company."

The boys decided to have a drink and a meal, so they headed to Ruth's Chris Steakhouse. Midway through their meal, Kory asked John James to walk with him to the outdoor deck. During their conversation, Kory spoke solely about his desire to take full control of Blake Industries and the brewery.

John James was twelve years his senior and very manipulatively smart. Nevertheless, Kory saw right through his bull. Just as all the other discussions, he promised he would soon be able to turn over full control of the Blake's shares, however he blamed the delay on paperwork; a legality thing impeding the alteration.

"We've been down this road a million times James and still, you preach bullshit. However, you know what?" Kory paused with a smile. "You know the leopard is the only thing I've come to know whose spots don't change. They also say nothing is permanent, but change, I will leave you with that to sleep on. Give my best to Elizabeth." He concluded leaving James stuck on stupid.

Chapter 13
Never Trust A Pretty-Face And A Smile

Like clockwork, the following morning after a small social gathering of colleagues, friends and maybe a couple family members, Clyde Barksdale loved a vigorous work out. Although he endured a continuous pain in the left side of his head, he forced himself out of bed. After a couple of Excedrin's and a hot shower, the migraine seemed to subside.

Clyde knew the extra shot of whiskey would definitely have him hung over in the a.m., but it did not stop him. He dressed in his normal workout gear and headed down to his kitchen. He needed his supplement of three-egg whites and a chilled piece of fruit before he headed out. It was not long before he was in traffic en route to Weaver High School to get in some laps around their huge track.

He wondered what the many motorists thought as they peered into his car window and saw him with a large hand towel draped over his head. The sun was shining with a radiance that seeped through Clyde's towel, rekindling his migraine. He cursed Earth's eye of day, begging for it to run and hide behind a cloud.

Clyde was aimlessly searching for a radio station when several angry car horns blared loudly. He had missed the trail of cars as they went through the light at Woodland

St. and Homestead Ave., which happened to be a lengthy one.

"Awe...Go to hell!" He shouted, flipping them all the bird.

When the red light switched to green, he sped erratically down Homestead, on the brink of road rage. Surprisingly, Clyde made it to the track without incident. The normal crowd was up and at it today. There were joggers everywhere. Some were just arriving, and some were already in stride. He saw two males stretching up against a brick wall that seemed enthusiastic about today's venture, but Clyde was still experiencing his ache. Get over it! His inner voice spoke loudly.

Clyde was 6'2", pale faced and well built. His constant regiment of calisthenics, laborious hours utilizing Weaver's large track and a nutritious diet, was enough to maintain his fountain of youth. At forty-seven, Clyde looked damn good for his age. He found his place on the track and began to stretch as always. A group of young females approached in a sweaty jog about to make the bend around the track and whistled at Clyde's masculine backside. He smiled as they passed.

"Alright old fella, let's get moving." He mustered, and then took flight.

His towel was tucked snuggly into his nylon top as he sported a dark pair of Ray Ban sunglasses to fight the bright daystar.

Three quarters around the track, Clyde saw a nice looking woman stretching her right leg on the fence. The woman sported an I-Pod clipped to her waist. Stuck on the camel toe bursting through her pink and blue biking shorts, he tripped and tumbled over. The woman caught the ending of his plunge and smirked.

She quickly ran over to help him up. "Hey are you okay?" She asked, extending her hand to him.

"Sure thanks. I…I must have loss my footing. These are some new track shoes and I'm not quite used to them yet.

"I can see. You sure you're okay? I've got a small first aid kit in my truck." She stated, noticing the nasty scrape on Clyde's knee.

When he looked down, the skin was chaffed and bloody. "Wow, I didn't think I caused that much damage and sure I'll take you up on that offer, Mrs.?" He probed. He was very captivated by her beauty, which is why he was caught up in his current situation now.

"Oh," she smiled gleefully, "it's Keonna, but my friends call me Kee."

"Keonna…I like that. My cousin has a stepdaughter named Keonna, though I've never met her and her brother." He admitted truthfully. He had only seen younger photos of them before the James' retained custody.

They were back in the school's parking lot exchanging light conversation as Keonna thumbed through her rear cab.

"Wow this is a nice truck, huge but nice." Clyde complimented. He had paid it no mind when he parked next to it earlier.

"Thanks Clyde!" She purposely said.

He was so into her curvaceous body that he hadn't noticed that he never revealed his name, somewhat ignorant on his behalf.

"Oh here we go." She said full of cheer.

Keonna suggested he sit on the passenger's side of the vehicle, so she would have a better advantage point at nursing his wound. She dabbed the nasty abrasion with an iodine swab, and enjoyed his boisterous outburst.

"Hssss!" He grimaced as the medicated swab brushed over the cut.

"Now c'mon Clyde, you're a big boy." She said, batting her eyes.

"Yeah, but it stings!" He defended.

Keonna then took an alcohol swab and squeezed the contents onto the scrap, sending Clyde into a frenzy.

"Ahhh!" He whined, resting his head back on the seat.

Perfect, she thought and eased a silenced.380 out from behind her back.

"Hey Clyde," she beckoned softly.

"I know, I…"

The look on his face was endless. He froze seeing the black metal pointed in his face.

"What's-" He began to say, until the hollow-point shells tore into his chest.

"By the way, I am the Lil Keonna you referred to earlier. See you in hell bastard." She whispered in a short breath, and then swaggered off covertly, as if death had not just consumed the high school's parking lot.

Though Keonna escaped the scene without incident, she played her rear and side view mirrors constantly as a precaution. In her mental rolodex, she checked off the ninth name on her list. It felt good to know that all of the people responsible in the undermining and demise of her parent's life would soon share the same fate. She desperately wanted to call and brag, per se, to Kory, but she needed a nice hot shower so she chose to head headed to her condominium. She would boast in his ear later on.

Chapter 14
The Art Of, Misconceived Swinging

It was 7:30 p.m., Sunday night, and Keonna had driven over to one of her brother's hideaways, as he called them, where she now enjoyed a glass of Red Marsala. She was elegantly wearing an open back dress by Vera Wang that stopped three-inches above her smooth knees. Her hair was pinned in a winding French bun, her accessories were priceless and she sported a black pair of designer pumps with a diamond-encrusted strap.

She grabbed the remote and flipped through the satellite channels, she was getting tired of waiting on Kory to get ready. She ended the surf on Lisa Raye's new series The Real McCoy; it was becoming one of her favorites.

"Dis bitch is fucking wild fo' real!" Keonna laughed hysterically.

"What's all the racket about Kee?" Kory asked, coming out of nowhere.

He was laced in an Armani Exchange eggshell white button down with a burgundy striped tie and a black two-piece. On his feet were some black square-toed ostrich shoes that completed his movie star appearance.

"You're looking real dapper tonight bruh! Oh, and I'm just watching Lisa Raye's, crazy ass!"

"Did you check the dinner arrangements?" He was concerned and wanted tonight to be special.

"Yes Kory and I spoke to the Dodd an hour ago. They'll be meeting us there, but I'd like to make a grand entrance, if you don't mind." Tonight meant so much to her.

"Oh, we're going to do that." He promised.

"How do I look?" Keonna spun around slowly.

"Stunning, darling," Kory answered, and then grabbed a cigar out of his humidor. "Shall we?"

He put his arm out gesturing for her to latch on and get things rolling. Tonight was going to be a mind-blowing experience.

For tonight's event, Kory made every effort to impress so they would be swerving in his Rolls Royce Phantom Coupe for the evening. Keonna wasted no time kicking off her pumps to enjoy the chinchilla carpeting throughout the vehicle.

Kory tuned into the oldies station enjoying some vintage Gap Band. Charlie Wilson was doing his thing back then, and in Kory's opinion, he could still do his thing today. The feel of the coupe's ride was almost like being in a Cessna high in altitude and inebriated from the finest aged wine.

L♥D~ L♥D~ L♥D

The Dodd's were being seated at one of the more valued tables at the Waterfront Bistro, a five-star restaurant in Windsor, CT. The establishment received highly accredited recognition for their menu; it was a grandeur place to dine.

"Ooh, I love this place Christian." Elaina Dodd complimented, on Kory's choice to dine.

"I'm wondering how long he's been coming down here. I've never heard of this place." Christian said to his wife.

The Dodd's had been married for six years now and were celebrating their anniversary tonight. The couple was young and spirited. They loved everything about life, especially sex and money. They were seasoned swingers and had finally gotten the Blake's to indulge.

Christian also made his large fortune in stocks, and a lot of it was through a wise decision to invest in Blake Industries. He became a self-made billionaire in five years, chancing his inheritance in 2002 as an investor.

"Are you nervous honey?" Elaina asked.

"No, of course not, sweetheart. I just need something to help me wind down." He assured her.

He always got this way on a swing date.

Elaina was the spitting image of a younger Cheryl Ladd when she was one of Charlie's Angels, only thicker. Though she could be extremely ditsy at times, her overall personality was sexually intriguing.

Now Christian was a young stud, and everyone was surprised when he tied the knot at nineteen years old but being twenty, he still had his clean boyish look and suaveness.

Elaina hailed down a server and asked for a bottle of Frascati and a martini. The server let her know that this was not her section and that Denise their server would be there soon.

"Sorry…"

Nevertheless, Elaina persisted and tucked a fifty-dollar bill in her apron. The server smiled and strolled off.

When the Rolls Royce pulled up to the entrance of the bistro, the gleeful valet, after helping Keonna exit the

vehicle, quickly rushed to Kory's door and accepted the keys.
"Thank you sir, enjoy your night!" The young valet said, then drove off.
Keonna latched onto Kory's arm and they made their grand entrance.
"Your table and party are ready as expected Mr. Blake. If you'll follow me this way please." The host requested, and then escorted them to their table.
"Oh there they are Kory," Keonna whispered.
Kory tipped the elderly host then acknowledged their guest.
"Elaina, Christian, how've you two been?" He said cheerfully.
Christian quickly stood up and pulled out a chair for Keonna, then gave her a light peck on the cheek.
"Thank you Christian, you look nice tonight." She flirted.
"Thank you but you...you're gorgeous."
He was mesmerized by her smooth skin and complexion; it made her almost look Brazilian.
"Stop...you're making me blush!"
Kory took his place next to Elaina and gave her a delightful compliment, then a sensual kiss on the lips.
"I see you've been sipping without us," he added.
"You know it takes Christian a drink or two before he fully unwinds," Elaina offered. "Here, have some, it's 1882 vintage." She held her flute up for Kory to try.
"Umm, this is great. You guys really know your grapes." He said. They all laughed.
During dinner, they talked and drank several Carafe's and bottles of the bistro's best wine, while enjoying the pianist as he serenaded them with some classic Sinatra.

"Well I think I'm ready to go, and take this party elsewhere. How 'bout 'chu?" Elaina slurred in Kory's face.

"Yes, it's about that time." He answered, rock hard from Elaina constantly rubbing on his thigh.

"Shall we?"

Keonna batted her light-brown eyes at Christian, which made him jump up.

After getting their vehicles back, the Dodds followed close behind the Rolls Royce, ready to swing.

Chapter 15
Black Roses

The crime scene took up the entire area of the Weaver High School parking lot and track field. It was 1:30 a.m. when a patrol car drove east down Granby Street, and noticed the GMC pick-up idle, which he found strange at such an early hour. He first thought it was some young couple out getting their groove on, until he flashed his light in the window.

Wayne Mosley was the first detective on the scene. He was beginning to wonder where his partner Yolonda could be, when her Maxima pulled up. He could see she was clearly worn out due to the homicides throughout the city and lack of sleep.

"Hey, I see you brought some Joe tonight." Wayne said, gesturing for a sip.

"Yeah, I had to make the stop or I wouldn't be standing and its straight black too."

"Just the way I like it!" He grinned.

"So what do we have?"

"Uhh, let's see. Patrol rode by, saw the truck idle, and decided to check it out. He expected to find some young kids playing nasty, and instead he found our vic' dead from a gun shot wound to the chest."

"Any I.D. on the vic'?" Yolonda inquired.

"Yeah, there's a wallet. Driver's license says he's uh, Mr. Clyde Barksdale, out of Bloomfield, CT." Wayne flipped over to another sheet of paper containing notes. "Check this out."

She followed Wayne to the truck. He moved over taking a stand next to the M.E., so his partner could get a better look. He also wanted to snap some photos.

"Is that a rose?" Yolonda asked.

"Sure is, and a black one. That's not it though, there's a card."

She put on a set of rubber gloves and picked up the white card.

"The letter 'K' and a set of lip prints." She was confused.

"That's what I said, but it seems to be our boy 'Killa', instead of the letter 'K' Killa, it just sounded more appropriate at the time."

"What the hell is going on? Moreover, what is the connection? We have to make some type of connection to piece this together, or we're gonna have black roses all over the city." Yolonda said.

"Excuse me Carin, but do you have a time of death?" Wayne questioned.

"Umm, I'd say, somewhere around 12:30 p.m."

"12:30 in the afternoon? Killa is getting quite bold. There must've been crowds of people out here; somebody had to have seen something!" Wayne said in a higher octave than normal.

The case was straining and stressful especially when your Chief was constantly breathing down your neck for an arrest, but all they could come up with was a footprint, a black rose and the gruesome letter 'K' that he often carved into his victims. Not to mention two cops were killed by him, which only fueled the fire.

"Carin, please notify us when and if you pull some prints." Wayne said, and then he ordered the patrol officers to go door-to-door with hopes that someone may have seen something.

Wayne told Yolonda she should go home and get some rest and they would start fresh tomorrow.

Chapter 16
Dead Ecstasy

"You've been quiet since we left the bistro, is something troubling you?" Keonna inquired out of concern. "Heavens no! I've been dying for this day, and now its here." Kory answered in a very calm voice, one that had puzzled his sister.

When the two were just small toddlers, Kory would always seem strangely calm, but defiant towards people who hurt or challenged him.

For instance, one day while playing cars with one of their parent's friend, the Bradshaws', son, Trent Trent used his fire-red no.14 box ambulance to destroy the towering Lego block structure Kory spent two long weeks building.

Boom! Crash!

"Yeah!" Trent yelled, feeling victorious with his accomplishment.

"Hey, why'd you do that Trent, that was my future house and it took me almost two weeks to build it?" Kory calmly asked, his tone subtle.

"'Cause I can, Kory! And you're never gonna have no house dummy, you have to have lots and lots of money like my folks!" Trent said hatefully. "Ah hah, ah hah, Kory's gonna be a bum!" Trent spat.

It didn't seem to bother Kory as much as it did Keonna. "Shut up Trent, you are so stupid and I hate you and your family!"

Keonna's words were like venom, but not as deadly as the pain Trent experienced from Kory's huge red plastic bat. He hit Trent repeatedly until Kline, Kory's father, snatched the large bat out of his son's hands. What really threw them all was Kory's cold stare as blood trickled down Trent's neck from his ear. The Bradshaw's never befriended the Blake's ever again. The Dodd's were rich and had similar ways like the Bradshaw's in Kory's book.

L♥D~ L♥D~ L♥D

Secluded in a pristine populated area of Simsbury, CT. rests a huge early English style manor. The manor rested on seven immaculately manicured acres of mint green lawn, surrounded by four-foot shrubs. The winding u-shaped driveway encased a large fountain with sculpted naked men and women in a subtle orgy, as thick streams of running water poured out of the men's penises.

The manor itself was dark, no lighting at all, but as the two-car cavalcade eased up the cold tarmac, and the expensive motion censored track lighting shone happily.

Both vehicles halted at the front entrance. It was extremely quiet. So quiet, you could hear the nightly crickets conversing in their specious way. Elaina stumbled as she stepped out of their four door Maserati Sport. She giggled like a catholic schoolgirl embarrassed after belching at the dinner table.

"You okay?" Kory quickly rushed to her aid.

"Yesss…" She slurred a bit. "Take me inside!" She ordered, as Keonna took up the rear clutching her speedy handle with an expensive pair of silk gloves. She smiled at Kory. The four finally made it inside and upstairs inside the Dodd's master bedroom. It resembled something Keonna vividly remembered on one of the Lifestyles of the Rich and Famous episodes. Nice crystal chandeliers were appended to the ceilings by gold riveted hooks. Their large king size bed rested in the center of the room. There was also a 40" plasma TV adjacent to the foot of the bed and the entire ceiling was plastered in beveled mirror, for optimal pleasure.

When Christian entered his home, he ducked off into his wine cellar and grabbed two bottles of 1921 Dom P., there were already flutes at the medium sized bar in the bedroom. By the time Christian made it to his bedroom, the festivities had begun.

The lighting was dim, but it was enough to see Elaina was in a very compromising position and enjoying herself pleasantly.

"Yea... Yea... Yeahhh..., Oooooooh." She exhausted on key.

While she had her mouth plastered in Keonna's moistened tenderness, Kory propelled his thick manhood deep into her tightness. It was obvious Christian was no match to Kory's measurements.

He drank from a bottle of champagne as he watched Kory destroy every wall or barrier Elaina had; while his dick erected quickly. It always turned him on to witness another man ravage his wife, but Kory was a beast. He stepped out of his trousers and briefs, then fondled his mediocre genitalia.

Keonna was enjoying herself as well. Elaina was so involved in Kory's back shot, that she had no choice but to devour Keonna's sweetness.

"Damn...You taste sooo, sweet!" She uttered between moans.

Keonna noticed Christian pleasuring himself and waved him over. He wasted no time obeying. He stood off to the side of the bed allowing Keonna access to his hardness. She greased her palm with her saliva then jerked his limb.

"Uhh." He moaned as she caressed his tool rapidly in a tight fist.

Christian's eyes locked with his wife's and her expression was one he had never seen before. Though it turned him on gravely, he was saddened by his shortcomings. Then his eyes met with Kory's. Kory smiled wickedly knowing what he was putting the virgin like womb through and it gave him the motivation he needed to stay focused.

"Uhh, Uh..."

Keonna had her fifth and final orgasm for the night. She continued the up and down motion on Christian just for Kory's sake.

"Fuck me harder Kory, harder! Give me all of it!" Elaina said and reached back and spread her ass cheeks so he could insert everything he had to offer into her wetness.

He would not talk; he instead latched onto her wrist and pulled her violently into his groin, as he thrust powerfully back into her sugar walls.

"You're killin' me, nooo, no, you're killin' me!" She shouted loudly, which made Keonna smile and Christian nut.

Smack! Smack! Smack! Was the sounds their flesh made as they collided at a fast pace. Kory was long dicking her and he touched her navel every time he came out and thrust back in.

"Oh...My...Goddd...Oh my God get it out of me!" she shouted in ecstasy.

Finally, a minute later Kory ejaculated all over Elaina's ass and back. He let her arms go and she collapsed onto her face.

"Wow...Oh my God! Ooooh! My little girl is still throbbing," she shared.

She was experiencing aftershocks–orgasms.

Kory thought it to be some of the best pussy he had ever had to date. He wondered what her head game was like, but Keonna shot him a stern look, she was obviously jealous. Although she got off, she saw right where his mind was as he caressed his length. It was not there first and probably would not be their last swing date, but there were greater things at stake tonight than a nut.

When he caught her growl, he unhanded his tool to proceed with their date.

"Hey Christian, can you get a coupla rags. Oh and some ice for your wife's you know," Keonna said as she empathized for Elaina's sore kitten.

"Oh, sure. Be right back."

As soon as Christian walked out of the room, Keonna slashed Elaina's throat with a razor she had in her mouth. Blood soaked the 3000 count linen sheets. Elaina's eyes were still closed; she had not seen her death in the makings. Keonna then carved a huge 'K' into her abdomen.

As Christian steadied his pace with the bottle of Dom tilted upright into the room, he received a half a clip from Kory's silenced .9 milli. The bottle dropped and shattered, as Christian's lifeless body fell into its remains.

"Hurry up, I wanna get outta here," Kory spoke.

"BullShit...You da one who tried to kill 'da bitch 'wit 'dat, thing of yours," Keonna said jokingly.

"Some of da best I've ever had," he admitted.

"I can see,"

Keonna went into her speedy and pulled out an average sized bottle of sulfuric acid and arsenic. She then douched out any trace of Kory's bodily fluids he might have transferred to Elaina, as well as wiping his semen off her ass and back. She also made sure to cleanse Christian's limp member as well. There could have still been a trace of her saliva on it.

Next, she hurriedly wiped down anything she felt they touched. She bagged the sheets and stuffed them into her speedy so she could destroy them later. Her final act would be a card with her kiss print on it and a black rose for the authorities to find, whenever they did.

"Shall we?" she said fully dressed, Chloe shades covering her upper facial features.

"I guess so. Damn…" He mumbled.

"What now, Kory?"

"Nothing, just a good piece of pussy down da drain." He shrugged.

Chapter 17
Departmental Fun

The Hartford police headquarters had a strict no smoking policy, so every so often Yolonda found herself sitting along the row of opaque stone lining the brow of the mystique structure. The building was molded in brick red stone with motion censored glass doors. In total, there were three floors, with the booking dept. on the second. Not far away was the Homicide Division, where her crammed desk sat full of manila files.

Yolonda was flush with anxiety over the serial killer case. It had her nerves going in so many different directions that coffee could not seem to jolt her awareness to much of anything these days. She was overexerted and heavily consumed with dead bodies, and she had very few leads to go on. She prayed for just one, just one lousy fingerprint, or something to that affect.

Chief Daniels dug deep into her and Wayne's hides on occasions, and she was tired of it. At this point, she often contemplated planting a fingerprint or some other incriminating evidence on a dirt bag from the inner city, but she lived by the code and honor of the department, but most of all, her integrity would not allow her to stoop so low; she was in it for the long haul.

It had been two long weeks since the Barksdale murder, and nothing came back on the card or rose. Funny she thought how a man was shot to death in a high school parking lot with not one eyewitness. Either people were outright terrified of saying something or this was the most evasive serial killer Hartford has ever faced.

As Yolonda watched the first shift turn into the second, several horns blew from cars with officers either going home to their families or pulling into the parking lot for their shift. It was 3:30 p.m., and she had been on duty since early roll call and did not plan to depart just yet. As a favor to her, some of her colleagues helped her out on many of her milder cases. She was elated to pass them over too.

"Oh well, let me take my butt back upstairs." She said to herself aloud as she put her Newport out in the tall ashtray.

Instead of using the tight elevator, Yolonda hiked the cold staircase. She was very fit and maintained a strict exercise routine and diet. Through the metal door, she entered into her division.

"Hey Yolonda, see you've been on nic-break. Case still got you tweaking huh?" Major Evans, a 3rd grade detective said.

He was cool, very conservative, however, he always smelled as if he had slept in cat-piss, and his breath continuously reeked of stale coffee.

"You called it Evans, but as soon as I fry his ass, I'm going to the islands for a month!" She responded. "Have you seen Wayne anywhere?"

"Yeah, he's been in the john since you stepped out; my guess is he's got the runnies!" He chuckled.

"You know Evans, you're too much," she joined in with a slight laugh.

Yolonda took a seat at her metal desk and put in her code to unlock her p.c. files. Killa was her new code, seeing it was what kept her ragged these days. She immediately began cross checking old murders with critical info she had compiled from the new ones, however, case after case turned up zilch.

Yolonda was so pissed she threw a crumpled piece of paper at the screen, and then sat back in her old squeaky chair with her arms cushioned behind her head. She was through.

"Whew! What da hell is that smell?" Ryan, a detective frowned as he entered the men's bathroom. He pinched his nose with two fingers to try to avoid the smell. .

"Awe shut up Ryan, I've got a little case of diarrhea going on, and that's between me and you got it?" Wayne warned.

"A little case, man you need some medical attention because it smells like something done crawled up your ass and died! As a matter of fact, whatever crawled up there must have moved in and paid the rent up for the entire year boy!" He continued to joke.

"Ha, ha!" Was all Wayne could muster.

Wayne finished his business in the bathroom and headed towards his cubicle next to Yolonda. He saw her exhausted, full of dejection, and spoke.

"Hey tutts, what's got `your panties in a bunch?" He toyed around like always.

"Same old stuff! Ooh, did you pass gas Wayne?" She frowned, as a foul odor invaded her nostrils.

"Uh, yeah. Sorry! Be right back." He said, and darted back to the men's room. He did manage to put a smirk on her face though.

While Wayne left to handle his odorous troubles, Yolonda's desk phone rang.

"Hello?"

"Hello, yes I'm looking for a detective Mosley or Long," The male voice said.

"This is Detective Long speaking. May I ask who this is and the nature of the call?"

"Sure. My name is Lloyd, Det. Lloyd Wolf from the Simsbury Homicide Division. I'm working on a sort of strange case which I strongly feel might tie into those recent serial murders that's been plaguing your city," he revealed.

"Umm...how do you mean?" She needed a little more info to feel interested. She had not known Killa, to go outside the usual circumference; he normally kept things in a specific radius.

"Well I tell you that this, black rose and card with the red kiss print ties instinctively into your boy, Killa I think you guys call him," he further explained.

"Can you please give me an address, fax, email, just please send me what you've compiled. I'll be there before you put a fresh portion of chew in your mouth."

"Great work detective." He said then ended the call.

Wayne was approaching fast. He caught Yolonda as she was shutting down her p.c., looking in a desperate rush.

"Hey tutts, what's crackin'?"

"Oh, I nearly left without you Wayne. I'll explain in the car, hurry, let's go."

L♥D~ L♥D~ L♥D

The air was subtle and seemed still, as the drive to Simsbury gave Det. Long time to think. Det. Mosley was in his own desolate world. He wanted the heartless bastard who called himself 'Killa', behind bars or preferably dead.

The Crown Victoria eased up route 44 towards Simsbury, cheating every red light that threatened their passage.

"So you think it's our boy?" Yolonda questioned, making small talk.

"Black rose, kiss print on a white card, yeah," Wayne answered truthfully. "The thing that puzzles me is the kiss. Why does that play any significance? Where does it fit in?"

Yolonda sighed, researched her notes, and disclosed that it was mainly found on all the male victims for starters, along with the black rose, however, most of the females had the letter 'K' carved into them.

"To be honest Wayne, this shit is starting to creep the hell out of me, let's see what's ahead and go from there, 'kay."

The road leading to the crime scene appeared to be recently paved, which gave the unmarked a pleasurable ride. The area was immaculate and affluent; the area reeked of prosperity at its highest level. They could already tell that someone of great importance and wealth lied dead by the hands of their serial killer, but what ushered their merciless marauder to these parts they wondered. A tale destined to be told.

"There, look!" Yolonda pointed.

"Whoa….," Wayne mumbled, "that's an extravagant house. Look at the…"

"I see the penis, Wayne, you're such a pervert!" She teased.

They double parked next to a Ford Taurus and got out, then followed the police trail inside the foyer of the house and were enthralled by the grandeur design. There were gold accents on everything. High cathedral ceilings and polished marbled floors lined the interior. They were so busy and engulfed by the manor's elegance, that they let a burly 6'2' white-guy creep up the rear and startle them.

"Hey!" They jumped, hearing the deep baritone.

"Whoa – take it easy," the man said.

"Hello, I'm Det. Wayne Mosley and this is my partner Det. Long."

"How are you two? I've spoken with Det. Long over the phone."

They all shook hands.

"Well follow me this way."

As they trailed the burly man, Wayne noticed large high gloss paintings of whom he knew to be some very, very wealthy folks dating back forty-years; he snapped a mental photograph for later reference.

"So Det. Wolf, how many bodies are we counting?" Yolonda queried, as she eased a pair of clear latex gloves over her hands.

"Two," he answered.

The spiral staircase brought the trio to the hallway. The smell coming from the master bedroom was horrifying. The stench was burning the tiny hairs of the detective's noses.

"Yeah I know, here are some masks, they should help," Det. Wolf said, tossing them two surgical looking masks. They wasted no time in dressing their faces with the protective gear.

"In here!" a blue and white said, and then stepped out of their way.

"Over here is the wife we presume. Her throat was slashed as you can see, and she clearly has that letter 'K' carved into her abdomen," Wolf spoke. "Over here is the husband. He sustained several shots, and get this, his penis was severed and placed inside his wife's vagina, testicles and all."

"This guy is fucking sick," Wayne, blurted out.

"My guess is, the perp made the couple have sex then killed them. There doesn't seem to be anything missing, but we're still running through this massive house."

"Any ID yet?"

"Yeah we were lucky seeing their stage in decomp, but we found some deeds, liens, and stock bonds with their names on it. Here take a look for yourself."

Det. Wolf passed Wayne the paper work.

"It says here that, um…It's Mr. and Mrs. Christian and Elaina Dodd. They seem to have several shares in James Electric, also Blake Industries. These young people were worth a ton of money," Wayne exclaimed.

"Well there's our motive, the great American dollar!" Yolonda exhausted.

"The Dodd's financial advisor had been trying to reach them concerning some money matters."

He used his two fingers implying quotations when he mentioned money matters.

"What's his name?" Yolonda asked.

"Umm, Harold, Harold…Peters." He answered.

"Alright, I guess we're done here. Please send me that info we talked about Wolf. In addition, we'll relay anything we come up with on our end. Thanks for your help, but we've got some other leads to catch up on," Yolonda said in a thankful tone, before the two strutted off.

Back in the car, they rode in silence once again; it was their way at piecing things together.

Chapter 18
Crime with No Ends, Only Means

John-James was an outgoing person, though he kept to himself on certain occasions. When not golfing with the boys or dining with hordes of uptight snobs, he and Bratford roamed the many acres of his huge compound. Money was like a breath of fresh air, he had to have it and lots of it.

He was also one who wanted full control over anything he was involved in. Power intrigued John-James; wealth tickled him and sex with young prostitutes relaxed him.

On many occasions, he would pick up whores off the streets. He assumed it much safer; escort services kept too many records for his taste, which could lead to a brick wall on his dying quest of monetary supremacy.

Currently, John-James was locked in his outhouse with Bratford, staring $1,000,000 in the face. It was the price Harry had to submit to enter into his world; a world of deceit, fraud, embezzlement, and crime with no ends. You would have to be willing to swim in a pool of sharks to feed and nourish your cravings and most desirable possessions, or you were not cut out to be in the "in" crowd as He called it.

For Harry, the $1,000,000 fee was just the admission charge; these boys spent $1,000,000 on summerhouses, boats, mistresses, etc...so Harry would have many other zeroes to bring to the table, or as they say, he would have never had the pleasure to voyage out to the blue sea alive. "Umm..." John-James uttered as he thumbed through the Hartford Courant and his palm pilot at the same time. Something quite intriguing stood out in the far right corner of the Courant, even still, he had an alert set up on his palm pilot when any crucial news erupted about the market. That being said, he chose to sort through his palm pilot.

After tossing the paper into a nearby chair, he began reading the caption.

Daily Stock Watch: "Drug and hospital companies led stocks higher yesterday after house lawmakers end months of uncertainty, and approved the health care overhaul bill."

"Blah...Blah...Blah...Who the hell cares." He cursed uninterested. It was news he had already heard about. He wanted the juicy stuff, so he scrolled down some.

"The approval late Sunday removed some of the anxiety that has dogged stocks on fuel and oil companies. The 10-year, $734,000,000,000 bill will extend contracts to over 25 million investors and uninsured Americans through a more diverse agreement. Though the price of gas rose 9% over the first quarter, they would anticipate more business. Those who fell because of a greater restriction imposed by the vast changes shall see a 3.2% relief; come the end of the 2nd quarter. Lastly; the Dow Jones closed at 10,796.78 – shares were up."

"Now see Bratford...That's the kind of news John-James needs to hear. Blake Industries falls dead in sync," He laughed, Bratford barking loudly following suit. "Yeah boy, Blake Industries shall be mine in a matter of time."

John-James was so enthralled into his palm pilot, that he ran out without reading the Courant's news heading, where a couple made the 18th and 19th victims of the mysterious 'K' murders.

"Corporate shareholders in James Electric and Blake Industries, found slain in an opulent manor deep in the Simsbury Hills. Anyone with any pertinent info leading to the arrest, please call 1-800-Crime-Stoppers."

Chapter 19
Meetings of Bosses

The Blake's, Kory and Keonna, had finally landed at the Bradley International Airport in Windsor Locks, CT., from California. The red fasten seatbelt sign in the G5 jet had went from bright red to non-existent as the two siblings descended the flight steps. A slender male presumed to be in his mid-40s escorted the two to a 62 Maybach. His name was Jeffrey and he was Kory's personal driver.

"Nice trip sir?" He asked as he opened the rear door.

"It's always good to visit my parents Jeff." He answered calmly.

Jeffrey then ushered Keonna to the opposite side and helped her settle herself inside. The car thrust forward at a fast pace, though it did not feel like they were speeding. All loyal consumers loved the fine comforting ride about the foreign car.

"Anywhere special, Sir?"

"Yes, my office. We have a meeting in half an hour," Kory answered. He then fixed him and Keonna a drink.

"Thanks bruh. So what do you have planned for this meeting? And how's the shares doing in Anheuser Busch and Westinghouse Electric?" She questioned.

She knew Kory kept an ace of spades card in his pocket at all times

"Now Kee, you know I never kiss and tell, but I will say that our shares are doing excellent as always. Now drink."

She laughed it off and swallowed her glass of Conjure`.

Blake Industries was located in the downtown area of Hartford at 8732 Pratt Street. The building was fourteen stories high and made up of all glass. The building had been constructed only seven years ago, when Kory felt his smaller office was no longer sufficient. The project cost over $2.3 billion to accommodate all of the Blakes wishes. The amenities were endless.

Kory's office was on the top floor and was the size of seven regular offices. He held certain private and important meetings in his personal office, which is why he demanded the space. The walls were a soft apricot, with plum molding. All the décor was designed to coincide with the walls. There was plush burgundy carpeting and a huge cherry oak escritoire that held his P.C. and phone.

There was also a glass display case with a vintage collection of knives and small swords. Kory was sort of a knife buff. He loved to watch sword fights, duels, etc.

The driver pulled into the lower level of the office building. He ushered the two to a secured elevator only used by those with a special key, then exited the garage. Unbeknownst to others, the elevator opened up into Kory's private office. The heavy coat of paint concealed the slim crack in the wall, leaving very few to know of its passage.

He took his place behind his desk and punched few keys on his P.C., and then the printer began spitting out sheets of colored paper. Some were copies of stock shares and prices; others were contracts he would use later.

Keonna took off her leather coat and hung it up, then made them both another drink.

"Here you go bruh."

"Jigga, huh?" He questioned her choice of beverage. "Ace of Spades seemed like it'd fit da moment," she said taking her seat at the large oval table. Fifteen minutes later, two gorgeous women strolled into the office and sat down. Then four men also found their places at the table. There was just one socialite missing to get things rolling. Lo Wen, the CEO and founder of Optical Tech located in Japan. He and Kory had become great friends over the years and had always hoped to do business someday and now that day had finally come.

Ceali, Kory's secretary, entered the room with bottled water and several small platters of fruit and deli sandwiches. Kory always catered to his people.

"Enjoy folks," he said, trying to stall time.

He constantly checked his Rolex for the time. Kory was not the type to wait on anyone, no matter how detrimental your addition to his plot was, and he would normally move on. "I think we'll begin without Mr. Wen," Kory said, obviously upset.

Keonna gave him a concerned look, but he nodded it off, it was nothing to worry about. She then placed a black laminated folder in front of each person to review. Inside was a prospectus with graphs, charts and prices on the insurance of which they would be buying into. Kory wanted them to salivate over this, hoping that it would draw them in like a shark to blood. Blake Industries had opened up a subsidiary called Korr-Tech. He explained that Korr-Tech dealt in three areas: fuel, oil, and insurance. During the presentation, the constant flash of the desk phone interrupted Kory's attention.

"Excuse me a sec, I have to take this." He picked up the receiver and listened to Ceali talk.

"Okay thank you."

Kory then picked up a small remote off his desk and pressed a button, which lowered a large 70" screen.

"My apologies people, but as you all know I was expecting one more guest, though his presence was greatly needed elsewhere, he's decided to conference in if you don't mind."

He looked around, accepted the nods of approval, and then proceeded.

The screen lit up and a round Japanese face appeared in front of their company logo.

"Sorry to interrupt people. There was an act of tragedy in the family, please forgive my tardiness." Lo Wen said.

"In front of you are the most accurate and defined proposals my family and I could come to terms with. You'll see for the 1st year, Korr-Tech wishes no profit, all profits shall be equally distributed to the shareholders," Kory iterated.

He paused to let them review further. He saw smiles on the men's faces, and wows on the two women's faces. It was a good sign. He turned his attention to the wide screen. Ceali took the liberty of faxing the proposal directly to Lo Wen when he was a no show. His angular shaped mouth quickly spread, symbolizing he too was happy.

"So Kory, what about your ties to James Electric?" Janet Atwaters questioned.

She was the CEO of a major corporation out of Colorado that was in trouble, and desperately needed in; and just to make sure she was not left out of Kory's proposal, she brought along her checkbook.

"Funny you should ask Janet." Kory paced the floor twirling his pinky ring around his finger. "To be honest, John James isn't trying to sell any more shares of James Electric and he has the prices so high at the moment, he's forcing me to pull out, but I'm still at the table with him as it currently stands." He spoke honestly.

Although he would never let on the true place, he held or would hold soon, no one wants the other to get rich over him or her. It was a game they played.

"Well I'm sold. I don't need to hear anything further. You can count us in." Phillip of Bayer Industries Inc. pledged.

"Me too." Albert H. also pledged. Slowly one by one, every member at the meeting signed on. The Blakes were on their way to defeating and avenging their parents' deaths.

"That's good to know. I assume you brought your checkbooks?" Kory smiled and the room erupted in laughter.

The first installment was to be made in check form for $10,000,000. The final payment would be a wire transfer of the remaining $40,000,000 to board the Blake's new ship. The people in attendance did not care, $50,000,000 was like taking a trip to Rome for a month, and they would earn that back in nine months tops. Nevertheless, the equity profit the Blakes would see would put their family fortune somewhere close to some of the world's wealthiest individuals.

Korr-Tech would be the new poster boy for Blake Industries and James Electric. Kory and Keonna drank themselves into a chuckled frenzy, as their new counterparts left. He noticed Lo Wen's money had been electronically deposited, the whole ten billion. It was clear they were now winning.

Chapter 20
Shook One

As the days went by, Harold Peters grew immensely agitated by the lack of follow through by John James concerning him becoming a board member, actually President of Blake Industries. He had done his part by giving the fee they asked that he submit over two weeks ago and still he controlled nothing. He had not even acquired a chair on the board nor sat in on a board meeting and it had him unbalanced in a great way.

Harold sat in his office reading the morning paper as usual. He was glad to get an opportunity to do so this morning because his schedule lately had been preoccupied with several concerned clients over the death of the Dodd's and their investments within his company. His understanding from the authorities had him to believe that it was a robbery homicide, but this morning's edition said otherwise.

It read: Simsbury, Ct.–Billionaire Couple found in what appeared to be a simple robbery homicide now determined by investigative detectives that they were actually the newest victims of the letter 'K' Killa serial murderer.

Detectives Wayne Mosley and Yolonda Long of the HPD coupled with Lloyd Wolf of the Simsbury Homicide Division yesterday ruled that the Dodd's death was strangely connected to the other cases. It has been ruled that all of the victims are connected in some way be it professionally, notability or ancestry.

It was their unmistakable findings, observations and experience in their careers that concluded the gruesome discovery. Furthermore, a task force has been formed in hopes to bring justice to all of the victim's families and to bring a serial killer to trial.

By Tyrone Mickens
Mickens@Courant.com

Harold's face was flushed with beads of sweat. The article threw him. He followed the news concerning the serial killer, but not to this magnitude. As he further studied the many profiles in the right corner of the article, he began to notice the many similarities. He even noticed a few faces he had seen before, all very prominent of course, some he had advised in the past.

"Oh my God!" He mumbled. "What does these killings have to do with all us? Who did we piss off?" He wondered. "Wow...What connection did Melinda King play in this, she's uh fuckin' news reporter. She's not into Wall Street or stock shares, or was she?" He continued to ponder the notion.

For now, Harold put it out of his head; he needed to remain focused on getting answers concerning his placement and leadership of Blake Industries. Harold quickly showered, then dressed according to the weather. Normally coffee and toast would be his morning nourishment; instead, he grabbed a warm piece of fruit and started for the door.

With his briefcase in hand, he quickly opened the front door, only to be confronted by a man and woman.

"Harold Peters," the woman began.

"Yeah I'm he, who's asking?"

"Hello, I'm Detective Yolonda Long and this is my partner Wayne Mosley. Would you mind if we took up just a few minutes of your time?"

"Um…I was on my way out. What is this about? I've paid all of parking tickets!" he said nervously.

Mosley shook his head at the stupidity of some of these rich, pompous bastards.

"This is far from a parking ticket. May we come in Mr. Peters?" His voice was powerful and demanding.

"Five minutes, then I must be going," Harold made clear to the detectives, he was nervous yet agitated.

They followed Harold into the den and sat on an auburn sectional.

"Nice place you've got her Peters. Live alone?" Mosley asked.

"All by my lonesome." He replied sarcastically.

"Pretty big house for one person, at least for me." Mosley added, but received no reply.

"So Mr. Peters, my sources tell me that you are a very successful advisor and investor, which I can see that for myself." Yolonda added, looking around at all the expensive trimmings throughout his den.

"I do okay. I'm quite sure you two haven't taken time out of your busy schedules to converse with me over how big my place is and the current finesse of my abilities, like I said, a few minutes are all I have to spare."

Their slow-witted line of questions were agitating him.

"Sorry," Yolonda said. "My sources say you advised a couple by the name of Dodd who were murdered days ago, also a Mr. Barksdale. There is also a host of others you financially advised in the past who have been victims of this serial killer. Do you have any comment on my findings?"

"Yes and no."

"What's that supposed to mean?" Mosley said sternly. He was playing bad cop here.

"Well it means yes, I have advised some of the people and no, it means nothing to me. I read the papers, and that reporter woman Melinda King had no ties to me whatsoever, so how would you figure that one detective?" He matched Mosley's sternness.

The two detectives looked at one another seeing his point. There were no ties between the two as they mentioned, which threw a monkey wrench into their theory.

"Well, Mr. Peters here's my card. Please give us a call if something jumps out at you, or someone. Have nice day," Yolonda concluded, and then shook his hand.

"You be careful now Peters, we don't know who's next on the list," Mosley gestured, with a smile. Peters frowned then slammed his door shut, then quickly used his cell phone to call a friend.

Chapter 21
So the Plots Thickens

Tonight would be one of many, but the first unified gathering in three decades of Blake history. It marks the first annual Gala of the 21st Century. Once again, Mr. Kory Blake had made every effort to impress and to ensure that all who attended enjoy a night of elegance and prestige in a ritzy way.

The affair would take place at the renowned La Renaissance off I-91 North in South Windsor, CT. The event was scheduled to kick off at 7:30 p.m. sharp, even with reports of severe thunderstorms.

Kory anticipated such weather conditions and hired two limo services two weeks prior to escort all who paid the hefty price of $10,000 a ticket. The service would carry its occupants to and from their doorstep, to the event.

As Keonna peered over the guest list, she noticed not one ticket went without being sold.

"Wow!" she uttered surprisingly.

She knew her big brother and his savvy aura that often rubbed off on folks, nevertheless, 1500 contributors dipped into their wallets to come out and strut with the Blakes.

"Don't seem so jarred sis, these people love us, and definitely know where a well invested buck belongs," Kory spoke, as he fixed the black bow tie around his neck. Armani draped him in a black tuxedo with a burgundy lapel. He also chose a classy Rolex with a diamond bezel.

"I can see Korr, but how do you pose you'll launch Korr-Tech with Blake Industries so broad?" Keonna was sweet, yet devilish and always wondered how Kory managed to do the things he did. How he so easily caught on to how the Wall Street game, considering he skipped college.

It was true, Kory skipped college around the same time their parents had their accident. He fell into a short depression and never made it to school. However, he managed to become an expert and genius with numbers. Trigonometry, Calculus and Geometry were subjects that came easy to him. In his younger school days, he was considered a mathematical wizard, people literally thought of him as a human calculator. Some even called him a mainframe or a number cruncher. Not long after, Kory took his father's seat in Blake Industries he learned of his inheritance and an empire he was preordained to rule.

"Oh...So cleverly sis, but you don't worry yourself with all of that. Make sure the James' are well tended to tonight, and fix your gown."

Keonna resembled a live mannequin out of a Dolce and Gabbana display window. A gold accented evening gown covered her bronze complexion. The split that rode the length of her right thigh, rose halfway up her curvaceous hips, while a huge dip in the neckline of the gown, exposed her plump cleavage. Her accessories were intact, which accentuated a gold stiletto heel. She was breathtaking to say the least.

"Don't 'chu worry about those James', I've got that. I think our ride's out front." She advised him.

It was like a red carpet affair as flash after flash brightened the entrance of the La Renaissance. The chatter was high and audible as the Blake's chariot halted and Jeffrey opened the heavy door unveiling its host. Kory and Keonna were stunning and deserved such grace being young, black and richly successful.

The Blakes sauntered inside the dimly lit atmosphere accepting many a wide smile of appreciation.

"Hey, there's the Cabot's," Keonna nudged Kory.

"I see them. Look at how they frown down at folks, sickening!"

Kory loathed the Cabots, but they were deeply interested in Korr-Tech so he allowed them to purchase two V.I.P. tickets tonight, which ran $35,000 a pop for them. He raised the price on them out of hatred.

Kory quickly switched facades as the couple strolled in their direction.

"Well hello, Keonna, Kory," Leo Cabot said cordially, blessing Keonna's cheek with a wet one.

"Hello to you Leo, Marge," Kory returned with a firm grip. He dared not smudge his Blistex on Marge's pale skin, although he would not mind letting her swallow a load.

"This Gala is it! I love everything you have done here Kory. So will you be unveiling Korr-Tech tonight?" Leo questioned. His curiosity had his balls in a bunch, prune like.

"Well Leo…I'm not one to kiss and tell, so you'll just have to wait it out."

Kory pulled his shirtsleeve a tad bit, his gold cufflinks sparkling brightly as he did so.

"You know this isn't about Korr-Tech, it's solely about Blake Industries. However, don't count your chickens before they hatch. You'll have to forgive me, but the host, must host," he concluded, and walked off.

Kory and Keonna hugged and swapped more kisses with their guests then took their place at the podium. The incandescent lighting now spotlighted their entirety, and then all of the chatter became faint.

"Thank you ladies and gentlemen for coming out and supporting my lovely sister and me tonight. "I'm quite sure the stipend for this event tonight won't put a dent into your wallets," Kory flashed the crowd a smile. This marks the first annual Blake Gala Affair. Our parents founded Blake Industries in the early 60's. Though they suffered a tragic death, Blake Industries lives on. I'd like to add a special thanks to the James' for a lifetime of friendship, trust and the opportunity to work together."

He paused to let the applause linger some.

"I don't see Blake Industries ever reaching the heights and accomplishments it's reached without the consolidation and dexterity of John James. They, the James', took us in when our parents passed, and for that they deserve another round of applause."

He paused once again.

As the applause ceased, Kory asked everyone to view the large 100" screen that scrolled down the wall.

"People, what you're about to witness is history in the making, and something you'll all be fighting to be a part of real soon. At the present moment, there are limited shares available" Just then, a large red banner with Korr-Tech in gold metallic letters tumbled from the sky. "Ladies and Gents, I present to you the newest expansion to Blake Industries, Korr-Tech, a corporate fuel, and insurance group of different magnitudes."

Whistles, cheering and applauding were all you could hear in the large room.

"Hey, I heard rumors about this venture, but I never guessed it was the Blakes behind it!" Ronald Weismann, CEO of Weismann Prudential said to his neighbor of the night, Tom Geico.

"Me neither, but they say their very well-funded and connected with some major insurance moguls," Tom added.

"I have to get with our lawyers and fast."

"How many shares are up for sale?" William yelled.

"William, you know we don't talk business so openly, I'm sure your lawyer has a working phone." Rudolph of the Mutual Life Insurance Group countered jokingly and the room fell into a deep laugh.

"Folks...Folks, as you all exit, there'll be apex digitally enhanced brochures for your taking, but tonight is about Blake Industries. I will say, the open bid is for 150,000 shares and up, which people, is at twenty-one now. But believe me, it'll be at sixty-four by next week." Kory ended, and then he and Keonna bowed gracefully and said their thanks for coming out. In addition, they made it perfectly clear that it there would be no more work related discussions tonight, it was time to party.

As they descended from the podium, Kory noticed the agitated mug on John James. Kory winked his eye and kept moving.

L♥D~ L♥D~ L♥D

The long ride home from the Blake gala seemed as if it took forever as the limo driver purposely drove through the city's most crime infested areas, which happened to be the scenic route for hoodlums. The driver was in tears, tears of joy as he eavesdropped and recorded the James' conversation.

Kory was always a giant step ahead of John James. He had to be, or the Blake legacy would tumble at the hands of the enemy. This particular limousine was bugged with the latest technology. He knew the James' would be extremely hurt and bias to the unveiling of Korr-Tech, so he needed an extra ear.

"I swear Elizabeth, that boy has undermined me on this one!" John James said through clenched teeth.

"Well you have to admit honey, Kory learned everything from under your tutelage and watchful eye. Hmm, and you should have seen something like this coming dear," she countered freely.

She knew the potential embedded within Kory and figured one day he would try something, but never on this magnitude.

"Humph..." He grunted. "We'll see how he does when the market crashes and prices drop so low he'll be giving shares away for free. No one outsmarts a James," he fired back disgustedly.

At the moment, he was picturing the two siblings on stage all high and mighty, like things were all cheery, but he had his plummet tucked away in his pocket and when it occurred, he'd turn his back on them forever.

When the limo finally halted curbside to their doorway, John James hurried himself out, not even waiting for nor helping his wife out. He disappeared into the large abode and took to his P.C., punching in numbers and words, as if he were taking a test. He was beyond furious and now seethed blood. Seeing that banner floating in midair with the words Korr-Tech, made him ill and overly nauseous.

John James opened a file titled "B.I.P.", then emailed it to an undisclosed address in Lower East Manhattan, New

York. Next, he went into his video live conference app. where he would express his true agenda.

The screen was snowy and obscured, and then a face appeared in an animated frame, it was his secret contact.

"It's rather late. I would assume your night with them 'went well?" The voice said.

"That's just it he's been very busy and has put together something major. He has several supporters too."

"So what do you plan on doing now?"

"I say we implement project "B.I.P," I've emailed you all of the files, so you should have the encrypted version. You'll have to use your fourteen digit code to open it, and then input their parents' name," John James instructed. He knew this would finalize something he began decades ago.

"Will do!" The voice said, and once again, the screen became snowy. Thereafter, John James heard a noise in the hallway. Being careful, he quickly shut down his computer.

"Bratford, is that you boy?" He called out, but received nothing back. "Maybe I'm hearing things," he calmly suggested, and left out heading for bed. When he entered his room, there Elizabeth was, stark naked lying across their bed, obviously horny.

"Not tonight honey, I've got too much on my mind. How about we try in the morning?" He said frankly, and then took his place under the covers.

Elizabeth laughed it off, and then headed downstairs still wearing nothing but her birthday suit. Not an hour later, he was sound asleep in dreamland, when he swore he heard the sounds of sexual delight and high-pitched screams from two female voices. He was obviously stuck in his secret videos of Girls Gone Wild.

L♥D~ L♥D~ L♥D

Deep in the mountains of Avon, an upscale and wealthy area in Connecticut, laid ten impeccably manicured acres of land. This particular piece of real estate, broadcasted a historic modern day theme, something you would find in your local brochure for tourist attractions. Traveling up the ground's winding road, were several Gothic sculptures lining the emerald green hedges, which helped the tour guide navigate to the main development.

After a forty second drive from the brow of the property, large white columns securing the architectures frame work stood out strongly, though the overshadowing of the large tinted rose and French windows nestled throughout the structure bestowed a since of mystery and fantasy within.

The place was utterly quiet and still, except for the light tapping of computer keys. The noise was coming from the study, well home office. The 14-digit code was keyed in and there it was the entire profile, logistics and fortune of Blake Industries. It contained all the sales, trades and virtual secrets of their legacy. This information could plummet everything concerning their dynasty into complete bankruptcy. However, the real info would appear after inputting the fore fathers' of Blake Industries name in the diminutive box in the task bar labeled 'Genetic Code'.

"Bingo!" A delighted voice uttered, as a photo of the late Nathaniel and Kaitlyn Blake consumed the large computer screen. It was finally, a day of retribution, a way to share the lap of luxury and most of all a chance to run Blake Industries.

Roman Blake sat in only a velvet red designer robe and fashionable house slippers. Jumping the gun, he lit a victory cigar and twirled some expensive cognac around in his mouth. For years, Roman begged and pleaded with his twin brother to share his triumph and power amongst the elite corporate men and women of Wall Street. None of that mattered, Nathaniel's' belittling and put downs subsequently drove Roman far away, where he strategically plotted his move. Years later, with the help of a family friend, he has everything he will need to take what is rightfully his, because the little that he's ciphered out of the Blake trust so far is only a fraction of what he'll receive very soon.

Chapter 22
Ass Chewing, To First Clue

The homicide division was occupied with their usual homicidal relations between rival street dealers and gang members, but all the tension lied in the unsolved case of the serial killings in and around the city of Hartford and its neighboring counties. The Mayor was bearing down on the Chief, because the Governor was chewing his ass out. Now the Chief was going to reciprocate all of his lashings and animosity towards those that he was in charge of.

In his close-knit smoke infested office, the Chief was reaming an onslaught of obscenities their way. They knew the Chief could get crazy, but the lewdness was over the top today. The pressure was thundering down from high up, so someone had to be held accountable for something and it obviously was starting with them.

"Yes Chief, were on this day and night, but from the shoe print, the single blood droplet found on the stem of the rose, to the lips on the card it is all just compiled evidence we have with no body to pin it on," Wayne said in their defense.

"You mean to tell me you have three sets of prints and nothing checks back from A.F.I.S. (Automated

Fingerprint Identification System)?" Chief Daniels said angrily, as his fists slammed onto his chipped oak desk.

"Uh...Yes." Yolonda answered sarcastically.

She was one of the very few who were not afraid to speak their mind in his presence.

"Excuse me young lady?" He rose up from his desk feeling she was challenging his authority.

Wayne nudged his partner with a stiff elbow before their eyes met. His stare said to relax a bit; he knew they had a serial killer to catch. Understanding, her posture seemed to go feather like for Wayne's sake.

"Sorry Chief, but we're dealing with a lot on this one, it's not like they're leaving a videotaping of the killing. We have what we have and it is obvious that there has never been a prior arrest because there's no record on A.F.I.S., or N.C.I.C. We're stumped for now!" Yolonda concluded.

"Well I suggest you two get back out there and canvass every scene, go door to door, because someone saw something. And the next time you attempt to go in on me, let it be known miss I'm your superior and I'll have you answering phones till' you're retired. Got it?"

"Sure Chief," she sassed, and strolled out the Chief's mildewed office switching a little too hard for both the men's liking.

When Wayne felt they were out of earshot, he yanked her by the arm.

"What's gotten into you Londa? You need to cool it and watch it with Daniels or he'll have you teaching back at the academy," Wayne suggested his words definite.

Yolonda shook her head. Chief Daniels did not scare her one bit. She grew up with six brothers, two young sisters and a stern set of parents, so the Chief was like a chore around the house, something easy at task.

"Wayne you and the rest of this division need to stand up to Daniels or he'll continue to fox trot all over your face!"

"I hear you Londa, but we've got a serial homicide to solve, all the rest will happen later," Wayne said. He was not the passive type, but he adhered to authority as he was supposed to.

"C'mon Wayne, I got a break on the shoeprint." She took off to her cluttered desk. Wayne followed close behind like a puppy dog. Once there, Yolonda logged onto her P.C. and searched the internet, which began to confuse Wayne.

"Uh, what are you doing sister?"

"Shut up Wayne and pay attention," she laughed.

Their relationship was close; sort of brother and sisterly like. Wayne was three years her senior and felt he had to protect her at all times. On many occasions, Yolonda would dine with the Mosley family. Sarah Mosley and their young girls considered her family, seeing she was all by her lonesome. She loved them vice versa.

"There," she said pointed, "that's our print!" She said gleefully.

"Trezeta Gore-Tex boot," Wayne repeated, his eyes fixated on the 13" screen. "It also says, out dated since 1998."

"Yes it does, but they have a website that bought the remaining sixty two pairs the company manufactured in '98. Hopefully the small company has a record of everyone they sold them to."

"Hey there's a number there, you want to give them a call?" Wayne suggested. No reply, just a crazy look greeted Wayne.

Ring! Ring! Ring!

The phone rang in the semi-large warehouse out in the industrial section of Astoria, Queens. Line 'Em Up, was a mom and pop business that sold all types of outdoor gear and similar things utilized when out venturing into the world's hot & cold climates.

"Hello!" A young energetic voice bellowed through the receiver.

"Yes, hello. My name is Yolonda Long and I'm a homicide detective in Connecticut. I just need a little bit of information about some of your internet purchases."

She waited hoping that they would not end the call after hearing the word, detective.

"Sure what do you need ma'am?" The young voice said.

"I'm interested in a person whom might've purchased a shoe that's out of date and out of stock."

"That should be very easy, if it's not over fifteen-years," he replied.

"Good. It's a Trezeta Gore-Tex boot. I learnt from the web that your company bought out the remaining sixty-two pairs. From the measurements I gathered, it's anyone ranging from an 11 ½ to size 12 shoe."

"Whew, that sure helped to narrow things down a lot. There was only one pair of 11 ½ out of the bunch, and surprisingly, no 12's."

"Do you have a name and address?"

She crossed her fingers as she awaited the response.

"Give me a quick second."

He thumbed the dark I-MAC keyboard in search of her request and quickly found something of potential.

"Here we go. The name is Jeffrey Gray and he lives at 54 Woodland Drive Hartford, CT. Does that help ma'am?"

"You just don't know how much sir. Thank you sooo much!" Yolonda yelled, and then hung up. "Let's go Wayne gotta name and address and you wouldn't believe who lives there!" she said holding up the small piece of paper with the info on it.

"Hey that's where…"

"Sure is my dear Watson!" Yolonda cut him off, and raced towards the cold staircase.

L♥D~ L♥D~ L♥D

As the dark Monte Carlo raced through the city, down Albany Ave., the detectives witnessed dope sales in plain sight, but drugs were not on the list of tasks in their job description, so they continued down the long two-way street. They took a left onto Woodland Street where a red light at the intersection of Woodland and Homestead Avenue stopped them. Once the two-minute light switched to green, they knifed over the hilly bridge, which brought them to a second light. Immediately to their right were projects full of red-bricked townhouse like apartments all cemented together.

They drove down the slight steepness of the smooth pavement and stopped at the first U-shape circle of buildings.

"Right there, Wayne."

She pointed at the white roofing hovering above the porch and front door.

"Looks like fifty four to me, tutts."

Wayne put the car into park and they hopped out and began an observatory stroll up the clam grey sidewalk. The long squared walkway ended directly at 54.

Knock! Knock! Knock!

Wayne pounded the large wooden door with a mail slot ¾ down its portal.

Nothing

Knock! Knock!

"Who is it?" A women's voice barked, obviously tempered by the pounding noise. "Who da fuck is..." She continued opening the red door but froze seeing a black male and female brandishing shiny, gold pieces of metal. "Um, can I help you?" Lareese questioned closing her robe, not wanting her goodies to be taking into account.

"Hello ma'am, we're from the Hartford Homicide Division. I'm detective Mosley and my partner here, is Yolonda Long." He offered his credentials then said, "Does a Jeffrey Gray reside here?"

"Jeffrey Gray?" Lareese paused and tapped into her mental rolodex, "the Grays moved out of here in the mid-80s, right after some woman was viciously gunned down by her estranged boyfriend. I haven't seen or heard nothing about them since," Lareese concluded.

Wayne looked from Lareese to Yolonda who appeared to be pissed the fuck off.

"Well here are our cards, if you see or hear anything concerning a Gray, please contact us," Yolonda said, in the midst of passing Lareese their business cards.

As the two started the long journey back to the vehicle, a cherry red Ferrari drove up the hill. By the time the detectives reached their car, the expensive car was gone.

"Wow, that was a very attractive car Wayne, but what is it doing down here? This isn't the type of neighborhood you would usually see such a car."

Wayne simply shrugged his shoulders, and then got in the car.

L♥D~ L♥D~ L♥D

Later that night, the two detectives found themselves back down the semi steep hill of Woodland Drive. Lareese took their advice and called them, only it did not pertained to the Grays, it was for some much needed help. When Lareese came home from a long day of swapping tainted currency for food at a McDonalds' just a fifteen-minute walk away, she found herself in a useless struggle for her aging life. When it was all said and done, Lareese laid ass naked in a pool of blood with the letter 'K' carved deeply into her torso.

"This is bad, very bad!" Wayne interjected.

Chapter 23
Good-Mornings

Kory sat in his kitchen crunching on a nearly burned English muffin, lightly buttered with strawberry preserves. Coffee was something he did not indulge in on a daily basis, but when he did, it was always a gourmet flavor. His mug contained a blend of blueberry coffee and French Vanilla Coffee Mate creamer. Sugar was cool, but he preferred three sugar twins.

Kory sipped his java while studying Ashanti's sleek tender body as she sat sexily on a stool wearing only a striped polo button down that she had found in his spacious closet. Her mane was silky and full of body. Ashanti knew she was extremely beautiful, not to mention in excellent shape, which drove brothers crazy. Lately Kory had been spending ample time with the stripper. He felt it was easy access, and he enjoyed her company. She was not plain, simple and ditzy as most dancers were. There was no sign of shallowness he could detect, so it was luck that she caught someone of his caliber.

"Here you go Korr."

"Good look ma'," he thanked, accepting the Courant as he quickly caught a crazy caption: Lawrence Taylor back in trouble once again.

"Oh shit, dis dude back messing with them drugs and hoes again. Damn Lawrence, a fifteen-year old girl though!"

Kory said in astonishment. It further read that he excessively beat and assaulted the teen and that he had sexual intercourse with her. "You really fucked up this time boah!"

"What about my Celtics?" Ashanti questioned with a large smile, her teeth white as tissue.

"Oh you got jokes huh? I lost eight grand fuckin' wit da so called King-James. It's all good, cause I'm about to take it out on you!" Kory said, then tossed the paper to the counter and attacked Ashanti's naked body.

"Hungry this morning aren't chu?" She teased, allowing him to fold her legs up into her plump breast. Kory then shook his head at the sight of her thick vagina, its face was burnt-orange with a tight smile.

Kory spit on his fingertips and lathered the head of his stiffness. Next, he positioned himself in her glazed opening and stroked her up and down tickling her button, which caused her to squirm and exhale deeply.

"Ahhhh!"

When he felt her inner cave was primed, he drove his pole slowly into depths she had not known were created. He was in uncharted territory, a place not found on her gynecological map. Kory was thick and filled her tunnel leaving no room for her fluids to leak out, except when he would pull his long staff out and droplets of her cream passion sailed south. He was too much for her. His pole was too big in girth, too long in length and his helmet seemed to be in doubles. Every time she licked or sucked it, it reminded her of two train track nails welded together.

"Ooooh Kory, oooh! Ooooh yeah, yeah Kory, fuck dis pussy! Get in there, make some room in there. Dis your pussy, oooh, I'm cumming again, Urggghh!" She grunted.

Kory had been fiercely jamming himself inside her cavern as she asked, only he was locked onto her waist and pumping like an oil well.

"Urggh!" He gritted through clenched teeth, as he nutted somewhere in her intestines.

"Boyeee... You gon' hava girl turned all da way out, you keep slinging dat gun around!"

Kory then sat her on the padded stool and brushed her teeth with his thick toothbrush. After swallowing a set of his triplets, they showered and proceeded to get dressed. When Kory attempted to push ten grand her way, she declined. She was content with him and would make her ends at his strip club, it was evident she was falling for her boss.

Kory knew this, but for the time being their relationship would remain as it is. He had too much going on now.

Kory was not consumed with having sex or going raw dog in one of his workers, nonetheless a gold digging stripper, but Mr. Blake has not come this far in the game to slip up now, besides Teezer'z maintains a very strict policy on disease control. Employees are tested upon interview, also weekly if employed, and luckily, for Mr. Blake, Ashanti had a clean bill of health.

After Kory dropped Ashanti off, he listened to the secret recording Jeffrey and he made of John James the night of the Gala. It was quite interesting, the deceit Mr. James harbored for him and his sister Keonna. The conversation had not disclosed in detail what he intended to find out, nevertheless, Kory knew it was something excruciating as far as Blake Industries was concerned.

Kory knew John James had no means or ways to tamper with the shares he held in Anheuser Busch, or

Westinghouse Electric, so he was cool there. However, John James was on the board of directors and owned 10% of Blake Industries, which posed a threat, nothing major, but enough to cause trouble. Kory was prepared he was always moving to gain an advantage over certain situations when it came to his business.

The vehicle disrespected the highways fast lane at 98-mph. Kory only drove his horse when he liked to speed and stunt a bit. In the flooring of the passenger seat was a leather suitcase full of cash. It was filled with close to a hundred grand, which happened to belong to his best friend and partner, Spade. He was on his way to meet Spades wifey, Mikia.

When the Ferrari exited the ramp, he thought about closing the top, but said the hell with it being he loved to profile and besides the weather was just right. It was not too hot and not too cold. As Kory pulled to the front of City Steam, a local restaurant, he noticed Mikia pulling up in a clean baby blue Bentley Azure. Kory grabbed the case, and then tossed the keys to the valet and Mikia did the same.

"Sup girl, I see you doing you!" He referred to the Azure. "I'm feeling that."

"Not too bad yo'self!" She countered. She had on a matching baby blue Gucci sundress on, with some black and baby blue Gucci sandals that laced up her thick calves. Her ice game was flawless, not to mention the new Gucci mambo clutch tucked in her arm. "You know the hubby would've had a matching horse, I can see y'all racing up the Merritt Pkwy going to New York,   or coming from the club," she admitted with a broad smile.

"C'mon, I'm hungrier than a hostage." He mentioned as his stomach growled. Kory sported some new construction Timbs, a pair of blue denim True Religion Jeans and matching zip up. Of course the hand he ushered Mikia into the restaurant with was drippin' in 10 carats of flawless diamonds, while the other holding the briefcase showcased a custom made Bretling full of princess cut diamonds. They both were wearing oversized shades, hers were Gucci and his were Bulvgari. They were the definition of pure money in motion.

After a good meal, conversation and a couple drinks they retrieved their rides and bounced. Kory had a rendezvous with Robert, his main man. Mikia rode off with the $98,000 Kory had for Spade.

L♥D~ L♥D~ L♥D

'I better have your lovin', I better find your heart!' Blared inside the speeding Ferrari Scagletti. It was Drake's newest single and one of Kory's favorites. The fluorescent clock on the dashboard read 8:30 p.m., and the sun had vanished as the dark clouds and anxious moon bullied its way around the spacious sky.

Tonight Kory and Robert had planned to meet and put the final additions down concerning John James and his delusive agenda. It was bad enough that he sent the Krammers into a spiraling downfall, which caused his wife to run for the hills leaving him with two kids to raise alone, not to mention all of the pain and heartache he had caused the Blakes over the years. Normally it is the other way around. Usually the man is the one packing up and leaving, however his wife was used to the good life and would not settle for less.

Robert and Kory's friendship was genuine. They have been tight for some time now and Kory was not going to sit back and let Robert wither away like some avid drug user. He had already given him his spacious abode out in Wethersfield and a quarter-mill' to live on for the time being, but he still felt like there was more that he could do for his old friend.

Tonight Kory was dressed down in a black and red LRG sweat suit with a black thermal underneath. Kory had a silenced .9 milli tucked in the lining of his waist, he was not sure about tonight's crowd at the club which is why he chose to carry tonight. Fridays tended to get crazy. He also wore a black and red Atlanta Falcons baseball cap and some platinum Cartier's with transitional lenses.

Pulling up to Teezer'z parking lot, he observed Robert's green Escalade parked up against the far wall. When he noticed the visors were down obscuring the view, he smiled knowing Rob was most likely getting some head.

Soon after, Kory entered through the rear entrance and was happy to see that the place was packed tonight; however, there were a lot new faces on deck. Ashanti was on stage sexing the shit out of the gold stripper pole, when their eyes met and she licked her lips erotically. It was something he did to her. Just the thought of sexing him, brought her to climax and the crowd went ballistic noticing the flow of thick cream trickling down her broad thighs. Bills were raining down onto the stage as if a hurricane had just swept through Teezer'z. Kory winked at her and she blew him an illustrious kiss.

"Hey boss, I guess you bring out the best in a girl," Mo'nay said as she walked up on him. She was next up, but did not think she would be able to top Ashanti's show, so she let Fantasia swap out with her.

"I guess so." He replied. "Ain't you up next?" He questioned, knowing the dancers rotation.

"Sure, but Fantasia begged me to go on next, so we swapped out. Is that okay boss man," she asked batting her round eyes, her lips puckered tightly.

Kory laughed Mo'nay's passiveness off. He knew what time it was and said, "Cool, but make this the first and last time you break rotation." He warned, and then headed for his booth. It was very rare that he used his plush office; he enjoyed the view from front row in case he had to make an example out of someone.

He watched as Mo'nay's substitute worked the stage, molesting the gold pole sensually. Fantasia, was 5'5" and curvaceously thick in the ass and breast. Her tiny waist looked as if she had been doing stomach crunches since birth. Her skin was a shade lighter then caramel and blemish free. Fantasia was a new hire, and if you must know, Kory sampled the goodies prior to her being hired, and he was very pleased with her performance.

"Damn Kory, who's the new dame?" Robert asked, after taking a seat in the booth.

Kory just shook his head because he knew Robert had an insatiable thing for black women and it was outside his nature to even look at white women.

"Her name's Fantasia and she's very blessed I might add for a white-girl."

"I got a coupla' bills for her, set it up for me bruh," Robert spoke through a sense of lust. "So what's up, we on?" He asked, though his mind was still on Fantasia.

"Drink!" Kory urged.

He wanted Robert to mellow out some. He is easier to handle when inebriated.

After a couple of drinks, Kory began. "For starters, Korr-Tech is up and running. Since the Gala, I have sold over 400,000 shares. The info I've gathered eavesdropping on

John James is suggesting that he is conspiring with one, maybe two others. I sense he will try to pose a trading scare, which will drop share prices drastically and then he'll back out, and that's where you'll come in."

"Sounds like some crooked shit he's into, but nonetheless, we'll be one up on whatever he throws at you." Robert responded.

He'd ride with Kory until the wheels fell off and the feeling was presumably mutual.

"I hope so Rob, because this experience doesn't involve whoring around all day and night. There's a lot at stake here and I'm putting all of my trust in you. After this, John will be begging to regain what has never rightfully been his. How are the kids?"

He suspected they were okay, but with Robert's wild side, he had to ask.

"They're cool bruh. They're staying with my folks for now. I will get 'em back once things fall into place."

Kory shrugged his shoulders and nodded his head in a sense of agreement with Robert's plans. Right now, things were crucial to a lot of people's livelihood and Kory thought his playboy of a friend, made the right decision to mask things from his off springs. This was not a children's game.

By now, they had downed both bottles of Rose` and also a coupla shots of Ciroc and cranberry. Tonight Kory had let his collar down by enjoying several lap dances from three different women. Robert was tipsy times two. As he saw Fantasia strutting by, he flashed a hefty knot in hopes of entrapping her. Sure enough, as money was the root of all evil, Fantasia swayed slowly over to their booth magnetized by the power of the almighty dolla.

"Hey boo, you feelin' lonely tonight? You lookin' to break bread?" She flirted openly, her gaze hypnotic.

"Yeah, I could use some company, all night matter fact!" His words spraying out in a slur. Fantasia smiled, and then glazed at her boss and Kory nodded in approval. "Just so you know white chocolate, I don't run cheap or quick so I hope you can go the distance!" She challenged his stamina, and then sat down on his lap. Her wide ass was planted dead on his stiffness. "Whew...We've gotta live one!" She said and began to buck and wind.

From where he was positioned, Kory caught a glimpse of an older gentleman walking from the bar with Teddy, a sandy brown mound of ecstasy. He also had a bottle of Cristal. The older man looked to be in his late 50s to mid-60s. His style was almost authentic. He wore navy blue slacks with creased pleats in the waistline and a cardigan sweater with a beige corduroy blazer. His feet were covered in a stylish pair of walnut brown penny loafers. However, what boggled Kory's mind was that dude unmistakably resembled a photo of his pops, Kline Blake.

"Man this liquor's got me bugging out, because dude looks just like my pops!" He said a little louder then he wanted to.

Kory and his parents were not as close as a normal family should have been due to their jobs and age, so trying to think back to a specific place or time they all shared together, and would just cause a major headache. Nevertheless, the photo in his head was almost identical to the man he just saw.

Although Fantasia was pleasuring Rob with a hand job under the booth's table, he heard Kory as if he yelled his statement over the PA system. When Robert glanced at the man, he damn near spit his entire drink in Fantasia's face.

He had seen the life like painting of Kline enough to agree with Kory.

"Wow…Kory, he looks just like your pops in a strange way." Robert said in truth.

His words were slur free; the older man damn near blew his high.

"Be right back," Kory said, then stood up.

He needed a closer look.

"Look at dis fool; he's all fucked up about my appearance, and why shouldn't he? I am his uncle. This is great and working out to be excellence at its best. What a way to meet your uncle for the first time in twenty plus years." Roman thought to himself. He knew exactly how old Kory and Keonna are.

Kory strolled by and peeked at Roman's table but kept it moving because he did not want to look too obvious. He went to the bar, which was at an angle where he could steal looks and not be open or seemingly stalkish.

"Hey boss, you need something?" Vanessa, the head bartender inquired.

"Yeah, you know what I like," he answered, peeking Roman's way.

Vanessa thought Kory was acting very strange. His suave-demeanor and swagger were leaning a bit to the left, a side she'd never seen before, and she was outright concerned.

"Here you go boss." She sat a glass of Ciroc on a napkin with a lime and some cranberry juice. "Hey, is that new guy causing trouble? I can get security to escort 'em out if you like!"

"Ahhh…Nah, I got dis. He's cool," he said and began his stroll back the way he came; only this time he planned to approach him.

Kory's mental seemed to be at the older man's mercy. He felt as if he were being attacked by a mob of angry Klu Klux Klan members after hearing one of their precious daughters snuck out and sexed a black man. As he grew closer, he took small sips of his concoction. His eyebrows flared with every step, seeing a human ghost of his late father. Finally where he needed to be, Kory looked the man dead in the eyes. He asked him his name after saying dad, but the words actually never left his mouth, it was all thoughts.

"Excuse me, may I help you with something young fella?" Roman questioned, using a familiar phrase Kline mouthed nearly a hundred times a day and it further spooked Kory.

"Uh umm, it's just you really remind me of someone very close to me. Is this your first time in here? I've never seen you before." Kory thought that maybe he had been through during the times he had not been around.

Kory downed the remainder of his drink and was now perspiring under his arms and around the brim of his forehead.

"People tell me that all the time, but yes this is my first night here. It's pretty cool in here too, I like your taste in women," he smiled.

"Well, make sure you enjoy yourself on me tonight. My name is Kory, and this is my joint." Although he maintained his composure, Kory spoke nervously.

"Thank you young fella, and I think I'll turn a coupla' buddies from my company onto this joint also. I'm quite sure they'll enjoy it as I do. Here, take my card, maybe we can do some business someday. I admire today's youth, real go-getters," he smirked.

When Kory made it back to his booth, he read the card and it said, 'Roman Blackwell, CEO of Blackwell Instrument. After reading the script, he looked back at Roman, who held up his glass and smiled.

"Aye Robert, I'll get up wit `chu in the a.m., I gotta move on. Fantasia," Kory called.

"Yes boss?" She answered looking his way.

"Go easy on 'em!"

"I'll try." She responded, while continuing her hand job.

Chapter 24
The Trap

Harold Peters, the advisor and investor in John James' newest scandal, was in a fit of rage. He had turned over a million dollars of his earnings, rather savings to Mr. James, and still nothing so much as a board meeting. Nothing in writing that tied him into what he so desperately sought after for two decades now. Blake Industries had been successfully trading on NASDAQ; earning the company well over 48, billion to date and he wanted in as promised.

Blake Industries had several tool and die companies across the globe, and as it is, they were a subsidiary of James Electric, which we all know is a magnet for business and currency. Though combined in marketing, Kory still planned to unhitch their ties, but in a schematic way. He planned to pass Blake Industries onto the Krammers. Korr-Tech would be more than enough trouble for him and Keonna to indulge in for the next four to five decades. Insurance was the in thing, as air was to the lung.

The motorist driving on the opposite side of the road looked on as Harold knifed his 2010 Ford SHO up Tower Avenue at a high rate of speed. He had a few things to run by him, maybe even an ass whooping, if things did not go as he expected. After several failed attempts at reaching John James, he decided he would head to a small pub in the downtown area of Hartford and throwback a few shots.

L♥D~ L♥D~ L♥D

It was rather late. The streetlights were radiant and powerful. Traffic was minimal around the city solely because of the heavy downpour of rain. Keonna maneuvered her mint green DB9 Vanquish with the skills of a NASCAR driver. Water brushed off her windshield, as the wipers fought and threw staggering left and right jabs in her defense against the torrent of droplets. Thus, her vision was impeccable in the storm.

"Speedster huh!" Keonna said to herself. "I wonder how fast you screw your wife. You're probably a fuckin' jack-rabbit," she further commented, as she stayed in great distance of the Ford SHO.

Keonna had been tailing Harold since he left his pitiful home in South Windsor, CT. Tonight would be his night to play corpse in the 'Game Of Death'.

It was no secret that he was conspiring with the James' to eradicate and overthrow the Blakes, and for that, Harold should dance with the devil. It was not by mere chance that Keonna popped up on John James at the service station that bright Saturday, when Harold had met up with him to make his last and final payment of one million dollars. She had been following both of them lately and learnt of their fiendish plot, and since all the males were Keonna's responsibility, she had to nullify their placement in life.

"Where are we going tonight?" She whispered. "You're going off course tonight my love."

Keonna slowed her pace seeing that the SHO had stopped at Club Velvet, an average sized nightclub in the downtown area. Although it was not the weekend, people often came in for happy hour, 1st Fridays, or to unwind and enjoy a cold draft. Keonna kept the engine running case that Ol' Harry made her, and tried to ditch her. She was an excellent driver, so either way Harold was going to cross into the Great Divide.

Something must be troubling my dear friend tonight, you're not your usual self. Club, bar, low lights, uh uhn, something's out of whack! She thought.

The driver's door opened and out stepped a burly Caucasian man. He desperately tried to fend off the heavy torrent of rain, as it rhythmically connected onto a daily edition of The Wall Street Journal covering his temple. As Harold made it into the small arching of the doorway, he shook off the loose drops of water in his salt and pepper pushback with his colossal fingers.

Keonna knew it was time to emerge from her latency and bond with her prey. She reached behind her seat, grabbed a Louis Vuitton umbrella, and snuggled her matching poncho close into her bosom.

There she was, off into the same torrent of water that pounced on Harold. However, she was protected, because there was no was way she was going to sit in someone's pub soaking wet. When she reached the arch, she clumsily bumped into Harold who was still attempting to wring dry himself off.

"Ooh, excuse me sir. I didn't know anyone was standing in here," Keonna apologized after delivering a stiff blow to his mid-section.

"No, No, I'm sorry! I shouldn't have been standing here as long as I was. I was just trying to dry off some," his voice bellowed with sympathy.

"Here," she said pulling out a cotton scarf and attempted to dry his face off a bit.

She caught a glimpse of Harold's eyes lusting at her plump cleavage as she tended to his dripping body. "This is going to be easier than I thought!" She snickered.

They both made it upstairs and realized that they were alone and possibly in need of some social companionship. Being a gentleman, Harold asked if he could join her, seeing she came to his rescue not moments ago. Keonna was more than happy to enjoy his company. They chose a medium size booth in the rear of the club, which was adjacent to the hardwood dance floor where a couple was engaged in a slow two-step.

The two exchanged names, and as time elapsed, they exchanged small talk over several shots of Patron Tequila. Harry seemed to be taken by Jose Cuervo's lofty proof, not to mention the blue dolphin Keonna covertly snuck into one of his shots as he cased her breast.

"You know I can't let `chu drive out of here Harry!" She spoke lowly, but audible enough for him to comprehend.

"Well…I   guess…You'll…Half   to…Drive   me, Sasha!" He slurred his breath very needy of a course mint.

"I guess so. You ready babe?"

She bent over to give `em a good shot of her goodies, which she called Venus and Serena.

"Do you promise to let me meet the sisters?" He asked and Keonna smiled. Harry was not only horny, but also drunker than a skunk at this point.

"Yes Harry, you're gonna meet the sister's. Here, lemme see your hand." She took his large hand and gently rubbed them against her breast. "You like babe?"

"Yes…yes, I like!" He sang joyously.

"Come on, you'll stay at my place tonight," Keonna insisted and helped him down the flight of stairs then into her convertible.

"Ahhh...I like this car, Sasha."

"Well if you like my whip, you're going to love my twin, Milli."

"Who's...Milli?" He replied goofily.

Instead of answering, Keonna backhanded Harry in the temple with the butt of her gun. "My .9 milli stupid!" Then she drove off into the thundering rainstorm.

Chapter 25
The Topple

John James was comfortably resting in his 3-way lazy boy recliner, with his nine and a halves elevated on his large desk. While he propped his feet up, he blew rings of smoke into the air. He loved cigars of all types, mostly Cubans but they had been hard to get lately. It had been two weeks since he had purposely been dodging Harold's calls. Harold was becoming a straight nuisance, a thorn in his side so he hid from him, but today he felt up to a little phone boxing.

"Lizzie, get Harold on the phone for me." He commanded over the intercom.

"Sure," she replied.

She tried the number for thirty minutes, but to no avail did she gain a connection. She wasn't tripping, but she felt she could be doing something much more productive, like surfing the many websites on the internet. Surfing the internet is something all employees do from time to time while at work.

"Dammit, where are you Harold?" She cursed under her breath.

As she dialed the number one last time, the recording said, "This number is no longer in service." She thought his service more than likely had to be from Sprint, because, they will cut your service off in a New York minute if your bill goes overdue by a red cent! "Lizzie, what's the hold up?" John James' voice echoed through the intercom. "Sorry boss, his number is no longer in service." "Thank you. Can you please get me a fresh cup of Joe?" He asked. John-James knew Harold more than likely had not stopped to add minutes to his throwaway phone his cohorts and he utilized when discussing certain business concerning Kory and Keonna.

His eyes were beginning to close from the potency of his cigar and the lack of sleep due to his wretched plot against the Blake's, it seemed like bringing Kory down was all he thought about and did on a daily basis. When his office door swung inward, he saw a familiar face holding his cup of coffee. "What are you doing here Hun?" His face full of surprise.

"Oh, I was just out running a few errands and thought I'd drop in. Why? You in here screwing your secretary?" Elizabeth questioned seriously. She wasn't getting any at home, and what heterosexual male doesn't cry out for sex on a daily basis? She thought.

"Come on now Lizzie, you know I'm not stepping out on you, but I'll take that java from you."

"I can't tell!" She said with heavy sarcasm.

"Please Lizzie, not at my office. You know how rumors around the office can be. Matter of fact, this is not even a topic of discussion. I'm not sleeping around!" He barked sternly.

"Well that's good to know James, you better not be!"

She then opened her full-length trench coat to reveal her naked goodies. Elizabeth was growing in age, her breast had sagged slightly, and her mid-section was somewhat flabby. Her pale off white skin was flooded by hundreds of burnt orange and red freckles.

James was shocked, but it did not halt his sexual hunger from lunging for his wife's nakedness. He took her lips and sucked them feverishly, his penis growing rapidly filling into the extra flab that housed his lady tamer. Elizabeth moaned softly in heat. She was finally feeling like herself, as his warm mouth made its way to her throbbing nipples.

"Mmmmm," she cooed. Her moans brought out the beast in James. Lizzie let out a fulfilling gasp of air, and then rubbed through his stringy hair.

Their encounter lasted a steamy thirty five-minutes with Elizabeth enjoying three much needed orgasms. She was overly satisfied for the moment, but there was still that wild side that to this date he would not cross. Oral sex was something that was nonexistent in their relationship, but that never stopped her from enjoying a good tongue lashing every now and then, just not with him.

They cleaned up and he turned the Glade Plug-in up full blast to overwhelm the smell of passion. Elizabeth kissed her husband deeply, said she would see him at home, and then left.

After Elizabeth exited, John James tuned into the Wall Street site. He wanted to check on some of his investments and the plummet of Blake Industries. Everything seemed to be normal on his side of things, but the oil spill in the Gulf was causing a wide scare to several seamen whom made their living in those very same waters.

Roman had successfully played his part in the topple of Blake Industries. As the flashing red ticker scrolled horizontally at the bottom of his screen, he smiled in divine happiness. The NASDAQ was showing that Blake Industries was dropping at a rapid pace, which meant shares would be sold at low prices. In addition, current shareholders were losing money by the minute. He immediately picked up the phone and called Roman.

Chapter 26
Female Chromosomes

As Wayne and Yolonda sat in the small coffee room at the station, they conversed on a few things concerning the serial murders. Wayne was all ears, and knee deep into a powdered jelly donut.

"Wow, there's a lot going on in the world, but we take certain things for granted." Yolonda spoke slightly above a whisper. "It appears that the number of deaths in the Afghanistan War has surpassed the war in Iraq by millions. This is some real bullshit!" She spoke candidly.

"Huh?" Wayne answered between bites, jelly dripping onto his light colored button up.

"Are you even listening to me Wayne? I swear whenever donuts are involved you go blank!" Yolonda blasted him, and then continued her news hunt.

"Sure tutts, I heard everything you said."

His smile widened as he concealed it behind the large green coffee mug.

Yolonda ignored him and thumbed through the USA Today. Her eyes roamed the front page like a high-end scanner, skipping the nonessential stuff to focus on the more drastic headlines. As she further reviewed the captions, she read the title U.P.I. (United Press International): Reports are that a savage murdered seven kindergarten school children and two teachers, then escaped life and prosecution by killing himself. China reports that there was a small quarrel over land with the kindergarten school and he felt he had gotten the short end of the stick, and took matters into his own hands.

"Wow!" Yolonda sighed heavily.

"What's the wow all about?" Wayne asked with concern, he felt obligated to help feed her crave for headlines.

"Do you know some lunatic went and hacked seven kids and two teachers to death at a Chinese school?"

"No, not until now, how tragic!" He sympathized. "What happened to the hacker?"

"Dead! Killed himself!" Yolonda answered shaking her head. "Just stupid, relentless and senseless!"

While the two detectives mourned the news, Ryan, another detective relayed to them that Wayne had a phone call.

"Thanks, I'll take it in here."

Wayne stood up from the round eating table, banged his knee hardly against the metal legs, and yelled out, "Shit...I'm really tired of this old ass table and its metal poles for legs!" He cursed. Yolonda laughed, as he limped over to the desk phone.

"Hello?"

"Hey Wayne, it's Carin down at the morgue!"

"What's good?" He returned, as the sharp pains began to subside.

"Well for starters, I did some checking after that couple out in Wethersfield was murdered and our killer is definitely a woman."

"How do you suppose?"

"Well, from the card with the lip print on it, I lifted a small piece of chaffed skin. When I ran it, I matched the chromosomes to a woman. In addition, that single drop of blood confirms my theory, not to mention the secretions Ronald found from a woman on the rug at the Chief State Treasurer's murder. We've got a real live one on our hands," Carin said.

"I'd say so myself. Okay thanks Carin, I'll be in touch," he said, and then hung up.

"So what was that all about?" Yolonda quizzed.

"The M.E. says it's definitely a woman behind our mystery killer."

"Shoot!" Yolonda shrugged.

"What's wrong?"

He was confused.

"Cause, I was hoping it was some deranged man who hates women. I should've known it was some freak ass broad running around screwing these men, cutting their peckers off, and then leaving black roses, and kiss prints on cards," she answered in frustration.

"Well what about the men who were killed? All of them sustained deep lacerations in the stomach and torso. That letter 'K' has to mean something tutts." Wayne added.

"Well the good thing is, I've tied a line and connection to some of these vics. They all had some stock in Blake Industries and James Electric. If you remember, Harold was the Dodd's advisor and their dead. Our Chief State Treasurer also had a nice amount of stock into Blake Industries, but get this…"

"C'mon, give it to me," he begged playfully.

Yolonda shook her head and continued.

"As I was saying, the Chief State Treasurer was also second cousin to John James, along with our news reporter, Melinda King. Also if you remember our vic from the parking lot of Weaver High School, Clyde Barksdale, he was

an investor in Blake Industries and a relative of the James';
some real family ties huh?"

"So you think this woman is killing off any and
everyone connected to the James' to gain control of their
business? That would be a whole lot of mula!" Wayne
pitched, as he sat down.

"Not sure, but we need to question the James' and
whoever runs Blake Industries."

"Let's get to it!" He ended with.

Chapter 27
Pillow Talk

The warmth of a Sunday afternoon is always appreciated by the cities ill-bred-blue-collared man, street-urchin, and bourgeois populace in and around the capitol. However, for this one particular servant, it was her day off and she planned to spend it exerting all of her reserved energy in a plush bed sweating and pleasing her stallion.

A servant pushing a new battleship grey 5-series BMW does not seem right, but this is not your everyday 9 to 5 helper. This servant happens to be 5'7" with copper skin, and her slanted eyes held an aqua tint. She was twenty sixty and full of beauty. Her hair touched the arc of her spine, which also matched her delicate skin, and to go along with all of those attributes, she was equally stacked in all the womanly places men loved.

Today she was laced in a tight fitting sundress and open toed sandals. A pair of Marilyn Monroe shades shielded her eyes, as a wicker bag hung from her arm. Her flimsy blue and white apron was sagging on a hook back at her employer's estate and would not see the likes of her until noon the following day. Picture that, the double life of a house maiden.

After speeding down I-84 west, the 5-series excused itself from the congestive highway and down the ramp. Farmington and Asylum Avenue was always a breath of fresh air to many motorists, being further down the road would become abundantly crowded at this hour. The sunroof was all the way back allowing the cool refreshing air to invade the foreign car's cabin.

Traveling up the inclined hilly road going southwest towards Park St., the battleship approached the fire red light and disobeyed the law by turning right, a traffic law that would surely earn a $35 to $70 ticket if a police officer were in sight. Now on the endless road, she came to Park St., and Pope Park Highway. The light was in between changes of caution yellow and fire red, and just as the one she disobeyed a few feet back, the sporty vehicle coiled right onto Laurel Street. The only car in sight was a S430, which she coat tailed into the Park Place Towers. She further pushed the Mercedes into the carport, and then found a lonely spot wedging her derriere nicely into an empty space.

After a quick sign in at The Towers security booth, she rode the elevator to the top floor. The mere fact that she obtained a key to the penthouse did not deter her from knocking; it was just out of courtesy. He could have a female companion inside. Noticing a shadow at the bottom of the floor from under the door, she smiled and held her breath, then it opened and there stood Kory, in nothing but a velvet Gucci robe and holding a tall glass of Mimosa.

"Hey sexy, I see you were expecting me," she said staring at his bulging erection with lust. "Here Papi, let mama taste my chocolate bar!"

Isabella wasted no time; she dropped to her knees and stuffed him into her warm mouth.

"Ummmm," Kory moaned, as Isabella slurped his manhood while jerking the end that could not fit in her mouth. "I see you've been practicing." He struggled to say, his eyes now shut enjoying the French house cleaner's mouthpiece.

"Yeah..." She looked up into Kory's brown eyes and said, "but Elizabeth doesn't taste as good as this," her accent traveling about the foyer.

Now massaging the length of his lil' brother with vigorous strokes, her silky palms juggled his tool bag softly. Not caring about the adjacent penthouse, their raunchy episode concluded with Kory shooting his warm load down her throat. When Isabella stood up and Kory's eyes opened, they noticed the young boy from across the hall. The boy's youthful eyes showed he was begging for a session with the French house cleaner.

Isabella smiled at the eight-year old boy then said," ten more years and I would let you come play, but you're too young honey!" She concluded honestly, and then walked into Kory's plush penthouse where they began to claw at one other like two wild animals.

L♥D~ L♥D~ L♥D

It was 8:30 p.m. when Kory was jolted out of his sleep by a surge of coldness, yet pleasure. He tried very hard to fight it, but the lock Isabella had on his pole was unforgiving, add that with an ice cube and you'll understand what Kory was going through at the moment. With Isabella it was always different, magnetic and risqué, which is why he kept her in his stable.

"Ahhhh..." His voice echoed out with extreme pleasure causing her to speed the strokes up. She felt the veins convulsing and constricting inside the thick pole and she jerked the serpent in a chastising manner. "Urggghh!" He belted, gripping the sheets for support. In the end, he always felt defeated, as if a mobbing crowd had beaten him up. "Whew girl, you just don't know. I'ma fuck around and have to marry yo sexy ass!"

"You play too much Kory," she uttered, knowing that is something he would never do or even contemplate for that matter. Their business was just that, business and occasional good sex.

"How you know what Kory is thinking?" He stared into her eyes waiting for a rebuttal.

"You don't want to marry a French girl, you want Americana," she replied through pursed lips, with her knees tucked into her bosom. She never figured she would ever escape the clutches of John James and Elizabeth's slavery, nor share a bed with a Blake, so any chance or opportunity that presented itself towards her, she promised to do well.

Kory and Isabella's relationship definitely crossed the bedroom border and even into the James' counterfeit concern for the well-being of him and Keonna. John James was living by his cunning wit, but even he knew deceit was just a lie that wore a huge smile, so in the end it was the possum that played dead that would prevail. With Isabella in place, Kory learnt things he would have never dreamed his supposed friends, the James' had up their sleeves. It was Isabella who stole certain deeds, paperwork and diaries from the James' that had belonged to his late parents and other important people. It was through Isabella's dutiful spying on the James' over the years, that helped he become aware of John James' role in his parent's demise and for that, he would endure the same fate tenfold.

As they lay in bed, Isabella informed Kory of the latest recipe that is brewing in the James' favor against him and Keonna. He considered John's plot to be clever, only it would never see daylight.

It would now boil down to whom was the better strategist between two dynasties, John James or Kory Blake. Now energized fully from the sudden plot, Kory hovered over the French maiden and entered her womb without protection and grinded until their excitement was expired.

L♥D~ L♥D~ L♥D

Later the same night, Kory left Isabella's naked body snuggled under the thick sheathing on his bed and drove to Teezer'z. Teezer'z is a place he knew he would be able to spark off his strategic scheme. Kory was dressed in black faded denims courtesy of Polo, a double X rugby and his Trezeta Gortex boots. It became habit for Kory to wear his thin black gloves after twelve. It was usually after twelve that his silencer spoke loudly and someone's blood drained into the city's sewage.

Just as he thought, the triple black Maybach with the German plates was parked in the grass directly in front of his lewd establishment. Kory used the rear entrance for specific reasons that entrance also led to his plush office.

The lighting inside his office was red, dim and dramatic. There was burgundy seating lining the walls that had rarely been used, except for during Kory's down time and his sexual episodes. The carpeting was thick and comforting to bare feet. On the walls were photos of his deceased parents and one of Keonna and him when they were just toddlers. Seeing his creators humbled faces made him grit his teeth a bit. The anger he had bottled up inside his heart was catastrophic, a wrath that he inherited from Nathaniel Blake. Up until now, no one dared cross him but John James. John James had not only provoked him, but he opened a box similar to Pandora's Box.

Kory looked through the two-way mirror while pulling on a Cuban cigar, his sharp vision yet to pinpoint that specific patron. The one body he left a good piece of ass sleeping for.

The more Kory scanned the salacious crowd, the more lightheaded he became from the cigar's potency, and then out of the darkness, his newest prey appeared.

"I knew you were somewhere amongst my horny partygoers," he smiled at the sight before him, though shocked by the company tagging along. "Who would've ever guessed you rocked with the other side, it doesn't matter now, it'll be two birds with one stone.

Kory watched the two like a hawk. He even put out the cigar that was bringing on his high from earlier, something he could not let interfere with his plans.

Time elapsed and it was time to shut the club down, it was also time for his prey to venture out into the wild. Using the same door, Kory climbed into his 7-series and laid back into the plush seating.

Both vehicles seemed to ignite simultaneously. Kory had to admit, the salacious taste of his prey was prestigious. The Maybach was clean and kicked up a small trail of grass as it peeled off. Kory knew his 760 Li could keep up if the 62 Maybach decided to act up, so he tailed his prey at a cautious speed. He also noticed the rear curtain cut off all visibility inside the house on wheels, so he knew the add-on was performing some kind of sexual act toward the driver. More and more, his prey displayed a defining attribute and just as all cats were gray in the dark, there was a definite parallel at the end of this estranged road.

When the Maybach turned into the large estate, Kory stayed back far enough to seclude himself from his prey.

"Wow!" He mouthed, in astonishment of the enormous abode.

It was the size of two of his honeycomb hideouts. Everything looked pristine and well groomed. Kory blacked all of that out of his mind, then just like a cat burglar, he crept onto the unsecured grounds, or so he thought.

L♥D~ L♥D~ L♥D

Kory maneuvered across the dark pastures with very little effort nor contingency, by now his skills were elevated to a higher plane. Those who were unaware that they were being stalked and hunted upon like wild game now lay six feet deep courtesy of his .9 milli and hunting knife.

With every step, his solid frame left permanent foot impressions in the thick brush. His adrenaline peaked with the anticipation of another kill. The 'game of death' itself was enough to exert one's stability, but two was a godsend in his realm.

Kory chuckle in a whispered tone, the acoustic sound too low for even the nightly insects to decipher. Now in range of the estates portal, Kory retrieved his life taker and chambered a round. There was not going to be any sudden blunders tonight. His new prospect was a bonus, but the add-on was a simple notch off his list seeing their name had made the team long ago.

"Here we go old tymer!" Kory uttered, and leant up against the brick stucco. Just as he was about to dive through the foyer window, the double French doors opened widely.

"Fuck," he thought. "Too slow!"

"See you this weekend," the female promised after a deep French kiss to Roman.

"I hope," he retorted, which caused Lasandra's head to jerk back in confusion.

"Excuse me? You hope. What's that supposed to mean Roman?"

She stood still waiting for his answer.

"Well, you know...Tomorrow is never promised. There was no real merit to the statement Sandra, so gon' get moving, I'm sure Alfred is worried sick that his wife hasn't arrived home yet. He's probably got the entire force out searching aimlessly for you!"

He tried to hurry her off before it was too late to escape hell, because it was just around corner literally, begging for her serum as a token of some sick game.

"Okay, now that you put it that way, I guess I'm off to my standard life with Alfred."

She did as she was told and stepped into her 2007 Volkswagen Beetle that had been parked there prior to them going out to the club, and escaped her one-way ticket to celestial bliss.

Once Roman was satisfied that the Beetle was on the road safely he called out to Kory.

"It's okay. You can come out now young fella!" His voice was full of humility and familiarity. "Kory, you can show yourself now, it's just you and I and I'm not bearing any weapons. Although it is you who cometh in hate, I still remain humbled." A dark figure then emerged from the shadows.

"How do you know my name? I shoulda known you had this fortress wired with some state of the art shit, but that still doesn't explain how you know of me. I think you better start talking and fast!"

"Come in young fella, we'll talk and get to know each other a bit. I promise this is one story you'll love or hate."

Kory took Roman up on his offer and crossed the threshold into Roman's world, weary about what the old man had to say.

Chapter 28
New Beginnings

It took some time, but finally Wayne and Yolonda got a break in this clueless drama. Through great detective work and their countless hours and tedious days & nights of investigation, things were beginning to look up for the duo. The two detectives had been clocking infinite time on the case, hoping for just a small lead and now they have come up on what they feel could put a dent into the faceless 'Killa'.

In East Hartford, fifteen acres of land housed 'Connecticut Limousine', which was owned by Javon Alexander, an ex-drug dealer gone legit, before the law had a chance to get a grip on him. When the Crown Victoria pulled into the property, they noticed a flock of various limousines that ranged from stretched Hummers, S600's, Cadillac Escalades, Range Rovers and a couple of stretch Maserati's and Porsches.

"He sure knows how to stock 'em!" Yolonda mentioned.

Wayne parked the car and they approached two Mexicans who were busy hosing down a chalk white Range Rover that was heading out tonight to usher some young rap artist, for an album release party at Vibz on Main St.

"Yolonda, lemme start this off as good cop and if things don't go as planned, I guess you can play bad cop," he said knowing how hell bent she could be during questioning.

"Sure Wayne, you know how I love to be the bad girl." She blushed and matched Wayne's stride.

"Hey excuse me, you two obviously work here, can you please tell me where I can find Javon Alexander?" Wayne asked.

"No...No speaka Ingles!" The shorter one answered quickly.

"How 'bout you, you speaka Ingles? He asked the other already knowing what his response was going to be. The shorter Mexican looked into his friend's eyes as if to say don't tell them anything.

"Hey, did you hear me? Do you spea..." Yes, he spoke very good English, but it was apparent that they both were in the states illegally and with that being the case they both shot out like sprinters in the Olympics hungry for 1st place.

What the sprinters did not know nor realize was that the two detectives weren't here for them and could care less if their entire ancestry was huddled in one of the stretch limos. They would not even break a sweat running them down, their capture was pointless. Now out of fear of being detained and deported, the immigrants would no longer have a job. They would be in constant fear that they would be back. All Wayne and Yolanda could do was shake their heads in amazement.

Forgetting about the two sprinters, they decided they would head towards the office of the establish to see if any more personnel were there, when a black Maserati coupe pulled up. Yolonda looked back hearing the revving engine, then tapped Wayne on the shoulder.

"Look, I'm guessing that's our boy!" She let on.

"Nah, no guess, I'm sure it's him." Wayne said, viewing the plates that read 'J.A.G.1.', It was obviously Javon's initials.

When the door opened, out stepped a black male, maybe 150lbs., brown skinned with prescription shades on. His attire was average everyday street fashion. The only jewelry he sported was a two-carat marquis diamond in his left ear. In his right hand, he tightly grasped an expensive looking attaché case and in his left hand, he held a phone that happened to be glued to his ear.

Noticing the two strangers, Javon quickly pegged them for plain clothed cops. He held his stride knowing everything was legit on his end, except for his hired help. As the distance between them shortened, Javon noticed his hired help, Mario and Pablo, was missing. The place was locked so he figured they could be inside, and then it hit 'em, Mario and Pablo had bailed possibly in fear of being locked away and deported. Javon shook his head and cursed the two strangers because now he would have to search for two more laborers.

"How may I help you?"

"For starters are you usually in the business of employing illegal immigrants?" Yolonda opened with. "And two, are you Mr. Alexander and please tell me you speaka Ingles!"

Bad cop was definitely on deck.

He smiled at the woman's questioning and was now very sure his workers ran off in fear.

"Yes I'm he, and as you can see I speaka perfect Ingles!" He emphasized the last three words. "How can I... Help you?"

"I need to know if you know, no let me rephrase that, do you own a pair of Gortex boots? Trezeta to be precise," she continued.

The hesitation said it all, and Wayne stole a quick glance at Yolonda. She winked back letting him know that she had caught it as well.

"Well, yes and no."

"What is that supposed to mean, it's either yes or no. Simple as that!" Yolonda urged.

"Well I purchased a pair off the internet as a gift for a good friend."

"Uhh…Does your friend come with a name? Because it seems like you're holding back some pertinent information which can be mistaken for obstruction of justice, and looking at your background," she paused and smiled, "we don't want any old business or illegal transactions to resurface now would we?"

"Listen copper, that doesn't faze me. I am cleaner than a whistle, but to end this little charade the name is Blake, Kory Blake. Now if you two will excuse me, I've got some paper to tie up!"

He raised the brown case up high to taunt the salary stricken officers and walked off leaving them stuck on stupid.

Back in the Crown Vic, they viewed their notes and realized that this Blake fellow's name continuously popped up during their inquiries. One thing is for sure and two things for certain, they would be heading down to Blake Industries before noon tomorrow.

"So who's first, Blake Industries or James Electric?"

"James Electric I guess! Yolonda chose.

L♥D~ L♥D~ L♥D

Monday 9:30 a.m., the cool breeze felt alluring and welcoming to the stragglers roaming the metropolitan section of Hartford, the downtown area of the city as most labeled it.

As the day was nearing lunchtime, various mobile food and fruit vendors set out to occupy their stake along the speckled gray concrete. On just about every hook and bending curve lied a place of nourishment, and come high noon the quest for supplement would tee off.

Behind the dark tinted windows of the Crown Victoria, Yolonda scanned her notes for the correct address to Blake Industries, while Wayne drove down Main Street.

"Dammit!" She cursed unhappy with her own penmanship, something she was always teased and ridiculed about in her wonder years.

"What's the matter now Londa? You jumped in the car this morning with an upsetting stare. Please tell me it's not…"

"No Wayne…It's not my period," she quickly stopped him from saying. "It's my freaking handwriting, I can't decipher if this is a four or seven. I got the Pratt Street down, but this one number is pissin' me off!" Her frustration was clearly getting the best of her.

"Here, let me see," he said, snatching the small steno pad from her grasp. "Looks like a seven tutts! 8732!"

"If you say so!" She snarled, and then snatched the pad back.

Turning off Main Street, then onto Pratt, their eyes surfed the shops and tenements for their numerical decal. Somewhere in plain sight, the tricky ones were in hiding, perhaps embedded into the inner wall of the entrance or worn and illegible unless a person was front and center under the buildings sign.

Halfway down the block and still no 8732. Now stopped at a red light, the car was in complete silence, Yolanda's fingers were clammy and jumpy, and to ease her edginess Wayne spoke out.

"I thought you suggested we do the James Electric first. So why are we downtown?"

"Beats me, guess I just wanted a fruit salad this morning," she shrugged.

"Well at least you're honest. Let's hit Chan's Fruit Stand and then retrace our steps. Sound good?" Wayne inquired, his heart always melting at his partners mercy.

"Cool!" she replied.

Just around the corner was who they felt was the best and most sanitary fruit vendor in the area. The Crown Vic' came to a halt parking just a few feet away from the fruit stand. Shortly after, they exited the sedan and made the short walk to Chan's Fruit Stand.

"Hello...Hello, what do you have today?" He smiled gleefully.

After just a moment of contemplation, Wayne spoke up first. "I'll have pineapple, grapes, kiwi and watermelon." Yolanda's attention was glued to the ruby red Ferrari at the stop light. "What 'chu having Londa?"

It took Wayne's baritone voice to snatch her attention away from whatever had her so drawn. Wayne had not noticed the vehicle.

"Oh, sorry, but that red vehicle is holding the stage right now. She's a real beauty."

"Scarlatti to be exact," Wayne mentioned. "I'd say...In my next lifetime, I just might be able to afford one," he said truthfully.

The mysterious horse ran close to $300,000 brand new. She frowned at Wayne's dry humor; even still, she kept her eye glued to the vehicle.

"So what are you going to have tutts?" He asked again, having never received an answer the first time.

"Anything, just get anything, dayum Wayne!"

Yolanda's watchers followed attentively as the stallion blew through the traffic light, clearly having no respect for the city's traffic ordinance. Surprisingly, the vehicle made a quick U-turn a short distance away, then pulled, rather double-parked in front of Chan's Fruit Stand. The facial expression on Yolonda's face was picturesque, on the verge of orgasm.

"Would you take a good look at this!" Her voice full of energy and excitement.

Wayne just chuckled. By now, he had caught on to her change in demeanor. When the suicide door rose upwards and the expensive sound system roared loudly. It was clean and audible. Yolonda could even decipher the rapper by the lyrics, the music so well invested. T.I.'s latest song, 'I'm Backkk!' serenaded the area until the owner pressed a button on his remote and the door closed.

"You couldn't have chosen a better time to crave some fruit tutts!" Wayne stated.

The unidentified male sauntered up the curb in a cocky swagger, too cool for most people. Yolonda thought the man was very sexy in his black UConn sweat pants and a matching zip up. Secretly she wished she could invade his privacy, but his eyes were concealed by smoke tinted shades by Versace. What really stuck out was his oyster perpetual Rolex with a full iced bezel and band. If it were any later in the day there would be a slight chance he would blind someone, the glimmer was so defined. Now standing beside

Yolonda, she was engulfed by his fragrance, John Paul Gautier, very expensive.

"Well how are you?" She spoke the first words, which could prove vital to their case.

He nodded instead of speaking, something she had not expected. She knew this was going to be very interesting.

"Sup Chan, lemme get my usual," he requested.

"Sure Mr. Blake, coming right up." Chan scurried to chop fresh fruit for his favorite customer.

Wayne and Yolonda searched each other for some sort of explanation. Why was Mr. Blake receiving fresh fruit, and theirs was coming out of the already cut up bowls. Besides that, Yolonda was so close to Mr. Blake that as he spoke, the smell of fresh mint escaped his mouth and made her tingle in all the wrong places. This was not good, seeing he just might be a person of interest in their serial killing case.

"So Mr. Blake," she started with, "please tell me you're not the one and only, Kory Blake, CEO of Blake Industries." Again nothing in response, at least not verbally. He nodded his head, the UConn decal dipping as his head tilted downwards.

Kory studied Yolonda very closely behind the tinted glass. She was very voluptuous, she was cute with an educated appearance. He paid close attention to her thick thighs and full lips. Then his concern switched to whom he presumed was her sidekick. He knew that although the Krispy Kreme's were beginning to take a vicious hold onto his mid-section, he just might pose a threat. Therefore, he figured small talk would be the only thing to take place, especially if there was no warrant on deck.

"How's my order coming Chan, I've got an engagement in twenty minutes," he said and then switched his attention to the woman with all the mouth. "So you know my name ma', what's next?" He smirked, his grin sexual and deceiving. "Well for starters, a coupla questions and answers, then you never know." She answered matching his stare; only she ran her tongue across her bottom lip with much sex appeal. He nodded in approval. "First, did you know or even realize there is a vicious serial killer running in and around Hartford County?" She wanted to get a feel of where he was at mentally.

"Sure do. I read the Courant along with other weekly-fabricated Journalism; it's all the same. I can tell you one thing Mrs…" He paused to welcome her name.

"Oh, it's Yolonda, Detective Yolonda Long, and this is my other half, Detective Wayne Mosley."

"Mrs. Long, I can tell you one thing, that curfew the Mayor implemented hasn't stopped your killer!" He smiled, which caused her to glance at Wayne. "I'm thinking it just might take a little more if H.P.D. plans on stopping this guy."

"I guess not. She has to be very calculative to rummage throughout the city without being caught don't you think?" Without even noticing, she revealed some vital info on their theory concerning what gender the killer might be.

"So you two think it's a crazed sister running around axing people up?"

It was then that she realized her slip, but it was hard to remain focused in Kory's presence. She wanted to strip naked where she stood and throw herself at his mercy, sexually that is!

"No, I guess that just slipped out. So what's your relationship if any to the," she paused and looked over her notes, her hand shaking, "the James'?"

"Oh my ex-parental guardians John and Elizabeth James, were cool, why?"

"Well it seems that most of the people now six feet deep were somehow work related or family linked to them and that it seems very odd don't you think?"

"I guess maybe from a detective's point of view." He answered just enough to fend off their speculation. "Well as I told my friend Chan, I have a previous engagement. So if you need me for any, and I do mean anything else, do not hesitate to holla! Here's my card ma'."

He then dug into his pocket and retrieved a gold money clip full of hundreds.

"Here you go Chan, take their orders out of that! Fruits on me guys," he ended by licking his lips, mimicking Yolonda's earlier sign of passion and desire, and then walked off.

"Will do." Was all she could say as he accepted his tin foil container full of pineapple and grapes? "Hey Kory!" She yelled out.

"What's good ma'?

He stopped, the suicide door rising behind him.

"Nice shoes, they wouldn't happen to be a size 11½ Trezeta Gortex boots now would they?" She continued to read off her scribbled note pad.

Kory looked down and smiled. He was just about to sit down, but he wanted to further taunt Detective Long.

"To answer your question, no they're A.C.G. Nike boots. You know something Yolonda…"

"What's that Mr. Blake?"

"You're very good, and seem to know a lot about me and my friends, all except that carnal knowledge!"

"Again, what's that Mr. Blake?" She smiled lustfully.

They openly flirted in front of her partner and Chan, only Kory now displayed a sexual hunger for Yolonda too. What really topped the cake was the lewd act he performed by gripping a good portion of his manhood and then he perched down into the seat of his sports car. With the push of a button, the engine roared loudly letting them know how much power it held.

As the stallion shot out of its halted position Wayne said, "Wow that was quite interesting!"

She again slipped, but tried to clean it up with a different frown, one less captivating. She tried her best to conceal her illustrious craving for the billionaire.

"So why didn't you intervene Wayne? Must I always do the interrogating?"

It was her only way of masking the obvious attraction she harbored for Mr. Blake.

"Because, you seemed to have it all under control tutts!"

In the midst of concluding his reasoning, he received a stiff jab in the shoulder. "Look, wonder boy even left a c-note for our bill. I can see this is about to get quite complicated, but very interesting!"

Chapter 29
Secrets

There was entirely way to much more going on with Kory today. He was on his way to meet with Keonna. He felt now would be the best time to reveal something extremely shocking, nevertheless enlightening, and besides either way, she had to know.

The little run in with the two detectives was not by mere chance and Kory knew better to think so. He understood he was now a potential suspect in the serial killing case, and possibly his sister. If Detective Long had not slipped up and mentioned the small detail about them having a woman pegged as the killer, it would not even be a topic for discussion. However, somewhere down the line, Keonna slipped up and left some sort of evidence behind he assumed, feeling as though his murderous expertise was beyond detectible. Not to mention hearing Det. Long inquire about his size and brand of shoe only meant that it was possible he had also left an unmerited token for the police to explore. Nevertheless, he actually knew where his fumble laid, which was at the Woodland Drive hit.

Kory Pulled the Ferrari into his personal parking space at Blake Industries' in the parking garage. In doing so, he noticed Keonna's Hummer parked in the spot next to his, which meant she was already upstairs. After a short ride on the private elevator, he stepped into his office.

"What's up bruh? You're late, and it looks like you're carrying some extra baggage wit 'cha!" Keonna said knowing him to a tee.

"You mind fixing us a drink?"

"Of course, why not? Now I know something's up," she muttered. "It's much too early to be tossing it up, bruh. What's good?"

After accepting his concoction, Kory sat comfortably in the leather chair behind his desk. "You wouldn't believe it sis, but you deserve to know," he said and began. First, he brought up the fact that he had met an older gentleman at his strip club a week or two ago, and for some odd reason he felt deeply connected to him.

He further explained that the man resembled their dad in a strange way, thus looking at an oversized painting on the wall only brought him back to last night when he invited him into his home.

"I thought you were off to kill that stinking bitch Lasandra Love?"

"If you let me finish, I'll put you up on game. I figured I could kill two birds at once and lay at the club for Old' boy first, then hit Ol' girl, but as I preyed on the look-a-like, I noticed the white bitch was his date...Crazy coincidence."

"You've got to be kidding me!"

"No shit! Anyways, I followed them back to his crib and crept onto the property unnoticed, or so I thought. Keonna, this place was something out of the DuPont Registry. I'm talking major scrilla invested in this place. Anyways, just as I'm about to hit the foyer window, the broad comes out and gets in her car, then sped off. But after she rode off, dude calls my name out twice, before I show my face, masked of course."

Keonna patiently listened for the moral and importance to Kory's story for a sufficient amount of time, and just hearing the crazy story was similar to reading an urban Steven King novel. "Wow!" Keonna was flabbergasted.

L♥D~ L♥D~ L♥D

The Crown Vic drove straight to the address they had on file for the James. As they entered the estate's grounds, they were mesmerized at how the wealthy class of people could spend their money as if it was nothing. Nonetheless, if in their shoes, they would not have done it any different.

They pulled up to the main entrance where the James' house cleaner greeted them.

"Hey Londa, you think she'll bail like that other Mexicans down at the limousine place?"

"Don't know, but I don't peg her as Mexican Wayne. All foreigners aren't Mexican!"

"Could have fooled, me!" He laughed.

"Hello detectives," she greeted in a heavy accent.

"Hello to you. We're here to see a John James," Wayne said.

"Please follow me." Isabella ordered, and began walking, which became a sexual trip Wayne welcomed, her thickness jumping with each step.

"Um, um, umm!" He mumbled, right before Yolonda shoved her right elbow into his meaty parts.

They were escorted to the patio where several lawn chairs rested in a row crowding the emptiness of an Olympic size pool. John James sat at a glass table under a grass green umbrella, sipping' chilled lemonade, his face stuck in the morning's edition of The Wall Street Journal.

"Mister James, you have company. Will you be needing me for anything else sir?" Her humbleness vibrant and worthy.

"No, no thank you Isabella," he laughed because those were the only words she seemed to know and speak.

"Have seat detectives. Cold lemonade? Our house cleaner, Isabella squeezed thirty lemons over a half an hour ago, and believe me, she can make some freshly squeezed beverages like no other. It's quite refreshing I must say."

"No thanks," Yolonda declined.

"Sure will," Wayne not surprisingly accepted.

"Help yourself. Now how can I be of assistance to you two?"

"Well I'm quite sure you've buried a few colleagues and family members behind the serial murders plaguing Hartford and its surrounding counties for starters."

"Yes, a terrible thing too. This serial killer you talk about, what's the connection to people I know or I'm related to?" he finally put down the WSJ to give them his undivided attention.

"Well Mr. James…" Yolanda began but he cut her off.

"John James, Mr. James works well for my employees.

"As she was saying, that's why we're here. Hoping you could help fill that void for us," Wayne finally cut in.

"You must have some knowledge as to why this person is going through lengths to kill people apparently close to you and your company."

"Do you know, a Mr. Kory Blake?" Yolonda jumped in tag team style.

Keep 'em off balance and sooner or later your opponent will tire and give up.

"Because we had a quick meeting with him concerning you, and your relations." Wayne interjected.

"Well then you should know I was their parental guardian after their parents passed, actually after my folks passed. It was then that my spouse and I sort of inherited them. When they turned eighteen years old, we relocated to Hartford and have resided here ever since." He explained hoping it was enough to send them on their way.

"So you and your wife took on their guardianship after your parents passed. So that would mean you also had full control of Blake Industries, am I correct?" She asked just to make sure all his explanations were credible.

"Yes!"

Wayne and Yolonda stole a quick glance in each other's direction, which stopped Mr. James' heartbeat by a few pulses.

"However, Kory regained seventy percent of the company once he turned eighteen, and once he became familiar with the way the stocks market works, he excelled making tons of money for him and Keonna"

"I see," Wayne nodded. "You know Mr. James, sorry, John James. I've got to be perfectly honest with you…I see some slight motive here. Quick question J., why would a person kill off your own people, doesn't make good sense does it? How 'bout chu tutts?"

"Well if you don't mind, I think I need to phone my attorney with that last accusation!"

"No need, we're leaving. You have a wonderful day and here's my card if you can think of anything pertinent to this case, or if you'd like to pass it onto your lawyer." Yolonda interjected before things got out of hand.

Yolonda stood up and laid the card onto the table then she and Wayne vacated the premises. Back in the sedan, Yolonda asked, "Did you have to pluck Mr. James' nerve?"

"It's what I do tutts!"

Chapter 30
Body of War

After a fruitful and prosperous day at work, Brice, Jordan, John James and Kory decided they would partake in happy hour down at Ty's Sports Bar and Grill. Kory, Brice and Jordan were full of laughter and deep into a conversation about golf and John James, who was late as usual, had fell into a ditch somewhere around the seventh hole.

"Boyee, was he pissed!" Brice said, and then drained his mug full of draft beer.

"Damn near sprained his ankle," Jordan slurred with laughter.

"Where is Ol' James anyway? Dude's always late when we meet up," Kory probed, and then downed his shot of Remy V.S.

"I'm right her Korr." John James answered, creeping up on them from behind, their backs turned away from the mahogany bar.

"Well it's nice of you to join us James," Kory said. "So what 'chu drinking sailor?"

"Umm, I'll take a draft for now. Can you handle that?" John James said, then took off his soaked blazer.

"Must you always start John?" Brice questioned.

"Pussy!" Kory thought. "Bartender, lemme get two pitchers and run the tab!" Kory added with an angered grin.

"Kory knows I'm just kidding around, after all, we are family." John James playfully hit Kory on the back.

Their outings always played as such, with John James being late. When he did finally grace them with his presence, he'd always nit-pick, starting with Kory then it would circle around. However, for the most part, Kory was the one who had to endure his corny and judgmental remarks.

"Hey Ty, isn't the bowl game on? I know we've missed at least the first half," Bruce asked.

"Yeah, I just figured the Huskies and Syracuse game would be much more interesting. I'll turn to it now though," Steve said.

He grabbed the remote and quickly turned to the Sky Bowl.

"Damn look at the score, looks like we missed a good one!" Jordan added. "Darn, I had fifty bucks on the Suns."

"Well Chad, it looks like sudden death between Team Sun and the Quarrel-Some Clouds. What do you have Terry?" John M. asked.

"I'm with you John," Bradshaw answered, and then John narrated further.

"Today marks yet another irrefutable win for the Quarrel-Some Clouds, as it fought a vigorous fifty eighty minutes in this muddy turf against the elusive Team Sun."

"Now John, you know with a great offense you can't count Team Sun out of the Sky Bowl, there's a lot at stake here!" Chad interrupted.

"We will see Chad, but, I've got all my chips on the Clouds," John M. boasted, then continued narrating. "Here you have it folks, Team Sun with the ball on their 44 yard line, 3rd down and 6 yards to the 1st and 1:05 on the clock. The score is 14 Quarrel-Some Clouds, Team Sun 12.

The whistle blew and the ball was snapped to Sunny, Team Sun's quarterback, who dropped back a good 5 yards. Two of the Clouds linebackers, Hazy and Opaque, zoned in on Sunny and saw a huge gap in between the Suns center and right-guard. Hazy dipped left and Opaque shot straight forward up the gut. Sunny anticipated their desires to add another sack for their team's records, and flanked wide left, his attention then zoned in on Bright-lights who was being defended by the Clouds safeties, so he shifted his focus on his wide-out Dusk. It did not matter, their cornerback Soggy had good coverage on him, and so he glanced further downfield and saw Dawn wide open with man-to-man coverage. Sunny cocked his right arm back and drilled the pigskin threw the air just in time, as Hazy tackled him thereafter.

The pigskin traveled long and high; the throw precise and catchable – one his best throughout the season. When Dawn looked over his shoulder, he alerted Foggy that the ball was in the air coming and heading in their direction, so he did the same. Foggy slowed his stride a bit anticipating they were going to overrun the throw. As Dawn kept his pace, it was Foggy who slowed and hung back some. The pigskin sailed and began to taper as expected, and then almost magnetically, the almond shaped ball of tough leather fell into Foggy's grasp.

"What'll you know folks, the final pass of this year's Sky Bowl has been intercepted by the Cloud's cornerback Foggy, who in-turn ran it all the way back an dove into the end zone for a touchdown," John M. broadcasted with much energy. "What a game folks. There you have it, the Quarrel-Some Clouds have won Sky Bowl-XX and now celebrate by showering the city of Hartford with a torrent of thunder and rain!" John M. concluded.

L♥D~ L♥D~ L♥D

Thereafter, the downpour continued for the next two days. Even through the heavy downpour, the city's sanitation crew made their runs throughout the streets and backyards of Hartford's tenements. They hurriedly drove through Hartford sweeping the rough tarmac, as rubber receptacles filled with rubbish were emptied into the rear of the moving trash compactor.

It was getting late in the midday hour and their roadwork was done. Now on an odorous journey to the city's landfill, the ground crew held onto makeshift metal bars for their safety as they slowly made their way through the city.

The large green dumpster pulled into the hideous dumpsite and Burt, the crew supervisor, flipped the lever inside the trucks cabin which released the malodorous package overtop a huge pile of garbage. After Burt finished, he hopped down out of the truck. As he walked past a small patch of dirt that had not been utilized, he noticed something very odd. Upon further observation, Burt saw what looked to be a human head. Burt, then radioed his boss, who in turn called 911.

What really struck Burt as odd and strangely peculiar, was that a single black rose was protruding out of the head's eye-socket. There was also a small card pinned to the forehead by a Phillip's screwdriver.

"What the fuck? This is some sick shit," Burt said through a sense of nausea.

It wasn't long before the proper investigators, along with the medical examiner Carin, crowded the carcass in awe. Wayne and Yolonda knew exactly who the UnSub was behind the heinous act of violence. They carefully collected their evidence and snapped several photos, then rode off quiet. They were stuck in their own thoughts and theories on why and who was truly behind these serial killings.

"Hey tutts, what's got your mind so clogged up? You've been extremely quiet since the dump." Detective Mosley asked, as usual, his concern for her was endearingly great.

Wayne was right in his assessment, Yolonda's mental was on a plane between business and pleasure, and Kory was the weight disturbing everything discernible at the moment. She had been feeling this way since he stepped out of his sports car a week ago. It was to the point that her work and better judgment did not rate as number one on her list of priorities anymore. Yolanda had a bad case of infatuation and lust, and there was only one way to nurture her fixation.

"I'm okay Wayne, just thinking that's all. I'm so sick of dealing with this animal, not to mention Chief Daniels."

"Don't worry Londa, she will slip up soon, but we have to keep an open mind on this. We're all going through the motions tutts. We're gonna get 'er!" He assured.

"Of course," She replied, and then there he was again, the most handsome male she had ever met, the young billionaire Kory Blake. What was crazy was that, Wayne knew what was haunting her day and night and he figured that one day her dream would become a reality.

Their fourteen-hour shift was over, so Wayne dropped Yolonda off at her home in Prescott Glenn, a residential area full of condominiums located in East Hartford, CT.

"See you tomorrow tutts," he said, and watched as she made it safely inside the glass doors.

L♥D~ L♥D~ L♥D

The hour had struck 7:00 p.m. eastern standard time, the chime of Kory's G-Shock was programmed to do so. In Animal City, a large pet shop, 20-gallon glass tanks housed a variety of different reptiles and exotic fish. A male employee was helping Kory as he scanned the many aisles for South African Cichlids.

After choosing two Red Devils, two Jack Dempsey's and four medium sized Pikes, he needed a hundred feeders for their delicacy.

"Just a hundred, sir?" The helper asked.

"Yeah, but I'll also take a large bottle of medium fish pellets." Kory responded.

"You like to see your fish devour the feeders huh?"

"All day long. I love to watch them run and hide for their lives, you know by morning there will only be about ten or twenty left fighting for immunity. Gimme a quick second, my phones ringing."

"Sure," he said and began trapping the orange feeders into a plastic bag with enough air for them to survive for a few hours.

"Hello?" He said not recognizing the number that displayed on his blackberry.

"Hello is this Mr. Blake?" The low female voice said, just above a whisper.

Kory laughed to himself now recognizing the sultry voice. 'Wow, she called, and with that low seductive tone I know she's diggin' da kid,' he thought conceitedly.

"Yes it is I, and what might this call be about, because as I told you and that pudgy Danny Glover I don't own a pair of those Trezeta, you called them."

"Well I'll say no, it's not basically about that, but if you're not too busy, I think we can cross a bridge and rule you off our chalkboard of suspects." She answered; her real agenda lied in the dark pastures of lust and sexual starvation.

"Sure, where should I meet chu at? Perhaps at the H.P.D. headquarters. And should I have my attorney present in case y'all attempt to railroad me?"

"No, there won't be any attorney's needed, I promise you." Her words reassuring, he thought.

Nevertheless, Kory was no dummy and knew he would have to summon his 'Halfway Crook' ass attorney Avante Taylor. He was back from the dead with a new license to practice, identity, and taking cases.

"So I guess I'll see you there in about 30 minutes."

"No, no, you can come out to Prescott Glenn apartment building 235, call this number when you arrive. See you then." She finished, and then hung up, she had some things to do before he arrived. Yolonda knew she was crossing the line when inviting Kory to her home, but she rationalized her sexual cravings over standard police policy not to get involved with suspects.

The one bedroom condominium reeked of cinnamon potpourri and pear sprits from Victoria's Secret. As Beyonce's 'Dangerously in Love' serenaded the spacious residence, Yolonda dried her smooth skin with a large bath towel. Standing in front of the double mirror fastened to the petite roll away closet doors, she admired her gorgeous physique. Her breasts were medium sized and perky, her stomach had maybe a ½ inch of fat to it and she cursed herself for missing her normal two days of crunches every week, but boyee was her ass phat.

Yolonda applied a soft touch of Curve 'Reality' in between her thighs and the nape of her neck. She wore a tight pair of low rise Calvin Klein jeans and a sheer blouse that displayed her alluring goodies. Just when she stepped into a pair of ¾ Enzo heels, her phone rang.

Grabbing her cell phone off the dresser, she answered sensually, "Hello."

"I'm here." Kory said,

"Be right down." She was consumed with joy.

Five minutes later, Yolonda appeared out of her lobby looking like a Lisa Raye double. It was not until she looked into the windshield that Kory noticed it was her.

"Damn…" He mumbled as he tripped the button for her door to open up. All he could do was shake his head at her stunning beauty.

"Hey there," she spoke, "How big is your stable?" She quizzed, eyes now raised into her forehead.

"What do you mean?" He was confused.

"This vehicle, what else do you have in your garage?" Duh… She thought.

"Oh, you're referring to my Lambo. She is nice huh. One of my fav's! Brand new, the fourth off the assembly line," he answered with arrogance. "I don't see a folder, briefcase… Nothing close to a line of questioning, so what's this about? Plus you got uh brother scooping you up at the crib, help me out ma'! Seems quite unprofessional."

He stared into her modest face waiting for her answer

Yolonda flung a few strands of hair from over her face, so she could return the stare.

"Well I was feeling a little bored in my place and I happened to trip over your business card and I'll be honest, I've been thinking about you since the fruit stand!" She answered with a hint of embarrassment, but she was so into Kory she could not find the right lie to pitch at him.

Kory studied her angelic face. He had a crazy fetish for strong black women with long silky hair. Her eyes were a glossy walnut brown and he could see the infatuation clear as a star in the night sky.

"Is that so? So you mean to tell me this isn't work related? No questions? No mug shots? Just a simple booty call?" He playfully asked, with a sexy smile.

"I guess so, and you don't have to be so arrogant Mr. Blake!" Yolonda said, twisting her neck left to right like a true sista.

"Feisty," Kory added, nodding his head up then down. "I think I'ma like you! Lay back and enjoy the ride," he commanded then turned up the radio, which was turned onto 94.2 FM, the Delilah Show. The group Nickel Back was blaring out of the concert sound system which really astonished Yolonda. Here it is, Mr. Kory Blake, billionaire and CEO of Blake Industries who probably had more ties to the hood than Robin, and he is mellowing out cruising the streets of Hartford listening to the Delilah Show. She was too stuck on him now and hoped his sex game was surprisingly satisfying as well.

All she could do was render helplessly in his clutches and obey for the time being. She had a job to do, and playing the part was already starting to test her virtue and morality.

L♥D~ L♥D~ L♥D

Things between Elizabeth and John James had really spiced up, especially in the bedroom. Since that seductive episode in his office, they had been going at it daily, in the car, in the backyard, in the pool and even the closet got a chance to welcome their erotic fascinations. John James even noticed his wife doing kinkier and borderline porn material things when they indulged. From the sixty-nine position, to doggy style and sodomy, she let James take her body and use it for whatever he chose. It really freaked him out when Elizabeth had given him a blowjob on the way home from the office. He actually was starting to feel like a cheap trick, but nonetheless, he was enjoying the new Liz. He became aware of Harold's death from the detectives. Of course, the two troublesome detectives harassed him with the normal line of questions when any murder was being investigated. Still, he had nothing for them. However, he did have a free million compliments of the deceased. Nevertheless, that did not deter the slight panic he had been experiencing lately. It was apparent everyone was being killed off that he associated with or who ever played an intricate role in Kaitlyn and Nathaniel's death.

Am I next? He thought. Is it possible for me to be attacked one night leaving work, kidnapped then murdered? Shot, stabbed or tortured to death? All of these scenarios played out in his mind twenty-four hours a day. He thought about moving away, but if they followed him to Connecticut, his past would forever catch up to him, so he remained in the Constitution State.

What he did do though, was buy a used gun from one of Jordan's friends for some added security. If he was going to go out, he planned to go out with style and grace.

It was dark out, the afternoon skyscraper had subsided and the crickets began to chirp, while lighten bugs fanned freely in the bushels lining his driveway and rose bushes.

Elizabeth walked into the den where he sat reading the day's edition of the Wall Street Journal. He would have surfed through it much earlier, but with Lizzie so needy for sex now, his body craved a hypnosis dose of sleep. When he reached the money section, his eyes bulged out with amazement. The NYSE had dropped by 508 points and closed down a whopping 22½% from yesterday's close, with

Blake Industries seemingly going belly-up. John James had finally won. He had finally accomplished what he set out to do two decades ago.

For some strange reason, he began to loathe Kory and his bratty sister, and vowed to turn their lives upside down and into sheer turmoil. He even went as far as to conspiring with a close relative of the Blake's with the promise that he'd retain full control and majority shares in Blake Industries and now that time has come.

"What are you so jolly about John?" Lizzie queried, with a straight face hiding the fact that she already knew. While he was somewhere in La-La-Land, she took the liberty of reading the newspaper.

"We've won Lizzie; I've finally got his black ass. Kory is going down. All he has now is his new prospect, that ridiculous Korr Tec, and once I tap into that and all of the investor's, that's going south as well. He was happier than a fag wit uh bag full of dicks. "So who gets control now?" She probed.

"Shit! I must call Roman before someone taps the bill. Hand me my phone dear."

"Sure, here you go."

The phone rang in the foyer of Roman's estate three times before he answered.

"Hello?"

"Hey, what's up Roman, good news. It's all yours, now all we have to do is sign my shares over to you and vote Kory off the panel." John James spoke energetically.

"When?" Roman asked.

"Now, we have to do this immediately. Where can we meet?" He was so anxious, he was shaking like the wet dog he is.

"How bout we meet at this strip club in the city, it's very classy too, not your usual hole in the wall type of establishment."

"Sure, I don't care, let's just get it done, because if I know Kory, he's looking for a loophole to salvage what's left of Blake Industries." He was actually viewing the Wall Street Ticker on CNN and it was declining at a rapid pace. All the major investors were pulling out by the doubles.

"See you there."

"So you know about this new club already?" Roman asked. He felt a surge of urgency and content in his voice.

"Of course, I know everything about Kory and Keonna," he laughed. "There's nothing I don't know and that includes the size of his third leg, as he calls it," he concluded. Just because he had never been invited to Teezer's before didn't mean he hadn't known about Kory's side ventures.

Elizabeth stood there shaking her head, she had a bad feeling about this, but John James was her true love, her first love her first everything, so she intended on riding the wave with him. Besides, her name was listed primary on everything they owned, it was something John James wanted and she went right along with it; there were no prenuptials when they tied the knot. It was a war against the James and the Blakes, another thing her devious husband created twenty years back.

"You take care tonight John, love you!" She made sure to mention that, knowing the risks and caliber of people involved. Becoming a widow was not in the plans.

L♥D~ L♥D~ L♥D

Every so often, Kory would glance over at the stunning detective as she lay back on the imported pig suede seats, her Enzo heels lost somewhere on the bearskin rug. She was not shy about her feet seeing she had just recently had a pedicure, something he also noticed. Being a homicide detective, time was of the essence, however, she managed to keep her femininity up to par at all times.

Yolonda was so relaxed; she drifted off into a light slumber. Not too surprised at the little growl echoing from her voice box, Kory smiled. He had been with plenty of women who snored, talked and held small conversations in their sleep, so Yolonda would just go down in history like all the rest.

"Oh excuse me!" She sat up quickly feeling embarrassed. "Tell me I wasn't just snoring, Mr. Blake! Oh my gosh," she thought.

"Just a little, I barely heard it," he lied.

He did not want her feeling some type of way. He actually thought it was good, because people, preferably women, who kept up small conferences in their sleep often, told a great tale, something always useful in his line of work.

Yolonda cracked her window a bit to let the cool air help flush her free of her tiring state. It was not her fault the therapeutic seats in his Lamborghini Gallardo, took over you the minute you sat down. Not too sure, how long she had been under, she checked the time on her Movado. It was only 8:15 p.m., good she thought, because that would mean she had been down for only nine minutes and she did not feel she rumbled off into a boisterous gurgle. From that moment on, she fought the urge to surrender to Kory's sedative seating.

Kory was all smiles, his grin charming as his swagger and now it was Yolonda stealing quick glances in his direction.

"So Mr. Blake, where are you driving to? It seems like we've been driving for hours." She was leery in a comforting way.

"Well first things first, I gotta get my little friends into some water before they die off."

He then reached behind her seat and grabbed the brown bag containing the freshwater fish he had purchased prior to their meeting. "Here take a look."

She took the bag then pulled the clear plastic bag out and admired the colorful breed of fish. "These as some gorgeous Cichlids Kory," she blurted out.

'Hmmm…Something else intriguing and desirable about my new woman friend', he thought. "So you know about South Africans huh?"

"Sure do. Got a 55-gallon full of Jack Dempsies and Fire Mouths. And yes, I feed them feeders maybe twice a month, it's their treat, I call it fish-day."

She could tell he was flabbergasted by her remarks towards the fish, because he hadn't retorted back. He just sat up some in his seat then pressed a button on the console of his vehicle. Yolonda was so into the fish, she had not noticed they had pulled up to a large black iron fence that surrounded a nice size manor fit for a family of six.

As the iron gate slid left, Kory eased up the short distance to the manor's portal.

"Please tell me, you don't live here alone Mr. Blake?!" Her interests were piqued; she never pegged him for being the family type.

"Of course not. My dear wife and three young boys live here with me," he answered with a straight face.

Yolonda does not quite know it, but she just revealed to him that she and her cohorts really had not been doing their homework on him as he had anticipated, or she wouldn't had proposed such a silly question. Then he optioned the fact that it was part of a ploy to dig into his realm.

"Coming in?"

"Do you pose that'll be a good idea?"

He gave no reply, just a sinister grimace!

L♥D~ L♥D~ L♥D

When the bluish green John-James' Nissan Titan pulled into Teezer'z parking lot, he noticed the striking house on wheels idled on the only patch of greenery directly in front of the club's entrance.

"That's either got to be Roman's or Kory's mini-limo," he assumed.

His head shook imagining how satisfying it felt footing the lofty price tag for the German car. After grabbing the dark, oil-blemished valise, he headed inside.

Immediately, he felt as if he were trapped inside a live taping of a Hollywood porn flick. Beautiful women of various nationalities pranced around in little or close to nothing in the club. Some were on the sleek stage engaged in your common girl-on-girl relations, as sex thirsty males lusted and carelessly tossed their hard-earned wages onto the stage's floor. So what he felt out of place not seeing many Caucasians in attendance, he had something to conclude. He was on a victory mission that would hopefully send Kory Blake into a spiraling plummet with no lifeline to pull him up.

"Hey there." Fantasia approached and said braless and wearing a lime green thong.

He was stuck for a minute, captivated by her seductive features.

"Uh...Hey there." Was all that escaped his squelch box. His bulging penile erection confirmed his lustful desires.

"Care for a lap dance?" She mouthed her lips glossy and pursed.

Again, he paused, but came out of his stupor much faster this time. "Sure, but I've got some business first. So, I'll catch you later," at least he hoped.

"Sure sexy." She walked off.

"Damn...I gotta come out to the city more often. Now where is Roman?"

He searched from left to right, his eyes scanning the dim crowd, then all of sudden they honed onto a quaint little area with a rotating bed for two and a small booth. In the booth was Roman. He had his large arm around Mo'nay as she licked and sucked on his neck and earlobe.

"You dirty, old man you!" She whispered.

John then began the short hike to what he presumed was the V.I.P. section.

"Hey Roman, it took me long enough to locate you in this dim light, but that's because your back here getting your sexy back, huh!" he smiled.

"Yeah, you can say that John. Have a seat. Is that what we need, rather what I need?" He mentioned, hoping what John had in tow was everything he would need to move on.

"Yes indeed."

"Well let's get down to business. Excuse me Mo'nay, but I have something I desperately need to handle, but you're welcome to come back in let's say ten to fifteen-minutes." Roman said.

"No need Ro, I'll do you one better." Mo'nay licked her full lips then undid Roman's trousers, then put his limp snake into her salivating mouth giving him a going away present. "Something to think about while you're handling your b.i., 'kay hon."

Roman was not too surprised by Mo'nay's actions. It was John-James who was in a mesmerized trance by her illicit mannerism.

"Shall we," Roman stated, adjusting himself in a more comforting position.

"Okay, here's everything tied into your brother's company. I am talking a list of all the remaining shareholders, deeds and your nephew's heir ship to Blake Industries. : In the wake of Nathaniel's death, his offspring's shall receive full ownership upon turning eighteen years of age. Now in the case of our deaths, the James' as it states or, they felt his off-springs weren't in tune and depth of running Blake Industries on any scope, then we the James' have the power to relinquish them of their place amongst the board, thus removed altogether. Furthermore, there would be a sizable tune of $10,000,000,000 deposited into an account for Kory and Keonna to live and do as they pleased.

In accordance to the agreement between the Blake's and the James's, any such infidelities, wrong-headed, unethical actions dealing or concerning the Industries' livelihood, would result in immediate ejection from the board and their seat within Blake Industries. "John James iterated some of the things he summarized   from past documents   that had been drawn up over two decades ago by Nathaniel.

"Here, you take a look," John-James passed him a folder out of his satchel, "and as you can see, I've already taken the liberty in putting my John Hancock on there," he smirked, overly thrilled with his act of deceit. "So now all that's left and needed is yours, my friend!"

Quickly thumbing through the folder, Roman found something of great importance and scanned the yellowish white document, his brother's handwriting causing him a slight sense of uneasiness. Flashbacks of them back when they were just young boys playing in the sandbox, then football, bike riding and then as they aged it was during their high school days together that they had begun to feud. With their good looks and comb-thru hair, they attracted many of the same girls, which they often used to both hook up with women back then. Their features were that close, but not identical, but just enough to trick the tainted hearts of lustful women. Subsequently, that is where their feuding turned into the worst betrayal that could be imagined.

As Roman stared at his signature, he felt what he thought was his blood pressure rising or even a heart attack approaching, when it was only a climax nearing. His eyes rolled into the back of his head, as his neck rested on the ledge of the round booth.

"Urggghh!"

A deep moan roared out of his mouth. There was no need for a napkin, Mo'nay sucked him dry. "You good, babe?"

"Like a person in remission," he gleamed.

"I thought you'd enjoy yourself hon. See you later?" She asked.

He nodded, trying to regain his composure.

What an epiphany he thought, because when he signed his signature on the document many years back, Kaitlyn was also pleasuring him. The only difference was her smooth skin gripped tightly around his hardness, gyrating up and down his length. They were young, in love, and freakier than a sideshow circus.

"To be honest, John, my signature isn't really needed at this point. As long as your John Hancock is legible and where it needs to be, we're good money." His slang was still intact. "Well Johnny, I have some where's to be so I guess I'll be in touch...Real soon!" His words a little course at this point, victory at its best.

Not comprehending, John answered, "If you say so Roman." Nevertheless, as he said, as long as he had signed it, Kory and his bratty sister were doomed. "Where you heading? I thought you an Ol' girl were going to hook up, she seems tight on you. You gonna just leave her hanging?"

Roman chuckled at John's shallowness. It was quite pathetic he thought.

"You can stay and play John! Let your nuts hang." Roman gripped his crotch to emphasize the suggestion. "Let loose and live a little, cause you only get one life and you should know that Johnny! Let us just be frank, you have gotten what you wanted. Kory is no longer your problem and you have milked my brother's corporation for well over $100,000,000. We both got what we longed for, so it's over," he concluded, and then began his victory stroll. "But if you must know, I'm going to see my children," he stopped and said.

The smile on Roman's face was broad and wide. He had finally won. He was victorious after all these years. He felt a sense of payback and closure for what Nathaniel and Kaitlyn did to him as a man. He was bruised. His self-worth was nearly dwindled down to nothing-zip, zilch, and zero!

Yeah, it was a selfish war he and Nathaniel endured, and sadly, it was over a woman they both loved with true endearment. If only he and his high school sweetheart Kaitlyn could have weathered the storm and explored life in divine holy matrimony instead of being entangled in a deceitful web of cruelty and adultery. To Roman, it almost felt like Kaitlyn called it quits as soon as she said I do! An immediate annulment to their commencement. However, he who laughs last indeed laughs best! Roman thought.

L♥D~ L♥D~ L♥D

With very little reluctance, Yolonda followed Kory into a world of trouble, so she thought, "My three inch heels will work well as a deadly weapon if the misses gets out of character." She wondered what Mrs. Blake would say once she entered her home. "What did Mr. Blake expect was going to transpire with me as his company? Would he introduce me as a friend, or as a homicide detective?" Several scenarios played out in her racing mind as he ushered her inside.

One thing is for sure and two thing's for certain, she was a cop and the badge of honor was a code she would break to solve this case, something she vowed to never go against until meeting Mr. Blake. In addition, she so desperately hoped Kory was so far off the radar that they would still be able to indulge in a casual, yet sexual fling.

"Here goes nothing!" She mumbled softly, but Kory's hearing was superb and he heard the low chatter clearly!

Through the large doors, Yolonda had her suspicions on what Mrs. Blake looked like, even his three boys. The place was expensive and immaculate; however, its manly feel had not gone unnoticed. It was missing that woman's touch. No floral prints or colors. No plants, no feminine drapes with matching valances. No, they were all leather right down to the furniture.

"Hava seat, make yourself at home. Care for a drink ma?"

She hesitated, but whispered, "Yes," Knowing it would help to ease her tension.

"What do you like?"

"You got some Tanqueray and orange juice?"

Kory nodded, his lips pursed.

"Thoroughbred huh?" He trailed off into the estate.

"Twenty-four-seven!"

Yolonda was beginning to think the little story about the misses and three boys was just a ploy to see if she was 'bout it-'bout it! It is obvious she was, because her heels were off and her tiny feet were lost in the thick carpeting. She did not care for the misses at this point, and she was already in the mood for whatever, not to mention totting her trusty sidearm for her defense. "Now how am I going to explain myself being in a suspect's home if I have to put one in his wife?" She contemplated.

After further observation, she knew for sure he tried to test her gangster. There was not one family photo or a single photo of Mrs. Blake nor his supposed boys in sight.

"Dat's alright Mr. Blake, I've got something for you," she purred. "You like games do you?" A smile formed over her face.

On a rolling bar, Kory ushered her drink and a small bowl of strawberries to where she was sitting.

"Is this man trying to woo me? Does he think he's getting some booty tonight? I hope not. Maybe some cuddling hugs and a passionate kiss here and there, but booty, nah?" She played in her mind.

"Here you go pretty lady."

"Thank you Mr. Blake. And might I ask, what the strawberries are for? Cause you ain't, hitting the kitty tonight," she said through pursed lips.

She really enjoyed Kory's smile, it was full of certainty, confidence and assurance, which tickled her nipples. She wondered if he noticed them at the fruit stand, or even now, because they were begging for his undivided attention. Her high beams were definitely on.

"Tell me that in that in the morning while you're naked cooking me breakfast!" He smiled.

"Hmmph!" She mumbled, feeling she was in full control of their destiny.

The night moved on, and after a few drinks, Kory put on some 'Sweat Hotel', which they slow danced too. Their bodies stuck together like a screw and a bolt. As her lips poked at Kory's neck, she noticed a very large photo of him at the children's hospital. There had to be over twelve kids with no hair surrounding him. They all had happy smiles on their faces even knowing the possibility that they would never see his kind and caring face again.

"Excuse me sir, but I notice more than three boys in your family photo. What's that about? And where's your wife?" Her inebriated curiosity highly piqued.

"Oh, those are my kids!" He replied, taking full responsibility for the little ones.

"How so?" She was confused. "There's no way all of those children are his," she thought.

Kory smiled. "Those are my children I sponsor and visit twice out the week. All of their hospital bills are paid for through Korr-Tech, my newest organization. They all have cancer, some with rare forms, and others who have until God requests their presence in the Great Heavens."

Detective Long was wowed to another degree. In her book, Kory was no longer a suspect in the serial murder case, and to make it official she tongue kissed Kory for almost five long minutes. With the soft music and the liquor in her system, she undid her blouse, and then her jeans flew across the room. For some reason she put her heels back on. To him it was more erotic, so she must have felt the same.

Yolonda was stark naked and a well-proportioned vixen, he thought. Next to Ashanti, Yolonda might be the next best thing to Lisa Raye.

Sucking her plump breast caused her to moan out in tongues. It turned Kory on to know he had control over her temple.

"Ooooh," she moaned louder, her breathing becoming heavy and labored to where she could not control it. "Uhh!" she gasped, while he softly traced the outer ring of her twin nipple.

While she enjoyed Kory's warm tongue against her breasts, she fought with his buckle. She desperately needed something to do. She knew he was holding by the bulge of his jeans. Kory finally undid his pants and she rushed to get them off. "Either the liquors got her in such a risqué mood, or she's a real freak," he thought.

With his jeans bunched at his ankles, lust and passion hovering throughout the room, Yolonda sprung her body upwards ultimately latching onto Kory's waist.

"Put it in, hurry! Hurry!" She begged.

He reached up under her buttocks, grabbed himself, and guided his staff into her moist slit.

"Ooooh…Shiiiitttt!" Roared from her mouth, as the tip of his snake attempted to enter into her wilderness.

"Damn is she a virgin?" He asked himself.

He kept at it though finally easing himself into her plush paradise. Slow strokes turned into long powerful thrusts, which she no doubt was beginning to enjoy. Five minutes into the session, Kory had brought her to two orgasms.

With a change of position, Kory bent her curvaceous frame over the ledge of the couch. With her legs spread as wide as they could go; she reached back and parted the red sea allowing him a clear passage into her murky waters.

"Ooh no, no, it's too big!" She cried, as his sailboat traveled deep up her channel. "Oh God...Ooh God please help me, please! It's too big Kory!" She continued to yell, as he pounded and thrashed her walls like a speeding car crashing into a solid brick wall. Her cries fell upon deaf ears and only fueled his assault. He was going to leave an impression on her and her vagina to embark on for future references. He was claiming the pussy his.

After the sixth orgasm, she lost count and let Kory have her any which way he desired. The next morning as promised, Yolonda was in those heels, stark naked, flipping flapjacks.

Chapter 31
Is It Too Good To Be True?

The killings seemed to stop and the city felt good about it. They felt safe again. The police presence in and around Hartford must have paid off, is what they claimed. The co-respondent, being The Hartford Police Department, were used to the public's bashing and trash talking to a degree where they exhausted all of their remedies and resources to make sure their streets and citizens remained safe. Now they have been presumably exonerated.

The letter 'K' killer was out on a limb and not a murder in weeks. Children played on the sidewalks and old ladies strolled the area pushing four wheeled grocery carts. The peanut lady was back in stride, moving the petite bags of shelled nuts like an eager drug dealer thirsty to trade their addictive substance for cash. Long story short, the Constitution State has for now won, only there has not been anyone captured and held accountable for the twenty-two deaths of innocent civilians in Connecticut.

A couple of weeks have surpassed and correct, not one sighting or homicide traced to their so-called serial killer. In view of the fact that this may appear true, the siblings are very much in plain sight and bloodthirsty, and things were about to turn up in Homicide Hartford.

L♥D~ L♥D~ L♥D

Both detective, Mosley and Long, had endured a very sensitive accommodation on their extensive police work involving the serial murders. Chief Daniels had respectively patted them on the backs for laying the groundwork and diligence needed to secure safety in the community. In consideration of their impeccable efforts, Chief Daniels felt they were in need of some down time with the option to decline. In either case, it would be with pay.

Wayne was against the option to recess, considering that no one had been arrested. At the same time, it was their sole case and had been since it began. Meaning, they were spared a heavy caseload, as their fellow colleagues suffered several homicides with no grace or special privileges. He was skeptic about the chief's offer.

Yolonda on the other hand was ecstatic, but she would never show it. A full seven days off with pay, she was so overcome with joy. She could have kittens and Kory most definitely would father them.

She hated that she had to hide and conceal their passion, lust and relationship, if that is what you call hot, erotic and spine tingling sex. The two would meet at some of the strangest places and engage in intense, mind-blowing sex where the dangers of being caught, seen, videoed and arrested for indecent exposure and lewdness meant nothing. For example: The park bench in the center of Bushnell Park on a crowded Saturday afternoon or the steam room at the Bally's Fitness Center, when movement was like rush hour traffic. These were just some of the places they frequented when they dallied in their sexcapades.

Kory was a very self-worthy individual and was content with himself. He never cared what people thought or the risks he took when playing life's roulette. His motto was,

'Chances make Champions'. Something he inherited from his good friend Spade before he fell into the B.O.P.'s clutches.

"So Londa, what'll you suppose we do? Stay on board or walk it out for the free seven wit pay?" Wayne asked.

He would not mind the time off because it would definitely give him ample time to relax and court his wife, Sarah. Also, time to take his three boys to the Orlando Magic and Boston Celtics playoff game. Then there was this deranged-asshole-killer, roaming the city freely, so he decided he would go off her judgment.

"Well Wayne, I'm sorta burnt out at the moment concerning our psycho!" She answered, trying hard to hide her hidden agenda.

"I thought you really wanted this scum locked up Londa, now you looking to halt our investigation?" His spider senses were tingling some. "I just feel we need to stick to the script!" He stated with heavy protest.

"Well Wayne, if you want to stay here and crash and burn, be my guest. I am taking Chief Daniels up on the paid leave. You know, relax a lil bit. And you know what?" She propped her hands firmly on her massive hips.

"What's that?"

He was all game for whatever she had to say, even though he knew he would not agree.

"I'll be partying for you!" She smiled, her devious mind consumed with the dirtiest thoughts a sex crazed woman cold fathom. Shit, Wayne's mind was there with her, but she was on the other side of town. She was beginning to fall head-over-heels for Kory and his black mambo.

Wayne just stood there in silence as his partner of almost a decade strolled off into her own unforbidden cosmo.

"Wayne has lost his last fuckin' marbles, if he thinks I'm about to stay cooped up in this congested police box and thumb through evidence that isn't there. Ut uhn, not me! Yolonda, is going to go get herself a pedi and a mani, then get me some good ol' hard dick!" She boasted her mind racing with thoughts of Kory knee deep in her guts. "Yes girl, let's get it."

Yolonda was not bullshitting. She logged off her P.P., locked up her desk drawers and then grabbed her large brown Coach tote bag. Being they had opted for a larger area to work out of, their cubicles were a couple of steps apart, so she had to pass Wayne's desk as she headed to the elevator and hoped he recanted just as she had, but if not, she was not changing her mind for nothing or no one!

Out of her small cubicle, she began walking, her DKNY sunglasses shielding her eyes, resting in her long mane.

The decisive moment was now five steps away. Her friend and partner sat in his chair surfing through his steno pad, which held all of his police notes. Reaching the edge of Wayne's cubicle, she gathered the strength to speak.

"Well…I'll see you in a week Wayney!" Her smile broad and friendly, cheeks flushed red. "Hey Evans!" She acknowledged the third Grade Detective, the divisions clown and prankster.

Wayney…never spoke, he just glared at her. He was trying to read his friend, but could not. He could not detect any trace of deception or anything even remotely close, but still he did not speak, just a cordial head-nod.

"Week off, huh? Have fun sexy!" Major Evans finally bided in her farewell.

"Oh, I intend to! Adios" She said with glee.

If she would have looked deep into her partner's eyes, she might have caught the disappointment and vice lingering, but she would meet that demon another time. Yolonda was off to the elevator, with her Motorola Razor phone in the grips of her soft palm. She was on the phone with Mrs. Wang trying desperately to schedule an emergency appointment for a day of pampering.

"Yes, Mrs. Wang now! Today! I need to come now!" She further pressed over the wire, continuing past the restroom, which was directly across from the elevators.

"Yooooou...Uh...Need Mrs. Wang, you need uh, Mrs. Wang early...Today! Right now! You pay Mrs. Wang, yooooou...Pay extra! Mrs. Wang needs double...For emergency!" she demanded.

"Okay Mrs. Wang, I pay...Extra! I give you ext..." Yolonda attempted to finish, but was attacked and pushed violently into the open doors of the elevator. Her cell phone crashing to the hard floor and tiny plastic pieces scattered throughout the enclosure. "Ahhhh..." Her once soft, sheer voice moaned in a low course squelch of anguish, because of the large hand overlapping her entire mouth. There would be no screaming out of Yolonda on this trip.

The metallic doors became one and inside the metal carriage, Yolonda was disoriented and unaware that she was caught up in a bad situation. Her flimsy floral print skirt, now hiked up to her trim waistline and her unmentionables were ripped to the side. There was nowhere to move, as her throbbing head and c-cup breasts were pressed evenly against the cold steel.

"Say sumphin or even yell, and I'll leave you slumped in this cold box…Understand!" The wretched voice warned, and then inserted his thick baby leg into her dry walls.

"Ooooh!" She moaned in pain, as she was being violently raped in the elevator of her workplace, the headquarters of the Hartford Police Department. Out of all the places to be assaulted, it had to be right under a 1000 guns, she thought.

"Urggghh, Urggghh!" The violator growled, as he dug his tip drill deep into her coalmine, his built pelvis rapidly connecting with her plump rear. The sound was repetitious and crisp.

Yolonda knew for this heinous crime to be actually a reality, her assailant was someone who had not valued authority or women, and was so frightened that he just might take her life, so she gave her body to the unknown. "Wayne where are you?" She wondered with fret.

The unknown took the liberty of placing the steel box on emergency stop, which was now in between the 1st and 2nd floor. The emergency stop alarm had been out of service for the past six-months, so anyone trapped, such as her would be doomed until their savior graced the stage.

"Urggghh, Urgh, Urgh." His grunting grew heavier, his warm, minty breath slapping the follicles of her hair. He then bit into her neck as he neared climax, compliments of her tightness.

Unconsciously, Yolonda tightened her pelvic muscle around the long bolt twisting inside of her. She also wound her hips a tad bit, as her thickness played patty cake against her attacker's grind. The veins in his rod began to constrict, causing the mambo to exert itself into its full length and width.

"No, no, please stop! You're hurt...ting....me!" She cried, tears flowing faster and more furious then in a motion picture.

She did not know how she would recover from this ordeal, but she really wished Wayne were by her side to make life easier. She felt her vulva splitting as each thrust rushed inwards through customs and across her sexual border. Yolonda was not sure how long they had been inside the steel cage, but as his pace quickened, she knew it was not very long until the curtain closed, so she attempted to hurry the assault by exercising her vaginal muscles in fear that it would never end. Then surprisingly, his body jerked once...twice...three times, and his muscular chest plated her sweaty back.

He made sure every drop of his tainted semen traveled up stream, then yanked out of her. As his head stayed pinned against the sweat-saturated impression, he vocalized a heed she knew was very authentic. In view of the fact that he was bold enough to commit such a crime here, she obeyed.

"I'm going to fix myself. If try to scream or do something to slightly agitate me, I will drive this metal rod deep into your neck. So don't test me lady!" His voice full of ill will and certainty. "You follow?" He pressed her face into her own sweat against the chilling steel wall.

"Uh, hunn!" She answered out of fear, tears flowing freely down her brown skin.

L♥D~ L♥D~ L♥D

"Damn, don't tell me the box ain't working again?" Jerry, the Desk Sarge said from behind the glass partition in the lobby of the police station.

He had been staring at one of the department rookies for several minutes as he waited like a fool for the elevator instead of using the stairs. "Lazy bastard, hope Cap' clocks your time too!" Jerry added, using the P.A. system to joggle the rookie's stupor. "Try the stairs Cal!" Calvin looked around for the voice but was so green Jerry had to yell again. "Over here Cal, behind the glass! Try using the stairs, they work just fine rookie"

Calvin smiled and quickly took his advice out of fear for his superior. "Fat fuck," he mumbled as he pushed the heavy door inwards and began his trek up in the cold stairwell.

L♥D~ L♥D~ L♥D

The jailhouse rapist eased out the box. He peeked left, then right. The coast was clear, so he dipped into the staircase in a hurry. There was three flights of concrete in which he conquered by two's. His mask was now concealing the better portion of his features, along with the black scully pulled low over his head. When the predator reached the middle of the last section of concrete, he and Calvin collided.

"Hey, hey, what's the hurry man?" Calvin asked in a controlled tone, but obviously bothered by his dance partner's clumsiness. Calvin was 5'11", white and on the meaty side of the bone. Although his badge entitled him to a sense and right of empowerment against civilians, he was still clumsy Calvin, as he had been all his life.

"Nah partner you need to watch yo' step!" He towered over Calvin in height, and the step only added to his elevation, which nerved him a great deal. "Fuck out my way pig!" He barked, and blew past 'em, then through the lobby doors.

If Jerry was not so laid back, he might have pursued the fleeing hooded man, but he saw no merit or cause to do so. Jerry thought he was just another civilian rushing to get out of the authorities' grasp.

As Calvin emerged through the staircase door, the elevator again smiled. He now knew what held the elevator thus far, and then noticed Yolonda crying while picking up the items from her Coach bag. He also noticed her hair was in disarray, unlike its normal keep.

"Hey detective?" Calvin said, "Are you okay?"

"I'm fine Cal. I mean, I'll be fine!" Yolanda assured, then pressed the highlighted button marked one. The doors closed and Calvin's red face faded to black. Thirty seconds later, the doors smiled once again and out stepped Yolonda. She looked to her right and saw Jerry, the Desk Sergeant, who in turn, smiled with a wave of the hand. Hooking a sharp left, Yolonda broke through headquarters feeling violated and very unsafe, her precious womb has been contaminated.

Yolonda squinted, as the midday sun beamed brightly on her face. Her eyes battling one on one, a war only her DKNY shades could defend. After carefully reapplying them to her face, she walked the short distance to the curb. It appeared timed, and on cue that an ebony-black Phantom coupe pulled directly in front of her obscuring all passage.

Without even a toot of the horn, Yolonda took her place inside the two-door chariot. She needed some serious medical attention, a.s.a.p. Her head was now cradled and wedged into the padded resting that would comfort her mangled body. What a coincidence Chief Daniels offered her some down time, because she was definitely feeling defeated. Yolonda was in shock, let alone embarrassed to report the atrocious act of violence she had just endured right under the noses of her gang.

"Can you please drop me off?" Her voice was low, almost inexistent, which left her driver confused.

"Sure, you okay?" he still managed to ask. "Where to?"

"Um, over by Mrs. Wang's." She replied, and then reached into her Coach bag, as the Phantom shot up the hill.

"No wonder," Kory uttered, observing her slip a fresh pair of panties on.

"Damn Boyee...Did you have to be so rough? My shit is killin' me!" She admitted, and then leant over to kiss her spring love.

She was not too sure, where the cruise line was heading, but since the all expense trip was paid for, she intended to exploit and make the most out of an unethical situation. It wasn't everyday a good cop got the chance to play bad girl and run rampant and reckless with the prime suspect in the city's most publicized serial murder case.

L♥D~ L♥D~ L♥D

In the shadows of the headquarters lobby, Detective Mosley cased the expensive flagship like a bank job as it shot up the steep hill with his best friend and partner who obviously has fallen victim to the Blake dynasty. Just as he paid very close attention to the enlarged taxi, a nondescript car trailed behind them as well. Safe in distance, Wayne was sure they were not friendly's or bearing chocolates, and knew Yolonda could be in the wave of trouble. The only thing he thought to do was trail them also.

The nondescript car traveled at a safe enough distance that the coupe would not detect it, and had been for several weeks. How could he be so shallow and stupid? How could he collapse and choose right over wrong? How could he love T-bone, over filet mignon? If he actually thought he would sail off into the sunset cherry, and full of triumph, he had another thing coming! The driver of the nondescript uttered.

On account of the tally being even at eleven-eleven, the opportunity to set the pace was a giveth and taketh meaning a simple kill could put one in the lead. Where at this current moment having the upper hand, proposed a leading chance to overmatch and throw the traitor into a spiraling plummet.

The temper of the driver was beyond rational thinking. As the soft flesh gripped the solidness of the course steering wheel, all thirty-two porcelain teeth bunched into an unpleasant fit of rage, pure anger and vengeance.

"Urggghh!" Both hands banged against the sternness of the steering mechanism.

On the cockpits passenger seat, sat a silenced, 17-shot .45caliber handgun. With one resting in the chamber, the nickel-plated four-fifth was ready to obey its master and eradicate any structure or form of life it met.

Just as any other day of surveillance went, the duo flaunted their explicit affair in plain sight unaware of the third party in tow. However, all of their candid actions would soon become non-existent. When the Phantom coupe stopped directly in front of Mrs. Wang's place of business, it took maybe sixty seconds before the passenger door opened outwards and Yolonda stepped out. She blew Kory a soft kiss, then waved farewell. He made sure she made it inside safely then, cruised west on Park Street. It was then that he realized the same Lincoln MKS, was shadowing him again.

"Changed whips huh?" Kory mumbled. The change from the red & white Mini Cooper was brilliant, but not enough to stay in hiding he thought. "Somehow, I knew it would come down to this. A sibling rivalry, but it has been since the playpen. It doesn't matter though; I know exactly how to get back at chu. This is going to hit chu where it hurts, Kory!"

A sinister laugh now wafted throughout the cabin of the MKS.

Chapter 32
All Is Fair In Love & War

Although the skies were dark and dreadful, the entire 12th floor of the children's hospital warded some very uplifting souls no matter what life challenged or threw out.

Directly off the elevator capable of ushering ten able adults, lied a large dayroom with various indoor activities from Scrabble, Checkers, Darts, Tic-Tac-Toe, Monopoly and Slinkies. The large space was encircled by twelve private quarters that practically had everything a one-bedroom apartment had, minus the kitchen.

The 12th floor was solitary for twelve very special children either dying or fighting to maintain youth. With spiritual help, praise and grace from God, some would survive to raise their own children and then you had those whom would not last through the night. A newly funded program called Kory's Kids provided the special needs, care, nourishment and love these special kids would require until passing. Korr-Tech being the founder covered all expenses including, doctor bills, insurance, etc...etc..., so a very huge burden was lifted off the families.

A light shower began to drizzle just as a new model Lincoln MKS halted in front of the children's hospital. Robert noticed the slender male was reluctant to getting wet, but soon trotted around to the driver's side door.

"How you doing, sir?" Trevor asked.

"Okay, please don't block me in, I won't be too long." Robert said, and then pressed a twenty into the boy's hand.

Robert hurried his pace not only to stay rain free, but also to do the manly thing and open the door for his female companion.

"Thanks Robbie, you're such a gentleman." She began walking into the revolving door.

"Don't mention it."

He watched as her phatty bounced with each step. Her shirt-dress high and tight around her curvaceous body, concealing all of her goodies.

"Hurry Robbie, you're getting soaked." She cooed softly, as her flirting smile teased him, one he had never seen before.

Robert was stuck until she called out to 'em. Little heads always at attention, overriding the big one, which always got men into a world of trouble.

Through the lobby, Robert led the way to the elevators. The bell chimed as the grey doors slid open and they entered. When the doors closed, Robert pressed the number twelve button, and then the large box shot upwards in a calming motion. When the doors slid outwards for the second time, the couple noticed a small boy who quit playing Uno, their heads bald from the obvious reasons.

"Come on beautiful," he advised, his arm outwards like a railing waiting to secure her step.

Her smile, there it was again, playful, yet sultry. She latched on tightly and let Robert direct her around the dayroom.

"Hi Mr. Krammer, it's good to see you on a Thursday," Conrad, a small nine-year old boy complimented full of joy. He wore sky blue and white PJ and was reading a comic on an orange sofa.

"Hey, little slugger. You feeling good today, I see you're up and about."

"I'm....So, so! A little queasy, but I'm cool for the most part," he answered, his eyes glued to the sexy schoolteacher look-a-like. She looked like a woman who called his name out every morning during attendance, before the malignant disease called out to him and commandeered his life.

"Well, you just hang-on in there. We gon' beat this thing together, okay!" He tried to console something he knew was weighing heavily on Conrad's mental.

They continued around the dayroom and spoke to all of the kids. Most of them engaged in a playful activity except one. He rarely participated with any of the groups kids. He was seven years old and a little ahead of his time. He was a favorite with Kory and Robert. He just had that effect on you. His name was Marlon Hamilton Jr.

"C'mon, I wanna introduce you to someone; he's like a son to me and Kory." Just as he started towards Marlon's room, he realized he had left a special gift inside the car. Seeing he made the early trip to surprise him, it was necessary he go and retrieve it. "Sit tight, I'll be right back, I forgot something in the car."

"Okay, I'll wait here. Can't afford to get my doo wet," she replied, even though she had a silk scarf bundled around her head protecting it from heaven's tears.

"Okay. Why do you still have those gloomy shades on inside? Can you even see?" He stated, and then darted for the elevator.

L♥D~ L♥D~ L♥D

Time had flown by and the clouds had gathered in the empty atmosphere, pushing and shoving each other for their turn to wring out their wet belongings. As the windshield wipers on the Dodge Challenger erased all traces of H2O away from the window, Detective Mosley's passage, became see through.

It wasn't hard at all to trail such a luxurious vehicle being Hartford didn't harbor too many 2010 Phantom coupes. That was some major shit, and only major Kats drove half-a-million-dollar cars as such. Wayne knew he was going off the deep end by trailing Kory and Yolonda, but his charismatic ways and nature wouldn't stand by and watch his partner just throw away a career she's worked so hard for. It was just something about Mr. Kory Blake that did not sit too well with him. His loud toys, big money companies, his arrogant attitude and hoodlum ways had Wayne on pins and needles, not to mention the fact the 'Blake Bug', which she seemed to not want a cure for, easily bit Yolonda.

"I've got a thing for you, Mr. Blake!" Wayne gritted. "You slipped up when you carved Melinda King up. You left your shoeprint when you murdered two of my friends." His anger heightened as he spoke. "That's right Kory, you left your calling card, and now it's time I use it!"

As Robert waited for Trevor, the valet to bring him the black K.B. Toys bag, he felt his phone vibrate. Unsnapping it from its cradle, he viewed the screen. It read 'Kory'. A little thrown back, he looked around nervously for anything remotely close to his best friend. He felt relieved and answered on the fourth ring, "Hey Korr, what's happening?"

"Same ol', same, what's the word with you? I haven't seen you since the club. Don't tell me Fantasia has you on lock 'n key?" Kory teased.

"Well... Yeah, you can say that if you want. She's uh fuckin' freak-a-leak. Where are you?" His voice timid and anxious.

Kory stayed silent for a moment to gather his thoughts. Something's out of place. His intuition told him it was serious. Heightened intuition was a gift-horse he obviously adopted from his pops.

"I'm around, why?" He retorted, his specs searching the rear-view, and that's when it hit him.

"Oh, just asking. Nevertheless, I have to go. Fantasia is calling big daddy!" He said hoping that would deter him from probing and end their small chatting.

"A'ight! I'll holla at chu!" Kory's phone flew towards the dashboard. He pressed a button up under the dash and tuned the AM station to 113.4 and a small compartment oozed out of the dashboard. He quickly seen what would soothe his tension and then his right hand became one with a silenced Glock .40, his pride and joy.

Robert took one last look before going inside. He knew Kory like the back of his hand. There's was no way he was going to let Kory find out about his sexual deceit. He was optimistic, but hell, it is what it is, no turning back now.

When he exited the elevators, he saw his guest playing 3-way Tic-Tac-Toe with one of the kids. He smiled seeing she was still bandaged in her clothing, her Marilyn Monroe's covering the upper part of her face.

"Hey you, having fun?" He asked now standing behind the multi colored table.

"Oh yeah, great, did you get what you left? You were gone for a while, Rob."

"Uh humph, just had a business call, so we can't stay too long. C'mon, I want you to meet Marlon."

As they walked away, a little girl in a wheelchair rolled up and asked Robert something.

"Robert, Robert... Is Kory with you?" Aaliyah asked, nearly hyperventilating. She loved when Kory came around; all of the kids did.

He tensed up briefly. His quest saw the change in demeanor and smiled.

"No, no Aaliyah, he'll be around on Sunday."

"O...Kay!" Aaliyah's voice trailed with sadness. She rode off, but not before saying, "Can you please tell Mr. Kory I said thanks for the ballerina dress and shoes. I really hope I'll someday be able to dance!" Her little heart felt broken. She had gotten word from her mom and pop that she might not make it through the night. Kory was very kind and had promised her she would be able to do Broadway when she got older, and now she might never get the chance to see him again.

"I will Aaliyah. I will tell him as soon as I see him. But don't worry little lady, you'll be able to tell him yourself come Sunday!"

"Hey Robbie, why don't 'chu just call him and let pretty little Aaliyah talk to him." His guest suggested with a cordial smile, but as she saw the fret in his face, little Aaliyah wheeled her little soul away.

"Just C'mon." Robert pulled her arm using some force. When they reached Marlon's doorway, they saw his parents sleep on a large couch, while Marlon did him.

L♥D~ L♥D~ L♥D

"Wow, Mrs. Wang, I'm really feeling rejuvenated. I needed this treatment girl!" Yolonda spoke with a bit of slang.

"I know...I know! Mrs. Wang, always do good job. You...Make appointment next time too!" The short woman wearing a floral print dress and open-toed sandals instructed.

"Okay, Mrs. Wang, I...Make appointment. Here's $150 and thanks a lot girl," she ended then pulled out her cell phone and dialed Kory's number.

L♥D~ L♥D~ L♥D

Not far away, the Dodge Challenger sat with the engine running, exhaust smoke blowing out of the dual pipes. The radio station was on Power 93.7 FM, but low in tone. As the driver's seat reclined back far enough where his eyes were level with his target and vehicle, he chewed on a Krispy Kreme donut.

Just as Kory dipped into his strip club's front door, his phone rang. "Fuck!" It was Yolonda calling. "She must be ready. Took yo' ass long enough!" He blurted.

He was agitated and burdened with too much at the current time. Robert was out on a limb chasing some ass, Keonna was nowhere to be found, Yolonda needed to be picked up, and now this fat fuck wants to play Cowboys and Indians!

Ring, ring!

"Hello?" His voice low and malicious.

"Hey sweetie, I'm ready if you're close by."

"Oh yeah, I'm very close. It's still raining out, so stay inside; I'll be there in a hot sec."

He pressed end, then darted out the rear door.

"Good thing this U-Haul spot is closed for the day and still full of trucks. Best cover I've ever had on a stake out." Wayne said to himself. It's true, the U-Haul store located on Capitol Avenue, was directly across the street from the new and renowned Teezer'z, Kory's place of business.

He actually contemplated walking up in Kory's club and jacking his ass right up, but there were too many witnesses, so he chilled out. His time was coming, he had his thermos full of Joe, and a dozen Krispy Kreme glazed donuts. He was content and ready to stalk.

"Now let's see how you like it, Mr. Blake!"

L♥D~ L♥D~ L♥D

Knock. Knock. Knock.

The loud boom broke the Jordan's slumber completely.

"Oh my, we dozed off! Wake up Marlon." Janet shoved her husband in the ribs.

"Woman, have you lost your damn..." He stopped midway in his speech noticing their guest in the doorway.

"Oh hey Robert, what are you doing here, it's not Sunday?" He sat up straight, his clothes in shams. Marlon Sr. was still half sleep, but knew it was not their usual day to visit, so he just asked.

"I can come back if there's a problem."

"No, no, come in." Janet urged, she started to pick up some around the small room.

Marlon Jr., was stuck in front of the tube playing 2007 Madden. He was a wizard at certain things and loved video games, which kept him glued to the TV instead of socializing with the other kids whom were in similar conditions.

"Well I just came to drop something off and introduce my friend to Marlon. She's never been up here."

"Sure, suit yourself," Marlon Sr. said. "Hey Marlon, cut the game off, you have guests and I've told you many times before that it's not polite to ignore your guest son."

"Dad...I'm in the middle of the playoffs, I can't break my concentration!" He answered back, growing frustrated with his father's request.

"Break you're what? Boyee...You better cut that damn thing off before I break yo' tail." He warned sternly, but playfully.

"Ahhhh!" Marlon grunted, his controller crashing into the thick mattress.

"Hey Rob, I mean Mr. Krammer," his voice full with sadness.

Video games were like a fresh breath of air to Marlon.

"Hey Michael!" He always called him Michael Jordan, because he really resembled him in so many ways. "I've got something you're going to love. Here, pop it open." He tossed the bag at him. Marlon knew it was something for his PS3, because it came from K.B. Toys. Robert gripped his lady friend's hand for support knowing how he would react once he looked inside.

"Hummph...Hummph!" He sang, as he dug into bag, his eyes closed. Once he felt the plastic and disk like toy, he yelled loudly. "You got it! You really got it! Thanks, thank you, Mr. Krammer! I love you Rob!" Marlon sang louder. "2011 Madden! It's not even out yet, how'd you get it Rob, sorry, Mr. Krammer." He again corrected himself, as his pops gave him that stern stare.

"Ol', you know me Marlon Jr., I get anything I want, and you do as well." Robert felt his hand lock up from the pressure of his female friend, she obviously felt warm inside from the affection between the two male species.

Just when Marlon Jr., ripped the plastic off and tried to pop the disk in, a nurse, Mrs. Ledbetter entered the room pushing a chrome wheelchair. It was time for his daily chemotherapy. Nurse Ledbetter was always nice enough to let Marlon Jr. play his videos all day long. She would normally wait until 7:30 p.m. to usher him to his destination, so you already know how Marlon was feeling now.

"No, I don't want to tonight. Please dad, tomorrow, please!" He begged shamelessly.

The nurse stared at Robert knowing he had something to do with Marlon's reluctance. Marlon Jr. always did this when Robert and Kory came with gifts.

"Now you know you have to go Marlon!" His moms said.

"No mom, I wanna play my video game, please!"

Her eyes watered, as did Robert's female companion. Women always melted for Marlon.

"Don't worry Jr., I'll be right here when you get back, I promise, Scout's honor!" Robert said, raising his two fingers up into the air symbolizing a great traditional code within The Boy Scouts of America.

"O-Kay!" Marlon Jr., said in defeat.

"Don't worry champ, I'll be right here warming up the joysticks for you!"

With that said Marlon Jr. climbed into the chrome chair and let Nurse Ledbetter chauffeur him away.

"Come on Marlon, let's go with him," Janet said, leaving Robert and his guest lonely.

L♥D~ L♥D~ L♥D

Like a thief in the night, Kory darted out the rear door of Teezer'z and blended into the pitch-darkness, his A.C.G. boots tracking muddy trails through the yards of nearby homes. A sleuth of angry dogs barked at the dark intruder trespassing through their comfort zone, a red beam lined up with their craniums to help guide the gold talons from Kory's Glock killing them instantly.

Kory hopped three fences and a small roof on a wobbly porch just to get far enough up Capitol Avenue to where he would be clearly shielded as he ducked into the backyards that led to the U-Haul parking lot. Satisfied with the point of attack, he looked around before hopping the two-foot barrier that separated the two structures.

When his feet touched down with the surface, he smiled knowing it was money, time to feed, and then out of nowhere his phone shook his waist, "Dammit, I forgot all about 'chu," he cursed before answering. "Wassup ma'?"

"Where are you boo, mama's waiting, and I think Ms. Wang's about to shut down." Yolonda replied.

He was not late or anything, she had only spoken with him seven minutes ago, so her urgency only heightened his thirst and adrenaline.

"Give me ten minutes, matter fact, go next door to the Broasterant, and order us coupla chicken breast dinners. Tell the elderly lady, Mrs. Silvia, it's for Kory and she'll know just what to do, Bye!"

L♥D~ L♥D~ L♥D

Back on the 12th floor, Robert inserted the 2011 Madden disk into Marlon's PS3, and fumbled with the joystick. Not paying attention to his surroundings, his female friend had closed the door and slid the lock so no one could gain entrance. She was intrigued by Robert's generosity, kind heart and affection towards the sick boy. It turned her on in ways he would soon appreciate, or not.

As the lights in the room dimmed heavily, Robert jumped as if he were afraid of the dark or someone, his face full of caution.

"Whew!" He mouthed his eyes wide as saucers. His lady friend's dress was high above her breasts.

"Hey, what's going on?"

"Shut up Robert, you know exactly what's going on. I have wanted to taste your semen in my mouth for a while now. I've heard stories about how long and thick your dick is, and now I want my turn at bat. Don't you want me, Robbie?"

She had one leg up on Marlon's bed exposing her shaved goodies.

His mouth salivated, his rod growing by the second.

"Yes!" He answered, biting hard into his bottom lip. "Yes, I want you, c'mere!" He demanded, tasting blood as he spoke.

"No, you come taste this pussy!"

"Ooh, you wanna be fresh huh?"

Robert crawled over to the bed and dug straight into her Jell-O Pudding Cup. His tongue easily sliding up and down her slit, grazing the tip of the shoreline, but enough to shake hands with the little man in the boat.

"Oooh yes, Robbie! Yes, just like dat! Ooh, Oooh!" She moaned loudly, as he tampered with her goodies in a special way, causing her to clamp onto his head nearly pushing his entire face into her womb.

With her free hand, she caressed her breast, which only caused her to pant louder. Robert was doing such a great job, she climaxed twice, and however, she needed to feel something stiff inside her dock.

"Lay down," she ordered, grabbing him then positioning him on his back on the edge of Marlon's bed. He felt funny about sexing on Marlon Jr.'s mattress, but she erased those thoughts after she yanked his trousers down to his ankles and took him into her mouth.

"You like dat, Robbie?"

"Yes…Yes, I like dat!"

She sucked him fast and raw, letting her teeth graze the length a little to invigorate his erection, something she learned from studying Kama Sutra.

"Urggghh…"

Robert whined like a little baby needing a warm bottle, only he was not hungry, he was satisfied. Just before she was about to end her fellatio act, she bit up and around the head of his penis.

"Urggghh!" His voice muttered with unknown pleasure, at least one he had never experienced.

In a swift motion, she plopped Robert's erection out of her mouth, then mounted him. His erection was sticking up at least eight-inches from his groin.

"Ooooh!" They moaned in unison, her walls gripping snuggly to his width.

"Ooooh yeah, yeah big daddy!"

She bounced up and down, twerked hard and fast, causing a loud slapping noise inside the room. The smell of sex lingered loosely about the room; sweat consumed their bodies, a sure inclination of their wrongdoings. However, the power of pleasure out ruled all of that.

"Fuck me Robbie! Fuck me harder!"

"Oh you wanna fuck, you want ol' Robbie to show you a good time huh? Take this, you slut! You dirty tramp!" He bluntly scolded her.

"Yes…Dat's…What…I'm…Talking…'Bout! Yes! Yes! Yes! Yeessss!" She yelled as Robert gripped her waist and drove his 9-iron deep into her caddy bag. "Oh my…Fucking…God! Uh hun, Uh hun…" She bounced hard onto his pelvis to make sure her last nut would suit her needs. Then as Robert thrusted upwards, and pulled her sleek body onto his, they both hymned a tune only known by the God's of erotica.

"Wheeew!" She moaned, hoping off him. Finally back on her feet, she pulled her dress down. She was not wearing any panties, so a quick cleansing with a few wet wipes and she would be okay.

Retrieving her bag, she reached inside while she watched Robert still in awe at the illustrious sex session he just endured. His eyes were closed shut, as he held his meat stroking what she thought was some extra nut he didn't get out, but hey, even better, she thought.

As was said earlier, the little head is always early for school eager to be first in line for breakfast, but always late for detention, which is why Robert's stupid ass was about to endure the most exhilarating nut to date.

Unaware his name was being summoned; Robert continued to jerk his length with great speed. "Robbie. Robbie." She called again just as he shot a stream of thick cum into the air, but he froze in a state of shock seeing the nickel-plated handgun pointed in his face.

"What's…?"

Psst, psst, psst! The silenced .9 milli spoke, sending Robbie on a one-way trip to hell! Before leaving the scene, she made sure to leave her mark; a sleuth of black roses now littered the area where Robert lay dead in pool of blood.

L♥D~ L♥D~ L♥D

Over the barrier, Kory now gravitated with the precision of a panther in the wild hunting for prey. The chattering drizzle played a concerto against the metal of the out of date moving trucks, the pinging sound similar to a winding clock.

He was now in direct line with the Dodge Challenger and immediately noticed the movement inside was very little, almost frozen in time. Kory had not felt the need to take any of his normal precautionary measures before attacking his prey, because any interruptions or intrusions, would also meet the same trip to hell as Detective Mosely was about to, he was never stingy about sharing his cop killers!

With the rain, the night and the dim lit area, he was shielded even though he stood out in plain view draped in black with a chrome .40cal Glock. Standing at the rear of the Challenger, he watched the droplets repel down his black sheathing.

"Never go to sleep on the job Wayne, you should know better than that. You haven't learnt a thing from Mr. Krugar I see!" He mumbled, and then tapped on the passenger window, startling Wayne. Wayne's box of donuts fell to the floor. "Fat fuck!" He smiled, as he dumped the entire clip into the window.

It was a farewell, a righteous sendoff, 17-shot salute. Kory's smiling face was the last image Wayne pictured before the 'Angel of Death' reached his glowing palm out for him to latch onto. He was there to make sure he made a safe trip to the great divide and would not try to dip-off in transport.

Kory checked his stopwatch and was pleased with his time. It only took 6 minutes total.

"Good! I must be getting better, plus this puts me in the lead with twelve kills' sis."

He praised his good work. Now back inside the dryness of his coupe he headed east down Park Street. He hoped his timing and hunch was as good as always, and if so, one more would be taking that short trip to hell.

He parked the coupe in front of the Broasterant, and then hopped out. As soon as Silvia saw her good friend and faithful customer, her aging smile widened broadly.

"Hi Kory, you've finally come home?" She casted a friendly vibe as she spoke.

"Come in, sit down and I'll fix up your booth," she insisted. She enjoyed chatting with Kory whenever he came around.

"Sorry Silvia, but I have to be some where's, like yesterday."

"Sure, sure. You send your wife in to order, humph." She indirectly asked, careful not to blow his spot up. "She's very pretty too."

"No Silvia, she's not my wife, at least not yet," He corrected and saw Yolonda's mood go from calm to ecstatic. Only she never spoke, she held it all in and would comment later.

"Well good luck and don't be such a stranger, Kory!"

"I won't, take care Silvia, love you."

He grabbed the bags, while Yolonda carried the two Snapple Iced Teas.

"By Ms. Silvia!" Yolonda whispered, not sure, if it was okay to do so. She did not want to intrude on their relationship any further.

Silvia smiled and nodded,

Inside the coupe, Yolonda finally spoke out. "She's nice and I can see she really cares for you."

"Yeah, Silvia's good people, you know the motherly type. One I've never really known." His words touching, this caused Yolonda to change the subject.

"So where we headed?"

"Gotta shoot by the hospital for a quick minute. You mind?"

"No, no, let's go. But what's wrong, you feeling sick?" She further probed.

"Nah, nothing like that. I just wanna to see something. It's my sixth sense. We won't be long, I promise."

"Okay, sure babe. As long as we're together, I'm okay."

A few minutes later, Kory brought the coupe to a stop at the corner of Madison and Washington Street, where he would be able to view the flow of traffic in camouflage. After three minutes, he saw not only what he was looking for, but also a wave of blue and whites racing into the lot around the children's hospital. Then from out of the valet area, a nickel colored Lincoln MKS, oozed out of the parking lot, and drove off Scott free.

When the MKS paused at the red light, Kory noticed the flickering of the neon headlamps, and then it sailed across Washington St. Kory smiled knowing what that meant. They were now even, twelve –twelve.

Chapter 33
The True Meaning of Reprisal and Victory

Once the Nissan Titan managed to escort John James within the secured gates of his property, he noticed the entire estate was in the dark, except the dining area. He had not found it to be out of place, nor strange, because he and Lizzie often retired early. It's just lately their sexual relations had factored back into their bedroom, so he knew she would be laying like a butterball turkey waiting to be based on Thanksgiving. However, he had another thing coming tonight. It was 4:30 a.m., and there was no way he would be able to get it up after what Fantasia and Mo'nay put on him. He was beyond drained and needed to soak old' Johnnie for a day or two before stepping back into Lizzie's pond.

Being somewhat inebriated, his steps were slow and staggered. His breath and attire reeked of high-end booze, his eyes stained red. He fumbled with the round key ring searching for the matching one to unlatch the bolt on the enormous door.

"Damn key!" He slurred loud and combative, as if his current condition were antagonizing him. In a sense of defeat, John James fell hard on his bottom, his legs too heavy to tolerate the 167pounds he had been harboring around on daily. In doing so, his broad shoulders met head on with the door, causing it to swing inwards. "This must be a godsend." He mumbled relieved that the door was already ajar.

He picked himself up with the help of the gold door handle and continued his stagger through the foyer and into the living room. "Lizzie, Lizzie!" He beckoned loudly, and kept it up knowing she would answer eventually. Instead of Lizzie's voice saluting at attention, it sang out in cries of pleasure. He thought his inebriation was starting to play tricks on him, but they were the same cries and laughs he had endured on many nights when he was too tired to sex his wife.

His interest was now very piqued and began to trace the echoes of lust. They were the same echoes he had caused hours ago just this morning, so he knew without a doubt what he was hearing.

"Where are you Lizz, where are you?" He yelled, continuing his search. "No one in the den! No one in the bathroom! No one in my office, so where? Where's it coming from?" He panicked knowing that someone was banging Lizzie's back out. Then it hit him, there was only one other room or quarters on the lower level of the estate. He quickly changed directions by skipping the library, and then crossed the cold tiled kitchen floor, which led to the last, and only room in the estate. When he reached the doorway, his suspicions were in reason.

"Yeahhh, get it in there! Ooh, ahhh, fuck! Ram that black dick in me! Ahhh, sssst!" She cried out trying to endure what Roman was doing to her. "Oooooooh! Oow, yes, hit it, hit it Roman, hit it, and hit it hard! This is…Your pussy!" She acknowledged through moans and loud grunts.

"Who's pussy bitch?"

"Yours Roman, yours! It is your pussy forever! I can feel that big black, dick. "She paused to get a breath or two in. "In, my stomach! Oh God!"

Lizzie was going through hell, but what woman do you know that can handle both of her private orifices being plugged and beat with by two enormous cocks?

Lizzie was not the only one going thru the turmoil now. John James was sick and now throwing up as he watched Isabella, the house maiden talk trash in perfect English as she drove a ten inch strap-on dildo into his wife's asshole, while Lizzie rode Roman, the man he signed over a $250,000,000,000 cash cow to a few hours earlier.

"No bitch...This is my pussy!" Isabella yelled, driving the dildo deeper into the black hole.

"Yes, yes Bella, it's yours too!"

"That's right, you white slut!" Isabella said.

With that, John started to cry as he fell to his knees. His life seemed to flash in front of him. Hearing the boisterous clamor from John-James, the threesome noticed they had a guest. Although Lizzie continued to cry out in ecstasy, she turned her head just enough to see her poor husband in a place she despised, on the bottom.

Roman excused himself from the ménage trios, because he had an old score to settle, something that trailed far back, but now he had finally, finally gotten his man. He grabbed the .45 off the nightstand already prepared for when John arrived, then walked and kneeled his nakedness beside him and said, "So, so now we can finally put things down and move on, but before I end your life as you did my Kaitlyn's, you should know that, I am Nathaniel. It was Roman whom you drove off that ridge in the San Fernando Valley that night, you conniving piece of shit! It took me all this time to plan how this would end and I must say, it was clever. Now that I have my company back and yours, thanks to Lizzie, I can move on! Never put all of you, meaning your company, into a women's grasp, idiot!"

Boom! Boom! Boom! Boom! Boom!

The loud echo thundered with each pull of the trigger, as John James' body absorbed each shell gracefully. It was truly the end of a menacing dynasty that had not only betrayed its closest friends, but the founding fathers.

There was no sense in letting some good pussy go to waste, so Nathaniel climbed back into bed and enjoyed the night.

First thing in the morning, after a quickie, then a shower, Nate placed two very large suitcases full of greenbacks in the trunk of a teal-green Bentley GTC, which Elizabeth and Isabella was to ride off in.

"So are you and the kids going to be okay, Nathaniel?" asked Elizabeth.

"Of course, and don't you two worry your pretty heads off thinking about us or Robert. I will have all this cleaned up within the hour. You're both Scott-free. Now get going before I change my mind and kill you both... You know, I really don't feel right leaving loose ends." He said truthfully, not seeing them as a real threat being they played a significant role in Robert's demise, not to mention the abundant amount of cash he laid on them to live off.

"Bye and thanks Roman, oops, I mean Nathaniel," Elizabeth bided.

Isabella blew Nate a kiss and then laid back in the comforts of the pricy shuttle ready to relocate and live life with Elizabeth.

L♥D~ L♥D~ L♥D

Several police officers, officials, reporters and Chiefs of Staff for the children's hospital swarmed in and throughout the entire structure hoping to find any clues to whom left a message that could only point in one direction.

"Something's gotta be done Daniels! This is unacceptable. It is far off the scale of murder," Mayor Marks scolded his Chief of Police.

"Yes Sir, I..."

"No! I don't want to hear your failures, I can see them. The public is in an uproar behind this one. I thought we had our community back, but this lunatic is still haunting our streets."

"Yes sir I know what..."

"I never said I was through, but I will not go down alone Daniel's Heads are about to roll, and it starts with yours!" The Mayor further scolded, and then walked away.

NEWS FLASH:

"Live on set of the 12th floor in the children's hospital lies what we all know to be the home for twelve very special kids ranging from the ages 4 – 14. This is also special in other perspectives such as how it is funded and whom from. The 12th floor is housing for twelve cancer recipients, whom live their everyday lives here free. Yes people, free. All expenses paid, rather funded by 'Kory's Kids', a subsidiary of Korr-Tech."

Nevertheless, a sick gruesome crime has interrupted the lives of these twelve innocent children. Behind me is the home of Marlon Jordan Jr., whom was a favorite of the proprietors of 'Kory's Kids'. What I hate to report is that, our serial killer has tainted the home of Marlon Jr., by leaving his mark and victim behind in a malicious way. Robert Krammer, best friend to Kory Blake, was found nude and shot twice in the head in a pool of black roses. There was also a card with a kiss print beside him, obviously a message to someone.

We have tried to reach out to Mr. Blake, but have not had any luck. Please, anyone with information connected to this heinous crime, please call or contact local authorities. This is Lasandra Love reporting to you live from the children's hospital."

L♥D~ L♥D~ L♥D

With nowhere else to be, Kory decided it was time to get it popping. He drove to one of his honeycomb hideouts where he and Yolonda were engaged in some hot sex.

Thump…Thump…Thump...Thump! Was the sound of the large headboard crashing into the wall, as Kory held Yolonda's legs wide and back into her chest just past her jaw line and parallel to her ears in the missionary position for the past fifteen minutes.

"Ooh, ooh, ooh, ooh daddy, bring it! You are tearing dis pussy, up! Ooh, ooh!" She yelled, and then grabbed her ankles giving Kory some extra passage into the depths of her womb. "Oooooooh…" Her voice trailed.

Call him crazy and deranged, but Kory always enjoyed sex or masturbation after a kill and Yolonda was enduring what he referred to as the after kill. Sweat beads were flowing off Kory's chest and forehead and onto Yolonda's body. They were drenched in each other's sweat and secretions, the smell of sex heavy in the air.

As the slapping sounds of both their bodies combined with his growls and grunts her boisterous moans and pants echoed as their souls connected in many ways. It was extremely frequent that they had sex. Lovemaking was very far from what this was or probably ever will be, however this was some hot and bothered fucking at the moment.,

Experience was key. Kory was a vet and turned her out each time they clashed. There was no hole Kory had not eaten, licked, sucked or plunged into, and right now, she was taking a serious beating.

"Urgh! Urgh! Urgh! Urgh!" He grunted in accordance with the thump of the headboard.

"Oh yeah, ooh yeah, beat it, beat it, it's all yours Kory! Fuck! Fuck! Fuck!" She was running out of things to say, so she just continued to scream, "Fuck, fuck!" Bucking back wildly.

After another two solid minutes of that, they both climaxed. His length still pulsating as his load sailed around her ocean with nowhere to go but up!

"Oh my, goodness!"

She began heaving and breathing fast. He had really worked her over this trip. Normally, she would get up to grab a warm, soapy cloth, but she was still having orgasms even after he pulled his beef log out of the oven.

"Don't worry, I got it ma'!" He assured, then stood up and walked into the large bathroom connected to his master bedroom. "You gon' have to get your own shirt though," he added.

She loved to lie down in one of his button-ups after sex; the smell of his cologne lingering in his shirts as she wore them was something that turned her on.

"All, right!" She sounded defeated, but reluctantly got up. "By the way baby, I've got something to tell you!"

"What? I can't hear you?" He yelled from inside the bathroom.

"I've got to tell you something," she repeated, as she threw her thick legs over the edge of the bed and stood up.

Through wobbly legs, she headed for the large walk-in closet. "Did you hear me?"

It was hard to hear anything due to the water running from the sink. Kory lathered up a black rag with soap and began to cleanse himself, and then he prepared a separate one for her.

"Disgusting!

Fucking...Down...Right...Disgusting!" Yolanda blurted out with hate and fury. "So you really thought you could hide this from me huh. Well...I have news for you Kory Blake! You think you have all the sense, but it is over and the buck stops right here! Never tangle with a scorned woman, asshole!"

"What did you say ma'?"

"Ohh," she couldn't believe her eyes.

"There it was! It was probably there all along, but I missed it. No, he did not really play me." She tried to make some sense out of this, but truthfully, there is none. "I can't, no I won't deal with it. Fucking disgusting." She mumbled more upset with herself, than him.

"Oh well, this is how we gotta end it bruh! Pitiful...what a fuckin' waste!" Another voice whispered undetected by Yolanda.

"Hey...Kory!" A pair of scorned voices echoed in unison, which had not sounded on key to Kory one bit. One was soft, the other sweet, though both sounded extremely agitated.

"Kory...!" There it was again, that frightening chorus, but the water enabled him to decipher it.

As Yolanda stepped out of the closet bearing arms, in the doorway of his private office connected to the master bedroom was hate, terror, craziness and what looked to be a large caliber handgun. Now four beady eyes crisscrossed with evil, rage and hurt. From one viewpoint, there was deception, from the other, revenge for betrayal, but when you summarize it all; it coils back to the same thing, Kory.

"Wow, she looks just like him, so she must be the female we have no prints on, but DNA," Yolonda thought. What no one knew or would ever understand is that only a ninja can kill a ninja! Only wit and diversity could conquer an army of soldiers. Lastly, only a true strategist could mastermind a dynasty through even a scorned and perfect world, and come out with the pennant. After all, nothing succeeds like success!

In the doorway of the master bath now stood six-inches of supremacy holding a fully loaded .45 desert eagle, stark naked.

"Ladies...Ladies!" Kory said. "I see we all hava problem on our hands," he mustered through a slight grin, his swagger always on tilt.

"Shut up Kory, you can't wiggle your way out of this, you betrayed me!" Keonna barked.

"You thought I'd never find out Kory, but those Trezeta boots are in your closet. You killed all those people, not to mention two cops, Kory. You're fucking crazy and deranged!" Yolonda yelled.

"Nah ma', make that three cops!"

"How do you mean?"

"You's, a stupid bitch! Your partner, Mosley. Yeah, while you were getting pampered, actually ordering chicken, he dumped a clip into your pudgy partner!" Keonna laughed.

Yolonda began to gasp and sigh, her eyes welling with tears.

"Tell me you didn't Korr; please tell me you didn't kill Wayne!" Pain and heartache began to cascade down Yolanda's face.

"Sorry, can't do dat, babe. He shoulda let things be. He's lucky I don't go and kill that Sarah and his three boys of his!" He said flat out with no emotion or regret. "You know Kee; killing Robert was cruel and fucked up. Something told me you'd use him to get at me and to achieve first place, but as you can see its twelve to twelve!"

"Twelve to twelve?" Yolonda questioned wearily. She knows she did not just hear what she thought she did. "Did you say twelve – twelve as in, you have twelve, and she has twelve? You two sick fucks are playing a fucking game with human targets?" Her .380 now raised, a torrent of tears pouring down her face.

"Of course it's a game bitch, and one I'm going to win," Keonna said and then raised her gun at Kory.

There it was, three deadly weapons being possessed by three postal shell-shocked individuals with their own agendas, but with Yolonda, it was deeper than we all know, because if what she now knew about the two siblings, it also meant there was a 99.9% chance her unborn child she was carrying held these similar traits. The question was, was she willing to raise a lunatic?

Yolonda took a good look at Kory then at Keonna and back to Kory doing the obvious.

"You did mention y'all were even, twelve to twelve right? Well you lose!"

Boom, boom, boom! The .380 sent three .9mm shells into Keonna's torso. Her body fell to the floor and shook violently. Thick globs of serum regurgitated up out of her mouth. She managed to somehow hold on to her defense - her pistol, but could not squeeze the trigger; that part of her brain was not functioning at the moment. It was definitely out to lunch; total unawareness.

Yolonda then took her place under Kory's arm, his warmth and touch protective, the one she would need soon. "Fuckin' bitch!" She spat.

Kory stared at Keonna's quivering body realizing what the game had boiled down to.

"Sorry sis, but as you know, this was just a game, so I win," He gently placed a kiss onto her forehead, whispered he loved her, and then fired a single shot into his baby sister's head right where he kissed her. It was done; Keonna's life was no more.

As Kory walked across the floor he said, "So what are we going to name my son?" His grin was wide and sinister.

He did not have to look at her face to know her beady eyes were double in size and full of wonder, shock and bewilderment. How was it possible for him to know being only forty five days into her 1st trimester? It was just his wit and intuition he and Nathaniel shared, very similar to that dreadful night back in 1963, when Nate tricked John James III into running Roman and his cheating whore of a wife Kaitlyn, off that cliff in the San Fernando Valley. Then he also constructed the scheme in which he would kill his own parents, Kline and Audrey James, and then take full control of the family business, only to later consume both dynasties.

Yolonda's mouth dropped when Kory asked her that. "Huh? Excuse me? I didn't hear you." She managed through a low whisper.

"Let me put it this way, do you have a name picked out for my, son?" He spun around. Her face flushed a deep beet-red. She was full of shock.

"Kory Jr., of course," She mumbled, knowing her response would please him.

"Kory Jr.," he repeated, smiling sadistically. "I wouldn't have it any other way."

The End

Victims of Seduction

J. ALEXANDER

Victims of
Seduction

J. Alexander

Victims of Seduction
By J. Alexander
Copyright 2014 by J. Alexander

This book is a work of fiction. The names, characters, places, and incidents are products of the author's imagination or have been used fictitiously. Any resemblance to persons, living or dead is entirely coincidental.

Published by Boss Life Publications

Follow us on Facebook and Twitter
Editor: Shelby Lazenby

Chapter One
Risky Business

As Carlos drove steadily down the evenly paved road, he paid very close attention to what the news radio broadcaster had to say. He was ten minutes late leaving his home, his midnight shift at the Detention Center would start soon. He knew if he drove a little over the speed limit, he'd be fashionably on time, but for some peculiar reason the broadcast held his undivided attention.

"Damn…," he uttered in response to what he'd just heard, "that's some sick shit," he finished, and then continued to listen.

"This is yet another heinous murder at the hands of a brutal animal that seems to subdue his or her prey in sick malicious fashions that results in a vicious death. With Sam Milner, being Number 24 on the capital's unsolved murder list, the citizens in and around the city live in fear. Some of those we've spoken to state they feel unprotected by the Hartford Police Department." Late night journalist Laura reported before changing subjects.

Carlos wasn't too interested with Laura's new choice of topics, so he switched the station to a pre-programmed channel which played his favorite oldies-but goodies.

Carlos was closing the lasting distance between him and the large bricked Juvenile Center and thought about his family. He felt through his pocket until he gripped the petite cellular phone. Next, he pushed the neon-blue button on the Bluetooth earpiece that clung to his right ear, and then voiced the name Creatia. After tossing the phone onto the plush leathering of his 300C, he waited for his love's voice to grace him.

On another side of the city, in the sleazy confines of a corner Motel-6 room, a fly- by- night sexed crazed woman was comfortably positioned on the floor, sitting Indian style with a large set of balls in her munch box feasting away in delight. A thirsty pair of blue eyes clocked her every move. Sexy, her name was, because she was just that. She was stroking the paleness of Conrad's semi stiff member, tickling the area surrounding his scrotum and shaft.

She knew without a doubt that Conrad wanted to shove all of him deep into her mouth, but he also knew there was another side to her which could be dangerous. He played along with her, taunting her as best he could.

"You like that don't you Conrad?" She teased, stroking him into full erection, their gaze conjoined in mid-air. Conrad sat on top of the rickety-wooden dresser with his back against the mirror. He was naked as a newborn baby; just the way Sexy liked him.

"Ahh…Yes Sexy, you know I enjoy when you lick my balls," he answered, winded. "Put it in your mouth," he uttered, resting his head against the glass.

The motel room was just like any other cheap, overnight hourly rated room. The place reeked of stale cigarette smoke and mildew. The burnt-orange carpet held countless traces of burn marks and stains. The furniture was fairly decent but outdated. There were two night stands, a queen sized bed and a brown stained table with two large chairs – no cushions. The only good amenity offered in the room was the 12,000 BTU air conditioner that was mounted high above the room door, that kept the room chilled and Sexy's nipples taunt and erect.

"We have all night for that boo, just enjoy the moment. After-all nothing lasts forever," she replied in a strange tone. Conrad never caught the change in her voice, because of the trance he was under; he was lost in the pleasure her touch provided. Sexy continued to jerk Conrad's tool while nibbling over his wrinkled sack. She reminded herself she was there on a mission and getting turned-on was not a part of the blueprint but if she kept the act up, it would only be a matter of time that the spark she felt in her pussy turned into a blazing inferno.

"Say my name baby, I wanna hear you beg," she demanded.

"Sexy… Sexy… Suck my dick, ooh…Please suck my dick," he said. Then suddenly excruciating pain shot through his groin. His heart raced erratically as his dick went numb. "Shit!" He cried, looking down at Sexy. She had his dick in one hand and a straight razor in the other that dripped with his blood. Just as Conrad went to yell and try to move, Sexy sprung up like a jack-in-the-box and slashed his throat leaving a huge gash that dispersed his serum like a running fountain machine.

Sexy side stepped Conrad's tumbling body and watched as his head connected with the hard floor. His body jerked for a few moments then became stiff. A large puddle formed outlining the circumference of his body. Sexy cautiously gathered what little belongings she'd brought along with her and then scanned the room to see what evidence she may be leaving behind. She was thankful there wasn't too much wiping or cleaning to do. Sexy was very contained and careful not to come in contact with any surfaces around the room, and not to mention when Conrad rented the room she'd made sure she was out of sight from anyone who may have passed by.

She forced small slits in the blinds to ensure no one was on the deck or in the vicinity in which her escape would be made. Sexy took one last look at the pool of blood, latched onto her satchel and exited the room.

Carlos tried La'Creatia cell phone twice after receiving the answering service at their home. When he received the same response, he said fuck it and chalked it up to her being sound asleep as usual. If he had not heard the Late Night episode from Laura, he might've just carried on with his agenda, but the broadcast left him slightly on edge and concerned.

He pulled into the parking lot of the detention center, and parked in his normal spot. He activated his alarm system and stepped into the building containing the habitual youthful offenders, he was employed to watch.

Through the gallery port doors, Carlos was greeted by Tacoma Red, his co-worker for the night who said, "Did you catch Late Night with Laura on your ride over?"

"Hell yeah, called right home after, too. Whoever that is murking off these niggas…Is straight 7:30 for real!"

"I'm talking Sybil, crazy," Tacoma replied, and they both laughed.

Chapter Two
I'mma Do Me Regardless Hon

"*D*amn Creatia, you lookin' spaced out this morning," Shauny said once she crept up to her catching her lost in space. La'Creatia stood behind the cash register in Wal-Green's, oblivious to the lengthy line of customers that were starting to form at the counter. She was daydreaming on the job, a habit which was beginning to become habitual for La'Creatia lately.

"Oh girl…I was just thinking about what my two bad ass kids could be doing at their granny's house. They're on school vacation and probably driving her crazy," she quickly answered, realizing there were customers waiting. Snapped out of her state of bewilderment, she began scanning items as fast as possible.

"So Creatia," Shauny paused, and then looked around before she spoke, "You heard about Conrad? They found his poor butt in some cruddy motel with his shit cut the fuck off. Yeah, somebody really sliced ol' boy up too, a damn shame to have such a good piece of dick go to waste," she added, whispering. It was true, around Wal-Green's Conrad was considered a ladies man and had gone around the block with just about every female employee there except Janice, the old pharmacist and of course La'Creatia.

"No, but I guess that explains why his smiling ass ain't ringing some of these people up." La'Creatia huffed, sarcastically.

Shauny looked at her strangely, because lately Conrad and she had been talkative and seemingly close, so it was weird seeing her react that way. However, she brushed it off as quickly as it came. Ten minutes later, they both shut down their cash registers and enjoyed a smoke outside.

A few hours passed and La'Creatia's shift was over. Her feet felt swollen and her head began to ache as she drove the short distance from work to her home. When she pulled up, La'Creatia noticed that her hubby's van was parked in the driveway; an indication Carlos was home. She hoped he hadn't fallen into one of his deep coma-like slumbers, because she was craving some male comfort and in desperate need of her favorite fix. Through the portal of their humble abode, she immediately picked up on the strong stench of marijuana which was Carlos' choice of drug – and not that cheap shit. Normally, after burning down a blunt or two, he'd ransack the fridge, indulge in a little video games, and then pass out. So she became pretty optimistic about his current state.

"CJ!" She called out, as she continued to strut.

No answer.

"CJ, I know you hear me babe. CJ," she yelled again approaching the oversized lounge chair he always found refuge in once his day was over. Seeing that she was coming from the rear, it was impossible to even tell if he was up or not.

La'Creatia rounded the lounge chair only to find her husband passed out with nothing on but his favorite briefs. She not only observed the blunt in the ashtray still lit with a good size piece of ash dangling into the fine crystal, but the huge bulge protruding through his briefs. This, of course, caused a small fire between her legs.

After setting her belongings on the coffee table La'Creatia raised her short denim skirt up to her waist, and pulled her panties to the side. With her middle and index fingers, she softly applied a light glaze of saliva onto her love-button which caused her eyes to shutter some. Gliding the tips of her pointers across her clitoris, she began to feel the euphoric pleasure she was thirsting. "Ahhh," she cooed softly as she fondled her breast with her free hand.

She continued to masturbate as she stared at her husband hoping he'd awake and punish her insides. "Oooooh, ahh, ahh…" She moaned and began winding her hips methodically to a rhythm only she could hear. Her lips began to swell in heat and she was enjoying herself tremendously, only she wanted her guts dug out. So she stepped close to her sleeping knight and lunged at the slit in his briefs..

Even without being erect, Carlos hung a good 5 1/2 inches down, which she loved. Next she easily unwrapped his serpent freeing him through the slit of his briefs and promptly placed all of him into her warm mouth. Up and down, she caressed his length until she thought he was growing in size and mass all while playing in her pussy.

"Ahh. What are you doing hon?" He questioned, in a tired state.

"Sucking your dick," she responded, then quickly stuffed him back inside her mouth. Her eyes told a different story as she pushed her fingers deep inside her womb satisfying herself until she grew him to his full potential.

"I'm sorry babes, but I'm tired, high and not in the mood," Carlos uttered, still groggy and out of it. He'd worked up until 11:30 a.m., and with that extra four and a half hours he really needed his rest for tonight's shift.

"Come on," she moaned, "I need my fix. Just a quickie baby...Come on..."

"Naw," he yawned, pushing her back and bringing her task to a halt. "I gotta get some rest before my shift."

"What!" She yelled, jumping up. "You is a sorry, limp-dick ass nigga, Carlos! Oh…So now you ain't got time to take care of home, our business and your marital obligations?" She further screamed. Carlos chose not to respond. "That's quite all right honey, I know who will," she threatened, licked the thick cream off her fingers, and then left the room, headed for her craft room.

"You'll get over it woman," Carlos muttered, then passed out.

Twenty some-odd minutes later, La'Creatia threw herself into the comforts of her oversized bean bag that rested in the corner of her office. Her craft room was where she spent most of her days and nights when home and not doing any household chores. The room was about the size of two children's bedrooms with everything you could think of in it to perform her tasks. She even had a small fridge and microwave that sat on a wicker shelf in front of a small back door no one had ever used and barely noticed for the most part.

La' Creatia, held one of her favorite toys in between her legs and then slid the rod up into her wet pussy, stroking until she reached her G-spot.

"Yes, whew, yes," she moaned, bucking against the dick fiercely. She took all her sexual frustration out on the tool, grinding on it like a dancer, desperately trying to make a few dollars. It only took seconds for her to reach her peak, for her to feel the tingling sensation that can only come when you bust a-long-awaited nut.

"That's it baby...That's it!" She screamed in pleasure.

Feeling appreciative and self-satisfied, she hurried and placed the 9" dildo back into the freezer, fearing it would thaw. "Damn Dave...You always take care of mama," her voice trailed as she spoke out. "Unlike my husband Carlos, but that's okay we just might get our freak on later. Ménage 'a trios maybe," she smiled.

It's very true. Whenever Carlos was tired and seemed he couldn't get it up for her, she'd retire to her sexual seclusion and handle her business with one of her favorite toys.

La'Creatia was in no way a slut or whore. If you asked her, she just loved her some good ole' fashion dick. All day, 24 hours a day if possible, and Carlos couldn't understand it one bit. They'd bang out for two, sometimes three hours, non-stop but that would never be enough for her. There were times when he'd wake-up and his rod would be fully erect and lodged somewhere in one of her many wet orifices. He enjoyed it the first two years of their marriage, but lately he felt like she was abusing him; basic in-house rape. "You might need some counseling," he would often say.

Her reply would always be "You must be gay CJ, most men would kill for a bitch like me." This statement was followed by her storming out of the room and locking herself in her craft room for hours.

Chapter Three
What You Won't Do...They Will

La'Creatia hadn't done any shopping in two weeks and the house was completely out of food. She'd planned to do it all week, but really didn't see the need considering that the kids were at her mother's for school vacation. Being that she never ate much beside fresh fruits and veggies, Carlos was left to fend for himself. He'd usually just eat before returning home, or would make a cold cut sandwich, however tonight it looked like his options were few.

"Dammit...," he cursed loudly in frustration as he ran through the entire icebox only to find some sausage links vacuumed sealed on the door of the freezer. "I guess this'll do," he said, then placed four of them into a pot full of warm water to boil.

It was just fifteen minutes pass the hour of eleven when Carlos rolled a nice size blunt to enjoy before his long shift. He was wearing a pair of holey sweats and an A-shirt. He sat at the dining room table waiting for his dinner to boil. He only planned to eat two, but he knew his buddy Tacoma would want some so he made extra.

He smoked the blunt halfway down, laced himself with his favorite cologne, and then stepped into his Guardian blues. He usually waited 10 minutes at the gate to apply two drops of advanced therapy Visine to both his watchers, but decided to get it out of the way now. Next, he placed all four sausages into a Glad Ware microwave safe container with three oversized helpings of sauerkraut over them, placed the bowl in his lunch bag, and then exited the house. He and La' Creatia were still on non-speaking terms, so he never yelled goodbye as he left. On his drive to work he listened to the Late Night with Laura show as always, and was stunned to hear about the newest 'Lady-Killer' victim. "Dis bitch is really sick and needs to be hospitalized quickly." He said aloud. "Damn, but ain't Conrad Wilkins one of La'Creatia's co-workers? Why didn't she at least inform me that it'd hit that close to home?" He wondered. So he decided to call home.

The phone rang three times before Carlos was serenaded with some Earth, Wind and Fire.

"Hello…"

"What?"

"What are you doing and why do you have the music blasting?" He questioned somewhat confused. La'Creatia only listens to her favorite pass time CD when she was horny or molesting him.

His first instinct was to turn all the way around and retrace his steps just to see what in the hell could be transpiring at his home, but he'd been late twice already this month and couldn't stand another write-up or his pay would be docked.

"I'm doing me, since you won't. But if you really wanna know, I'm dancing in the dark, nude with Ryan, Will and Roy," she giggled, while Roy tickled the edge of her nipple gently.

"You know what Creatia," he paused, wanting to gather his words because he was tired and fed up with her sudden mood swings when it came down to sex. There were times when she'd pour cold water on him while he was dead sleep just to let him know what it felt like to take a cold shower when she was trying to shake her horniness. Then there were times she'd leave the house and wouldn't return for hours without any regard for his feelings or an explanation as to where she'd been, and he was tired of it. "You need psychiatric help for real," he said, shaking his head.

"No, I need a man who knows how to please me," she snapped. "A man who knows how to handle his shit! Not some lame nigga who I have to beg to fuck me."

"Go get you one," he blurted, pissed from her disrespect. "I'm sick of your bullshit La'Creatia. Matter fact tell the mutherfucker, I said hello!" He hung up before she could respond. "Stupid shit," he grumbled, continuing towards his destination.

The air inside the room was chilled with the temperature at 55 degrees. The lighting was dim, but seeable for all parties in attendance. This was the perfect atmosphere for La'Creatia's orgy with her special guest.

Ryan was the first to enjoy the warmth of La'Creatia's sauna, while Roy pleasured her back door. Neither of the pale men felt out of place as she cradled Roy in a padded chair; his length just inches away from the cold stiffness of Ryan's meat stick. There was no way she wasn't going to enjoy the fulfillment of all three rods, so she feverously fed, Will, into her mouth whole.

She began to pant but even with three large dicks stuffed inside her, she craved more. She was loving the feeling they provided and cried out loudly just to show her gratitude as she climaxed heavily. "Yesss…"

Afterwards, she slurped every drop of her sweet cream off Ryan's penis, and then cooled them off. "Thanks guys," she smiled, returning the dildos to the fridge.

It was 3:00 a.m., break time at the Juvenile Detention Center and a few of the CO's broke into the lounge to have a quick smoke, coffee or whatever they'd prepared for lunch. Howell, Banks, Jones and Willard, were just finishing their rounds around the facility, when Carlos and Tacoma Red strolled into the smoky room.

"What's up fellas?" Carlos tossed.

"Hey Cee," Banks returned, and then stood up to leave. He had to get back to the East Wing, his post for the night, rather than the entire quarter.

"Ain't sheeit, bout to warm some links up before breaks over. Y'all heard about the new dude that got sliced up? Dude worked with La'Creatia too," Carlos said, his voice somber and weak.

Willard was the first to speak up. "No doubt, I heard about dat crazy shit on the news through Late Night with Laura. So ole' boy worked with the wifey?" Willard mused with wide eyes.

"Hell yeah, I just found out. You know what's really strange bout dis shit – she's killing all white men, so you and Jones betta be on high…fuckin'…alert." Carlos clowned. He and Tacoma laughed as if their stomachs would flip out.

What stopped them from laughing was the sound of the large commercial microwave beeping loudly. For some reason Carlos didn't feel hungry anymore knowing there was a wild crazed woman at large slicing white men's penis off and leaving them for dead, so he and Tacoma raided the vending machine instead.

"Hey," Howell called out just before they broke sight. "What about your links CJ?"

"Y'all can split 'um, just clean and return my damn bowl, greedy." Carlos said, before he and Tacoma walked out the door.

"Kool…" He replied, and the three of them ravished the thick pale sausages like they'd never eaten before.

"Damn, these links are good! Tough…But good" Willard boasted, shamelessly devouring his and Banks' share.

"Dey got a funny taste and smell to 'em. And why so many damn veins?" Howell questioned vaguely remembering that he had a tough time with his first bite. "And why's yours bigger than mine, Willard?"

"Shut up and eat it dummy," Jones added, a piece of kraut dangling from his thick beard, as he spoke.

"Sheeit…What if it's a dick, Howell?" Willard shot. "You know one of those that's been severed by ole' girl, 'The Lady Killa'?" He teased, paused for a brief moment as the room became as still as air; each one in their own thoughts – then seconds later they all erupted in laughter.

"You's a sick son-of-a-bitch, you know that Willard!" Howell said.

Chapter Four

Betrayed, Too Close to Home

Although it was Happy Hour at the Sisson Street Tavern Bar & Grill, the night was as young as a virgin's innocence. The establishment was at room temperature, packed even for a Thursday night with men and women clad in their work attire anxious for relaxation. Cold chug-a-lugs lined the glass-stained bar filled with various brands of beer. Next to them, were baskets of fresh fries, dipped in their special house batter; beer of course. But it was the beauty of one sexy lady with glassy light brown eyes and auburn colored hair that flowed freely passed her broad shoulders that magnetized every man in passing.

She'd been occupying her position at the bar for the past forty-five minutes and had easily turned down offers from six different men. Even with the pleasant smile she courted them away with, the bartender saw different. Maybe it was her intriguing pink, off-white albino colored skin that attracted a crowd of men like ants to crumbs or the way she twirled the straw around her glass with her teeth that made them desire her. Whatever it was Ralph, the nightshift bartender, didn't like her.

"Can I please have another apple martini?" The woman asked politely, as Ralph began wiping down the bar area where she'd been loafing since entering.

He gave her a stern, but friendly smile, and then said, "Sure lady, coming right up."

He quickly returned with her order, and a fresh basket of house fries but not before a gentlemen who looked to be in his mid-thirties grabbed the seat next to her and engaged in some pretty sensual small talk from what Ralph could discern.

The gentleman was also gracious enough to pay for her drink. He placed a wrinkled twenty onto the dark wood slab and said to keep them coming.

One hour turned into two, and then three, and before you knew it, it was closing time when the two of them stumbled out of the Tavern. As they were just out of the front door, the woman glanced over her shoulder and licked her tongue seductively, then winked at Ralph. He simply shook his head, and continued his clean-up.

The two were now in the parking lot of the Tavern trying to decide where their night would end, and surprisingly she chose her home, but quickly remembered her other half was there. So she followed her new friend to his crib on the South End of Hartford.

The police had been combing the city day and night searching door-to-door for any clues as to who had been splicing the male organs off Hartford's male citizens between the ages of 18 to 42 years old. Up to now, they had not one clue except for a young couple that had been out late pumping gas at a Texaco Service Station. The couple heard a man yelling from the rear of his sedan like he was in pain, and then witnessed a light colored woman with a red ponytail poke her head-up, then lower it back down as if she were performing a sexual act. They later learned the man had been murdered and stripped of his manhood. The next night the same couple returned to the service station and they noticed the same woman, this time dressed in black, and wearing a long blond wig. They reported it, but when called on to give a brief, but composite sketch of the woman in question, they couldn't be found.

So all the authorities, news broadcaster and journalist had to go on was that this woman was about 5"7', light in complexion, possibly a Caucasian and wore a variety of different colored wigs, not to mention she was strikingly beautiful. This sketch was now ready to hit every news channel, local gas station and store front, even small billboards running alongside Hartford's many bridges and under passes.

"Hey, can you grab me another brewski while you're up Banks," Carlos asked. He and the boys had the night off, all except Jones. He'd used up all his comp time, so his new days wouldn't kick in until the next quarter, so they all thought. Carlos and the rest of the boys decided to have a couple beers at his home while watching the game.

"I gotchu," Banks replied, keeping his stride into their kitchen. Before La'Creatia had left to go out for a few drinks with Shauny, her BFF, she'd prepared a nice size portion of kielbasa, wild rice and stewed vegetables, Carlos' favorite; which seemed to be his buddies as well. They couldn't eat the sliced beef sausages fast enough.

"Yo, Tacoma, pass the smoke partner," Carlos said. Tacoma had a habit of hoggin' up the weed, only to pass it when it was nearly ashes.

He pulled deeply twice, and then passed the blunt off, "Here," said Tacoma, his eyes stained menstrual red.
"Sheeit...You might as well roll-up another one, this shit here is about to burn out!" Carlos said.
"My pleasure," Tacoma fired back, and began splitting a Dutch Master.
"Aye CJ, you think you can get the wifey to make a huge batch of this to take home for the freezer? Dis shit is good-as-fuck!" Howell claimed, scrapping his plate.
"Sheeit, that goes for me too," Willard added.
"I'll see," CJ answered as he blew out several rings of smoke. "Might cost you guys a bit, but I'll definitely holla."

Simultaneously, both vehicles pulled into the narrow driveway of Midget's home. Midget was a nickname for Marlin Jones. He wasn't too short, but his frame made him carry his body strangely. Midget wasted no time locking his car doors, then ushered his friend inside. Once inside, Midget admired her sculptured temple and began to salivate at the mouth, as always.
"Stop drooling and come get this pussy Jones!" She demanded with a guiding finger. He again wasted little time undressing himself bareback, then racing over to where she stood. Now directly in front of her, he began fondling her goodies. "Slow down, give me a kiss sexy," she requested. "You're gonna treasure this one."
They kissed briefly and when Jones went to suck in the saliva he formed in his mouth, he tasted blood, his own. Somehow during their intimacy, he'd been cut, but it didn't deter his sexual cravings and lusts. He did notice that

something sharp had nipped his tongue while kissing her, but his libido was rising and he needed to fuck.

"So Jones, let me ask you something."

"Shoot," he said licking the nape of her neck.

"You think your boy would trip out if he knew you'd been bangin' his wife on your days off?"

"Yeah! But who cares at this point. You ready to suck this dick?" He pulled his wood up, caressing the head slowly.

"As ever as I'll ever be, Jonzy," she smiled seductively.

Midget enjoyed what pleasure he could from the fellatio act he was receiving, up until he felt his staff being gnawed at, and then pulled away with ease. He screamed in dire pain. He went to feel for his little man, and felt nothing but flesh and blood. He fell to the floor, now drenched in a pool of his own serum and cried out sorrowfully, "Ahhh...You fuckin' bitch! I'll kill you!" He yelled loudly, and then attempted to say something else. "You're the, 'Lady Kil'..."

"Yes..." She finished, and then drove a steak knife into his chest. Afterwards, she spit the home made razor mouthpiece, into a plastic bag along with some ragged pieces of Midget's penis. The only thing for her to clean up was knee prints – she'd never touched anything in Jones' place that night.

Chapter Five

One Crazy Ass Night

$\mathcal{U}$p until this very moment, no one, not even Carlos' best friend from work, Tacoma Red, had actually seen La'Creatia up close and personal. They'd heard on numerous occasions how stunning and sexy she was, and easily resembled an exotic model from overseas, but to actually get a face-to-face was something similar to shaking Obama's right hand.

It was a little past the hour of 2 a.m. when La'Creatia casually strutted through the solid wood door, lugging what appeared to be a briefcase of some sort. Everyone was sort of star struck seeing the beauty held within Carlos' other half, and smiled in fascination. "Oh...Hey fellas, I thought you guys would have been gone by now," she asserted, surveying the room.

"Hey boo, they were just leaving," Carlos replied, staring at her strangely. "Weren't you fellas?" He said louder than needed seeing they were still staring at his wife.

"No need, I'm just gonna shower and finish up this storyboard for a girl at work, then I'll join you upstairs honey," she smiled devilishly. "Bye fellas..." The words echoed as she sashayed through the room.

All eyes were glued on La'Creatia's rear as she strolled past them, which Carlos hadn't paid to close attention too, seeing he was trained on the trail of water droplets that shadowed her every step. What the fuck is leaking from your case ma? He wondered silently. He was still woozy from the liquor and hash they'd been smoking, so he wasn't too sure he could rely on his eyes solely. So he quickly got on all fours and traced her steps all the while examining the droplets with the tips of his fingers.

"Man what da fuck is wrong with this fool!" Banks the loudest and the most boisterous one of the bunch barked.

"Dude done lost it, for real. Get up Craig," Howell joked, trying to impersonate the father from the movie Friday.

Carlos suddenly snapped out of whatever trance they assumed he had been stuck in. He stood up still clenching his fingers together now sure that there was indeed H2O lining his hardwood floors. "I'm cool chump. Dropped my contact," he said in response to their comments.

"Yeah right!" Willard spoke. "C'mon fellas, I think we need to get moving, it's pretty late and wifey seemed a bit horny if you ask me."

"Shut the fuck up smart ass!" Carlos yelled out. They couldn't decipher if he took Willard's remark offensively or not, so they all stood up gathered what belongings they'd brought and walked to the door.

"See you at work tomorrow?" Tacoma asked.

"Yeah, no doubt champ. Oh, and I didn't forget about the food request either."

"Preciate you, those links was on point!"

"Yeah, yeah. I'll holla now get out!" Carlos frowned playfully, slamming the door behind them.

The house grew quiet. Nothing could be heard except the moaning of the beloved winds tugging the gutters and storm boards around the house. Outside La'Creatia's and

Carlos' home, Howell questioned Banks and Willard to the fact if they noticed CJ's wife was an Albino.

"Whatever that woman is…She's drop dead gorgeous. I'm talking straight out the magazine fine," Banks said as they rode off.

Carlos' company had vanished, leaving him sole clean-up duties which he had to suck up. He placed all of the dishes into the dishwasher, and then wiped down all of the glass surfaces with some 409 and a dry cloth. Next, he wrapped the cords of the PS3 joysticks, placed them back into the entertainment center along with each game. The console itself stayed out for DVD use, so there was nothing left to do except fall back and enjoy the piece they all neglected to burn when La'Creatia interrupted their night. Carlos retrieved the blunt from the ashtray then sparked it up. The blunt became a fiery-orange glow stick as Carlos puffed intensely through the other end. He inhaled deep and long until he felt his lungs couldn't reserve anymore. Then after maybe 10 seconds of withholding the extreme pressure, he blew out an enormous cloud of white smoke. His eye's doubled over with glaze. They shined with a sparkle of reflection releasing a fence of tears as he tried to fight the blinks. He hit the blunt again, and then thought he'd check on the Mrs. because now he was feeling frisky and ready to fuck. He pulled off all his clothes, leaving them on the floor.

After swigging the last of his Cognac, he travelled stark naked, blunt in hand through the house and down the basement stairs. He stood at his wife's craft room door listening for voices, but only heard the softness of hers, but whom was she talking to when she requested that he fuck her harder?

"What the fuck?" he thought. "Fuck is she doing in there?" He wondered silently, then pushed the door open slightly so he could get a good look inside, which he'd forever regret for the rest of his eternal days on earth.

When Carlos glanced through the small slit in the door; he saw his wife plunging a long dick into her rectum, while she held another in her hand that she used to rub against her oiled chest. What really threw him was how she stuck the one she had in her ass into a medium size Igloo cooler before grabbing a fresh one out and deep throating it. After a few deep long strokes, she then inserted the stiff cock into her pussy. "Ohhh..." she moaned, the tip of the ice-berg was when she began beating and smacking herself across the face with the other dick she held in her hand.

"Dis bitch is fuckin' loony for real," he whispered, only his erection grew larger as he eavesdropped on his wife. As he continued to watch her dance around with a variation of color and different size dicks, he jerked himself into a lasting nut. "Ahhh..." He uttered, shooting semen onto the door; it slowly dripping downward onto the floor.

After his enjoyment was complete, he felt strange about what he'd done and saw, and tried to creep off, but she heard the faint steps as he crept away. La'Creatia rushed over to the door and pushed it open.

"Now that's a naughty boy, CJ," she said noticing the puddle of sperm under her feet. She kneeled down then dipped her finger in the slick liquid. "Very naughty," she giggled. She rubbed the remainder of it over her clit, then chest and went back to play.   It was nights like this, La'Creatia loved to fuck. A half an hour later, she made her way upstairs where she found Carlos sound asleep and fully dressed, obviously frightened from what he had witnessed earlier.

Chapter Six
A Waste of Time

When La'Creatia woke the next morning she rolled over to find her husband gone. She smiled brightly knowing he was shook from the show she'd given him just hours before. What she didn't know was what he'd actually seen and how much. So now she'd have to play this by ear. She in no way felt threatened by Carlos' findings, because love would cost him his life if he became a problem, she swore to it.

After a fifteen minute phone conversation with her two kids, Shelly and Shavon, she drifted into a deep comatose sleep.

La'Creatia might've thought her husband was long gone, but unbeknownst to her he was right under her nose and creeping around in her craft room searching for anything out of the ordinary.

He made it through the locked door with ease, seeing as he'd used her key. Now in the abyss of her private sanctuary, he began rummaging through any and everything.

When Carlos glanced at his Chrono Swiss watch, he realized he'd been in La'Creatia's dungeon for over twenty-five minutes and hadn't noticed a thing, so he slowly retraced his steps making his way up the basement staircase.

Once Carlos made it to the top of the steep landing he was met by his wife's naked body. Now startled and shook, he tried to conceal the obvious.

"Hey babes, you're up pretty early." She spoke calmly, her eye's trained on his hands.

"Oh morning pooh. I was just downstairs looking for that pack of new shimmies I brought last year. I think I'll wash the van today," he fired quickly, but with a sense of nervousness in his tone.

"Well I see you couldn't find it," she nodded towards his empty grasp with a cunning smile.

"Naw, I didn't. I'll just stop at Auto Zone and buy some new ones on my way out. So what's gotten you up so early?" He questioned. His head was still throbbing from all the liquor and weed the night before. He still wasn't quite sure if what he'd witnessed was real or a dream, which is why he'd rushed out of bed to search La'Creatia's craft room before she'd awakened.

"Oh nothing…Just rolled over and noticed you were gone. Thought maybe you were preparing breakfast in bed, then a little morning sex." She answered rubbing her right breast.

"Creatia, you know there's nothing in this damn fridge but sausage links, so what am I to cook? Which reminds me, the fellas love your kielbasa put down and wonder if you can whip up enough to send them off with. Do you have enough links, or should I hit the deli?"

La'Creatia smiled candidly at her husband's request, she thought it to be extremely hilarious, but said, "No babes, I've got enough for all of them. They can come and pick it up tonight. I was only working a half shift today. Now as to your question about what to eat, you can have this…"She cooed, then stepped back into the kitchen and climbed up on the breakfast nook, spread her thick legs and parted her pussy lips.

Carlos was stunned, but rose to the occasion quickly. He viewed the way her clitoris stood out openly in the thickness of her diamond, shining brightly with the reflection from her piercing and juices. He moved in between her thighs and got on his knees as if he were proposing for marriage and attacked her insides feverously.

"Yes baby, lick this pussy. Yes, CJ, Yes!" Her voice echoed with lust. Her insides soon to overflow with pearl lava. He continued to savage her womb with fast, swift strokes across her clit then inside her cave plunging his tongue deep within. She moaned grabbing onto his head, then ears for dear life chanting out obscenities. The pleasure was monstrous. "Fuck!" She exploded into his mouth, pulling his face nearly into the depths of her erupting volcano. "Oh baby put it in please!" She further begged.

After stepping out of his cut-off sweats, he never took the time to moisten the head of his dick and drove his wedge deep into her awaiting pussy. "Ahhh," he bit his own lip. Her pussy was wet, but snug, just the way he remembered it. After a few strokes it seemed to expand beyond his girth which he never knew it could do.

He sped up his thrusts pounding away like a jack hammer in a cement block. Her secretions dripping down his legs like running water. He could hear the squishing sound their organs made as he traveled in and out of her soaked container, then he slipped out as if he were too small to float in her ravine, which caused him some physiological issues.

"C'mon baby, hit it harder!" She demanded biting her nipples harder. "Fuck me nigga!"

He pulled her by the waist locking his grip in addition to gyrating his hips wildly. Now feeling like he'd gotten back in the race, he stroked and stroked, until he nutted inside her.

He collapsed onto her sweaty chest heaving in and out, then took turns biting both of her nipples. "Damn honey, you wore me out," he whispered his breathing slow and labored.

"Sheeit, you did all the work babes. Now lemme taste that dick," she said pushing him away with force.

Carlos didn't know where he'd gotten the added strength to go the extra mile needed to cum in his wife's mouth, but he did and was satisfied that he'd put the mack-game down superbly for a change. Only thing is La'Creatia was far from over. "Put it in my ass now!" She ordered, but he was too limp to even think about sex.

"Baby, gimme 'bout twenty minutes," he looked her dead in the face.

"You've got to be kidding me!" Was her reply. "See…This is why bitches, not me, cheat! Because you sorry ass nigga's can only fuck long enough to get your one little nut off then it's a wrap. You need help CJ, cause I'm not going to keep stuffing dildo's in every hole I got because you can't satisfy me properly," she yelled and walked off leaving him looking and feeling stupid and inadequate as a man.

As La'Creatia stormed off, Carlos' mind clicked back to when he saw his wife with some dicks in each hand fondling, talking and placing them in every hole she was birthed with just as she'd said. He was a complete mess, totally flabbergasted at the things she so unthoughtfully barked at him. His ego was bruised and his manhood tainted. He then grabbed his rod and massaged it carefully trying to get it to harden, but there was no use, he was dead.

Moments later, he crawled into bed beside his wife and tried to cuddle with her from behind only to receive a stiff blow to his mid-section. "If you're not hard and ready to ass-fuck me, get the fuck off!" she concluded and fell asleep, content.

"Bitch!" He mumbled.

Chapter Seven
One More for the Cemetery

Days later, after missing several unreported shifts, the Lieutenant at the Detention Center inquired about Officer Jones' whereabouts. He questioned everyone at work especially Johnson and Babbs. They informed him that they hadn't seen Jones since last week, the previous Wednesday that they had all worked. So he called the authorities and requested that a patrol car be sent by his place. This is normal procedure when an employee is absent without cause.

Officer Fallen and Officer Dickey responded to the call and arrived at Jones' apartment. They checked the windows for movement, and the doors to see if they were unlocked, which they weren't. One of the patrolmen radioed into dispatch that everything looked clear, that there seemed to be no hint of foul play, so they were cleared to leave.

"Excuse me officers," a little old woman called out softly. Her cry was almost too low and withered to hear. "Excuse me," she yelled again and Officer Fallen, the lagging officer, turned around quickly now caught by the old woman's glare.

"Hello ma'am, may we help you with something? Is everything okay?" Fallen's softer side appeared. A side much smoother than the arrogant, street side he showed around the city throughout his tour.

"I'm quite all right young man thank you, but I noticed that you handsome fellas were checking in on that nice security guard for the young boys' over at the Broad Street Detention Center."

"Yes we were," Fallen continued, "have you heard or seen him lately?" He asked as he peered into the elderly woman's eyes closely.

"Not in a couple of days, which is not like him? I usually hear him go out between 11 & 11:25 for work, and returns around 8:00 a.m., but he hasn't been out to even collect his mail from the front box for a few days. Do you think he's okay?" Her aging crow's feet crinkled as she spoke.

"And what is your name ma'am?" Fallen's partner finally spoke.

"Oh...Silly me. Everyone knows who I am, but, you two sweet boys. It's Ms. Scholtz, but you can all me Pam," she smiled, her top teeth missing.

"Thank you Ms. Scholtz," he shot her a warming smile.

She quickly cut the officer off, "I said to call me Pam. All the neighbors and officers call me, Pam!" Her voice now cracked in slight agitation and disrespect from the young patrol man.

Fallen had to turn his head in order to halt the uncontrolled burst of laughter that was sure to spray the petite woman smack dead in her kisser.

"Sorry Pam," he apologized, but his small frown hid nothing short of his anger and embarrassment. "Do you know where we could locate the property manager?" He probed solemnly, slightly upset.

"Yes, but Tim, the owner, is off with one of his many tramps in Hawaii, being a freak. But...." She paused and dug into her flannel gown that had more color than a kaleidoscope, and retrieved a small ring of golden keys.

Both cops studied each other for a brief moment, and then Fallen spoke up. "Pam, I take it Tim left you in control of his property while he's away." He said as a statement, more than posing a question.

"Why yes, handsome. And if you like, I'd be very happy to open the apartment belonging to Jones for you." She again flashed her topless row and Fallen broke, he chuckled innocently.

"What's so funny young man?" Her gums were now exposed.

"Oh nothing, would you please show us inside?" He replied, his face still fixed with laughter.

"Humph…"She sighed. "You're not so cute anymore mister! But follow me." She swung her linty gown inward, sucked her teeth, the bottom one's of course, and stepped to Jones' door. She jingled the keys for a moment until she found the one labeled #121, she stuck the small key into the lock, and then stepped aside. "All yours humph!"

With a semi-serious face, Fallen ordered Pam to step back a little more, opened the door and immediately smelled the familiar stench of death. "This is a police matter now ma'am. I'm afraid I'm going to have to ask you to step back into your apartment and please refrain from exiting until further notice." Fallen ordered his voice now active and full of policy statement, going strictly by the book.

Now inside, the fumes from Jones' decomposed body began to burn the tiny hairs that lined the inside of both their noses. They quickly yanked out handkerchiefs from their pockets and covered their mouths and noses. Fallen went one way, while Dickey, his partner, fished the opposite way. Both were in search of a body they knew they were destined to find.

Fallen's search resulted in nothing but drug paraphernalia. It was Dickey's hunt that stumbled across Jones' horrendous corpse, now overcome by maggots; a dead body's secret lover. If it wasn't for the large bath towel that lined the gaping hole between the floor and the pastel yellow bath door, he might've never looked down in passing the bathroom door. Between the heavy scent of death and the Glad Plug-In's that were placed throughout the place, Dickey could no longer contain his lunch.

By the time Fallen reached Dickey, he was kneeling over staring into a pool of his own vomit. "So I see you've found our missing person," Fallen pinched his nose as he called dispatch exiting back out to the fresh air of the cool hallway at the same time.

Meanwhile on the other side of town, downtown to be exact, Shauny, La'Creatia and Carlos, were perched in a large booth at the Sports Bar & Grille across from the city's local train depot. They all happened to share the same day off this week. Shauny needed a drink and also a chance to hunt some fresh dick, so she invited La'Creatia, who in turn, insisted that Carlos tag along. He only agreed because he felt it could help their relationship out some, and God only knew he needed it.

Ever since the day she elbowed him, things had been on a rocky slate. Arguments over silly things had substituted quiet cuddly nights. An elbow here and there, replaced soft hugs and kisses, and "Fuck you CJ" was now commonly used instead of, "I Love You'".

It was March Madness, and everyone's attention was focused on the University of Connecticut's men's game. Their tables were plastered with all sorts and style of wings, cheese sticks, sandwiches and pitchers of beer. There was also some downed shots of Cognac. They chose bar seats which was much closer to the large 100' wall screen that showcased the game in HD.

"Okay UConn!" Shauny boasted, as her team advanced to the playoffs. "Yes..." She nearly tipped her tray of wings over as she jumped out of her seat.

"Yeah, they got to see Butler now," Creatia added, as if she'd known a thing or two about college ball. They both looked at her in shock, her outburst really shook them.

"I thought you didn't care for college ball, Ms. Kobe Bryant!" Carlos teased, all up in her face.

"Yeah, yeah, there's a lot you two don't know about me, hump..." She returned, and sipped her Naked Lady.

"You're right," Carlos eyed her suspiciously. Just then the bartender used the large universal remote to surf through the satellite stations. Not too long after that he freeze-framed the channel on the 'Eyewitness News' logo and the room seemed to quiet in unison.

"Shut up and look, there's been another killing. The 'Lady Killer' struck again," someone in the large establishment shouted loud enough for everyone to hear. All eyes were glued to the plasma, which showcased a lofty brick building taped off with the mustard colored tape labeled, crime scene.

You could clearly see various men and women scurrying about the vicinity in which the alleged crime took place. Everyone knew once they'd seen two persons bearing blue lab jackets with 'Coroner' in blocked white decals, someone had indeed bit the bullet. Who, was the million-dollar question? The two techs hoisted the metal gurney that secured the deceased now strapped and enclosed in a black bag. They rode off hastily with the wagons lights spinning and flashing. It was then that the mouthwatering report was delivered to the public.

"Here we are again, me, you, the citizens surrounding what some call, 'Homicide Hartford', and others the 'Constitution State', on the scene of yet another gruesome murder at the hands of a malicious killer. The police are working this one as what we all know to be attributed to the 'Lady Killer'. Citizens, what the authorities have allowed me to reiterate as helpful information to you, is that our killer has changed her preferences, meaning it's not just Caucasian males she's attacking anymore. This victim just happens to be a middle-aged African-American whom was identified as an employee of the Juvenile Detention Center, just a few blocks away on Broad Street. I'd also like to add that there are minimal clues, one being our killer hunts at night, possibly starting in our local bars and wears various styles and colors of hair pieces. If anyone has any information that could possibly lead authorities to our killer, a substantial reward will be granted.

Please contact the Homicide Division at the Hartford Police Headquarters, on Jennings Road (860) 555-6000."

"Hey...Isn't that your buddies crib?" La'Creatia's hand rested on her husband's knee as she spoke. She'd been in the car one night with Carlos when he had to drop him off, being that Jones' lousy car had broken down on him.

Carlos was stuck in another world since the beginning of the broadcast. He'd caught on to the building immediately, but was praying Jones' absence had nothing to do with the breaking news.

He felt crushed. A thousand things travelled through him, orbiting around his mind like a shuttle in space. He was so far and high in altitude, that he hadn't heard his wife's question, or noticed her hand was pinching his thick skin.

"CJ!" She stood and jumped into his line of sight, breaking his trance. "Hell—lo...," she boomed.

"What? What is it?" His body jumped and caused her to fly back into her seat. Some of the nearby patrons were being drawn to her sudden reaction.

"Yeah, yeah, I'm cool. I'm sorry babe, but you startled me. What were you saying?"

"Never mind, let's go!" She evil-eyed him, stood up and dragged her Fendi duffle as she stormed out the door.

"What was that all about, CJ?" Shauny probed.

"Not sure, but..." He paused because there was still the fact that somehow his buddy had become victim to the 'Lady Killer', and it fucked him up. "I'm not sure," he said.

Once they reached outside, they found La'Creatia visibly upset and shaken smoking on a Newport. Now in front of her, Shauny noticed her hands trembled, and her right leg wouldn't stop twitching. Shauny was scared for her BFF and asked Carlos to do something with the hopes of calming her down.

Many of the bar patrons began to exit the place. As they strode by, they gawked and whispered. They saw that La'Creatia was going through a spell as she shook and tapped her foot against the grey concrete, smoke billowing around her.

"C'mon, keep walking honey," one nerdy white fella suggested to his wife. She's either having some sort of seizure or hoping for another hit of some sort of drug."

"Dat's right fag...Keep it moving, before I fuck one of you up" La'Creatia suddenly snapped back to reality as she threatened the scrawny man.

"Creatia!" Carlos called out embarrassed. "What's gotten into you?" He addressed her, unsure of La'Creatia's bewildered state.

"Can we just get the hell out of here?" She flicked the burning cigarette in the couple's direction glaring menacingly at their backs as they walked off.

"Yeah CJ, let's just bounce," Shauny added in her ghetto fashion, pulling La'Creatia towards the car. "For we fuck some shit up!"

Once in the comfort of CJ's 300C, La'Creatia said, "and what I said was...Wasn't that your friend's crib on the news."

Carlos looked at her with a very confused stare, but what really threw him was the fact that she even knew Jones' place of rest. He slowly pulled out of his parking space and into traffic, then it hit him. He actually remembered how she could know such info about his buddy. "Yes it is babe, sorry about earlier. I guess the sudden news fucked me up," he said, and rubbed her knee softly as they drove away.

Chapter Eight
Reminisce

*A*fter dropping Shauny off at her place, La'Creatia and Carlos rode home in utter silence, both completely doomed in their own thoughts. La'Creatia's head leaned up against the Chrysler's window, her knee's knotted. Carlos went to steal a quick glance at his wifey and didn't see the nearing pothole promising to corrupt the smooth ride.

Booommm! The 300C's front end hit hard, Creatia's head tapped the thick glass with a loud thud. "Jesus Christ CJ!" She barked extremely loud, her voice full of venomous poison, as her normal embracing eyes shot menacing daggers his way.

"Sorry sweetie. I never saw the pothole," he said with hopes that she'd accept his humble apology. "You all right, though?"

"Fuck no, duh…" She spat. "I just banged by fucking head!" She was holding the sore spot.

He couldn't believe his beautiful wife sometimes, it was like she had several different passports with different lives which were triggered by a deep-rooted anger and also being deprived of sexual intercourse. Crazy, he thought. "You're over reacting as usual, Cree," he reasoned.

"Yeah whatever," she snapped. "Just get me home."

"Gladly," he mumbled in privacy, only she'd heard every crossing breath.

"Oh, this muthafucka thinks he's got all the damn sense these days," La'Creatia thought, still feeling the after effects of her sudden trauma. Strangely though, it brought her to a place and time when she was a little girl.

It was around the years '91 and '93, she couldn't really compute, but she'd definitely been in Junior High at Quirk Middle School, a rookie, not to mention one of the prettiest specimens walking the dense corridors between both grades. School had only been in session a few months, maybe the ending of the first marking period. Her grades were on a scholastic level, she was honor roll bound for sure. A's & B's in the high stats and very much a pleasure to have as a student, all her teachers thought. It was some of the envious females who'd begun to feel threatened by her suave, good-natured aura that enticed everyone who came in contact with her. Not to mention the captive hold her alluring, devil-green eyes held on most of the boys as well as the girls.

La'Creatia was an excellent swimmer, sort of like an aquanaut, only she didn't reside under water. She quickly became the captain of her swim team after her coach saw the way she handled the pooling waters. This drew even more attention to La'Creatia's status throughout the academic quadrangle, drawing a pivotal axis of hate directly towards her.

One day after a swim meet against Fox Middle, off of Albany Avenue, some of the girls were changing out, lathering away the filmy stench of chlorine from their adolescent bodies. She was very secure about her growth, plus Mother Nature had done her great justice to say the least. She was completely lathered in an apricot body wash and her eyes sealed shut shielded from the stinging suds, so she never saw or heard when her attackers snuck inside the shower room until it was an instant too late. Then she felt several different hands over her dearest pleasures.

"What the hell!" She yelled furiously. "I said STOP!" She further insisted, her voice a cross between anger and fear.

"Shut it up, Ms. Goodie-two-shoes," one of her assailants shot back. "You're going to enjoy this white girl."

"Fuck you!" Creatia said. "Stop! Stop it," she said tussling for freedom to no avail. She then began to cry and scream loudly, but all of the showers had been turned up all the way and the hot water drawing a dense fog throughout the room. Then everything went blank, but just before she crossed over into unconsciousness, she muttered, "No please no, not again. God, please no!" La'Creatia woke up maybe thirty to forty minutes later feeling spent, extremely sore in the southern region of her body with both of her orifices bleeding profusely. Struggling to her feet, La'Creatia tried her best to rinse away the grime she felt inside her vaginal womb. She'd most likely have to defecate loose whatever was lodged up inside her rectum. Boy, did her ass and pussy hurt, she thought, as she stumbled into the near empty dressing room naked.

When she finally got to her locker, the last two girls stared at her with a blink of sadness because they'd heard her cries. Her attempts to call for a savior; but being unpopular around school and terrified to death of the 'D-Squad' who'd warned everyone to-fall-da-fuck-back while they handled their business, kept them still as statues. Even so, they'd stayed behind. Funny thing was, they'd also been violated and raped by the 'D-Squad' not weeks ago, so they just had to make sure she was all right, but that would be as far as it would go – nothing more, nothing less. "Are you okay?" One of them questioned somberly.

"Why didn't you help me? You guys let them rape me? You two just stood out here and listened to me scream, holler, beg and cry…While whoever had their way with me?" Said Creatia in a very tearful voice. "Never mind," she said, "but to answer your dumb-ass question, no I'm not all right. But I will be! I promise!" Those were the last words they heard her speak also the last time they would ever see the likes of her again.

La'Creatia never reported the rape to the school officials, to the authorities nor to her parents in fear that they wouldn't believe her. They never did, not even when it happened as a young girl, so what would make this any different. That day after school she just went home, bathed for what seemed like an eternity and cried herself to sleep. The following morning, she begged her mother to let her go and live in Albany, NY with her granny, which after several phone calls became a reality. Within two weeks, La'Creatia was enrolled in a good school and back to her norm, only her norm now consisted of vengeful thoughts towards those who'd wronged her. She'd been dramatically scarred and the childhood blemish had taken a meandering effect on her everyday life.

Either way, a lot of people even if falsely accused or randomly selected had to suffer for years of regressive vendettas, it was just the way the ball bounces.

While Carlos parked the car, his wife stormed out of the car letting the heavy door slam hard with a loud thug. He shot an insane, vulgar curse word at her back as her head became smaller and smaller with each step.

"Yeah…This bitch has gone straight, Tweety-Bird, Loony Tunes for real."

Chapter Nine
Double the Pleasure

The city had become a grievous bed of roses, a deplorable happiness. The medical examiner's office was flushed with countless corpses with only one explanation for the Homicide detectives assigned to the heinous murders, as the many funeral homes gained an all- time high percentage in business for the year. You'd think that with all the new arrivals of gangs and drug related murders in the capital that the numbers would be more elevated, but that wasn't the case one bit. The 'Lady Killa' had emerged. Yet invisible, in a class above all, she had been undoubtedly crowned one of Hartford's most feared women they've ever encountered.

Vital information and warnings in adherence to the city's safety had been reeled off over numerous broadcasting elements, The Harford Courant, local satellite radio, in addition to vigilant marches in an around most of the areas where the atrocities had transpired. But even in the light of this latest darkness fear hadn't kept the night owls from hooting and howling in the raunchy cabarets. The lights were in a dim glow. Music blared crushingly with every beat, symbolic to a symphony of out of control drummers, violinists, and trumpet masters coupled for one last impromptu. There were shirtless men galloping after shirtless women. Some wore glow-in-the-dark rings around their necks, a good depiction of the walking dead, basically zombies stoned on prescription pills and booze. But the most intriguing acts that took place throughout 'FREEDOM', the cities raunchiest nightclub, was the wide open sex. Sex was very exclusive in this dive. Any and every one at some point and time engaged in some sort of sexual act from the monogamous couple, to trading saliva, to the two Asian kittens bumping and grinding rhythmically to the funky-tempo, to the two males who swung around like two lily-feathered lovers in ninety degree heat rock hard, and all smiles. But the tip of the iceberg was the ménage 'a trios that was in full stride.

"Damn!" A passerby thought as he stared in lustful awe while two extremely beautiful women handled a six-foot man like he was a blown up doll. His shirt and slacks had been tossed to the ground beside him, where he now only had a pair of flannel briefs covering his personals. "How can I get in on that?" The stranger pondered. He just knew his eyes were deceiving him that is until the lighter one dropped to her knees and took him into her waiting mouth as her friend tongued him down feverously. They did this until each one got their fair share of Vitamin E, then the trio eased away. "Woooow!" He shook his head in disbelief, but he had seen far worse, just never a two-on-one.

The trio decided to take the party home, rather to a telly, he paid of course. It was a cheap dive in East Hartford on Main Street, run by some Indians. Inside, the shoddy room reeked of low budget cigarette smoke, Sunlight detergent and sex, but they'd just come to add to the smoldering odor, so they didn't mind. There'd be more than enough for the house maid to clean up come checkout time tomorrow.

Things jumped off almost instantly only at the present moment the fight was fair, a straight one-on-one. While Lavish, the less attractive of the two felines squared off in naked erotica, Sexy was using the bathroom. They heard the toilet flush and the water ran gushingly out of the rusted colored spout. Scott was too busy to even begin to question what the one he truly desired was held up doing in the bathroom because the intensity Lavish was sending his way was overwhelming. "Damn ma", he lowly uttered out, "you really know how to work your hand," he quipped, thinking he'd said something phenomenal or flattering of her craft.

"You haven't seen nothing yet, sweetie," Lavish remarked, and sped up the elevator ride on Scott's manhood. "Just lay back and enjoy yourself, boo. You're headed for an unforgettable trip to paradise," she smiled wickedly as he slumped onto the unpleasant, thinning mattress.

"Well after the club and this, I don't see it getting any better lovely," Scott snorted, feeling close to a nut, his eyes tightly shut anticipating his rising bliss.

Scott was so spent off Lavish's hand job, he hadn't noticed the loudness of the sink water turnoff, nor Sexy standing over him. "Damn…", thought Sexy as she stared at the Lego-block before her. Yeah she'd just swallowed every inch of him, but for some reason he hadn't grown that big, maybe he had been too frank and reserved to openly engage in the act, she considered. "Poor baby was a little skittish," she smirked, but she was remotely turned on, thus feeling the need to get her some.

Lavish watched as Sexy hiked her leather thigh high skirt up to her petite waistline and yanked her thong to the side; the nipple of her privacy glistening with sweat. Lavish continued to jerk Scott vigorously while she fingered Sexy briefly. Sexy gave her a succulent caress on the lips and let her body slide down Scott's throbbing pole. She let out a pleasurable sigh, grinding fast and hard on his lap. At this point, Jonas opened his shutters realizing it was the woman he'd desired since he'd stepped inside the telly. "You feel good, ma'." He praised, thrusting his body upward which drove his wedge deeper upstream.

"Just don't come in me, baby...Ooh, ooh, oooh," she cooed. With the friction from the arm like a plunger struck in her drainage, in addition to Lavish feasting on either nipple, she was seconds away from an explosive climax. "Oh, fuck...This dick is the bomb!"

Hearing this, Scott gripped her thin waist and pulled her strongly with every thrust, the crown of his scepter promising a pleasurable rendezvous with each other's pasteurized milk. Just when Sexy went to tell Scott to let her know when she should hop off, he pulled her violently into his pelvis, drove himself into the VIP section of her depot and bullet trained a stream of protein deep inside her. "Ahhh...," he yelled in mid-flow, his grunt showcasing satisfaction.

Her mind was saying no, but her body and mouthpiece was screaming, HELL YEAH! Then she exploded with an eruptive flow of built up passions, creamy lava. It wasn't until after she'd released every drop, that she realized she'd let Jonas nut inside of her.

Scott was in a deep exhausted pant as Sexy climbed off of him. She looked down in pure disgust and nodded to Lavish, who used a seven-inch razor blade to slice off his still hardened penis at its base and then slit his throat before he barely had time to take a deep breath. Being that his eye's still remained closed, he hadn't seen his death approaching. The irony behind his demise was pleasure, lust and the fact that he'd let the two felines seduce him to his death. But without a breaking and entry charge into his satisfying estate, there was no way possible that he could've heard the grim reaper knocking.

"C'mon girl. We need to get the fuck outta here," Sexy said sashaying out of the bathroom fully cleansed in a hasty- trek. "I said, let's move!" She barked again.

Lavish was confused at Sexy's temperament. Of all their kills together, not once had she reacted this way. But she knew her girl and obeyed like an expensively trained Shih Tzu.

Like two thieves in the dark night, Lavish and Sexy escaped the scene of the city's 28th murder of the year, leaving a small trail of droplets from the leakage of water from the plastic satchel with melting ice and Scott's stiff penis.

Chapter Ten

One of Their Own

Last night's malicious act of violence which resulted in a gruesome murder with the victim's private dismembered and now absent from the scene made this a yet another high priority and sensitive case. But it wasn't the facts of the case that required the red-tape on this, or the nature of it, it was the mere fact that the tragedy had hit home. Claimed one of their own, and that was just unacceptable.

It was early this morning at approximately 9:43 that a member of the hotels cleaning staff went into Room 116 to service it, and discovered a lifeless body in a small reservoir of blood. Her screams drew nearby renters and the hotel manager. The authorities were alerted, as well as the Medical examiner's office and as Homicide examined the scene the conformation was made. His body and case would be treated with the utmost respect, in addition to the definite perseverance in solving his death.

The Governor had just ripped the life out of the Mayor, who then had Margaret Pettihall, his mid-forty year old secretary patch him through to the Commissioner who endured an offensive, verbal onslaught like a lecture from a notable professor at a prestigious college. But there was no doubt that the buck wouldn't halt there. The Commissioner made it his personal agenda to skip lunch and had his driver take him H.P.D. Headquarters on Jennings Road.

All four wheels hadn't come to a full stop before his greatness bolted out of the rear seat. His footsteps appeared to be four-at-a-time in a 'Spike Lee' world, he moved so fast. In the elevator, he pushed the second floor button. Next he found the Chief in his office peering out of the vast window of his cluttered expanse.

"Uh hum..." The baritone voice gurgled, startling the Chief out of his reverie.

"Oh, hey...Sir," he spoke stuttering, his facial expression clearly showcasing surprise. "What brings you all this way sir?" Asked the Chief, trying to mask the abruptness of the Commissioner's visit.

"First of all," he began after a deep sigh, "I'm quite sure you're aware of the nature of my presence. But if not, you should know that I've only had to make this trip twice during my tenure and personally, I don't like it," he emitted slamming his large hand onto the Chief's cluttered desk.

"But..."

"No buts, Chief. There's a maniac, a psychopath, a loony, having her way with the citizens of my city, and you and your department of so-called cops and detectives are being made fools of!" He spat, particles of his saliva showering the Chief's face. "What leads do you have?" He demanded to know, drumming his stubby fingers over a thick manila file that sat atop the Chief's desk.

The Chief felt like a mouse caught in a real life glue trap desperate to be freed. "Sir we have minimal leads at this point, but I have every available body working the streets as of early this morning. So I'm very hopeful that something will turn up."

"Not good enough, Chief." The response came quick, almost prearranged, and read off a teleprompter. "Results Chief, results. That's all I damn well want to hear concerning this. A damn woman?" He stated, eyebrows raised in awe. "She's touched home base and has the entire department looking like fools all the way up to the Mayor and Governor. And when it's my ass on the line getting chewed out then it's going to rain asses on you. And let me remind you, it's election time, so think highly about your little cul-de-sac here, catch my drift?" He stood to leave.

"I don't like threats, Sir, but I read you loud" he nodded, "and clearly," said the Chief reassuringly, as he watched the Commissioner disappear like a coin in an elusive magic trick. "Asshole!" The Chief paged his secretary and had her summon the entire Homicide division; it was a chain of command, a domino effect and their turn to experience the wrath of his anger as he did from his higher ups.

When they were all assembled in a larger enough room, he gave out all the new contingency plans and orders. They were to canvass every known murder scene of each victim. Every local bar and grill in the city, also the more discreet nightclubs until they had answers or no one would be going home. "Ah Chief," one detective belched out. "I've got my kids graduation today."

"You had. Now get!" He barked. As the room cleared of all personnel, a call came from the M.E. with some vital information that could be detrimental to the existence of the case.

That's very good Elaine. Very good!" He exclaimed, and then got in touch with the lead detectives on the case.

"Yeah Chief." Brunson said, as he and Edwards were just about to hit the pavement.

"Elaine down at the Morgue says she found traces of a woman's secretion on Scott's pubic hairs. Ol' girl has finally slipped up and I want her ass!" The Chief gritted nearly cracking a few teeth as he spoke anxiously.

"Well God willing, she's on our database and it'll probably take the Lord to make that a reality, Chief. Cause if not, we're still stumped," said Brunson. He was five foot seven, 173lbs with a balding head and had been the department's most valuable player the last three years. He was holding a good track record for solving some of the city's most elusive homicides.

"I'm feeling that way as well, Brunson," said Ursula, his partner of two years now. "I don't think this woman has a record, she appears to be way too smart. But as you said Chief, she left us her calling card, so who knows, we might just get lucky," Ursula finished. She was second fiddle to Brunson, 221 lbs., with a keg-of-beer shape and dark grey-smoky eyes. Her hair normally stayed cropped in a wet curl that fondled her broad shoulders. Other than being pale-pink and freckled with pimples, she was somewhat cute, and that was on a good day; which were few.

"Well enough talk, I need my two best detectives out there on this," the Chief proclaimed.

"Need I remind you it's an election year and heads will roll if this sickly woman isn't apprehended soon?"

Brunson shook his head no, and then he and Edwards broke wind. But not before Edwards said "Don't worry Chief, the public likes you. Those last two dips weren't cut out for what this dangerous city has to offer. Just don't sweat it, Bro!" Then they disappeared.

Once in their nondescript car, Brunson cut into his partner.

"Why must you always bust the Chiefs chops, Ursula? You know you've only been a detective for twenty-four months now and you'll be the first to go when heads roll."

"So what, screw him. I've been offered a job with I.A., so let him try. Revenge is always best served with conviction. Now let's hit some bars," suggested Edwards, lowering her dollar store shades over her gazing watchers.

After the duo canvassed the fifth location on their list of places to check out, they still hadn't come up lucky. No one had any clues to offer the detectives. "Thank you and here's my card. You can reach me 24 hours a day." This had been the same old song and dance thus far.

"What's next?" Brunson inquired, as he drove steadily through the sluggish traffic.

Edwards flipped the wired steno pad. Edwards' smoke-grey pupils scanned its lettering until they fell upon the name 'Sisson Street Tavern Bar & Grill'. "Shoot over to that spot on Sisson Street," Edwards directed.

A short distance later the sedan pulled up curbside in front of two frequented establishments, the 'Wood Tap,' the other, the 'Sisson Street Tavern'. Brunson thought it was strange that two popular dives would operate so close in proximity, but that was probably because of the possibility that there was one sole proprietor between them, he thought. "You wanna split up or tackle this together," he questioned, even though he was lead. He wanted to feel comfortable with her and by doing so from time to time, would enable just the security he desired from her.

Brunson didn't have to ask twice as Edwards responded, "Sure, we'll meet back in the car." She strolled off towards the Tavern with a sense of acceptance from her two year partner. Brunson smiled as he walked into the 'Wood Tap,' finally giving her some much needed freedom to investigate.

Brunson had interviewed the entire wait staff, bartender and owner, thus coming up empty. The staff on deck swore they hadn't seen or remembered anyone strange and out of the norm frequenting their establishment, and were sorry they couldn't be of much help. Feeling drawn, in addition to the fatigue he was beginning to undergo, he retired to the car, tilted his seat back in a restful position as he waited for Ursula to return. "Well scratch the 'Wood Tap', he said and drifted off.

Inside the Tavern, Ursula was questioning someone from the bar.

"Are you sure?" Detective Edwards asked with urgency.

"Without question," the head bartender beamed as he cloth dried a few tumblers and mugs. "I can even see her as we speak, a real looker, strangely alluring in a bad way."

"So you know what she looks like?" She quizzed, with hope.

"Humph, get me an artist, and I'll have a composite sketch for you in no time," he promised. "I'll never forget her pretty face."

"This is just the break we needed. Thank you Lord," she praised and squawked giddily over her radio summoning a department sketch artist. Within eighteen minutes, Judy Cruz and her canvass were aligned on the five foot bar sketching what, George, the bartender vividly recollected about the woman in question.

"Got it!" shouted Judy, proud of the depiction of an urban, Mona Lisa she'd masterfully sketched in charcoal. When George saw the composite rough-in he nodded with definite approval.

"Good," exclaimed Detective Edwards. She thanked George as she passed him her contact card hightailing it out of the dim lit Tavern. Back at the nondescript sedan, she noticed Eric trying to steal a little z-time and banged on the window with her stubby palm.

Startled out of his wits, Eric jumped up, the steno pad taking flight landing on the floor of the sedan. "What's your problem Ursula?" He barked heatedly, "and it better be fucking good!" he snarled.

The car door slammed. She tossed the Picasso in his lap to let her work show for itself. His cue balls bulged with intensity. He glanced at his gold Seiko and realized he'd been asleep for over forty minutes. He was about to question how she'd gotten the composite and whom it was who drew it up, when Judy, along with her drawing kit strolled out of the Tavern. She smiled at him in passing, then skirted off into traffic as if she'd never been there.

Edwards sat with a huge grin plastered over her face, then suggested they get the sketch out over the wire, news and anything else they could think of before their 'Lady Killa' struck again.

"You did good, Ursula. Very good," he praised, driving away from the curb.

Chapter Eleven
Composite Progress

The composite had been mass produced over the TV networks as an interrupted broadcast along with the news and local radio stations. This was an emergency that needed to be addressed by all media outlets to show progress in the eyes of the public. All the way up the chain-of-command, phones rang off the hook with applause for the new leads and dedication by the Homicide Department; because when one team did well, they all looked good in the eyes of the higher ups.

The fact that Scott was an off-duty officer out having a good time and had become a victim of circumstance, pushed the department to storm the city for answers. His death regretfully gave them the break they'd longed for since the first murder occurred, and was the push needed to bring face back to the Chief, Commissioner, Mayor and Governor.

Willard, Howell and Banks were watching Tiger swing a 9-iron at the small golf ball. With the night off, they had gathered for fun. Banks had just purchased a 52" HDTV and was showing off the quality of the new VIVIO technology when there was a break in the show. The men clad in plaid, button-up short sleeves and caps, were substituted by a petite woman, in her early thirties who was now directing the viewers to a black and white sketch of an obviously beautiful woman. She then said, *"To the left of me on the blue screen is a composite sketch of who the authorities believe is the woman wanted for questioning in the multiple homicides committed throughout the city. I'm going to say this with heavy emphasis people, please take a very good look at the drawing, dig deep and try to focus on if you've seen this woman before. If so, if you have any pertinent knowledge about this woman, do not hesitate to contact the homicide division at 555-6000 X477. Now back to our local broadcast..."*

"Man, do you see what I'm seeing?" Willard stated his eyes still wide as silver dollars.

"Hell yeah, that's La'Creatia, CJ's wife to a tee," Howell chimed in.

"Without a doubt," Banks' seconded the motion. "Damn she's the one killing and cutting off people's swipes?!"

"So what'll we do?" Willard questioned. "Let's not forget, Jones became one of her victims," he added. They all shook their heads agreeing.

"I say we call CJ" Banks suggested.

"No! He'll just protect his wife. And we damn sure can't call Tacoma, you know they're fuck buddies," he smiled, not meaning it sexually, but just very tight in friendship.

"You're right. We have to phone the police", boomed Willard.

They all agreed, but since it was Willard's idea, it would be up to him to call. He actually felt it was a privilege to call the anonymous tip in. Picking up his cordless house phone, he dialed the homicide division, pressed in the extension and asked to speak with someone of authority. Minutes later, he was patched into Brunson's cell line. He then explained his relationship to the Johnson's especially the fact that La'Creatia was a stunningly beautiful albino and seemed to be the woman in the photo. Detective Brunson relayed everything to his partner as he steadily drove towards the address given, while Edwards called it in to the Chief. Moments later, they were parked directly in front of the house, checking the clip of their service weapons at the same time. They contemplated waiting for backup, but this was a collar that would result in promotions they figured, and said to hell with waiting for backup, and moved with extreme caution towards the house.

"Get back here CJ," La'Creatia threatened angrily, "I'm not through with you limpy," she scolded, the remark cutting him deeply. They'd just worked up thirty-five minutes of sweat trying out various positions which ended in Carlos shooting his coconut-rum all over her back after pulling out of her ass. When she went to give him some head, he declined and started for the shower feeling drained as an empty well.

"Go play with your dildo's honey, I'm done."

"That you are," a sinister sneer crossed her mouth. A vivid picture he'd seen almost daily for the past three months now.

She decided against playing with one of her dildos and instead chose to call her friends. After speaking to Shelly and Shavon for 15 minutes, she dug into her pocketbook where the finely sharpened serrated knife lay dormant awaiting its next slice. Her alter ego was calling out to her damn near demanding that she answer. La'Creatia held the long eight-inch knife with pleasure. She felt they were one and the same. It gave her power and sadly the power she feigned to kill the one she loved with all of her heart, but first he'd be treated just like the rest. His love trophy would now be available to her whenever she saw fit, as it would remain stiffly frozen in her secret sexual habitant.

"Damn, she just doesn't get enough," thought Carlos aloud as he was drying off from a quick shower. The house was quiet – a little too quiet for him, but he liked it. He made it to his room and crashed to the bed ass-naked and drifted into a deep sleep. He was far off into a horrible dream. A dream where he was being chased by a group of devil midgets with knives demanding he sex them, men and all, or his dick would be cut off. Surprisingly, he felt his throttle shifting back and forth becoming hard with each wiggle of its length. But he was dreaming – it couldn't be real. So he hadn't resisted as the little woman massaged his manhood.

La'Creatia studied his facial expressions and wondered what sick ass realm he could've drifted off too, but to tell the truth, she really didn't give a shit. Fuck him! It was coming off. The mirrored blade seemed to smile at La'Creatia as the angular-tip and serrated edge brought to surface the demon within her. She'd brought Carlos deer leg to its heightened potential, grasped the large blade and said, "See you in hell, hubby," then took a slow slice at the base of his tree trunk, blood spewing sporadically, as he began to squeal in a high pitched tenor.

She'd sliced him out of his sleep. "Ahhh...Ahhh! You fucking bitch! I'll kill you," he yelled peering down at the bloody stump where his penis used to be.

"Not in this lifetime, babes!" She then jabbed the sharp stiletto into the ridge of his neckline twice before he sunk to the floor like dead weight in an open bay of water. Proud of her work, La'Creatia trekked off to place Carlos' length and girth in her ice-box. It would be her most favorable congealing piece to date.

.

Outside Brunson and Edwards drew their guns as they heard the screams from within the house. "Did you just hear what I think I heard?" Ursula whispered. "Yeah I heard it," Brunson answered. "Step back," he ordered. After taking two steps himself, he lunged forward with his right foot and sent the low budget wood door straight to the floor. "Watch your ass, Edwards!"

"You do the same."

Together they stormed the house. Like pulling an order out of a ballot box, Edwards was assigned the upper floor, while Brunson would search the bottom for any signs of foul-play. The screams were no doubt authentic, so something wrong had transpired in here he thought waving his 9mm side-to-side through the living room and now the dining room. Nothing, he proceeded to the kitchen when he heard a low thud come from behind a door by the cream colored range. Upon further assessment, he learned it lead to the basement, and more than likely where the noise originated from.

He carefully descended the squeaky steps one by one, his gun oscillating slowly like a pendulum on a grandfather clock. If someone was actually down here, it wouldn't be a surprise whatsoever because each step he took was coupled with a squeak of aging wood and then he tripped. He tumbled to the very last step, his weapon now two feet away as his nugget thumped rapidly. Then a sharp jab in his chest caused him to bellow out softly; moans of pains nearing unconsciousness consumed him as a whole. From the new body piercing he just received without signing a waiver or consent form, now had him on borrowed time bathing in his own blood.

La'Creatia stood over him with the serrated knife ready to claim yet another victim. He was fading in and out of reality, and then the squelch of his radio startled her. "You're a fuckin' cop!" She mouthed. "Guess you're a little too late to save CJ and early for your own funeral. Hmmmm, I wonder what you're working with down there, coppa?" Out of curiosity, she gripped a nice handful of his crotch and felt it wasn't worth cutting off. Instead she began perforating his chest and stomach with the stiletto. Watching the detective take his last breaths was enough to draw an orgasm and she began to shudder violently, only it was the infinite array of slugs entering her legs. She dropped to her knees, the knife by her side as blood seeped from the wounds.

Even in the academy, Ursula had been a lousy shot, and being that she was shooting downward at a funny angle in a dim light, she hit her target three times; enough to incapacitate and immobilize her. She then eased down the steps, kicked the murder weapon further away from her reach, and cuffed her. Moments later, their backup had finally arrived. While she was upstairs, she'd located Carlos and radioed everything in. The EMS team hurried into the basement, but it was too late for Detective Eric Brunson. La'Creatia had killed yet another, only difference, she'd killed another cop.

Luckily for La'Creatia the paramedics arrived when they did, or Ursula would've finished the job. Upstairs Carlos was wheeled out on a gurney with the help of a portable respirator. As he was lifted into the mobile hospice, he and La'Creatia locked eyes. Her malicious grin sending a throbbing chill threw his entire being.

After a thorough search of the house, Rugby, a cadaver dog, sniffed out La' Creatia's secret room behind the wicker stand where she had a small generator relaying power to a wall-size freezer with every missing penis from her previous victims.

"Wow" one officer yelped. "Hey, Marty, check her husband for a missing pecker, this one's fresh. She might've snipped the ol' boy's wood off." He shook his head in bewilderment.

Chapter Twelve
The End of Crazy

Several weeks later as La'Creatia lay impotent and strapped to her bed in a thick off-white straight jacket, she reminisced back when it all began. She was six-years old. Her three older brothers by seven years would take turns molesting her to see and experience what it was like to have sex. This went on till she was fifteen years old. The last episode resulted in her being pregnant and secretly having an abortion. That coupled with the rape in high school drove La'Creatia madly insane. No one listened to her back then, and they damn sure hadn't now.

They craved answers as to why she did it, not what drove her to the pivotal point of murder. Tired of their queries, La'Creatia spared no detail on each of her killings. They ended with her serenading them with a sick chuckle, and some words of wisdom. "I'll admit I'm more than a little bit promiscuous, it's a vain glorious feeling I've come to sit well with. However, two heads are very much better than one, and I'm not the only girl in love with a big dick she finished and slipped into a sickening snicker. "Ha…Ha…Ha…"

After a superior court judge sentenced La'Creatia to the County Insane Asylum for the duration of her life, Carlos, felt it was okay to bring the girls home.

He had surgery to have his severed penis reattached to his stub. His wounds to his neck weren't that deep, though he received several stitches, he was going to be fine. He maintained his correction officer position and raised his two daughters back to the normal life they were used to. During this time he chose to fall in love again and share his home and heart with a longtime acquaintance. She was bold and sexy like La'Creatia and Carlos was convinced he had finally struck gold. The woman being Shauny, understood when Carlos didn't want to make love and empathized with the psychotic-bullshit he had endured at La'Creatia's hand. Despite all he had endured, life was now good.

A few months passed by and Carlos regained full erectile functions in his groin and Shauny was extremely pleased. "He seems to be working just fine honey. I even like the tattoo the stitches left behind, sweetie," she said and swallowed him whole. She deep-throated his member, giving him head worthy of applause and making him feel irresistible.

"Yeah, baby...Yes," He moaned. "I love that shit Shauny."

"Don't call me Shauny," she said, pulling away and then looking up at him. "Call me by my pet name."

"You keep doing that shit and I'll call you whatever you like! Just tell me your pet name."

"Good," she laughed, loudly. "Call me Lavish." She winked her eye then wrapped her lips back around his dick, devouring him again.

BOSS LIFE
BOSS LIFE PUBLICATIONS
PRESENTS
RAISIN'
HELL
J. ALEXANDER

RAISING

HELL

J. ALEXANDER

PREFACE

The year was 1988, a day that was supposed to be filled with joy, endearment, and celebration, where life was being bestowed upon earth in a parallel way. It was April 17th, to be exact. Obscuring clouds hovered over Hartford's most prestigious medical facility, where a beet-red Cherokee swerved erratically into the U-shaped exterior of the parking lot. Lightning began to glisten in the opaque skies. Booms of thunder fought each other to produce a sonorous concerto of fret equivalent to a horror flick. However, it was the extraterrestrial rumble within Aruby's belly that heightened.

"Ahhh…oooh!" Her dismayed squeal shivered with each kick. Then, like an off-switch, the rumble subsided for the moment, only to kick start minutes later. Aruby actually cursed herself for consuming the pepperoni pizza last night, knowing it would cause a major case of heartburn and indigestion later.

Shaun Hellum Sr., Aruby's husband and sperm donor, smiled as he rubbed the knot protruding from her oversized button-up.

"Would you stop it, Shaun!" she spat, annoyed to the point that any little thing Shaun said or did plucked her last nerve - not to mention she was not a fan of maternity wear.

Shaun was ecstatic. His eyes were glossy, pupils dilated, and he seemed to be sweating a lot more than her for obvious reasons. Aruby secretly held some disdain for him. "Relax, babe, we're almost there. Just hold on." Shaun's words did nothing to cease the repetitious kicks to Aruby's abdomen. The FICA Soccer Championship proceeded on schedule.

Up ahead, the brightness of the neon red and yellow script etched into the emergency room sign gave Aruby a sense of salvation. Shaun nearly left the Jeep in drive in his attempts to rush to her aid, stopping directly in front of the crowed vestibule.

"Please help!" he shouted. "My wife's in labor!" He held onto his wife's hand gently, beads of sweat trickling from his brow with every step. He resembled a slave perspiring on a plantation.

With the doctor's help, a wheelchair was quickly rushed outside for her to sit in. Aruby was gingerly seated in the two-wheeled car and then ushered inside. While the chrome sedan dashed to the pipe-grey vertical carriage, Shaun retrieved her overnight bag from the car.

Upon entrance into the hospital, he was informed that he needed to fill out all the necessary paperwork for Aruby's admittance, which took him about seventeen minutes.

Before catching the next flight up, Shaun visited the hospital's gift shop. He purchased two matching teddy bears, both baby blue, a vibrant bouquet of flowers for Aruby, and two jumbo-sized balloons bearing the phase "It's A Boy". It was his last $85.00, which he had planned to score with, but as he rode the distance from their home on Asylum Avenue to Washington Street where the hospital lay, he sacredly declared that he would cease all involvement with drugs.

"Hmm, I can do this," he told himself, knowing that his wife and kids would need his support and getting high would hinder any chance of him doing so if he remained high 24/7.

Once off the elevators, Shaun noticed a familiar cry which resonated throughout the entire floor. It was Aruby belching out God's name, asking Him to please stop, to end the seismic tremors tornadoing within her womb. Shaun blew by the receptionist, who tried diligently to indicate whom he was there to see, but to no avail.

"Excuse me, Sir," her voice echoed loudly.

Shaun ignored her and followed the howling pitch that continued to resonate throughout the entire sixth floor. Aruby had made it to the hospital just in the nick of time. Her uterus was at full dilation - 10 centimeters - and her boys wanted out, as if they had somewhere to be.

"There you are!" Shaun's labored tone vibrated in the air. Surveying the room, Shaun noticed that the clock read 4:14 p.m.

"Are you the father, Sir?" a woman in pink scrubs and a full surgical mask questioned.

"Yes, I'm Shaun Hellum Sr. and she's no doubt my wife." He used the term "Senior" because one of his boys was going to inherit his name.

The woman shrugged her shoulders and then yelled, "Well, get over here, Sir!"

Taking heed of her orders, Shaun took his proper stance beside the medical chaise lounge after placing the gifts he had purchased down onto a table in the corner of the room.

"Wow, already?" Shaun's facial features showed his surprise. "I can see the head." He stared dumfounded in between Aruby's legs, which were spread eagle in the metal stirrups as she blurted loud obscenities into the air, her head thrashing from left to right as if possessed.

The delivery commenced with baby number one entering the world at 4:17 p.m. He weighed 6 pounds even with a distinctive birthmark on his face and he was christened Shaun Hellum Jr. In an encouraging burst of energy, the delivery room nurse muttered, "C'mon, Mrs. Hellum, push!"

"You've got to push harder if you'd like to get your second baby out," Doctor Malloy urged, her eyes fixated on Aruby's Good and Plenty's.

"You push, bitch! Get...this...thing...out of me..."

The room lit up with smiles at Aruby's outburst, unbeknownst to anyone but each other because of the surgical masks they wore snuggly over their mouths.

Exercising the coaching skills he'd learned in Lamaze class, Shaun shouted, "C'mon, baby girl, push. You're almost there!" The beads of sweat descending from his forehead were now drenching the rim of his shirt.

Through a tight gasp, Aruby's voice flared, "If you don't shut your mouth, Shaun! Ahhh!" she yelled.

That's when Vaughn, baby number two, slid down the slick canal and into Dr. Malloy's grasp, weighing only 3 pounds, 6 ounces with a head full of curly hair and deep dimples. What struck Dr. Malloy as being a true gift from God was the size of baby Vaughn's enlarged genitalia. You're going to make some poor girl very happy one day, she thought.

Then something dreadful all doctors feared took place. Vaughn's tiny heart was so underdeveloped that it wouldn't be able to ensure him a prosperous life.

Beep...Beep...Beep...

The sounds of the heart monitor echoed slowly. The fading drum of baby Hellum's heartbeat was dying with each squelch as the neo-natal monitor orchestrated a withering concerto. A desolate soul was ending. After doing everything possible to save Vaughn's life, it appeared that the medical staff's vigorous years of schooling didn't work. Dr. Malloy then left baby Vaughn in Aruby's soft cradle to mourn.

Now realizing the tragic misfortune, a rapid downpour of hurt, despair, and pain ran from Aruby's tear ducts. One tear turned into a stream, and then the stream erupted into a woeful river, which in turn formed an ocean.

Sadly, Vaughn Hellum only lived a mere two minutes outside of the cozy womb nineteen-year-old Aruby Hellum had nursed him in for 37 weeks. A part of Aruby's heart died as the beeping ceased. It was too much for her young soul to bear.

ONE

The funeral for Vaughn Hellum was held at Clark & Bell Funeral Home. At the time of his death, neither Aruby nor Shaun Sr. was drowning in money, so the State ended up paying the bill. It made for a cheap ceremony, leaving only immediate family to mourn his unfortunate passing during the after-service.

Since the time Vaughn's tiny soul entered the afterlife, Shaun Sr., had been acting very strangely, a side Aruby wasn't very familiar with or accustomed to. The older man she'd grown to love and adore was slick, vibrant, outgoing, and engrossed with energy when not trapped in his glass house. Aruby could see that today her husband was sober, yet pain-stricken, for lack of better words. His eyes glossed with uncertainty, widened with disbelief, but as Aruby struggled to remain focused and maintained, Shaun Sr. would slip away with every inhale and exhale of breath.

In a cold sweat, Aruby sat on the secondhand store recliner in a world of grief and despair, where she fell into a deep nod. Her mind fell victim to months of remembrance.

It was actually two years prior, 1986. She had met Shaun Sr. when she'd turned a youthful seventeen, him being older at twenty-four. He easily captured her innocent heart at a neighborhood garage party after she mistakenly spilled her Orange Cisco all over his outfit.

"What da fuck?" he barked angrily until her stunning ambiance stole every vein that coiled in his heart. His upset scowl soon formulated into a forgiving smile.

"Please excuse me, someone bumped me in passing," she apologized. She tried dabbing at his checkered sweater with the napkin she held.

Shaun flashed a perfect set of pearly whites while checking out her measurements. "No need, cutie, I'm good. What's your name though?"

"Aruby," she quickly answered, her shallowness evident.

He was completely confused by the reply, his expression vividly depicting his perplexity. "A-Ruby? What kind of name is Aruby?"

Although her mood seemed to lighten on account of his gaping smile, she was livid inside. She'd always become offended towards people who frowned or joked upon her birth name and she often became hostile. "For your information, it's 'uh-ruby'! The 'A' is silent and passive. My father named me Aruby. Why, you don't like it?" Her petite hands now rested on the curve of her hips, awaiting a reply, as her small neck snaked left and right.

"Whoa, cutie, I'm actually digging it, to be honest. And he damn sure knew what he was doing when he gave it to you."

Aruby began to relax a bit as a cordial gap substituted for the evil, smug smile she wore. "So what's your name, Mr. Smooth?" asked Aruby, crossing her arms over her young, tender C-cups.

They were just the perfect size that made Shaun a sucker for love and young women. She was like sexual kryptonite, but in a good way. "Shaun...Shaun Hellum," he answered with a hungry bravado.

Aruby said to him in a cordial tone, as their eyes locked on cue, "Well, it's nice to meet 'chu, Shaun, even under the circumstances. Sorry about the clumsiness. Like I said, someone bumped me."

"And like I said, don't sweat it, cutie. Let me stock you up." He nodded at her plastic cup, seeing she was green to his lingo.

"That's okay, maybe it wasn't meant to be. Plus it's getting hot and crowed in here." What she left out was that it was funky.

When Shaun peered into the massive crowd, he shook his head, agreeing. "That's cool, but can I at least get a dance?" Shaun's eagerness was very broad and enticing.

Aruby knew he had it bad for her, but he appeared much older and she wasn't going to play herself out like that. "Sorry, Slick, not gonna be able to do it. But..." She paused with a contemplating smile. "You can have my number though. Do you think you can remember my number or do you have a pen and piece of paper?" she asked through a slick grin, assuming he did this with all of the ladies. She looked at her best friend Ranette, who was dancing erotically with two strange boys, one in the front, the other in the back - your average bump and grind during parties.

Shaun answered with a nod. His low Caesar tapered just the way his first baby mama Eboni liked it. It was actually what entrapped her dark hazel eyes in passing while he toured the marbled flooring throughout the Westfarms Mall. He thought about just giving the P.Y.T. (pretty young thing) his pager number, but he wanted her to have a direct connect to him. "See, you're not all young and green like a lot of today's chicks. But yeah, I've got a cell. What's your digits, ma?"

After keying in her math, Aruby said goodnight and left Shaun her thickness to study as she danced slowly over to her friend. She broke up the vulgar threesome, pulling *Ranette towards the garage opening where they'd head home. "C'mon, Ra, let's go."*

"Who was that old-ass dude you was kicking it with?"

"He did look kinda old, right?" Aruby pursed her mouth and tilted her nose up in the air as she spoke. "But to answer your question, his name is Shaun, and he may be the father of my children someday," Aruby smiled. "Dat nigga was finer than Christopher Williams."

"He was a cutie, girl!" They shared a high five. "But your baby's daddy? I don't think so. Your parents would murder you the second they noticed your little-ass belly starting to bulge," Ranette warned knowingly.

"Not now, silly!" Aruby giggled. "Later on in life. Now c'mon, let's break out."

As the two sisterly friends walked from within the crowded space, Aruby turned back to look one last time and caught Shaun gripping his crotch, all the while layering his bottom lip with saliva as his tongue rolled over it.

"Bye!" Aruby's soft voice carried through the distance.

"Aruby...Aruby!" Someone tapped her shoulder, snapping her out of her reminiscent state. "You okay, poor chile?" an elderly family member inquired with worry.

"Oh, hey, I'm fine. I must've drifted off." She stretched with a strained yawn.

"Well, you need to go and lie down, chile, you look exhausted. I'll clean up and come check on you and Shaun Jr. in a little while."

Aruby was more appreciative than it could ever possibly show. She and Shaun Jr. packed up and retired to her cluttered makeshift room, where they both fell into a deep slumber. But before that happened, she said a small prayer, not only for Shaun Sr. to get his act together, but also a heavenly cry for her late son, Vaughn Hellum. In addition, she praised the Lord for sparing her firstborn and asked that He watch over and protect him until it was time to come home.

She then kissed Shaun Jr. on the nape of his neck and the crown of his unshaped head. She enjoyed the new birth scent he exuded unknowingly, and then they fell asleep in the comfort of each other's warmth.

TWO

Aruby awoke to the belching cry of Shaun Jr. He was probably hungry since he'd skipped his last two feedings. Just as she was taught at birth class and from a nursemaid at the hospital before being discharged, she pulled her left breast out of her V-neck nightshirt. She grimaced as Shaun Jr. latched onto her swollen nipple, although it made her feel much closer to her child. He sucked until his tiny eyelids began to flutter back and forth. He was obviously still beat from his long travel into this world. Aruby burped him and then laid him on his side in between two fluffy pillows so he wouldn't roll over or smother himself while she went in search of her husband. One last peek at Shaun Jr. and she was off.

Shaun Sr. sat in the driver's seat of a puke-gold Plymouth Reliant, the engine running, music loud enough to agitate the neighbors. But because of the young couple's tragic loss, they overlooked the boisterous intrusion. It was actually Shaun's place of solace, his personal smoke house whenever he chose to indulge. But oddly, Shaun Sr. kept his word of staying clean. Right now, he was intoxicated by anguish. The loss of a child bore deep into his soul and triggered a reaction that would do more harm than anyone would ever anticipate.

Shaun felt that it was his fault that Aruby's pregnancy was complicated, that she had delivered one healthy boy and one with an unrepairable hole in his tiny heart. Vaughn Hellum died before getting a good chance at enjoying life, which Shaun Sr. attributed to his perpetual crack addiction.

To the right of Shaun Sr. sat a pint of brandy - E&J, his favorite. The bottle became an escape from the dour reality that he'd killed his boy. He, Earl, and James became intimate, although during their intoxicating intercourse, Shaun was the only one who spoke.

"James, my friend, why are you so dark in color?" Shaun slurred. "Earl, do you have any kids? Boys?" Shaun's speech grew deeply gurgled with each query. "That's all right, fellas, you don't have to answer me tonight because it doesn't matter anymore." The soot-black .38 sneered with jealousy that Earl and James held all of Shaun's attention at the moment as he sat quietly between them.

Shaun decided to rid Earl and James of their brown serum. Their lifeless bodies tumbled to the mat-less floor. With all of his devoted brain cells now trained on "Azrael", the petite, black, one-eyed passenger, he understood where his fate lay.

"So this is how we part, my friend?" questioned Shaun. "Only you know best. Take care of Shaun Jr. for me." He pulled Azrael by his collar, gripped the thickness of his neck, and squeezed him with all his might.

A splatter of ruby-red sap spewed freely from Shaun Sr.'s temple as he tinted the windshield of the family's car with gore. He'd been sitting in the left side front when he blew the large hole through his right temple, leaving him parallel with Earl and James on the nasty floor.

Aruby had been wandering around the house in search of her husband and was on her way back up to bed when the shrilling clap of gunfire halted her travels. Aruby knifed through the house until she reached the garage, where her dreadful steps stopped at their vehicle. When she approached the driver's side window, her heart nearly burst in two. She screamed loudly and called to the neighbors for help.

Aruby had only hours ago buried her offspring, and now she would have to do the same for her husband of two years. Her entire world was crushed. She was young and uncertain how her life would turn out for her and her son. But later that very night, she promised Shaun Jr. that she'd protect him from every bad thing the cold world had to offer. Soon she'd realize that "raising Hell" would not be an easy task – nor godly – but just a realization of "Hell on Earth."

THREE

*I*n spite of all that had transpired in Aruby's young life, she tried her best to remain focused. She had a son to raise and she would do so justly. As a start, Aruby had the car cleaned and detailed. She planned to conceal all traces of what had happened a year ago between Earl, James, Azrael, and Shaun Sr. It would be a dark secret that would stay nestled in Pandora's Box for all eternity, never to be told by way of her voice.

Shaun Jr. was strapped into his car set as Aruby sailed the Jeep Cherokee into the parking lot of the WIC program located on Pak Street. After that, she would head over to a job interview at Friendly's, her fourth one this week, in hopes of finally being hired. Aruby had been out on a limb in the months after Shaun Sr. decided that life was too unbearable to endure.

The Cherokee now rested in a tight parking space. The engine coughed heavily as it attempted to settle down from the intense beating it had endured in the mere five miles it traveled across town from Aruby's driveway. When she went to unstrap little Shauny, his face was painted a sticky orange from the Cheese Doodles that he greedily tried to stuff into his tiny mouth. His sticky orange palms also showed trace evidence of such doings.

Aruby used a few wet wipes to get little Shauny cleaned up and then headed inside. Finding two empty teal-green chairs, Aruby sat with little Shauny in her lap, her makeshift diaper bag in the other. After obtaining her number from the desk where she checked in, she waited to be called. To the left of her sat a Hispanic woman in her mid-twenties who cradled a toddler. Aruby cordially smiled at them, bouncing little Shauny on her knee. The two little ones locked eyes, caught in a world unbeknownst to all adults. Gibberish utters of nouns and verbs gurgled from their traps, almost as if they were having a dispute of some sort. But to the mothers, it appeared to be nothing but a cordial befriending, so they placed both toddlers on the tiled flooring to let them frolic about.

The two moms engaged in light conversation while the little ones crawled around, aimlessly doing what cradle jumpers should be doing at that age. It was the coming years that would be problematic for parents.

"He's so cute!" The Hispanic woman looked on with favor at little Shauny.

"Thank you," Aruby cordially expressed her gratitude.

A shriek of lung power belched out from Santos, the little boy who was now trapped under a few pounds of the heavier Shaun. Slobber drooled from one petite opening to the other. It was apparent that Santos wasn't too thrilled about the saliva bath. The two mothers quickly jumped up to rescue their kids. The Hispanic one actually had a great reason, seeing that Santos was on the downside of the infantile war. Aruby did it more to bottle up her growing pains. It seemed like her little Shauny was growing a temple of trouble with a fierce attitude.

"Shauny, stop that!" Aruby shouted, embarrassed, as the many gawkers looked on, some awestruck, the others chalking it up to kids being kids. "C'mon, Shauny, let's go."

She lifted him off the poor child and he squirmed out of her hands and onto the floor in a steaming fit.

Instead of chastising her little one in the open, she simply left the building and returned to the Jeep, seeing as how his fit wouldn't stop and she had missed her appointment altogether. She silently wept as tears trickled down her face, not knowing how she'd be able to get formula, cheese, eggs, and cereal for her and her child. The price of Similac was far too expensive for the few dollars the state awarded her each month, even with her living in a Section 8 apartment.

Aruby wiped away her sullen tears, turned over the ignition, then peered over her shoulder to peek at little Shauny. He was fast asleep, but the shocking trip of her day would be the single eye that slit open, his mouth framing a sinister smile, which frightened her. It was just the creasing of his tiny slash that made her heart flutter uncontrollably.

Soon after, the Jeep sped away hastily. Aruby had an interview to catch.

FOUR

*O*n April 17, 1990, little Shauny fell into the terrible two stage - not that being two was any different from how his aura and behavior was at one. He was knee high to a grasshopper, a rug rat, an ankle-biter, but nonetheless, Aruby loved him unconditionally. He'd learned to walk at thirteen months, became potty trained at eighteen months, and began to formulate words and babble sentences.

"Ma, Ma, hungry!" or, "Play – Shauny, play." And of course, there was his favorite catch phrase. "Fight, fight," he constantly pitched.

It was breakfast time for little Shauny. He sat in his high chair, waiting impatiently as his plastic spork drummed against the white tray.

"Coming, baby," Aruby assured him. She was cutting a single fish stick into small pieces so he'd be able to use his spork to gather up his eatables without her help. She wanted him to grow up independent and to never need a soul. A moment later, the drumming grew intensely loud. When Aruby turned to view the racket, little Shauny appeared to be giggling and talking to someone she couldn't see and it threw her. "Baby, you okay?" she cooed, concerned, as she stopped the cutting.

In a heartbeat, little Shauny's neck swiveled in her direction as if he were possessed and he cried out, "Eat, eat, eat, eat!" His spork danced in rhythm with each word. Then he once again returned his gaze to what Aruby assumed was an imaginary friend right there before her, only she couldn't visibly see him or her.

"Shauny!" She let her emotions take control, yelling out, but to no avail. He just began to giggle as if he was being tickled. She finally placed his plate with the cut-up fish sticks on it and also put his favorite sippy cup full of unsweetened apple cider in front of him.

Fully aware of the fresh catch before him, Shaun's attention reverted to his mom and his food. "Umm," he mumbled, seeing his favorite drink and food. "Umm, Mommy."

"You okay, baby?" Aruby questioned. She laid the back of her hand over his forehead, checking for a fever. Seeing that there was none, she started to settle down.

Little Shauny began stuffing his mouth with a few pieces of warm fish, and then it was like something became sour in his mouth because he spit every bit of it back on the tray. He shoved the plate and its remnants to the floor then began to sip from his cup as if he'd done nothing wrong. After a few good sips and swallows, he titled his small frame to the left and began laughing along with whoever was now his so-called friend.

"Oh my precious Lord!" Aruby cried. "What's wrong with my child? Please help him! It's not his fault," she prayed. "It's not his fault."

FIVE

It had to be one of the coldest winters ever and it was also little Shauny's fifth Christmas. The terrible two's had long since been a frustrating afterthought in Aruby's mind, and to say times grew harder would be an accurate statement. She'd been waiting tables ever since three days after her initial interview at Friendly's back in 1989.

Shaun had grown a few more inches above the green jumper with stringy legs. His vocabulary was beyond imaginable for a five-year-old, and Aruby often contemplated a soapy beverage as a lasting deterrent to rid him of his foul dialect. For a while, Aruby let his hair grow, maybe three inches off the crown of his head, but after the constant visual of his best friend's hairstyle, he demanded his mother cut the small afro off so he could fully resemble his pal. To save arguments and a series of fits from her baby boy, Aruby gave in and had Venoris, a local barber, bring it down to a number one style length.

Mother and son had finally completed putting the finishing touches on the battered pine tree that had been donated by the Salvation Army just around the corner. Aruby asked little Shauny if he wanted to hit the switch to the light show. She hoped he'd be amazed at how many different hues shone brightly.

To her surprise, little Shauny replied, "No, I want Blake to do it." His eyes squinted into tiny slits as the furry bushes over his lids furrowed. He then looked to his left and asked Blake if he'd like to plug the extension cord into the wall, still holding his frown.

Over the years, he and Blake had become best friends. They were both actually the same age, only Blake was older by a few minutes. They wore similar hairdos, low cuts with waving follicles. Their skin tone was sandalwood brown, eyes the hue of spring acorns with manipulative characteristics if caught in a contentious stare-off, and flaring temperaments that could easily slip into a quivering burst of rage at the drop of a dime. All in all, the two could undoubtedly pass for brothers.

Staring back at Shaun, Blake passed on the idea. He was just a friend and didn't want to intrude on the moment. He had other plans.

Finally, Shaun answered. "I guess I'll do it," he sighed. "Blake says it's a family thing, and he's just a friend."

Aruby had seen this side of her son too many times to count and she didn't want to ignite his ill-mannered rage, so she overlooked his answer. However, she stared at him with moist eyes, not understanding why her beloved son was displaying signs of schizophrenia even at such a young age. With no insurance but what the State offered, she never sought help for little Shauny. She just hoped and prayed that it would subside – not likely! She did all that was possible to refrain from crying and in a soft whisper said, "Okay, honey, maybe Blake can do it next year. So go on, plug the cord in."

Shauny did as suggested. She was happy to see the wide-eyed expression plastered across his handsome face as the array of bright hues dances around the small living room. For once, Aruby felt like everything was in order instead of in dire straits.

"Cool!" Blake shouted in awe, the kaleidoscope of colors dazzling to the eyes.

"Look at 'em blinking, Blake. That's cool!" Little Shauny stated looking to his left.

Not able to undo or change Mother Nature's prediction of rainfall, the downpour of pity ran down Aruby's defeated face. With only one rational thought at the moment, Aruby said to the boys, "Okay, it's getting late, and if you guys want Santa Claus to come and bring your presents, we have to get to bed." She wiped away all the tears she could.

Blake stared into her face, moved by her pain, but what about his? He no longer had a set of parents he could run to if he scraped his knee or if he had a vicious cold, no father figure to model after to teach him how to ride a bike or box. So just as easy as his compassion arose for his friend's mom, it disappeared. A wicked sneer replaced the look of pity he'd just showcased.

"Santa Claus!" Blake snarled. "He's not real! C'mon, Shaun, if you believe that fat ol' man is the real thing, you're as crazy as her!" He nudged his head in Aruby's direction, smiling at how disturbed she appeared to be. Blake and Shauny had made a pact several years ago and it would forever remain solid. It could never be broken by or for anyone, not even his mother.

"Yeah!" Shauny also snarled. "He can't be real, Mom. Look at all the presents we already have. Blake's right. Santa's fake and we wanna open our presents now!" he demanded. His spring-acorn eyes bulged with rage, the inner demon now topside.

Aruby couldn't believe her eyes or ears. Why had Blake planted such a thought into her baby's head? *Why is this happening to my family on Christ's birthday?* Her mind wandered, but being the parent, she had to try and regain order. "Listen to me, Shauny, there is a Santa Claus, but if you're not—"

"No...there... isn't!" Blake shouted.

And with that said, Shauny ran up to the already-battered tree and pushed it with little effort until it lay horizontally on the ground, where he performed a raging pow-wow over the tree and gifts. Blake looked on with sheer happiness at his pal's doings. He thought that now was a good time to let them be alone and he slipped out of the room unnoticed.

Aruby entered a wailing fit of wet emotions while Shauny continued into his pow-wow.

Merry damn Christmas!

SIX

"Shauny, please make sure you bundle up this morning. It's supposed to be pretty chilly out today!" Aruby yelled from inside the kitchen.

It was 6:32 a.m., 1998, the first day of school for Shauny. Yes – just plain ol' Shauny. He and Blake thought that since now they were fifth graders, the "little" had to go, which was a hard task for Aruby. But with some reluctance, she'd gotten use to the change.

"But Mom, I hate those itchy sweaters and they're too tight! The kids might laugh at me," he reasoned. He was walking around his bedroom in his favorite boxers, no shirt. His denim jeans were laid out across the bed next to a button down shirt. No name, of course, at least not one to be proud of.

"C'mon now, Shauny, you're going to be late on your first day and you still have to eat something.

"Do we have any Toaster Strudels, Mom?"

"I'll warm them up, but only if you hurry and promise to wear the sweater…"

"It's ugly, Shaun, they're all gonna laugh at you." Blake made a silly face at the repulsive top after speaking.

It made Shauny upset that his pal would flat-out laugh at his Goodwill-like attire. "I told her – you heard me. You heard me tell her, Blake. I told her they'd laugh at me and that it was tight," he barked defensively.

"Yeah, but so what? You're still going to put the damn thing on. Just go eat some Strudel!" Blake concluded tauntingly. It was his nature to push his buddy to the edge, which would normally result in rage.

"Oh yeah?" Shauny questioned. "Watch and see!" He then chucked the repugnant garment out of his bedroom window without a care as to what his Mom would think.

The two sauntered into the kitchen. Aruby wore a burgundy skirt with the Friendly's apron tied around her waist and a white cotton bra. She was pouring a glass of milk and pulling Shauny's Toaster Strudel out of the oven when they walked in. She heard the footsteps and turned around briskly. The first thing she noticed, of course, was Shauny's attire. He was draped in everything she'd laid out last night except the fuzzy sweater. Her temperament was always subtle and giving when it came to him over the years, but his constant defiance was beginning to bore a deep hole in her heart.

"Shauny, I thought we agreed that you'd wear the sweater? It's supposed to be chilly out."

Normally when school started in September, it was warm, but with all the latest global warming and inconsistency in seasonal climate control, September had mixed feelings about which side of the thermometer it wanted to rest on.

"I'm not wearing that ugly, itchy sweater!" Shauny declared, picking up the small glass of milk and layering his top lip with its froth. "I'll be okay, Mom."

"You're not listening to me, Shauny." Aruby held herself back from getting loud. It was something she'd never really done, not wanting to be a pressing parent. There was no way she'd lose the only thing worth living for. But still, she was the parent – not her son. "No sweater, no Strudel!"

For the first time in ten hardened years, she was giving her son an ultimatum, and it finally felt like she'd taken parental duties to its proper perspective.

So she thought!

"Mom, you're not hearing me - you never do!" Shauny's young voice rose. "Whenever I try and ask you things or tell you certain things, you never hear me. I'm not little Shauny anymore, Mom!" he barked. "And stop eyeing my mom, Blake – perv!"

"That's right, Shaun, let her have it!" shot Blake, loving the morning protest. "And I'm not a perv! She should be wearing a top."

"Shut up, Blake! You know it's ugly and itchy! Why don't you tell her instead of always laughing?" Shauny raged, a wicked sneer now dressing Blake's mug, happy to have set off the little engine that could.

It had been some time since Shauny had spoken of his so-called friend and this actually frightened Aruby. She'd always thought it was just a phase he'd soon grow out of, but here it was months after he turned ten and he still proclaimed to have an imaginary friend.

"Shauny!" her voice shrilled with tension. "There will be no more talk of Blake! He's not real! Blake isn't real! He's just a figment of your imagination. And if you don't quit it here today, I'm going to bring you to see someone, you hear me?" she shouted. Aruby hated to lash out, but she wasn't about to let the schools continue to threaten her and her boy with psychological evaluations.

"You see, Shaun? She doesn't believe; she never has. But I'm telling you the truth! She's been lying to you, bro. Ask her," urged Blake. "Go ahead, ask her, scaredy cat!" Blake taunted, making Shaun extremely pissed.

It wasn't the first time he had tried to provoke his brotherly friend with mysterious accusations about his mom withholding pertinent info about his life, but when Shaun would ask her, she'd say it was nothing or say, "Shauny, you're just too young and your tough little mind is being jolted with nonsense."

"Who cares!" shouted Shaun. "Maybe they need to come and take me away. I feel like I'm crazy. I'm seeing people no one else can see," he explained, pacing back and forth, bumping into Blake with every pass. "And why does Blake look so much like me? Huh? Answer that! Can the doctors tell me that, Mom?" He was like a raging bull. He tossed his glass of cow piss across the room and then ran out with great speed, leaving his mom stuck on stupid.

Aruby fell into a fit of crying. She didn't know what to make of this. Blake stood there watching her weep, but he felt absolutely no pity for her. He was bonded to Shaun in so many ways now, and he would do whatever was necessary to protect him. A devilish simper groomed his pouty mouth. He winked at Aruby, and then shadowed Shaun's footsteps until he found him in the den, rocking in his favorite chair.

Thirty minutes later, Aruby steered the Cherokee to Martin Luther King School. They still had a good ten minutes before the bell would sound off. Aruby eased into a tight space in front of the school and watched the youth as they scurried about, various book bags lining their backs, some toting lunch boxes, some hoping for reduced lunch. And during this tranquil time, Blake, Aruby and Shauny all sat deep in their thoughts as Johnny, the aging crossing guard, ushered kid after kid across the broad street.

When Aruby glanced at her watch, she decided it would be a great opportunity to break the ice. "Listen,

Shauny, I'm very sorry for this morning. You know Mommy loves you dearly. I'll never let anything happen to you."
"Yeah, right! Tell some other kid that bull crap, Mom," Blake chimed in.
"Shut it up, Blake. I'm warning you!" snapped Shauny. "That's my mom!"
"Son, please, try not to bring Blake up while you're in class. I don't want any phone calls from your principal," Aruby softly spoke. She'd been down this troubling highway his entire school life and had shielded him from too many evaluations prompted by the school officials to have it all rekindled like some undying flame.
"But Mom - "
"No buts, Shauny!" she demanded sternly. "No Blake, okay?"
"Sorry, Mom, Blakey is here to stay!" shot Blake, his frowning smirk enough to drive Shauny over the top. But for some strange reason, he held back at the moment. Maybe being older came with maturity.
Shauny looked over his left shoulder, where Blake was propped up with a mean mug. Yes, they'd become best friends, become blood brothers, but his mom would always be his mom. She truly loved him, he knew. Blake always made him angry and thirsty for a fight, kept him in an agitated state since befriending him. So after weighing the options, Shaun calmly said, "Okay, no Blake," and then left the Jeep, as happy as a kid could be on his first day of school.

The bell had rung fifteen minutes ago and all prospective students were in their assigned homerooms in their choice seats. When Mrs. Gregorsky finished gathering all of her curriculums and the attendance sheet, she asked each and every student to come up to the front of the class and introduce him or herself properly to the class. Within several passing minutes, over half of the class had done as instructed. Margie Reed had just given her subtle speech of how she was nine years old going on ten in a few days and was ecstatic about making some new friends.

Next up was Phillip Crooms. He was a short, stubby kid with braces. He wore his hair in a bushy 'fro and wore tasteless clothes compared to some of the other kids, but he was geekishly handsome, to say the least. He began, "Hey, class, my name is Phil – "

Shauny never got to hear the ending of his name due to an obnoxious outburst.

"Phillip the overweight nerd!" laughed Blake. In spite of the fact that Shauny shot Blake the most menacing stare ever, he continued to snicker at his own statement. "Phillip the nerd! "Phillip the nerd!" His laughter continued.

"Stop it! Don't start your crap, Blake. Leave the kid alone!" His voice caught the attention of not only the students, but the ears of Mrs. Gregorsky as well.

"Excuse me, young man?" She became leery of what the young kid belched out so openly. "What did you just say? What is your name?" She shouted question after question. "As a matter of fact, you're next. Please sit down, Phillip."

Shauny stood and made his way through the close-fitting aisle of desks, chairs, and dangling feet protruding from underneath them. He scowled towards those who thought their steppers would remain blocking his passage. They quickly retreated - with good reason.

Approaching the head of the class, Shaun looked Mrs. Gregorsky dead in the face, their visual receptacles locked in for the long haul, neither of them budging for the other. But it was the shaken feeling she received when Shauny bit down on his bottom lip, drawing a tiny speck of blood along with that exercise-like scowl, which proved the young man had prevailed. The short-winded, asthmatic woman quickly rested her bosom over the shuffled papers on her desk and tried to regain a controlled level of respiration. Seeing he'd triumphed over his teacher, Shaun continued as directed.

With an excited demeanor, Shauny vouched that his government birth name was Shaun Jermane Hellum Jr., that he was ten years of age and he desired to be a professional basketball player someday. Then he awaited a response from his new classmates.

"Now that was, L.A.M.E. – lame, bro!" shot Blake. "I thought you wanted to be a gangsta, or even the next Jay Z, but a sports dweeb? Nah, bro, you don't have the crossover for that." Blake shook his head.

Whispers grew from the classroom about what their new classmate was so preoccupied with to his left. Shaun's gaze was stuck on Blake, who was kneeling low to the ground. Shauny's shapely noggin shifted left to right in a fit of shock.

"What's he doing?" one boy said to his neighbor.

"Beats me," the neighbor responded.

"You see that, Ivy? He's lost it," Charles whispered, not wanting to be caught talking about the disturbed kid.

"Yes, and that's not nice, Chucky! Shut up! What if he hears you?" Ivy warned in a murmur. For some strange reason, Ivy felt drawn to Shauny. She could feel his inner pain, the exhilarating force troubling him, and she warmed to his stressed apparition. In more ways than one, they were two and the same.

"I'm whispering, Iv' – he can't hear me. But the dude's a complete freak job." He laughed softly as Ivy sent him a cold stare. He didn't care; he was used to her after being in the same classes with her over their time in Martin Luther King.

When Ivy grew tired of the class's disrespect and silence towards Shauny, she said, "I think it's cool you wanna be a basketball star, Shaun," and smiled broadly.

This made Shauny snap out of his questionable silence with a smile as well. Finally, someone agreed with his thoughts and his presence period, and he welcomed it with grace. "Thanks." He didn't have a name to go with the gratifying gesture.

"Ivy. My name's Ivy, and I'm ten years old. I'd like to play the piano like Alicia Keys, and also tennis. I think I can, and will, someday beat Venus Williams," stated Ivy with a smile.

"Would you stop being all weird, Ivy!" Charles boomed. "I hate it when you're this way! Venus? Yeah, right! I'd love to see that, Ms. Skinny Minnie," he further teased.

"Cut it out, Chucky, I mean it!" she tried to whisper, but everyone looked.

"Thanks,, Ivy. I kinda think it's cool," said Shauny. "But you don't think you're a little too young to catch Venus?" His little bushy brows furrowed.

"That's right, tell her, bro!" exclaimed Blake. He was enjoying everything up to the point where Shauny seemed to be making a breakthrough or a real friend besides him.

Shauny looked to his left and gave Blake a serious lashing. He was so severe that he sent chills into everyone in the room except Ivy, who actually appeared to be poised and relaxed with Shauny's verbal onslaught. Frightened now beyond belief and realizing that this kid needed some serious attention, Mrs. Gregorsky's snuck out of the classroom and headed down the tight hallways headed for the principal's office to seek help. Using the wall phone in her classroom might've set him off even more, so she did the next logical thing.

Within minutes, Shauny was dragged out of the classroom, where he now sat amongst the clutter in the school guidance counselor's office. Ms. Eady's twelve line GE desk phone was overflowing with important calls from other school officials as the constant light show blinked in rotation, alerting her. But she was hardly interested in those calls. She wanted to speak with the parents of Shaun Hellum Jr., and fast.

Aruby arrived within forty minutes of being called, the Jeep Cherokee nearly on its last curve-bending journey. She knifed through the mini crowds of adolescents trudging about. Rushing into the school's main office, she rapped, out of breath, "Hello, I'm Aruby Hellum. I'm here on behalf of my son, Shaun Hellum."

"Oh, okay, Ms. Hellum. I'll let the guidance counselor know you're here," said the school secretary with a peculiar frown before switching away.

A few minutes slipped by before Aruby was led into the cluttered office of Lattice Eady. She'd been a fourth grade teacher most of her career up until six and a half years ago, when she decided she could do more for her students as a counselor. "Ms. Eady will see you now," the nosy young secretary stated as she arm-guided Aruby inside and then turned on her heels to leave.

"Hello," Ms. Eady cordially spoke. "Come in and have a seat."

Though a little hesitant because of the worried stare Aruby held on her son, Mrs. Eady kept her composure and pretended to rummage through Shaun's file. She was actually feeling the mother and son team out, just doing a little personal PI work.

"I'm sorry, Ms. Eady...you said that was your name?" Aruby questioned, never taking her eyes off Shaun.

Shauny sat in the comfort of a plaid loveseat all by his lonesome. His face was in a tight scowl, coupled with a sense of uncertainty - the same uncertainty that Aruby often scared him with when telling him to cut out all the Blake stuff. But now he'd finally gotten the school officials involved and Aruby only hoped she'd be able to cut through the same old red tape bullshit, as always. To date, this would mark the third time Aruby had been called to a meeting regarding her son and Blake.

"Yes, I'm Ms. Eady, the school's guidance counselor. His teacher has brought to our attention that your son Shaun might be in some kind of trouble. Is this something new to you, ma'am?" Ms. Eady thought she'd take the light approach. She didn't want to trigger anything in either of them.

Ignoring the counselor, Aruby addressed her child. "Shauny, are you okay, honey?"

"Uh, yeah, Mom. Why did they make me come here?" he questioned.

"I'm not sure, honey, but I'll find out. You haven't been - "

"No!" his childish voice boomed with anger. "No, no, no!"

Ms. Eady looked on in awe. She could now understand Mrs. Gregorsky's reasoning for having Shauny brought out of her classroom and into her office. "Relax, honey, everything's going to be okay," Ms. Eady chimed in, feeling her words would have a good effect on him.

Unsure of how the woman's words would impact Shaun caused Aruby to feel like she was on the borderline between hopeful and disastrous. Aruby had lived with her child for ten years now and knew that the latter was more probable.

"So you're going to just sit there and let that bitch tell you to relax? You're losing it for real, bro!" snapped Blake. He was now in a world of desolate anger with only one real person to lash out at. "You'd better wise up, bro, or they're gonna lock you up," Blake warned.

"You've said that before. You're always saying dumb things. Maybe it's you that's lying all the time and I'm sick of it!" Shaun stood, rushed to Ms. Eady's desk, and with a single swipe, relieved it of its contents. Each and every stack, pile of information, phone, clock, keyboard, and the family photos crashed to the carpeted floor.

The scene was enough to frighten Ms. Eady. She began to think that maybe she should've stayed teaching fourth grade. Never in all her years had she ever encountered such a disturbed child. And to be honest, she didn't plan on it going any further than it had already.

"Um, Mrs. Hellum, I think you need to get your child some proper help. But for now, you are free to take him home."

Aruby was busy picking up the pieces from the hurricane that had just ripped through the office as Ms. Eady spoke. "Let me finish up down here!" Aruby said.

"That's perfectly okay, Mrs. Hellum. Just please get some help for your son before it's too late.

"Help?" Blake uttered. "No one can help him but me!"

SEVEN

*I*t was 2004, six years later. Life for Shaun and Aruby had somewhat gotten better. Aruby was now a major factor at work instead of just a plain ol' tip girl wiping tables and serving meals. She had been promoted to shift supervisor/manager of the fast food/dessert establishment. They could now afford better meals, and to some extent, more fashionable clothes, not to mention a new set of used wheels. Life with the old Jeep Cherokee had come to a close two years prior when it became ill with a terminal disease. With a couple of thousand Aruby had saved away, she had miraculously obtained a small loan at her bank and bought a 1997 Subaru Legacy. She still hadn't dated, thus far, partially because of the love she still harbored for Shaun Sr., and, sadly to say, because her son was enough for any one woman to handle by her lonesome. Shaun became her main man.

Shauny had grown up to be a surprising 5'11" tall. He gained mass in the muscular department as well, and he now carried a picture perfect physique. Just as he had aspired to growing up, he had become a well-defined ballplayer for A. I. Prince Tech, and he had been crowned co-captain of the junior varsity team since he was a freshman. He was now a sophomore. He maintained a B-/C+ average in spite of his brewing altercations with various students. He academically held his own. But his new love for hip hop prompted his choice of shop-class being Music 101. If it wasn't basketball, music, or hanging out with his BFF, Ivy, he was more likely to be knuckling up against some kid in a battle of brawn to prove his manhood. And moreover, Shauny would always be the victor.

He'd been to the principal's office too many times to count and had enough inside and outside detention enough to be expelled, but Coach Calhoun always fought for his existence with all he had. The earnest efforts by Coach Calhoun were what actually saved him over his time at the technical school. He was a great asset with promising skills. Coach Calhoun hoped Shaun would push above and beyond. He wanted to see the young man become what he'd dreamt of being since a youth. His only flaw would be his attitude, his ill-mannered temper towards his peers and staff, and, in addition, his pal, Blake – the ignition behind his raging fury.

It was game day for the A.I. Hawks. They were playing their rival, Chaney Tech, out of Manchester, Connecticut. The winner would go on to play against Hall High, the leading team of the division. The freshman team had smoked their game, winning by 22 points, and the varsity squad had shamed the school by losing with a deficit of 47 points, being mercy-ruled for the first time in history. But for the school, it was expected. The varsity squad wasn't worth the surname or moniker written and plastered throughout the academic quadrangle. No, this highlight belonged to Paul, the captain, and co-captain Shaun and their junior varsity squad. Everyone in attendance was actually there to see the J.V. squad get down and take home the title.

The tip-off was set to start in 40 minutes. The intermission was in full swing with swarms of spectators galloping about the densely-crowded hallways in search of a snack and beverage.

Ivy, Charles, Shauny, and Blake stood off to the side, shooting the shit. Ivy was telling Shauny how she knew he was going to do well tonight and that she'd be right there in the front row cheering him on, which made Charles jealous. It had been this way since the first time they had met in school and hereafter.

"I don't think he's that good," Charles snapped in an opinionated tone. "What's all the hype? I don't even think he can dunk the rock," he continued to whisper in Ivy's ear.

Ivy had had enough and said, "Quit it, Chucky! Shauny is the best, period. You'll see tonight." Ivy was loyal to Charles a hundred percent, but it was different with Shauny, her best friend and confidant. They'd shared some of their most intimate feelings and insecurities with each other, so it wasn't like anything was a secret – nothing. And Shauny knew exactly how Chucky felt about him even if he always expressed it in a discreet whisper.

"It's always 'Quit it, Chucky! That's enough, Chucky! Stop it, Chucky!' when it comes to the loony-toon," he said in his own defense.

"You all right, Ivy? Charles getting on your nerves?" asked Shauny. "Well, don't let him. He's no different than Blake."

"Don't put me in this weird triangle, bro. I'm thinking it's her that's a little disturbed from all the strange things you've told me!" shot Blake. He was grilling Shauny, angry that he had even let Ivy into their circumference to begin with.

"That's it, Blake! You're over-stepping your boundaries. I won't have you disrespecting Ivy for one moment, you hear!" Shaun snatched her by the hand and dragged her into the gym full of fans and family members and the many ballplayers ready for some intense full court excitement.

Once through the heavy metal doors, Shauny paused, looked into Ivy's alluring eyes as his sexual desires rose rapidly. In the heat of the moment, he pressed his thick lips against hers. She surprisingly welcomed the passion by probing his mouth with a salacious dance of her tongue.

As the two shared an incessant French kiss, standing off to the side in utter shock and anguish stood Blake and Chucky, scrutinizing the game of tonsil hockey. Once the buzzer sounded off, indicating that there were only five minutes left before both teams would face off, the predestined love connection ceased.

"Wow!" blurted Ivy. "I wasn't expecting that, Shauny."

"I've wanted to do that for years."

"Why now?"

"Don't know."

"Well, you better get moving, Casanova." Ivy smiled, her perfect teeth resembling a roll of cool mint Dentyne gum.

"See you after the game?"

It was clear to Ivy that her best friend wanted seconds. She smiled happily without speaking.

"Well?" Shaun was in a rush and needed to change into his purple and yellow uniform before he messed around and didn't start behind his tardiness.

Not wanting to wait, Ivy blushed, feeling the sleeping muscles come to life. "I'll be here, Shauny. Have a good game." She swatted his butt as he took flight for the dressing room.

As Shauny ran with great speed to the locker room, Blake caught up to him and blatantly voiced his opinion. "So this is how it's going to be, bro? You going to take up with Little Miss 'I wanna be Alicia Keys? I think I can beat Venus Williams'? Downright pitiful, I tell ya! I'll tell you something though, bro, I'm not having it. I love you, but I won't let some fly-by-night trick destroy our blood!" Blake barked heatedly. He knew he held the power over Shauny - the power to finally corrupt everything his Mom tried to shield him from, the power to bring forth all the answers he questioned over the years. If things didn't happen to Blake's liking after the game, it was on and poppin'.

"Just go somewhere, Blake. I've got a game to win!" Shauny shot and dismissed Blake altogether.

"I'm sorry, Chucky, maybe it's meant to be. It's been a long time since I've really had a dear friend such as Shauny who could really relate to my troubles beside you," Ivy said as Charles questioned her to death about what he had just witnessed. "If anybody should know, Chucky, it's you. Please don't be mad," pleaded Ivy.

Charles was actually the only brother-like figure she'd ever had growing up. He was and had been there since she could remember and she loved him for it, but as they became toddlers, then kids, then preteens and into teenagers, the time would surface where even friends and siblings had to part. Ivy hoped this wouldn't be theirs, but if it was, then so be it.

Charles felt her pain as it were telepathically distributed to him. He thought long and hard, and then uttered, "Okay," to his counterpart. "I really hope you know what you're getting into, Sis." Then he smiled at her widely.

They went into the stands and took seats next to Blake, who sat fuming.

"I've got something for all of you!"

EIGHT

The score was tilted in the Hawks' favor. Shauny led his team with twenty-two points, four rebounds, seven assists, but no blocks as of yet. He normally finished every game with a triple double and at least three blocks, but the Cheney Tech squad harbored a majority of 6'5" to seven-footers. It was all good, he thought, because he'd punish them in points, rebounds, and assists.

The fourth quarter was coming to a close with a minute-thirty on the game clock and thirty-two on the shot clock. The Hawks had just turned the ball over - a good steal by Cheney Tech's 5'7" point guard. He dribbled the rock up the court and was exhibiting some stylish craftwork with the ball, going behind his back and under and over each leg like it was human nature – a gift he'd developed in the womb, perhaps. The opposing shooting guard came at him, lunging for the ball, but was easily crossed over, left to view the back of his jersey as he blew past him. Next, he repeated a similar move, only this time he caused the young teen to trip over his own feet. He was discombobulated by the ankle-breaking move.

The entire place went into a boisterous frenzy. The Cheney Tech bench nearly raised the roof with their ooh's and ahh's. Feeling like an NBA draftee, the ball handler became caught up in his own hype. The shot clock was down to seven seconds due to all of his fancy footwork.

"Pass the ball!" his coach yelled from the opposite side of the court, but to no avail.

"I got dis one," he muttered to himself, studying the final seconds. He backed up to his hot spot behind the three-point mark, measured his range, and took flight into the air, using every calf muscle he had. He had a star-studded form, picture perfect for scouts as he went to release the leather ball. His wrist flicked as always. He saw a clear path straight into the netted rim.

But then out of nowhere, a figure wearing purple and yellow appeared in the direct line of fire. A large palm attempted to swat away the clutch shot like a nagging bug. Like always when Shauny rose to the occasion, his blocking slump was no more. He sent the ball into the stands, where it came close to hitting a small child dead in the face.

"Oooh!" the crow blared as the Hawks stole possession.

The ball was checked in and brought down the court as the clock now read fifty-nine seconds and counting. The Hawks were down by two with a good chance to tie it or win with a three-pointer. The play was set up. They were going for the tie. The players passed the ball around, cautiously looking for an open shot or lay-up, but when the rock reached Shauny, he had other plans.

"Okay, let's see whose da man!" he said, performing some impressive Globetrotter moves that had everyone in the bleachers on their feet.

"Whoa, would you look at this kid?" someone shouted. "He's nice!"

"Shoot the ball!" a woman who lived for the game bellowed loudly.

"Look at the clock, dummy!" another barked, annoyed at the display.

"Get 'em bro! Take it home, Shaun!" Blake yelled out. "You rock, bro!"

"What's he waiting on, Ivy?" Charles asked.

"Shut up, Chucky, he's got dis," she replied, on edge. The final seconds of the school year now rested in Shauny's hand. He wasn't about to pass the rock, and the difference between the game and shot-clock was seven seconds. Shauny had full control. He peered at both clocks and timed everything down to the wire.

"Time for the money shot!" He taunted the defender before him with a broad smile.

Four, three, two – the clock blinked and Shauny raised several inches off the maple flooring, releasing the ball with an accurate spin. It sailed towards the netted rim. The throng of onlookers became still in silence, the anxiety of the shot consuming the air.

One! The Spaulding NBA official ball flew through the circle, bouncing on the side of the rim, appearing to be on its way down. But surprisingly, it hopped out and into the hands of Cheney Tech. The rebounder passed the ball to his forward, who then dished it off to their point guard, who rode the fast lane down the court. He scored two points with an explosive windmilling dunk.

The entire gymnasium erupted into a boisterous cheer. The buzzer sounded, indicating the end of the game. The Hawks's nearly flawless record and season was over. Shauny stood in awe, his sights on the kid who had scored the extra two bone-crushing points to solidify the win.

"What happened, bro? Why didn't you just pass the ball?" asked Blake. "Now look, you let the team down all because of her!"

This enraged Shauny. He looked into Ivy's pretty brown eyes and could swear he saw a sign of disappointment. He then looked at Blake, who was grinning while shaking his head as if to say, "You never listen, Champ."

But this time he didn't have to. He had so much of Blake scribed into his block and mental side that he already knew what to do. Charging at the kid who scored the winning shot, Shauny clotheslined him, bringing the limelight onto the hardwood with shocking speed.

"Hey, look!" someone from the boys' team shouted.

The entire team raced to the aid of their fallen teammate and then all of the Hawks followed suit. The gym became an all-out free-for-al, team against team as well as some parents against parents. Ivy and Charles were in awe. Blake seemed to be enjoying himself to no limit.

"Get him, bro! Kick his ass!" Blake boomed.

Tired of watching the rumble, Ivy pulled Shauny from the pile of brawlers, escaping unscathed. They met up with Blake and Charles in the teacher's parking lot, jogging away while the ruckus back inside the gymnasium continued.

NINE

A block away from Shauny's house, the quartet stopped to catch a breath of fresh air before they all collapsed from exhaustion. Ivy knelt over, her sleek palms resting over her knees. Her breathing was erratic as she searched for a steadying breath. Blake mimicked Shauny's actions as both their muscular chests heaved in and out rapidly, a fight to capture the main source of life.

"Always the clown, huh, Blake?" shot Chucky. He'd been fed up with him for some time now. It was Ivy who often mediated their peace, unbeknownst to Blake, but the gripping seriousness of what had just transpired and the revelation of his sisterly friend and Shauny hooking up, caused him to finally lash out.

"What, you got a problem? You got something on your chest, pansy?" snapped Blake. "Well, c'mon, c'mon, buddy. Put 'em up, put 'em up," Blake challenged in the voice of the Cowardly Lion from the Wizard of Oz.

"Cut it out, will ya?," Shauny boomed at Blake.

"Oh, so you wanna take Casper's side?" Blake was growing angrier by the second, a side Shauny hadn't seen in years. "Huh, bro? Answer me!" he demanded. "I'm the one who protected you when we were little, the one who chose to eat all the garbage your so-called mom tried to feed us. I was your pillow and blanket when we lived in that tiny, cramped enclosure she claimed was a bedroom. Who feeds a kid pepperoni at such a young age, huh? What mom would put her young'uns at that risk, knowing they'd be trying to kick all that salty acid from their blood stream the next day?"

Blake was on a roll at this point. He was tired of holding in all of the built-up hatred. His malevolence had finally reached a combustible stage and it was the things he reiterated that brought forth that same hidden rage. Those same queries that lingered somewhere deep in the back of Shauny's mind, the untold answers Aruby refused to relinquish.

Ivy stood there in a downpour of tears. For the first time in a while, Chuck was silent. He had no comments, no slick remarks to dish out. He was too frightened by Blake's barking.

Shauny began pacing back and forth over the steely-grey surface. He was stepping with such velocity that a dust cloud hovered around the area, creating a trail of microscopic debris. If possible, Shauny would have choked the life out of Blake, but instead, he was finally going to confront his mom. However, totally overwhelmed with exhaustion, he was going home to rest first. The rest would take its course once he felt rejuvenated.

Shauny tried to send Ivy away so he could have time to think, a minute of solace, but she wanted to tag along. And wherever she went, Charles made it a habit to shadow her, sort of like her guardian angel. In a state of reminiscence, Shauny felt the blissful sensation of Ivy's kiss and he gave in, which actually calmed his angry temperament some.

When Shauny made it home, the place was as quiet and lonely as an empty house of worship. You could hear the basements pipes whispering softly and the tingling of the wall heater casually burping. After calling out for his mom several times with no response, he realized she was still at work doing overtime.

"Hey, you thirsty, Ivy?" Shauny asked in a calm tone. His earlier demeanor was an afterthought, so long as nothing else transpired and sent him off the deep end.

"Sure, I'm feeling a little dehydrated after all that."

"Cool. What would you like?" asked Shauny, walking into the kitchen. "We have –" He cut off abruptly as he noticed they were out of Kool-Aid, juice, and soda. The only drinkable substance was H20 and the remnants of week-old milk.

"Something wrong?" she quizzed, noticing the blank stare and change in his subtle posture.

Shauny's chest began heaving. His nostrils flared broadly. The embarrassing notion of offering Ivy some water was belittling in his mind, but to save face, he did. "Mom must be at the grocery store, so all I can offer you is water."

"Water's fine, Shauny, thanks," she accepted with a smile, again defusing the ticking bomb in him.

"Humph!" Blake snorted. "No water for me? All of a sudden you get into a tongue-dueling death match with a dark-skinned Sanai Latham lookalike, grow your first real hard-on, and you're the man?" Blake rapped furiously. "Blake doesn't exist no more? Well, I've got some news…for…you!" he concluded and stormed away.

Shauny thought about chasing after his friend, but knowing Blake would never leave his side, he decided against it. "C'mon, Ivy, I could use a good nap."

With that said, Shauny led and Ivy followed, admiring his shapely butt for a boy. They reached his shack-like bedroom, which was full of wall-to-wall posters of the NBA greats and a few gangster flicks, all memorabilia he'd collected since a kid. It was sort of like he was filling the fatherless void in his life, because for him not having the opportunity to experience what it would be like to have one around, or actually knowing much about his, caused a deep pain in his inner soul, a scar that would remain for as long as he existed on earth.

These were some of the questions that Aruby constantly refrained from answering for hm. She'd simply say that his father left when he was a few months old, that he didn't want to man up and be a father to his child. With each long, thought-out lie, they both would plunge into a private world of emotions, Aruby for flat-out lying and Shauny because he'd felt unwanted and unloved. But in spite of the fact that these findings had been embedded into his mental vortex since being able to comprehend such rational answers, he always felt they were false.

While Ivy studied the memorabilia with an eagle eye, Shauny looked to the corner of the room like he always did each and every time he entered. He stared long and hard, feeling like something was really missing, like something should've been in its place instead of a dresser. On the parallel wall sat a ten gallon fish tank, but again, he felt something else belonged in its place. Lastly, he stared at the tiny closet only physically capable of catering to one, which he'd always felt should've been enough for two, and this by far fucked him up bad every time he walks into his room.

Shauny nearly became dewy-eyed, as always, and Ivy rushed to his side, quickly consoling him with a bear hug.

"Listen, Shauny, the heart has its reasons for which the reason knows nothing about. It's just the way it works," she spoke caringly. "Some things we'll never understand, me and you, but it doesn't mean we're any different from anybody else. You and I are very much alike and I'm glad to have met you and to have been your friend over the years."

Shaun's heart nearly burst, he felt so mushy, but instead, he accepted her soft embrace. Their lips entwined like two-way sticky tape, threatening to cement their mouths together for all eternity. Feeling the rise of the Titanic, Shauny felt it was a good time to break up the tongue dance before they got into trouble. "Thanks, but I'm pretty tired," he lied.

"Yeah, me too." Ivy blushed, nodding towards his private area, letting on that she noticed. She had felt him growing against her lower midsection. "I'll join you."

As the two young sparrows laid in the plush nest like coupling spoons in a true lover's knot, one set of eyes watched them from across the room as another scrutinized them from outside the bedroom window in a fit of anger. Within the next few hours, the events predestined to take place would determine their existence on earth.

TEN

The next morning, Saturday, at approximately 8:42 a.m., Aruby awoke with a pounding headache. She was drenched in her own perspiration, saturated to the point where the ripe peach and fern green bed sheets were now a drab hue where she lay. She was exhausted from the double shift she had been required to cover when two of her co-workers up and quit at the last minute with no explanation as to why. As the shift supervisor, it was her duty to continue the normal operations of the restaurant. Stumbling in after a sixteen hour shift, Aruby never thought of checking in on her son. Aruby had simply lined herself up with the full-size bed and plunged into a tired coma.

Finally fully awake, Aruby realized she had missed her boy's final game of the year and she started to feel guilty. After a quick hygienic cleansing, Aruby headed for Shauny's room to apologize for her absence.

"Oh, this is going to be great!" shot Blake as he trailed in Aruby's footsteps. The anticipation of seeing the reaction on her face when she opened Shauny's bedroom door and saw a young woman in her son's bed was similar to watching a new blockbuster release in the theatre. "All hell's gonna break loose in the place today!" Blake laughed hysterically.

Every Jack must have a Jill, as the magic of first true love is an ignorance that can never end. Ivy went to turn over from her lock in Shauny's muscular arms so that she could snuggle closely against his chiseled torso when the door creaked open and a feminine voice called out! Her voice changed from calm, cordial, and loving, to an upset roar in a matter of seconds.

"Shauny, Shauny!" Ivy whispered while nudging him in the side. "Shauny, get up!" Her voice trembled in fear.

"Hmmm?" he answered tiredly.

"Boy, you'd better get your butt up now!" Aruby boomed loud enough to snap him out of his stupor.

"Oh, shiiiiit!" Shauny's eyes zeroed in or Aruby's statuesque framework.

"Sounds about right to me, bro," Blake added in a pool of laughter.

Aruby stood in the entryway, her sleek hands rested on her petite waist. "Oh shit is right! What the hell is going on, Shaun?"

He knew his moms had lost it when she referred to him as Shaun instead of Shauny. It was one of the few times she had done so over the years. "Nothing, Mom, we fell asleep after the game, that's it," he explained, hoping she'd buy it.

"Try again, bro! Mom looks pretty ticked off," said Blake, standing by her side.

"That's it, Blake! I'm tired of you nit-picking all the time!" snapped Chucky. "You really need to fall back."

"Care to do something about it?" Blake ran up to Chucky's face, smashed him, and waited for a counter measure, but just as he thought, Chucky was all talk. "I thought so, punk!" he grimaced.

"Hmph, it could be innocent," Aruby reasoned. They did have clothes on and it appeared to be the truth, but she didn't want to look like a mother who just let young girls sleep over in her son's bed at their convenience. "Well, get up, and I mean now! Me and you are going to have a long chat, young man," Aruby stated firmly as she watched the two adolescents climb out from under the covers, fully dressed down to their funky yesterday-socks, and stand embarrassed before her.

"Can it wait 'til later, Mom? I wanna walk Ivy home."

"Now, Shaun!" The nerve of him! she thought.

"I said I wanna walk Ivy home! Didn't you hear me?" Shaun's voice raised in a turtle's snap.

"Shauny! What's wrong with you? Don't talk to your mom like that," Ivy chimed in, feeling embarrassed by his behavior.

"Stay out of it, Ivy," said Chucky, finding his voice again.

"Did I tell you to speak, choir boy? Well then, shut up!" Blake barked. "Hey, bro, are you going to finally ask her? You need answers, bro. Make her tell you, Shaun! There's no better time like the present," urged Blake. He'd been pushing Shauny to confront his mom for years, but now that he was at a ripe enough age, he felt it was best to become well informed of his past. "Duh, earth to Shaun! Hello, anybody in there?"

With the loss of his game, the weight he'd carried on his shoulders since the leather sphere had bounced out of the rim coupled with his mom's authoritative tone of voice, snappy demands, and Blake's persistent nagging, caused him to finally blow a major valve. His calm, subtle eyes were now a vibrant hue of red. Beads of sweat could mistakenly be perceived as steam, he was so agitated, and like always, he only knew one way to express the emotions he was feeling.

Shauny's eyes darted from Ivy to Blake and fell on Aruby. His breathing and heartbeat weren't in sync. However, as Blake could feel and see this, he became pleased. "Okay, Mom, you wanna talk? Let's talk. Why do I feel so alone when I shouldn't be? Can you answer me that?"

"Riddle me this, riddle me that," Blake joked, mimicking the Joker from the movie Batman. "Ah, I love my life," he sang.

"What do you mean? You have me. I'm here for you, Shauny," Aruby answered solemnly. "Where's all this coming from?" Her interest was piqued.

"That's not what I meant, Mother. I always feel like there should be someone else in my room, that there should be two beds, two dressers, matching closets, clothes, someone waiting to go into the bathroom in the morning or in the room when I come out. You know, like a sister or a brother," he rapped on as if he were reading straight from a teleprompter, bombarding her with a whirlwind of questions.

With the help of Blake, Shaun always felt something was wrong, out of place, but he could never put his finger on it for the life of him. Nobody ever told him – Mom didn't, Dad couldn't. Hell, he had always known his father had abandoned him before giving him the proper chance at becoming his little slugger, or even his hero and idol. And as Blake said, it was about time Shauny knew the truth and sought out vengeance - his vengeance - for things that should be, but weren't!

"That's it, boy," praised Blake, beaming with pride.

"You really need to calm down, Shauny," Aruby spat out, feeling disrespected.

"She's right, Shauny," added Ivy.

"She lied to you, bro." Again Blake tried to pour gasoline on the brewing fire.

"Don't say that!" yelled Shauny.

"Are you gonna believe your brother or your lying mother?"

Shauny felt like he was trapped in time, stuck in a glass bottle with no exit, chucked into the sea on an endless journey around the globe. His eyes squinted into slits. His thin cheeks raised into a menacing scowl as his brown fists folded tightly into two balls, drawing every blood vessel to a head. "I told you before not to say that! You're not my brother!" he shouted to his left.

Aruby knew this day would come sooner or later, and this was the first time ever that she had heard of Blake supposedly being his brother. Shauny had never once referred to Blake in that manner – just as his friend. Could it be true? she pondered. *Could it really be?* "Listen, Shauny, I'm not having this conversation with you. I've told you before, your father left before you were born. He left us, okay!" Screaming, Aruby then stormed off into a world of anguish, a part of her life she never desired to relive – ever again!

By this time, Ivy was also drenched in her own tears. However, when she went to gather some affection from Shauny, he shoved her almost to the point where she fell to the floor. "Get away!" roared Shauny.

"Hey, don't put your hands on her!" shot Chucky, not believing Ivy was on a one-way course to the floor.

"Relax, Chucky, it's okay, I'm alright."

Shauny paced back and forth as he normally did when feeling angry and ready to hurt something. Arguing with Blake would make him feel good, but it would still leave his questions open with no answers, so he set out for the one and only person who could open up the can of worms.

ELEVEN

*T*aking giant steps throughout the house, Shauny yelled his mother's name, desperate to talk. "Mom, Mom! Where are you?" he continued to bark, searching every inch of the house to no avail. "Where is she?" he asked himself, coming up blank.

"Try the basement, bro," pushed Blake. He figured that with all that had transpired over the last few minutes, she'd retreated to the place where she normally did before bed. It had been a ritual since early 1989.

Without answering Blake, Shauny shot past him in the direction of the basement door in the kitchen. He never broke stride, rushing to his destination. Reaching the clam-white door, he latched onto the unpolished knob, twisted it, and pulled outward. He then raced downward, taking three sets of stairs in a single descent. The basement was still a work in progress, but it did contain a small non-working one person bathroom, a larger room which would one day become an entertainment alley, and a diminutive room with one dresser, a bed, and a large closet. Scanning the most common areas of the damp, cemented enclosure, he came up empty. Then he crashed Aruby's pity party inside the small room.

Shaun was immediately serenaded by soft sniffles, low, whispering moans and "I miss you" to the point where he almost felt sorry for her. When Blake urged him to pursue the reasons for her pain, Shaun walked up close to where she sat Indian style, knees bent, hands together, and he noticed she was cradling a 10x13 photo of some sort.

"That's right, go on, bro. Take a good look and you shall find all that you desire," Blake promised. "Go on."

At that point, Aruby hadn't noticed that she had acquired any company. Shauny leaped over to where she sat like a grasshopper in a field of foliage, surprising her like a cat burglar.

"Oh shit! What're you doing down here, baby?" Aruby's voice quivered with each word.

"Oh shit is right!" Shauny said to her, retorting with the same phrase she used on him not more than twenty seconds ago. "What's that you're gripping so tightly, Mom? Let me see it. You okay?" A softer side of him appeared upon seeing his mother in a fit of disparity.

"Here you go, always going Mr. Softie on me. You might as well get you a line of Good Humor trucks and serve the community ice cream and soda pop, bro. Pitiful!" stated Blake, tired of Shauny's passiveness for a weak moment. "Would you look at the damn photo, bro?"

Aruby saw that her son was peering to his left side, which meant Blake was putting things into his head at the moment. Noticing the squinting of his eyes, the tightening of his lower jawbone, and the pursing of his pouty lips, she knew the whispers were all bad.

"Who's the photo of?" asked Shauny. "Can I see?" he asked, reaching his hand out calmly.

Feeling like she had no other choice in the matter, tired of holding back all the secrets, Aruby cautiously handed over the old photo to her son. Grasping the brass framework, Shauny studied the aged photograph with keen eyes and a dour expression. As the mental activity churned in Shauny's mind, distilling thoughts of betrayal, his overall reality became gloomily silent. He then spit to the ground, experiencing a sour grape taste when swallowing, all because of the familiarity in the spooky eyes. He was looking death straight in the face.

"Please, tell me this isn't my father," Shaun said as he continued to study the photo.

Aruby turned up the volume on her live sob-cast, but refrained from answering.

"Mom!" Shauny let the word linger before continuing. "Is this my dad or what?"

"Sure looks like it to me, bro!" Blake shot sarcastically. "But that's just the beginning."

Ivy and Charles stood in the doorway, feeling sorry for Aruby as she wept uncontrollably. Then a cold chill wafted through the dank basement. But there were no windows, no air conditioning or central air, so what could it be and where could it be coming from? Everyone except Shauny mulled this over. He was too busy rummaging through the floor closet in search of anything else his mom held in secret.

Three inches from the bottom of the chest, a satin, lace-trimmed blanket graced his clammy touch. Showing a piqued interest as to what was beneath the covering, Shauny hastily yanked the silk covering away, which up until now was where all the most important answers to his life lay dormant. The first thing he noticed was two teddy bears, both with a baby blue hue. They still had a sort of fresh off the assembly line look. He pulled them both out, only to place them on the floor beside him. Next he gripped two long-deflated identical balloons bearing the catch phrases "It's A Boy" across the belly, and lastly, two matching baby books, also a soft baby blue.

With all of the items strewn on the floor, Shauny became hot - hot as in an angered state of being. Aruby was so absorbed in a pool of hurt, shame, and soul-stirring grief that she really hadn't noticed the classified, her-eyes-only critical pieces to an untold story before her.

"Mom, what's all this? This is my father, isn't it?"

Aruby finally looked up and into a younger though splitting image of her late husband. The swagger, voice, posture, and choice of words was a hundred present identical to Shaun Hellum, Sr. She was so enthralled and captivated by the aura of her son that she almost smiled, thinking it was actually her late companion before her, but luckily she caught herself. Instead, she let a muffled one word response escape her oral cavity. "Yes."

Shaun's frown morphed into a slow smile. He was happy to now know he actually had a Pop, happy to now know the exact details of his facial design, the color of his skin, style of hair and the hue of his eyes. These things brought him a sense of peace, understanding, and closure. Then all of a sudden he could distinctively hear his mom telling him since he was old enough to understand, "He left us, baby…he left before you were even born…he never gave you a chance, Pooh."

So much of Blake was embedded in Shauny that there was no need for his best friend to speak out. His cordial frown easily turned into a menacing scowl, compliments of Blake and his sinister implantations.

"So you did lie to me? I can feel it, Mom," Shaun said. He picked up the cuddly teddy bears and studied them as if they could tell a tale of truth versus deceit. From the teddy bears, his gaze shifted to the two jumbo-sized balloons, which caused him to nod up and down a few times. Dropping the two tiny grizzlies on their heads, he picked up both baby books, sat down on the fold-out cot and began a no-return journey to Hell.

"What's he looking at, Ivy?" Charles asked. He noticed how Shauny's keen awareness surveyed the scrapbooks.

"Shhhh!" she mumbled, not wanting to disturb Shauny.

As Shauny looked over the books, his jaw began to tighten, marking a chiseled beeline to his lower neck if looking at him from a profile angle. He was done looking through his supposed book of memorabilia and he flipped open book two. The opening page gave him the shock of his life – the truth to years of lies and deception.

Under the name category, it read "Vaughn Blake Hellum". His weight was listed as three pounds, six ounces, his hair black, eyes brown, and his gender male. At that point, Shaun was curious about what else the deceptive dictionary would reveal. Flipping the page, he saw a footprint which appeared to be a tinier version of the one in his book. The next page had a scrawny, dark, circular object which he knew was a belly button stump, again like the one in his book. The last and only differences between the two life journals was the dark curly lock of hair that was bound by a sea-blue ribbon.

Turning to the last page, Shaun found a small laminated card. The heading "Death Certificate" stood out in bold print. Viewing the name on the card explained everything he'd been looking for all his life, everything Blake had been trying to tell him over the past sixteen years. They'd been friends, twinning, but mainly womb-buddies, which was now evident. Peering at the bold print, Shaun saw that the date of the deceased read "April 17, 1989", which only meant that Blake - Vaughn Blake Hellum - was indeed

Shauny's brother, the twin brother he'd been dreaming about every night since an infant, the twin brother he'd been best friends with since he could remember, the twin who'd been pushing his buttons for the duration of his life. But even though Blake had only started off as a figment of his imagination, a vivid life-like ghost who appeared to his left whenever he looked, he had been a guiding light to him.

With this realization of things, the evidence of truth, Shauny fell into a furious rage.

"I told you she lied, brother!" Blake uttered. "Dad loved you, Shauny. He only left because of me."

"Is that true?" Shaun snapped at his Mom. "Is it?"

"Is what true, baby?"

"About Dad! What happed to my pops?" Shaun asked, his voice at its highest octave.

"He took his life the same night of your brother's funeral." Aruby began to sob louder and then slowed down to finish the story. "He felt it was his fault for Vaughn's death and took his life to go and take care of him in Heaven. I'm sorry, honey. Mommy's very sorry I kept this from you, but I didn't know how to tell you," she admitted truthfully. She had contemplated on several occasions whether or not to just confess, answer his questions to the full extent, but she was overprotective as most mothers are with their boys, so she chose not to.

"So you've been lying to me all of these years about my pops? I had a good father and you dressed him in a monster's suit? You kept the fact that I also had a twin brother who died at birth - the only person I've grown to trust and love other than you, Mom. I was really beginning to think I was loony for real until I met Ivy and she said she'd been going through the same exact things. She had a twin who died at age two and she could see and hear him!" Shaun rambled off, pacing back and forth.

"I tried to tell you, bro, but no, you didn't wanna listen. But now we must take vengeance against the woman who's fault this is," urged Blake.

Shauny glanced into the baby book one last time and recorded some vital information in his mental Rolodex. Then he threw the lost treasure against the sheetrock wall with a force that created an eight inch hole

In his fitful rage, he looked at his mother and then attacked her. Unable to dodge the first smack across the face, Aruby stumbled into the wall, which broke her fall, leaving her in a stunned upright position to endure another whaling from the two-piece across the jaw. Those two crashing strikes landed with Aruby right-side-up on the floor.

"Urggghh!" Shauny roared as he towered over her breathing heavily.

"No!" shouted Ivy. "She's your mother, Shauny!"

On account of Ivy's pleading voice and words, Shauny left the basement, stepped through the living room, and out the front door on a new course of action.

Blake looked at his Mom, then at a shaken Charles, and simply shrugged his broad shoulders before trailing in his brother's footsteps.

"See ya!"

TWELVE

*W*ritten in the stars, a million miles away, a voice tried to whisper in Shauny's ear with the hopes of cleansing the vengeful thoughts he now harbored before it was too late to undo the upcoming events. But it was like he'd activated a force field of some sort, a jamming device for such intrusions. The thing is, this was the voice of the lost treasure he'd searched for his entire life: his father's voice, Shaun Hellum Sr. Truth be told, he could hear his father's cries, but Shaun Jr. was faithful to one person and one person only. Now it would be the moment of retribution for both Shaun Hellum Sr. and Vaughn Blake Hellum.

Like two track stars racing over the unleveled asphalt, Shaun led the way towards their destination, but seeing that they'd be getting nowhere at their slow gait, Blake suggested something Shauny would've never contemplated on his own. "Don't worry, bro, we'll be okay," he persuaded, as always.

Shauny nodded, feeling the reality in his brother's suggestion.

The two slowed to a halt at the corner of Farmington Avenue directly at the top of May Street, where an elderly woman sat inside her Jeep Cherokee, warming its engine, obviously not paying attention to her surroundings. Shauny crept up to the driver's side of the truck and gave Blake one last look. He gave the go ahead. Shauny then latched onto the door handle and not only yanked the door open, but pulled the elderly woman out of the vehicle at the same time. "Ahhh! What's going on?" she cried, hitting the ground fast and hard. "Please don't kill me, young man!" she pleaded, staring into the cold slits before her.

Without any response, Shaun hopped inside and then he and Blake sped off, committing their first brotherly carjacking.

"Wow, bro, you're crazier than I thought," said Blake, kicking his size nines up on the dashboard, enjoying the erratic driving skills Shaun displayed.

Reaching their destination, Shauny whipped the Jeep Cherokee into the U-shaped driveway and parallel parked beside a Ford F-150 pick-up truck. He slammed the gear shift into park, hopped out, and stormed into the emergency entrance of Hartford Hospital. Trudging past all the chaos of the people scattered about in need of medical attention, he located the large pegboard enclosed in glass with all the names of the doctors, nurses, and so on, and the respective floors in which they labored. "Bingo!" Shaun nodded, made a few steps for the elevators, and waited for the vertical carriage to appear.

Ding! The chime signaled that the chariot had reached its desired stop. The doors of the steel box yawned widely and Shaun and Blake flew out like two vampires after midnight, literally on the hunt for blood. A left off the elevator brought him to the main desk, which was deserted. Shaun did take notice of a half-eaten chicken club sandwich on potato bread, an all-white iPod with a pair of earbuds beside it, a stack of mail about two-inches thick, and a stainless steel letter opener on top of the pile of correspondence or perhaps bills.

Shauny didn't have to think twice about his choice of weaponry. He quickly grabbed the letter opener and dashed away from the nurse's station. In slow motion, he and Blake glided down the iodine-scented hallways, reading the name tags of every woman clad in a white trench lab coat, hoping to come up lucky.

They must have passed maybe five different women, most extremely desirable to the eye, before finding the one they'd longed for.

"That's her, bro! Get 'er!" Blake barked.

Like a trained pitbull, Shauny attacked his prey with no regard as to who saw the blatant seizure.

Subdued and pinned to the mosaic tiling, Dr. Malloy squirmed on the waxed floor like a sea trout caught in a fisherman's net. Although Dr. Malloy was being held at knifepoint – in a state of shock - she every so often tried to muffle out a plea for help.

But that all ceased when Shauny punctured her abdomen with the sharp steel. "Shut up and keep quiet!" he snarled into her ear in a threatening tone. He then looked at her name tag once more just to be sure she was the one in question. After reading the name correctly aloud, he became satisfied. "You killed my brother, lady!"

The doctor looked baffled. She knew without a doubt that she'd never purposely taken a person's life, caught a vehicular homicide, or anything to that affect during her twenty years of practicing medicine, so this crazed young man had to have the wrong person.

"I'm very sorry."

"I told you to stay quiet!" Shaun jabbed her again, this time in the leg and then a few more times in the mid-section. "See, Blake, I've got her, just like we planned brother," he stated, peering towards his left while Dr. Malloy was in a world of pain, squealing like a mammal being slaughtered for the reproduction and sale of its precious skin. "That's right," Blake answered. "Now ask her why she didn't save me? Then let her know that our father committed suicide after I died and we blame her! She must be held accountable for both of our deaths, brother! Kill her so me and Dad can kill her again in Hell!" growled Blake with urgency. Blake was only sharing parts of the story. There was much more than Shauny could fathom right now; should he know the truth, it could hinder Blake's plans.

"You heard him! Why did you kill my brother? Why didn't you save his life when he was being born, lady? Why?" Shaun yelled in her face, spit spewing all over her. "And did you realize that because you couldn't save his life, our pops killed himself?" "Huh!".

"It wasn't my fault," the frightened physician answered as if she really knew whom they were talking about. It was just a ploy to stall for time. She hoped someone saw when the young man had attacked and for the moment abducted her, or at least heard her muffled cries. But what she did find to be the most disturbing thing out of this ordeal as a whole was when the loony teen had said, "You heard him." At that point, she really didn't see herself coming out of this alive.

As the life seeped rapidly from the puncture wounds Shauny had inflicted upon her person, Dr. Malloy shook dubiously as she prayed to the most high. She asked that her life be spared as well as that of her attackers, but as reality set in, her consciousness slowly faded away with every fighting breath, every withering blink of the eye nearing the point of final closure, never to re-open again. She screamed.

Down the hall a male guard and two plainclothes officers had wheeled in a suspect in an armed robbery. The perp was handcuffed to the mobile bed in a world of bloody pain. He had taken four .9mm slugs from one of the officer's service pistols during a desperate getaway attempt and was now subject to being the only one prosecuted because his band of thieving brothers had deserted him when attempting to flee the scene. With one foot in and one foot out of the all-black cargo van, he'd become the target of two different laser beams from two different caliber handguns, which led to his apprehension.

"Officers, as I said before, we can't operate with you two crowding in here. I'm afraid you're going to have to wait out there," the attending head physician said.

"But we need names! We need to question this punk!" one of the officers responded vehemently.

"Well, I'm very sorry, but - " The poor doctor halted as he heard the wailing of a familiar voice. There was no mistaking that pitch because he distinctively remembered it every time she had to administer the insulin shot to her co-worker, since she was extensively squeamish when it came to needles and herself. She'd never once since being diagnosed with type II diabetes been able to administer her own meds.

"Mark, can you cover in here? I think - no, I know - I just heard Dr. Malloy yelling down the hall."

"Sure, go!"

The two officers trailed the man straight to the low pitch, and through a tiny slit in the beige mini blinds, they could now see the cause of the screaming.

"Oh my God, do something!" the doctor demanded, shakier than a crackhead crawling on the ground in a desperate rock hunt.

Inside the hospital room, Dr. Malloy had become anti-social because of the blood loss and beating Shauny had given her. When she wouldn't answer his questions, he assumed she was ignoring him and being stubborn, but he was wrong. The pain and shock had caused her to fall unconscious, so Shaun began to bang her head against the unfriendly floor.

"Answer me!" he shouted repeatedly.

"What are you waiting for? Do something, or he's going to kill her!" shouted the attending physician as he came upon the scene.

The shorter of the officers noticed the piece of steel the attacker carried and knew that restraining him would probably require deadly force. Drawing the same exact Browning .9mm handgun he'd used to drop the bank boy earlier, he burst through the swinging doors, his life taker now trained on Shauny's chest. "Freeze!"

Shauny looked up from the bloody mess before him with a devilish simper that even frightened the cop. Rising up, steel in hand, he stood in a sweaty pant, sizing the cop up for the kill as he stared into his eyes.

He'd finally snapped. He had finally been pushed beyond normalcy, had reached his limit of sanity, and in doing so, someone would never make it out of the room alive.

The cop took into account that the youngster before him wasn't going to back down. It was as if he had some kind of death wish, another place he wished to be besides earth, and he'd happily be willing to send anyone who desired a free one-way trip to the "Mist of Darkness."

"You've got three seconds to put the steel on the ground, place your hands behind your head, and get down on your knees, son!" the officer boomed.

But there was no complying on Shauny's part. He blatantly disrespected the direct order from the cops.

"One...two..."

"I'm with you brother. Kill him, then her!" Blake whispered.

Looking to his left, Shauny said, "I love you, Blake," then faced the cop with a crazed smile, a smirk that said this was it.

"Save some room for me, bro!"

"Three!"

Shauny lunged at the cop with the intention of taking his life, but as the thunderous roar echoed from the high-powered Browning .9mm, Shauny was cut down by two heat seeking missiles. His body fell limply to the floor. As blood began to spew out of the two holes, the cop's partner finally rushed into the cramped room along with several doctors.

As the two bodies lay on the floor, there was no possible way to determine whose blood was whose since there was an ample amount of serum pooling below them both.

Death, a probability for both victims, floated about.

EPILOGUE

*O*ne operating room, two patients.

"Hurry, what blood type is he? C'mon, we need the blood or the boy dies," a surgeon shouted through his surgical mask.

"Here you go, Doctor, it's B negative," a nurse gave the info. She hung three packs of blood to the metal post beside Shauny's bed.

"How're you looking, Dr. Swanson?" the surgeon inquired about the work being done on Dr. Malloy's puncture wounds. In spite of the fact that she appeared to be in dire straits, she only required stitches. Being a diabetic caused her to bleed out as if her condition was far worse than it seemed. She'd be just fine with a little intensive care.

A smile was all the surgeon needed to see. He went back to working diligently to save Shauny's young life. "Hurry up, we need more blood! I'm losing him. Let's go, people!" His voice boomed with urgency.

Shauny's body started to convulse. He shook violently, causing the IV's to pop-out of his arms like buttons on a shirt. It took three people just to strap him down so they could finish working on him, but by then, it was far too late.

Beep...Beep...Beep...Beep...Beep...Beep...,

The fading sound of Shauny's unforgiving heart ending was all the medical staff needed to hear to call the time of death.

"You want me to call it, Doc?" a nurse asked.

"Sure." He lowered his surgical mask in defeat, threw the bloody gloves across the room, and sighed heavily. "No one deserves to die, even in the attempt to take another's life," he concluded, staring at Shauny's lifeless body, wondering where he was headed - Heaven or Hell?

"Hey, brother, you're looking good," Blake whispered to Shauny.

"Where am I?"

"You died on the table – we're together now. It'll just be a little while longer before you cross."

"But how can I see you in this form now?" Shaun quizzed Blake as he floated effortlessly in the air.

"Shhh or he'll hear you, bro!"

"Who – who'll hear me?" Shauny asked, peering around.

"Too late, Vaughn, I've finally caught up with you. How ironic it is that here we are, in the same hospital you died in sixteen years ago, just a mere baby waiting to be born?" The voice cracked. "But fate had it all written out in a different scenario."

"Who's he, Blake?" Shauny wondered, staring at the specter.

"Never mind, bro. Just stay quiet and we'll both be out of here shortly."

"So you don't know, do you, Jermane?" asked the voice.

"How do you know my middle name?"

"I know everything about you, Shaun Jermane Hellum, Jr., and I'll be glad to elaborate since your older brother chose to keep you in the dark."

"Older?" Shauny looked baffled. "There's no way Blake could be older, because I saw the time of death on the certificate. I was without a doubt born first. I'm the junior, not Blake!" Shauny grew angrier by the second.

"That's where you're wrong, son. You see, you and your brother were so tight, so close, even closer than most twins today. And during the stay in your mom's womb, he protected you at all times. When your mom would ingest salty foods, spicy things such as hot sauce, jalapenos, the wrong types of beverages, the secondhand smoke from your pops marijuana habit, amongst other things, your big brother accepted as much of it as he could, which is why he developed a small hole in his heart early on in the pregnancy. You see, Shaun, Vaughn had already figured out that his life wouldn't amount too much, but he would've survived simply due to the fact that he would've been older – born first. One of you was pre-ordained to live, the other to die, but the catch was that the first shall live and the second would perish."

"So you're saying…"

"He sacrificed his life for yours. Like always, he was protecting you. The real complication would've set in when they tried to deliver the second child as they did, with the end result being you going on to become Shaun Hellum Jr. - your brother's gift to you."

"That's enough!" Blake fired loudly. He'd never wanted his brother to know the truth. He just wanted some vengeance on the doctor who didn't save his life, causing Shauny to grow up fatherless in the process. And there she was in the hospital operating room, looking over at Shauny's lifeless body in tears, now realizing who he was. There it was again; she'd never forget the small, unusual birthmark over his right eye.

"Just shut up! We're leaving," stated Blake as he reached for his brother's hand.

"You're very right about one thing, Vaughn, but only one of you will be passing on. And just because of the situation, I'm going to let you two make that decision. One of you must come with me, today, now," he made clear, his voice now sternly convincing enough for both of them.

For the past sixteen years, Vaughn Blake Hellum had been hiding out in limbo, on another plane, in hiding from what was destiny. But now the gig was up. Vaughn mean-mugged the powerful man before him, then stared at Shauny, trying to capture eons of remembrance until it would be time to reunite. Without another second lost mulling over what needed to be done, Vaughn agreed to move on and stop hiding out as a spirit and cross over into the great divide.

"Listen, brother, I've been with you for all this time. I will never leave your side, but so you can live a productive life, I must go home now."

Shauny began to weep, unsure if he'd ever see Blake again. "No, you can't – "

"Whoa! You're a Hellum, and Hellums always overcome diversity, so suck it up! We'll be together again; I promise. You just promise me that you'll make a good life for us both. Take care of Mom. Tell her that I'm sorry for blaming her and that it wasn't her fault. Tell her I love her" said Vaughn as his image slowly began to fade away.

"If somehow I get out of this crazy predicament, I'm going to make you proud, bro! I love you, Blake. I promise to become something great. Check the sports section of the

Hartford Courant and USA Today." Shauny wept harder the more he thought about never seeing Blake again.

"I love you too, bro!"

Beep...Beep...Beep...Beep...Beep...Beep...Beep ...Beep...Beep...Beep...Beep...Beep...Beep...

As the life seemingly began to pump back into Shauny's body, he watched as his brother was ushered away by the Angel of Death.

Hearing the sudden beep of the heart monitor, the surgeon shouted, "Okay, people, let's move it! I don't know how, but we've got a live one!"

By that time, Aruby, Ivy, and her ghostly twin stood outside the window of the operating room, watching as Shauny miraculously came back to life.

"Thank you Lord!" the two women cried out as they wept with happiness.

THE END

Boss Life Publications Presents a Compelling Novel of Redemption
By: J. Alexander...©2014

www.ingramcontent.com/pod-product-compliance
Lightning Source LLC
Chambersburg PA
CBHW060153260626
47160CB00001B/249